I0678758

THE UNIQUE MAGAZINE
Winter 1992-93

ISSN 0898-5073
Art by Bob Eggleton

MIDNIGHT MASS . . . . F. Paul Wilson 14
Was evil victorious precisely **because** *men doubted the power of God?*

MIRROR, MIRROR . . . . Tina and Tony Rath 44
Even wicked stepmothers have to keep pace with the times.

SIRENS . . . . Steve Rasnic Tem 47
The figure in the darkness sang to her . . . of death.

YELLOW ROME,
          OR, VERGIL AND THE VESTAL VIRGIN . . . Avram Davidson 62
Of magicks, mysteries, and tender mercies.

WHEN HE WAS FAB . . . . F. Paul Wilson 72
His life, his career, his charisma went right down the drain . . . literally!

VERSE

MONSTERS by Joe Haldeman: 56. WINTER by Kathleen Youmans: 61.
CONAN POSTMORTEM by Ann K. Schwader: 71. AURALINCUBI by Keith
Allen Daniels: 71.

FEATURES

THE EYRIE 4
SHADOWINGS . . . . Douglas E. Winter 10
WEIRD TALES TALKS WITH F. PAUL WILSON . . . Darrell Schweitzer 49
BIBLIOGRAPHY OF F. PAUL WILSON 57

Publisher: George H. Scithers. Editor: Darrell Schweitzer. Managing Editor: Carol Adams. Assistant
Editors: Leslie Smith, Dainis Bisenieks, Diane Weinstein, Don Keller, & Nicholas Beauchamp.
Production: Michael W. Betancourt. Circulation Manager: Tina Hoffman. Computer Consultant: David
J. Williams III. Typesetter: Owlswick Press & Campus Copy Center. Printer: Malloy Lithographing,
Inc. Mailing: Unit Packaging Corporation. Manuscript Submissions: Yes; we read unsolicited
submissions — **but only if** they are in standard manuscript format. To survive, all editors insist on
a few Rules: each submission must be in proper format and must include a return envelope
addressed to you with enough postage affixed to bring the manuscript back to you. If you want us
to discard the manuscript if not bought, tell us so, but include a business-letter-size envelope with
postage affixed, addressed to you, so we can send you our comments. Please: no loose stamps, or
registered or certified mail, which would make us wait in line at the post office. We cannot be
responsible for manuscripts in our hands or in transit. *Weird Tales®* is published 4 times a year by
Terminus Publishing Co., Inc., PO Box 13418, Philadelphia PA 19101-3418 (4426 Larchwood Ave.,
Philadelphia PA 19104-3916). 2nd Class Postage paid at Philadelphia PA & additional mailing offices.
Single copies, $4.95. Subscriptions: 4 issues (one year) $16.00 in U.S.A. & possessions; $20.00 in
Canada & Mexico, $22.00 elsewhere, in U.S. funds. Postmaster: send address changes to *Weird*

THE EYRIE

Welcome to *Weird Tales*® #305. There have been some obvious changes, not all of which we ever intended. Quite frankly, with the weak economy causing poor subscription renewals, we found ourselves, despite encouraging bookstore sales, between the proverbial rock and hard place. Something had to give, and what did was our beloved, traditional pulp-sized format, which was just too expensive. The perfect binding, in particular, was killing the magazine. Either *Weird Tales*® had to become less costly to produce, or there would be no more *Weird Tales*®.

We think you'll agree we made the right choice. Henceforth, the magazine will be published in a standard magazine format. Price and subscription rates will remain the same. You still get a color cover and approximately the same amount of text each issue.

We may have lost our famous red spine, but we still have yet another issue we're justifiably (we trust) proud of, complete with what we believe to be *the* finest portrait of Cthulhu ever done. And we are similarly proud to have F. Paul Wilson as a featured author. He is simply one of the very best horror writers active today and more than deserving of the honor.

We're somewhat less proud of a couple of **ghastly errors** that crept into last issue's editorial section of The Eyrie.

The first was brought to our attention by the featured author **John Brunner,** who hastens to point out, lest he seem vain and inclined to claiming honors which are not his, that he was *not* Guest of Honor at the 1990 World Science Fiction Convention in The Hague. He was merely present, one of many distinguished program participants. The writer guests of honor were Joe Haldeman and Wolfgang Jeschke.

So we'd like to set the record straight and apologize to all concerned.

We're less apologetic about the other error, since it doesn't change our thesis any, but when last issue's editorial was written, we had not seen *The Horror of Dracula* in perhaps ten years. We saw it again recently. Guess what? There is *no* trans-European, hyperspatial carriage chase anywhere in the movie. But our basic argument, that somehow Hammer Films couldn't make the *real* world convincing (however well *The Horror of Dracula* maintains its classic status due to brilliant performances by Christopher Lee and Peter Cushing) remains as valid as ever.

Now we're left wondering why all these English people (Luca, Mina, Arthur Holmwood) *just happen* to be living in a small German town within a day's ride of Castle Dracula. (Transylvania is an ethnic patchwork. There *could* be such a town in such a place.) In said town, the signs may be in German blackletter, but both undertakers and street urchins speak broadly-accented British English, even

Cockney. No wonder we remembered it as England. As for what border-gate everybody went crashing through, that likewise remains a mystery, since in the late 19th century Transylvania was part of the Austro-Hungarian Empire, and the nearest international border to Castle Dracula would have been the Turkish. Maybe it was a McDonald's drive-through that was closed for the night.

Censorship Rears Its Ugly Head quite a lot these days, in the films and TV, but especially in the schools, where so-called educators who haven't managed to understand the text try to ban *Huckleberry Finn* as racist or Shakespeare for being racist, sexist, politically incorrect, and unkind to puppy dogs.

None of us can ever let our guard down. The thought-police have a way of turning up in the most unlikely places.

We encountered a quite trivial bit of censorship ourselves recently. Jason Van Hollander and your editor have taken the "Corpse Who Dances" Weirdism from issue #296 and printed it on a t-shirt bearing the legend: **Tibetan Olympic Corpse-Wrestling Team.** This has proven a popular convention item, for all that, by the standards of what our fellow horror professionals wear at the Northeast Regional Fantasy Convention (NECon) every summer, it's not merely tame, but almost classically sedate.

Despite which, the shirt was recently banned by the board of directors of a local science fiction society. Why? Because someone decided it was in poor taste, "Like making jokes about Jews in gas chambers," as someone put it, recalling the oppression inflicted on Tibet by China in recent years. Of course the *rolang* ceremony has been a part of Tibetan magical lore for centuries and was first documented by Alexandra David-Neel in *Magic and Mystery in Tibet* (translated into English, 1925), from which H.P. Lovecraft learned of it and jotted down a note in his *Commonplace Book*. The Weirdism, and the t-shirt, have as much to do with contemporary Sino-Tibetan struggles as the song "Zombie Jamboree" does with the dictatorship in Haiti.

But the censor didn't bother to ask what it meant. The censor merely presumed to know.

Ah. Censors always do.

A much more serious case of censorship, of a story originally published in *Weird Tales*®, has come to our attention. The Philadelphia *Inquirer* for November 19, 1991 carried an article entitled "Whose Values?" with the sub-headline, "Even in a seemingly homogeneous place such as eastern Lancaster County, there is dissension over what the schools can teach." It's the usual, sad story of ignorant, self-righteous parents in the Conestoga Valley School District trying to keep their children equally ignorant by banning texts they find threatening.

Such parents — yes, religious fundamentalists — generally attack mainstream classics — Shakespeare, J.D. Salinger, Mark Twain — but have their sights especially set on anything *imaginative*, since the imagination is our chief tool for liberating our minds from such straitjackets as, well, religious fundamentalism. In this case the special object of their wrath was **Robert Bloch's** "Enoch," which originally appeared in *Weird Tales*® for September 1946 and is very much the sort of story we'd be proud to publish today.

Those militant parents wouldn't approve of *Weird Tales*®, we can be fairly sure. They'd take one look and say, "Satanism," to which we would have to reply, "Satanism as a religion is protected by the Bill of Rights, just like Christianity. What are you, un-American?" *Reasoning* with these folks, trying to explain to them what the magazine is really about, what fantastic literature is really about, would be a hopeless exercise. Extinguished imaginations cannot be rekindled. The fight is to prevent the parents from extinguishing their children's imaginations too.

What was the objection to "Enoch"? That it did not teach what the parents understood to be "values." Theirs, of course, which are to be forced on everyone. "Enoch," by the way, is a story about a man haunted by a malevolent little man who lives inside his head and compels him to commit murder. You can find it in *The Collected Stories of Robert Bloch*, published by Carroll & Graf. Not once does the author or even the character suggest that murder is good. It's a *horror* story, after all, and the protagonist's uncontrollable urges cause everyone involved a great deal of dismay.

For children, this story might be described as reality-training. It teaches us that there are bad things in the world, which we can't always control. Bloch, incidentally, is a rigorously moral writer, with a strong sense of good and evil. In his books and stories, evil is usually defeated, or if it wins, this is seen as a *bad* thing, never to be celebrated.

The irony is that the story is fully as moral as the parents, who may not have even read it, want it to be. After much wrangling, the school board re-instated several of the imaginative stories which had been attacked (including one about a future society that eliminates overly-bright children — What a far-out fantasy! We wouldn't know anybody who would want to do that!), but the Bloch story remained on the banned list. (Bloch facetiously asks in a letter to *Weird Tales*® whether this tale, "cunningly calculated to encourage immoral behavior and provide rôle-models for innocent youth" contributed measurably to juvenile delinquency among the students in question.)

We can only hope that those kids went to the nearest paperback bookstore and bought up all the Bloch, King, Koontz, Skip & Spector, F. Paul Wilson, Schow, Richard Laymon, and Rex Miller books they could find, the more "un-wholesome" the better. If this is the beginning of those bigoted parents' loss of control, if the children deliberately sample the forbidden fruit as an act of defiance, then some good may come of the whole affair, and some of those juvenile imaginations may not be snuffed out after all.

We already know of one top-flight horror writer who survived a horrific Christian fundamentalist upbringing — to the point that when his neighbors found out he was writing horror fiction they tried to murder him — and, who knows? Maybe in a generation there will be a few more coming out of rural Pennsylvania.

There is no possibility of compromise. The censors, be they religious fanatics or arbiters of Political Correctness from either end of the spectrum, are The Enemy of all artists, all writers.

What to do? Our solution is to antagonize them as much as possible. Keep them *angry* all the time. Never cave in. Provide them so many targets that they can only waste their energy and look ridiculous in public. What did we do about the t-shirt ban? We arranged to have as many people as possible show up at the next meeting wearing the thing, and explained to all and sundry. The culprits ended up looking quite silly.

All those kids in Lancaster County should buy books, precisely the ones their parents don't want them to read.

And if anyone accuses *Weird Tales*® of being part of a Satanic/Commie/dero/men-in-black conspiracy which killed the Kennedys, kidnapped Elvis, and conceals space-alien xenoproctologists on a secret Air Force base in the Bermuda Triangle, well, we aren't going to deny it.

Simon MacCulloch writes us from Edgware, England:

Many thanks for your special on Thomas Ligotti — the second horror writer this century to excel Lovecraft (Ramsey Campbell being the first).

One minor correction: "The Lost Art of Twilight" (the best vampire story ever?) first appeared in the Summer 1986 issue of Dark Horizons, *the Journal of the British Fantasy Society, then edited by David Sutton. Carl Ford's* Dagon *did a Ligotti special (No. 22/23), to which I contributed an essay on "Lost Art," but did not reprint the story itself.*

You're right about the central place of mystery in supernatural horror fiction, and the distinction between mystery and murk is worth making. Ramsey Campbell's Midnight Sun *may be the genre's greatest example yet of an overwelming sense of mystery conveyed with flawless lucidity — a seeming paradox as rare and spectacular as the phenomenon from which it takes its title.*

Having said that, consider the following excerpts from Walter De la Mare's rules for ghost stories: "The reader's imagination . . . must be furtively quickened by a series of almost imperceptible hints, decoys, innuendoes, into a peculiar sensitiveness. . . . When the story is at its proper dusk, and the footlights burn murky, and the pupils of the writer's (and the reader's) eyes resemble a cat in the small hours, precisely the right kind of characters must be in alarmed or stealthy movement on the stage . . ." The story that is impossible *to follow is undoubtedly a failure, but a degree of* difficulty *characterises a number of masterpieces by De la Mare, Aickman, and the early Campbell. And, as Mr. Ligotti mentions in your excellent interview, the best of Poe is "poetic and obscure." The reader who wants to be led into the heart of darkness*

should not always expect to be handed a flash-light on the way in.

As for sex and violence in horror fiction, I recommend Tennessee Williams's "Desire and the Black Masseur," which remains the most terrifying and illuminating study of the subject(s) I have read, precisely because it reveals their role in the context of the functioning of the human imagination. It also happens to be lit throughout with clinical clarity, proving that the choice between murky footlights and the hard glare of the operating theatre must ultimately rest with the writer's judgment of how best to present the material in question. As Ligotti says, it's in the act of "processing" that unique literature is conceived.

We would certainly agree that the delver-into-darkness doesn't need a flashlight, but somewhere along the way *enough* should become clear that the reader has at least an emotional sense of what is going on, as is the case with, say, De la Mare's own "Seaton's Aunt." The deterioration of the title character is clear enough, and the reader's sympathy is engaged, for all we're never *sure* the Aunt is the actual, supernatural creature she seems to be. For the characters in the story, the distinction ultimately doesn't matter.

Scott Robert Ladd adds to the chorus of praise for Thomas Ligotti:

Issue #303 was wonderful! I was particularly overjoyed with the work of Ligotti, Hoffman, and Taylor. I was impressed by Ligotti's use of color and texture in his writing; reading his work reminded me of reading Lovecraft for the first time.

Artist **Denis Tiani** comments on both art and writing in #303:

I am a Ligotti fan and it was nice to see an issue devoted to him. I especially liked "Nethescurial," and I would probably give it my best-story-in-the-issue vote, except that I also liked "To Become a Sorcerer" very much. The Schweitzer story has a nice flow — moving in and out of different realities — and it's really very beautiful and thoughtful. Even the scary parts are made beautiful by the story and ideas. I guess I'll have to split my vote between the two.

Illustrationwise, the issue looks great. Koszowski and Van Hollander work well together.

The cover has a nice macabre sense of humor to it. It looks like there's a little more Van Hollander than Koszowski there, although the faces have Koszowski-like expressions. The division of labor is more clearly defined in The Classic Horrors, and it works very well — with Van Hollander's background complementing Koszowski's foreground figure.

That one of Harry Morris's on page 23 is the scariest of the lot and the best of the issue. It's a masterpiece. In the best H.M. tradition, it offers ambiguous and suggestive implications that draw the mind as well as the eye.

Along more clean-cut lines are Stephen Fabian's two "Sorcerer" illos. There is a serene weirdness in Fabian's clean style that goes well with the story.

Janet Aulisio's has a nice ghostly quality about it and the three indistinct elements — night sky, grass, and human figure — create a striking effect.

Anyhow, all the art is great and all the artists are giving Weird Tales® *their best. And the diversity of styles from different artists is, to me, far better than one-artist issues.*

As far as we can tell on the creation of the cover for #303, Schweitzer — who draws about as well as a bear rides a bicycle — made a rough sketch of the design, based on the description in Lovecraft.

Koszowski did the main pencil drawing; Van Hollander refined the faces and did most of the color work. The two conferred many times. Whether or not they, like Pickman, posed or photographed their subjects from life, we think it indiscreet to say.

All of the reports — whether true or not — that your editor was subsequently carried off and eaten by ghouls are emphatically denied.

Kristine Farrell addresses us as "My Friends at *Weird Tales*®":

I just read The Eyrie of issue #303 and I cannot believe my eyes. How could there be any question that the small press has a place in the literary world? To quote Jim Morrison, I believe the small press allows new writers to "perform their art and perfect their lives." How can a new writer expect to break into the BIG press (the call of fame and fortune), before cutting his teeth on the SMALL press (modest and unsteady beginnings)?

The core of the controversy is simply this: many writers *do* sell immediately to professional markets. A generation ago, there was no small press, so anybody who made his or her debut before about 1970 did so in the professional markets. Therefore — many professional writers hold — wouldn't new writers of today be better off simply polishing their tales until they're good enough for the big markets, rather than settling (perhaps forever) for second-best in the smaller ones? The other side objects that the stories in the small-press magazines aren't necessarily rejects from the big ones, but stories which fall outside the range of what the big markets will take.

Our own view is that both arguments have some validity. But certainly enough stories from the small press make it into anthologies like *The Year's Best Horror* to demonstrate that small-press magazines don't subsist on professional rejects. Then again, maybe some of those stories could have been sold to professional magazines, if the authors had only *tried*.

The best procedure for writers is to submit stories to the best-paying and most widely circulated magazines first, then work their way down the scale. But much excellent fiction appears in the little magazines. There's certainly no stigma attached to them.

The Most Popular Story in #303 was something of a surprise, like an upset in a political primary. Darrell Schweitzer's "To Become a Sorcerer" drew a lot of early praise, but by the time the votes were counted, Thomas Ligotti's "Nethescurial" was the clear first-place winner, with "To Become a Sorcerer" a moderately close second, Nina Kiriki Hoffman's "Visitors" third, and everything else trailing far behind. Ω

SHADOWINGS
from a Whisper
to a Scream

by Douglas E Winter

To be violent, or not to be violent: that, it would seem, is the question confronting the literature of horror as the millennium draws near. Certainly it is a question asked repeatedly in author interviews, debated at conventions and in letter columns, and invoked in every other book review. Indeed, if recent genre wisdom were to be believed, horror fiction may be divided neatly into two components — "quiet" and "loud" — each with its own writers and readers, editors and publishers, cheerleaders and naysayers.

In this often heated discourse, "quiet" horror is postured as a product of the old school, the firmament of the weird tradition, and thus allied with the elusive literary hopes and dreams of horror. Particularly when known by the genteel rubric of "dark fantasy," "quiet" horror is identified with Charles L. Grant, whose long-running anthology series *Shadows* took as its manifesto that: "What really frightens us, for the most part, is . . . all that we do not *see* even though we know it is there. . . ." Grant, an unassuming, fortysomething former schoolteacher whose hair and beard are salted with grey, is seen by some to represent a kind of staid establishment bent on preserving the halcyon days of the supernatural tale — this in spite of his fervent rejection of Lovecraft and Howard, his unswerving support for new (particularly women) writers, and his own fiction, which echoes Hawthorne but little else of horror's traditional roots.

Set in opposition to "quiet" horror, we are told, is the aesthetic of "loud" — better known, as the Eighties progressed, as "new" horror or "splatterpunk," and personified by Clive Barker and the rude dudes in black leather, David J. Schow, John Skipp and Craig Spector. Embraced by some — and denounced by many others — for its insistent violence, sexual explicitness and bad attitude, "loud" horror is linked with rock-and-roll and revolution, and has been championed as a new wave, if not a full-blown movement.

Virtually every contributor to Paul Sammon's *Splatterpunks* (1990) denied the monicker, and for good reason: any "movement" afoot was the continued liberation of acceptable art and commerce, pioneered not by genre fiction but by film and music and stand-up comedy. A mere glance at the envelope-pushers of the past decade distills the many impulses at work, from the crass (Andrew Dice Clay) to the sophomoric (2 Live Crew), the sublime (Robert Mapplethorpe) to the inevitably ridiculous (Annie Sprinkle).

The same impulses, emboldened by the violently liberating special effects of contemporary cinema, are manifest in "loud" horror, which glories most of all in the showing, not the telling. And it rarely proved unique; indeed, most of this fiction is highly imitative, yet another take on existing iconography — particularly vampirism — but with more explicit sex, explicit violence, explicit intent.

Yet "loud" fiction, more often than not, was horror's cutting edge in the late Eighties; and as it attracted the eye of publicity, we witnessed the tragic irony of writers who claimed dedication to a fiction bent on exploding the taboo speaking out in antagonistic and repressive tones against the aesthetics of "loud." (I recently sat in stunned silence on a convention panel as an esteemed novelist deemed *American Psycho* "pornographic" to enthusiastic applause. The same writer had once expressed surprise and outrage that the "dirty" words had been stricken from a library edition of one of his books.)

What is at once amusing and alarming is that this debate is neither fresh nor particularly meaningful. Those naïve enough to believe that splatterprose is something new should check out Matthew Lewis or "The Copper Bowl" or, in more recent years, Britain's bestselling writer of horror fiction, James Herbert, who ripsawed his way through the Seventies with ultraviolent abandon when some of the "splatterpunks" were still sucking milk through straws.

Similarly, to suggest that "quiet" horror is *passé* is to reject out of hand the power of the written word — to buy into the growing American nightmare of conformity, in which every entertainment called horror must be "R" rated. Just as Robert Wise's brilliant film *The Haunting* demonstrates convincingly that one could make an effective G-rated horror film (if only Hollywood's shopping mall demographics would allow it), new novels and stories are published every year that succeed, critically and commercially, without explicitness — while endless "loud" fictions fail.

The fallacy of classifying — and judging — fiction by its imagery is underscored by the latest novels from the writers said to represent the ultimate in "quiet" and "loud": Charles L. Grant and the writing team of Skipp & Spector. On close reading, these books share so much in common that one wonders just what the fuss is all about.

Something Stirs (Tor, hc, $19.95) proceeds from a premise that is archetypal, if not stereotypical, Charles L. Grant: a small town in New Jersey; an oppressive autumnal night; a clique of alienated teens; a fringe of the elderly and outcast; and a mystery shrouded in shadows, both real and imagined. This précis alone should suffice for most prospective readers. In recent years, Grant has seemed intent on delivering novels meant for a cultivated palate — as with a second taste of sushi, you know before you bite whether you will like it or not; there is no real middle ground.

Blood is shed in the opening act. One dark evening, a skittish high schooler named Joey Costello walks the streets of Foxriver, one of those pastoral small towns that seem only to exist in television commercials and horror fiction. Like Grant's own Oxrun Station and Stephen King's Castle Rock, Foxriver has survived the past forty years without ever seeming to change. Joey Costello is also a throwback to the Fifties, dressed in black leather jacket and jeans, hair ducktailed — thanks to his friend Eddie Roman, a literal Leader of the Pack, so obsessed with the Eisenhower Era that he has persuaded his friends to form a gang and adopt its styles: hence the James Dean couture, girls in poodle skirts and saddle oxfords . . . and a fierce and fatal haunting.

Screams pierce the distant darkness. When Joey runs to Eddie's house, he finds his friend, hatchet in hand: "The blade was dark, and dark dripped from the steel, the haft, and the hand that held it. . . . 'Got him,' Eddie whispered."

Eddie's father is dead; then Eddie. And as the screams continue, invading the teens' sleep, others die. Fears have come out of the peaceful past — mundane childhood fears, brought somehow to life: big bugs, colossal men, things in the cellar, darkmen . . . and most of all, the unseen, the faceless dark, the shadows. "Which," Grant reminds us, "is what it all boiled down to — having an imagination."

For Grant, brooding atmosphere is as important, and as prominent, as story, and his mystery unfolds in characteristic shades of grey: ambiguity and abstraction abound. There is no doubt of the power of such elusive prose in Grant's capable hands. The reader is set adrift in the manner of the best conspiratorial suspense novels, wondering at how and why the puzzle parts must fit together. Grant also strives mightily to make us feel for his characters, imbuing them with mundane humanity, the trivialities of daily experience. Yet the reader is left with an overwhelming sense of introversion — that an inner logic, rather than plot, has driven this novel, and that the real story has never quite been made known. One can almost feel Grant shrinking from his readers, erecting buffers of small talk, sunset and shadow, to fend off those innermost feelings that he can't quite dare onto the page. Along with his reliance upon what is now a too-comfortable setting, this is the salient obstacle that has denied Grant the kind of commercial success that he well deserves.

While *Something Stirs* cloaks itself in shadows, Skipp & Spector's **The Bridge** (Bantam/Spectra, pb, $4.99) is the fictional equivalent of a Klieg light, a bold and bright end-of-the-world extravaganza that echoes *The Night of the Living Dead, Miracle Mile,* and *The Toxic Avenger.*

The literal bridge at issue is a backwoods dumping-ground for hazardous waste — a short span over a Pennsylvania creek that has become "a sin-eater for the Industrial Revolution." When, on one fine evening, some good old boys feed another truckload of barrels into its maw, the creek vomits back the New World: a sentient slime that transforms all that it touches, twisting vegetation and inanimate objects into virulent warmongers, humans into toxic zombies. The bridge thus also becomes the novel's driving metaphor for the unsteady structure of waste that we are building from now to an uncertain — and, for Skipp & Spector, unremittingly bleak — future.

Merely embracing the socially correct side of an issue does not make for good fiction, and Skipp & Spector dance perilously close to a preachment. From page one, there is no sympathy for their devil — each environmentally unsound character is part of a chain of fools leading inexorably to disaster. Indeed, *The Bridge* is virtually devoid of character development; instead Skipp & Spector embrace character transformation, a hallmark of their more unrelenting film influences and, of course, Clive Barker.

What makes *The Bridge* work, and work well, is its unabashed pluck: Skipp & Spector manage to generate a kind of manic propulsion, moving the book forward in a single-minded, damn-the-torpedoes rush. If not all that happens can be forgiven, most is forgotten in the mad rapture of the moment. It's a bit like watching good live rock-and-roll: although lacking in precision, the unabashed vitality makes this book memorable.

Both *Something Stirs* and *The Bridge* proceed from the time-honored template of *Salem's Lot*: a multiple viewpoint exploration of a small town besieged and overcome by evil. But this is only the first of their similarities.

The toxic zombies of *The Bridge* are driven by an unexplained (and indeed superfluous) "Overmind," apparently created by the writers to personalize their horror. A like entity exists, although unstated, in *Something Stirs,* as if Grant, too, were uncomfortable without a focus for his animus. What is noteworthy is that neither novel chooses to personalize good. Absent from each book is a conventional religious underpinning; while Skipp & Spector take pains to ridicule organized religion, for Grant, God is simply missing in action. The novels infuse their characters with an impulse to do what is "right" — to confront and defeat the evil that has been visited upon them — but what is important, the writers stress, is personal choice, a kind of moral courage in the face of an increasingly hostile, if not vengeful, universe.

In *Something Stirs,* there is a counterbalancing of sorts: a suggestion that hope and love, and the confrontation of our personal fears, will engender a transcendence. *The Bridge,* on the other hand, is aggressively nihilistic: after dispensing with God, the writers offer a semicomical discarnate entity, channeled by an earth mother, whose magick is strong enough only to allow the plot to play out to its bitter end. Otherwise, love and hope prove quixotic impulses, savagely frustrated by a world gone wild.

Both novels are influenced heavily by film. Grant presents a world without color, without contrast, a mist of grey in which even the characters start to blur and fade. With each recent novel, he has explored an increasingly minimalist horror, black-and-white vagaries inspired by legendary Forties filmmaker Val Lewton. In *The Bridge,* Skipp & Spector paint with the most vivid of colors, a psychedelic light show that melds the garish bloodletting of Herschell Gordon Lewis and the antic cartoons of Bob Clampett with an in-your-face plea for social consciousness. As should be obvious, there is little room for subtlety here: eyes burn with "napalm pain"; fear pumps bladders "full of lava"; and as for faces, "At least a dozen mottled golfballs of pus jutted out from his greasy post-Elvis complexion" — whatever that may mean.

And yes, of course — if indeed you are wondering — Skipp & Spector again go too far. This time it is their grand finale, a buckknife Cæsarean that produces that nervous feeling one gets when watching a film like *Caligula*: amazement and laughter and a sudden self-loathing. It's a cheap shot — not a sucker punch, for the astute reader will have seen it coming — as unnecessary to concluding this novel as a fatal injection is to a hanged man; but there is no doubt that it is of sublime necessity to the writers' aesthetic.

At a recent World Fantasy Convention, John Skipp argued that his fiction was intended to slap people on the side of the head. There is no doubt that *The Bridge* does just that. Whether this is the best means of making a wake up call to the conscience is another matter.

The Bridge is intended as polemic; the book includes, as an afterword, a pocket guide to environmental action, complete with addresses and alternatives. While the gesture is worthy — as is the generosity of Bantam Books in allowing it — one wonders whether, after reading the nihilistic bloodbath that precedes it, anyone will be interested in activism of any kind, or simply throw up their hands, grab another Big Mac, and watch the rain forests burn.

The apocalypse envisioned by Skipp & Spector is internalized in *Something Stirs*; for Grant, emotional violence is the most deadly kind. His wounded heroes struggle for identity as ferociously as Skipp & Spector's strive to survive. Thus *Something Stirs* is by no means the comfortable ghost story that critics of "quiet" horror have come to imagine, but a slashing of psyche rather than skin.

While these novels thus work at virtual antipodes of imagery — horror at its most extroverted and introverted — together they celebrate the remarkable diversity that this fiction offers. In both books we witness committed talents intent on pushing and pushing their singular visions in pursuit of the concerns that challenge them most; and both offer proof positive of what should have been obvious all along: the question of violence is not one of the lady or the tiger.

The simple truth is that the aesthetics of a story govern its imagery. A writer should neither shrink from indulging in the explicit nor become so overwhelmed by imagery that he or she cannot seduce readers through restraint. The fleeting moments of overt violence in *Something Stirs* disturb the reader by their very rarity; and Skipp & Spector produce, in *The Bridge,* a reunion of doomed lovers that is one of the most powerful set pieces in recent memory: a convergence of sentiment and terror, beauty and horror, that defies any description of "loud." Thus Grant could well write splatter with the best of the punks, just as Skipp & Spector could probably weave the most delicate of dark fantasies — if that was what these writers desired.

These are novelists who, like other writers of conscience, are exercising their substantial talents to entertain and enlighten us in ways that are uniquely their own. Each is pursuing an intensely personal vision, not one that is "quiet" or "loud," but one that is Charles L. Grant, and another that is John Skipp & Craig Spector.

It is time for us to learn again to judge a book by its contents, not its cover — to forego this senseless and divisive debate about what a fiction shows us and to focus our attention upon what it tells us. Ω

We know it's been a long time between issues — but you must still avoid the Awful Curse of the Undelivered Subscription: when & if you remove to another lair (a couple-three weeks beforehand, if you possibly can) do let us know: When you will move, from Whence (with complete old address and ZIP/Postal Code), and Whither will you go (new address and ZIP/Postal Code). Many thanks !

MIDNIGHT MASS

by F. Paul Wilson

It had been almost a full minute since he'd slammed the brass knocker against the heavy oak door. That should have been proof enough. After all, wasn't the knocker in the shape of a cross? But no, they had to squint through their peephole and peer through the sidelights that framed the door.

Rabbi Zev Wolpin sighed and resigned himself to the scrutiny. He couldn't blame people for being cautious, but this seemed a bit overly so. The sun was in the west and shining full on his back; he was all but silhouetted in it. What more did they want?

I should maybe take off my clothes and dance naked?

He gave a mental shrug and savored the damp sea air. At least it was cool here. He'd bicycled from Lakewood, which was only ten miles inland from this same ocean but at least twenty degrees warmer. The bulk of the huge Tudor retreat house stood between him and the Atlantic, but the ocean's briny scent and rhythmic rumble were everywhere.

Spring Lake. An Irish Catholic seaside resort since before the turn of the century. He looked around at its carefully restored Victorian houses, the huge mansions arrayed here along the beach front, the smaller homes set in neat rows running straight back from the ocean. Many of them were still occupied. Not like Lakewood. Lakewood was an empty shell.

Not such a bad place for a retreat, he thought. He wondered how many houses like this the Catholic Church owned.

A series of clicks and clacks drew his attention back to the door as numerous bolts were pulled in rapid succession. The door swung inward revealing a nervous-looking young man in a long black cassock. As he looked at Zev his mouth twisted and he rubbed the back of his wrist across it to hide a smile.

"And what should be so funny?" Zev asked.

"I'm sorry. It's just —"

"I know," Zev said, waving off any explanation as he glanced down at the wooden cross slung on a cord around his neck. "I know."

A bearded Jew in a baggy black serge suit wearing a yarmulke and a cross. Hilarious, no?

So, *nu?* This was what the times demanded, this was what it had come to if he wanted to survive. And Zev did want to survive. Someone had to live to carry on the traditions of the

Talmud and the Torah, even if there were hardly any Jews left alive in the world.

Zev stood on the sunny porch, waiting. The priest watched him in silence.

Finally Zev said, "Well, may a wandering Jew come in?"

"I won't stop you," the priest said, "but surely you don't expect me to invite you."

Ah, yes. Another precaution. The vampire couldn't cross the threshold of a home unless he was invited in, so don't invite. A good habit to cultivate, he supposed.

He stepped inside and the priest immediately closed the door behind him, relatching all the locks one by one. When he turned around Zev held out his hand.

"Rabbi Zev Wolpin, Father. I thank you for allowing me in."

"Brother Christopher, sir," he said, smiling and shaking Zev's hand. His suspicions seemed to have been completely allayed. "I'm not a priest yet. We can't offer you much here, but —"

"Oh, I won't be staying long. I just came to talk to Father Joseph Cahill."

Brother Christopher frowned. "Father Cahill isn't here at the moment."

"When will he be back?"

"I — I'm not sure. You see —"

"Father Cahill is on another bender," said a stentorian voice behind Zev.

He turned to see an elderly priest facing him from the far end of the foyer. White-haired, heavy set, wearing a black cassock.

"I'm Rabbi Wolpin."

"Father Adams," the priest said, stepping forward and extending his hand.

As they shook Zev said, "Did you say he was on 'another' bender? I never knew Father Cahill to be much of a drinker."

"Apparently there was a lot we never knew about Father Cahill," the priest said stiffly.

"If you're referring to that nastiness last year," Zev said, feeling the old anger rise in him, "I for one never believed it for a minute. I'm surprised anyone gave it the slightest credence."

"The veracity of the accusation was irrelevant in the final analysis. The damage to Father Cahill's reputation was a fait accompli. Father Palmeri was forced to request his removal for the good of St. Anthony's parish."

Zev was sure that sort of attitude had

something to do with Father Joe being on "another bender."

"Where can I find Father Cahill?"

"He's in town somewhere, I suppose, making a spectacle of himself. If there's any way you can talk some sense into him, please do. Not only is he killing himself with drink but he's become quite an embarrassment to the priesthood and to the Church."

Which bothers you more? Zev wanted to ask but held his tongue.

"I'll try."

He waited for Brother Christopher to undo all the locks, then stepped toward the sunlight.

"Try Morton's down on Seventy-one," the younger man whispered as Zev passed.

Zev rode his bicycle south on Route 71. It was almost strange to see people on the streets. Not many, but more than he'd ever see in Lakewood again. Yet he knew that as the vampires consolidated their grip on the world and infiltrated the Catholic communities, there'd be fewer and fewer day people here as well.

He thought he remembered passing a place named Morton's on his way to Spring Lake. And then up ahead he saw it, by the railroad track crossing, a white stucco one-story box of a building with "Morton's Liquors" painted in big black letters along the side.

Father Adams' words echoed back to him: . . . *on another bender* . . .

Zev pushed his bicycle to the front door and tried the knob. Locked up tight. A look inside showed a litter of trash and empty shelves. The windows were barred; the back door was steel and locked as securely as the front. So where was Father Joe?

Then he spotted the basement window at ground level by the overflowing trash dumpster. It wasn't latched. Zev went down on his knees and pushed it open.

Cool, damp, musty air wafted against his face as he peered into the Stygian blackness. It occurred to him that he might be asking for trouble sticking his head inside, but he had to give it a try. If Father Cahill wasn't here, Zev would begin the return trek to Lakewood and write this whole trip off as wasted effort.

"Father Joe?" he called. "Father Cahill?"

"That you again, Chris?" said a slightly slurred voice. "Go home, will you? I'll be all right. I'll be back later."

"It's me, Joe. Zev. From Lakewood."

He heard shoes scraping on the floor and then a familiar face appeared in the shaft of light from the window.

"Well I'll be damned. It *is* you! Thought you were Brother Chris come to drag me back to the retreat house. Gets scared I'm gonna get stuck out after dark. So how ya doin', Reb? Glad to see you're still alive. Come on in!"

Zev saw that Father Cahill's eyes were glassy and he swayed ever so slightly, like a skyscraper in the wind. He wore faded jeans and a black, Bruce Springsteen *Tunnel of Love* Tour sweatshirt.

Zev's heart twisted at the sight of his friend in such condition. Such a mensch like Father Joe shouldn't be acting like a *shikker.* Maybe it was a mistake coming here. Zev didn't like seeing him like this.

"I don't have that much time, Joe. I came to tell you —"

"Get your bearded ass down here and have a drink or I'll come up and drag you down."

"All right," Zev said. "I'll come in but I won't have a drink."

He hid his bike behind the dumpster, then squeezed through the window. Father Joe helped him to the floor. They embraced, slapping each other on the back. Father Joe was a taller man, a giant from Zev's perspective. At six-four he was ten inches taller, at thirty-five he was a quarter-century younger; he had a muscular frame, thick brown hair, and — on better days — clear blue eyes.

"You're grayer, Zev, and you've lost weight."

"Kosher food is not so easily come by these days."

"All kinds of food is getting scarce." He touched the cross slung from Zev's neck and smiled. "Nice touch. Goes well with your zizith."

Zev fingered the fringe protruding from under his shirt. Old habits didn't die easily.

"Actually, I've grown rather fond of it."

"So what can I pour you?" the priest said, waving an arm at the crates of liquor stacked around him. "My own private reserve. Name your poison."

"I don't want a drink."

"Come on, Reb. I've got some nice hundred-proof Stoly here. You've got to have at least *one* drink —"

"Why? Because you think maybe you

shouldn't drink alone?"

Father Joe winced. "Ouch!"

"All right," Zev said. *"Bissel.* I'll have *one* drink on the condition that you *don't* have one. Because I wish to talk to you."

The priest considered that a moment, then reached for the vodka bottle.

"Deal."

He poured a generous amount into a paper cup and handed it over. Zev took a sip. He was not a drinker and when he did imbibe he preferred his vodka ice cold from a freezer. But this was tasty. Father Cahill sat back on a crate of Jack Daniel's and folded his arms.

"Nu?" the priest said with a Jackie Mason shrug.

Zev had to laugh. "Joe, I still say that somewhere in your family tree is Jewish blood."

For a moment he felt light, almost happy. When was the last time he had laughed? Probably more than a year now, probably at their table near the back of Horovitz's deli, shortly before the St. Anthony's nastiness began, well before the vampires came.

Zev thought of the day they'd met. He'd been standing at the counter at Horovitz's waiting for Yussel to wrap up the stuffed derma he had ordered when this young giant walked in. He towered over the other rabbis in the place, looked as Irish as Paddy's pig, and wore a Roman collar. He said he'd heard this was the only place on the whole Jersey Shore where you could get a decent corned beef sandwich. He ordered one and cheerfully warned that it better be good. Yussel asked him what could he know about good corned beef and the priest replied that he grew up in Bensonhurst. Well, about half the people in Horovitz's on that day — and on any other day for that matter — grew up in Bensonhurst and before you knew it they were all asking him if he knew such-and-such a store and so-and-so's deli.

Zev then informed the priest — with all due respect to Yussel Horovitz behind the counter — that the best corned beef sandwich in the world was to be had at Shmuel Rosenberg's Jerusalem Deli in Bensonhurst. Father Cahill said he'd been there and agreed one hundred per cent.

Yussel served him his sandwich then. As he took a huge bite out of the corned beef on rye, the normal *tummel* of a deli at lunchtime died away until Horovitz's was as quiet as a *shoul*

on Sunday morning. Everyone watched him chew, watched him swallow. Then they waited. Suddenly his face broke into this big Irish grin.

"I'm afraid I'm going to have to change my vote," he said. "Horovitz's of Lakewood makes the best corned beef sandwich in the world."

Amid cheers and warm laughter, Zev led Father Cahill to the rear table that would become theirs and sat with this canny and charming gentile who had so easily won over a roomful of strangers and provided such a *mechaieh* for Yussel. He learned that the young priest was the new assistant to Father Palmeri, the pastor at St. Anthony's Catholic church at the northern end of Lakewood. Father Palmeri had been there for years but Zev had never so much as seen his face. He asked Father Cahill — who wanted to be called Joe — about life in Brooklyn these days and they talked for an hour.

During the following months they would run into each other so often at Horovitz's that they decided to meet regularly for lunch, on Mondays and Thursdays. They did so for years, discussing religion — Oy, the religious discussions! — politics, economics, philosophy, life in general. During those lunchtimes they solved most of the world's problems. Zev was sure they'd have solved them all if the scandal at St. Anthony's hadn't resulted in Father Joe's removal from the parish.

But that was in another time, another world. The world before the vampires took over.

Zev shook his head as he considered the current state of Father Joe in the dusty basement of Morton's Liquors.

"It's about the vampires, Joe," he said, taking another sip of the Stoly. "They've taken over St. Anthony's."

Father Joe snorted and shrugged.

"They're in the majority now, Zev, remember? They've taken over everything. Why should St. Anthony's be different from any other parish in the world?"

"I didn't mean the parish. I meant the church."

The priest's eyes widened slightly. "The church? They've taken over the building itself?"

"Every night," Zev said. "Every night they are there."

"That's a holy place. How do they manage that?"

"They've desecrated the altar, destroyed all the crosses. St. Anthony's is no longer a holy place."

"Too bad," Father Joe said, looking down and shaking his head sadly. "It was a fine old church." He looked up again, at Zev. "How do you know about what's going on at St. Anthony's? It's not exactly in your neighborhood."

"A neighborhood I don't exactly have any more."

Father Joe reached over and gripped his shoulder with a huge hand.

"I'm sorry, Zev. I heard how your people got hit pretty hard over there. Sitting ducks, huh? I'm really sorry."

Sitting ducks. An appropriate description. Oh, they'd been smart, those bloodsuckers. They knew their easiest targets. Whenever they swooped into an area they singled out Jews as their first victims, and among Jews they picked the Orthodox first of the first. Smart. Where else would they be less likely to run up against a cross? It worked for them in Brooklyn, and so when they came south into New Jersey, spreading like a plague, they headed straight for the town with one of the largest collections of yeshivas in North America.

But after the Bensonhurst holocaust the people in the Lakewood communities did not take quite so long to figure out what was happening. The Reformed and Conservative synagogues started handing out crosses at Shabbes — too late for many but it saved a few. Did the Orthodox congregations follow suit? No. They hid in their homes and shules and yeshivas and read and prayed.

And were liquidated.

A cross, a crucifix — they held power over the vampires, drove them away. His fellow rabbis did not want to accept that simple fact because they could not face its devastating ramifications. To hold up a cross was to negate two thousand years of Jewish history, it was to say that the Messiah had come and they had missed him.

Did it say that? Zev didn't know. Argue about it later. Right now, people were dying. But the rabbis had to argue it now. And as they argued, their people were slaughtered like cattle.

How Zev railed at them, how he pleaded with them! Blind, stubborn fools! If a fire was consuming your house, would you refuse to throw water on it just because you'd always been taught not to believe in water? Zev had arrived at the rabbinical council wearing a cross and had been thrown out — literally sent hurtling through the front door. But at least he had managed to save a few of his own people. Too few.

He remembered his fellow Orthodox rabbis, though. All the ones who had refused to face the reality of the vampires' fear of crosses, who had forbidden their students and their congregations to wear crosses, who had watched those same students and congregations die en masse only to rise again and come for them. And soon those very same rabbis were roaming their own community, hunting the survivors, preying on other yeshivas, other congregations, until the entire community was liquidated and incorporated into the brotherhood of the vampire. The great fear had come to pass: they'd been assimilated.

The rabbis could have saved themselves, could have saved their people, but they would not bend to the reality of what was happening around them. Which, when Zev thought about it, was not at all out of character. Hadn't they spent generations learning to turn away from the rest of the world?

Those early days of anarchic slaughter were over. Now that the vampires held the ruling hand, the bloodletting had become more organized. But the damage to Zev's people had been done — and it was irreparable. Hitler would have been proud. His Nazi "final solution" was an afternoon picnic compared to the work of the vampires. They did in months what Hitler's Reich could not do in all the years of the Second World War.

There's only a few of us now. So few and so scattered. A final Diaspora.

For a moment Zev was almost overwhelmed by grief, but he pushed it down, locked it back into that place where he kept his sorrows and thought of how fortunate it was for his wife Chana that she died of natural causes before the horror began. Her soul had been too gentle to weather what had happened to their community.

"Not as sorry as I, Joe," Zev said, dragging himself back to the present. "But since my neighborhood is gone, and since I have hardly any friends left, I use the daylight hours to wander. So call me the Wandering Jew. And in my wanderings I meet some of your old parishioners."

The priest's face hardened. His voice became acid.

"Do you now? And how fares the remnant of my devoted flock?"

"They've lost all hope, Joe. They wish you were back."

He laughed. "Sure they do! Just like they rallied behind me when my name and honor were being dragged through the muck last year. Yeah, they want me back. I'll bet!"

"Such anger, Joe. It doesn't become you."

"Bullshit. That was the old Joe Cahill, the naive turkey who believed all his faithful parishioners would back him up. But no. Palmeri tells the bishop the heat is getting too much for him, the bishop removes me, and the people I dedicated my life to all stand by in silence as I'm railroaded out of my parish."

"It's hard for the commonfolk to buck a bishop."

"Maybe. But I can't forget how they stood quietly by while I was stripped of my position, my dignity, my integrity, of everything I wanted to be . . ."

Zev thought Joe's voice was going to break. He was about to reach out to him when the priest coughed and squared his shoulders.

"Meanwhile, I'm a pariah over here in the retreat house, a goddam leper. Some of them actually believe —" He broke off in a growl. "Ah, what's the use? It's over and done. Most of the parish is dead anyway, I suppose. And if I'd stayed there I'd probably be dead too. So maybe it worked out for the best. And who gives a shit anyway."

He reached for the bottle of Glenlivet next to him.

"No-no!" Zev said. "You promised!"

Father Joe drew his hand back and crossed his arms across his chest.

"Talk on, O bearded one. I'm listening."

Father Joe had certainly changed for the worse. Morose, bitter, apathetic, self-pitying. Zev was beginning to wonder how he could have called this man a friend.

"They've taken over your church, desecrated it. Each night they further defile it with butchery and blasphemy. Doesn't that mean anything to you?"

"It's Palmeri's parish. I've been benched. Let him take care of it."

"Father Palmeri is their leader."

"He should be. He's their pastor."

"No. He leads the vampires in the obscenities they perform in the church."

Father Joe stiffened and the glassiness cleared from his eyes.

"Palmeri? He's one of them?"

Zev nodded. "More than that. He's the local leader. He orchestrates their rituals."

Zev saw rage flare in the priest's eyes, saw his hands ball into fists, and for a moment he thought the old Father Joe was going to burst through.

Come on, Joe. Show me that old fire.

But then he slumped back onto the crate.

"Is that all you came to tell me?"

Zev hid his disappointment and nodded. "Yes."

"Good." He grabbed the scotch bottle. "Because I need a drink."

Zev wanted to leave, yet he had to stay, had to probe a little bit deeper and see how much of his old friend was left, and how much had been replaced by this new, bitter, alien Joe Cahill. Maybe there was still hope. So they talked on.

Suddenly he noticed it was dark.

"Gevalt!" Zev said. "I didn't notice the time!"

Father Joe seemed surprised too. He ran to the window and peered out.

"Damn! Sun's gone down!" He turned to Zev. "Lakewood's out of the question for you, Reb. Even the retreat house is too far to risk now. Looks like we're stuck here for the night."

"We'll be safe?"

He shrugged. "Why not? As far as I can tell I'm the only one who's been in here for months, and only in the daytime. Be pretty odd if one of those human leeches should decide to wander in here tonight."

"I hope so."

"Don't worry. We're okay if we don't attract attention. I've got a flashlight if we need it, but we're better off sitting here in the dark and shooting the breeze till sunrise." Father Joe smiled and picked up a huge silver cross, at least a foot in length, from atop one of the crates. "Besides, we're armed. And frankly, I can think of worse places to spend the night."

He stepped over to the case of Glenlivet and opened a fresh bottle. His capacity for alcohol was enormous.

Zev could think of worse places too. In fact he had spent a number of nights in much worse places since the holocaust. He decided to put the time to good use.

"So, Joe. Maybe I should tell you some more about what's happening in Lakewood."

After a few hours their talk died of fatigue. Father Joe gave Zev the flashlight to hold and stretched out across a couple of crates to sleep. Zev tried to get comfortable enough to doze but found sleep impossible. So he listened to his friend snore in the pitch darkness of the cellar.

Poor Joe. Such anger in the man. But more than that — hurt. He felt betrayed, wronged. And with good reason. But with everything falling apart as it was, the wrong done to him would never be righted. He should forget about it already and go on with his life, but apparently he couldn't. Such a shame. He needed something to pull him out of his funk. Zev had thought news of what had happened to his old parish might rouse him, but it seemed only to make him want to drink more. Father Joe Cahill, he feared, was a hopeless case.

Zev closed his eyes and tried to rest. It was hard to get comfortable with the cross dangling in front of him so he took it off but laid it within easy reach. He was drifting toward a doze when he heard a noise outside. By the dumpster. Metal on metal.

My bicycle!

He slipped to the floor and tiptoed over to where Father Joe slept. He shook his shoulder and whispered.

"Someone's found my bicycle!"

The priest snorted but remained sleeping. A louder clatter outside made Zev turn, and as he moved his elbow struck a bottle. He grabbed for it in the darkness but missed. The sound of smashing glass echoed through the basement like a cannon shot. As the odor of scotch whiskey replaced the musty ambiance, Zev listened for further sounds from outside. None came.

Maybe it had been an animal. He remembered how raccoons used to raid his garbage at home . . . when he'd had a home . . . when he'd had garbage . . .

Zev stepped to the window and looked out. Probably an animal. He pulled the window open a few inches and felt cool night air wash across his face. He pulled the flashlight from his coat pocket and aimed it through the opening.

Zev almost dropped the light as the beam illuminated a pale, snarling demonic face, baring its fangs and hissing. He fell back as the thing's head and shoulders lunged through the window, its curved fingers clawing at him, missing. Then it launched itself the rest of the way through, hurtling toward Zev.

He tried to dodge but he was too slow. The impact knocked the flashlight from his grasp and it went rolling across the floor. Zev cried out as he went down under the snarling thing. Its ferocity was overpowering, irresistible. It straddled him and lashed at him, batting his fending arms aside, its clawed fingers tearing at his collar to free his throat, stretching his neck to expose its vulnerable flesh, its foul breath gagging him as it bent its fangs toward him. Zev screamed out his helplessness.

Father Joe awoke to the cries of a terrified voice.

He shook his head to clear it and instantly regretted the move. His head weighed at least two hundred pounds, and his mouth was stuffed with foul-tasting cotton. Why did he keep doing this to himself? Not only did it leave him feeling lousy, it gave him bad dreams. Like now.

Another terrified shout, only a few feet away.

He looked toward the sound. In the faint light from the flashlight rolling across the floor he saw Zev on his back, fighting for his life against —

Damn! This was no dream! One of those bloodsuckers had got in here!

He leaped over to where the creature was lowering its fangs toward Zev's throat. He grabbed it by the back of the neck and lifted it clear of the floor. It was surprisingly heavy but that didn't slow him. Joe could feel the anger rising in him, surging into his muscles.

"Rotten piece of filth!"

He swung the vampire by its neck and let it fly against the cinderblock wall. It impacted with what should have been bone-crushing force but bounced off, rolled on the floor, and regained its feet in one motion, ready to attack again. Strong as he was, Joe knew he was no match for this thing's power. He turned, grabbed his big silver crucifix, and charged the creature.

"Hungry? Eat this!"

As the creature bared its fangs and hissed at him, Joe shoved the long lower end of the cross into its open mouth. Blue-white light flickered along the silver length of the crucifix, reflecting in the creature's startled, agonized eyes as its flesh sizzled and crackled. The vampire let out a strangled cry and tried to turn away but Joe wasn't through with it yet. He was literally seeing red as rage poured out of a hidden well and swirled through him. He rammed the cross deeper down the thing's gullet. Light flashed deep in its throat, illuminating the pale tissues from within. It tried to grab the cross and pull it out but the flesh of its fingers burned and smoked wherever they came in contact with the cross.

Finally Joe stepped back and let the thing squirm and scrabble up the wall and out the window into the night. Then he turned to Zev. If anything had happened —

"Hey, Reb!" he said, kneeling beside the older man. "You all right?"

"Yes," Zev said, struggling to his feet. "Thanks to you."

Joe slumped onto a crate, momentarily weak as his rage dissipated. *This is not what I'm about*, he thought. But it had felt so damn good to let it loose on that vampire. Too good. And that worried him.

I'm falling apart . . . like everything else in the world.

"That was too close," he said to Zev, giving the older man's shoulder a fond squeeze.

"Too close for that vampire for sure," Zev said, replacing his yarmulke. "And would you please remind me, Father Joe, that in the future if ever I should maybe get my blood sucked and become a vampire that I should stay far away from you."

Joe laughed for the first time in too long. It felt good.

They climbed out at first light. Joe stretched his cramped muscles in the fresh air while Zev checked on his hidden bicycle.

"Oy," Zev said as he pulled it from behind the dumpster. The front wheel had been bent so far out of shape that half the spokes were broken. "Look what he did. Looks like I'll be walking back to Lakewood."

But Joe was less interested in the bike than in the whereabouts of their visitor from last night. He knew it couldn't have got far. And it hadn't. They found the vampire — or rather what was left of it — on the far side of the dumpster: a rotting, twisted corpse, blackened to a crisp and steaming in the morning sunlight. The silver crucifix still protruded from between its teeth.

Joe approached and gingerly yanked his cross free of the foul remains.

"Looks like you've sucked your last pint of blood," he said and immediately felt foolish.

Who was he putting on the macho act for? Zev certainly wasn't going to buy it. Too out of character. But then, what was his character these days? He used to be a parish priest. Now he was a nothing. A less than nothing.

He straightened up and turned to Zev.

"Come on back to the retreat house, Reb. I'll buy you breakfast."

But as Joe turned and began walking away, Zev stayed and stared down at the corpse.

"They say they don't wander far from where they spent their lives," Zev said. "Which means it's unlikely this fellow was Jewish if he lived around here. Probably Catholic. Irish Catholic, I'd imagine."

Joe stopped and turned. He stared at his long shadow. The hazy rising sun at his back cast a huge hulking shape before him, with a dark cross in one shadow hand and a smudge of amber light where it poured through the unopened bottle of Scotch in the other.

"What are you getting at?" he said.

"The Kaddish would probably not be so appropriate so I'm just wondering if maybe someone should give him the last rites or whatever it is you people do when one of you dies."

"He wasn't one of us," Joe said, feeling the bitterness rise in him. "He wasn't even human."

"Ah, but he used to be before he was killed and became one of them. So maybe now he could use a little help."

Joe didn't like the way this was going. He sensed he was being maneuvered.

"He doesn't deserve it," he said and knew in that instant he'd been trapped.

"I thought even the worst sinner deserved it," Zev said.

Joe knew when he was beaten. Zev was right. He shoved the cross and bottle into Zev's hands — a bit roughly, perhaps — then went and knelt by the twisted cadaver. He administered a form of the final sacrament. When he was through he returned to Zev and snatched back his belongings.

"You're a better man than I am, Gunga Din," he said as he passed.

"You act as if they're responsible for what they do after they become vampires," Zev said as he hurried along beside him, panting as he matched Joe's pace.

"Aren't they?"

"No."

"You're sure of that?"

"Well, not exactly. But they certainly aren't human anymore, so maybe we shouldn't hold them accountable on human terms."

Zev's reasoning tone flashed Joe back to the conversations they used to have in Horovitz's deli.

"But Zev, we know there's some of the old personality left. I mean, they stay in their home towns, usually in the basements of their old houses. They go after people they knew when they were alive. They're not just dumb predators, Zev. They've got the old consciousness they had when they were alive. Why can't they rise above it? Why can't they . . . resist?"

"I don't know. To tell the truth, the question has never occurred to me. A fascinating concept: an undead refusing to feed. Leave it to Father Joe to come up with something like that. We should discuss this on the trip back to Lakewood."

Joe had to smile. So *that* was what this was all about.

"I'm not going back to Lakewood."

"Fine. Then we'll discuss it now. Maybe the urge to feed is too strong to overcome."

"Maybe. And maybe they just don't try hard enough."

"This is a hard line you're taking, my friend."

"I'm a hard-line kind of guy."

"Well, you've become one."

Joe gave him a sharp look. "You don't know what I've become."

Zev shrugged. "Maybe true, maybe not. But do you truly think you'd be able to resist?"

"Damn straight."

Joe didn't know whether he was serious or not. Maybe he was just mentally preparing himself for the day when he might actually find himself in that situation.

"Interesting," Zev said as they climbed the front steps of the retreat house. "Well, I'd better be going. I've a long walk ahead of me. A long, *lonely* walk all the way back to Lakewood. A long, lonely, possibly *dangerous* walk back for a poor old man who —"

"All right, Zev! All *right!*" Joe said, biting back a laugh. "I get the point. You want me to go back to Lakewood. Why?"

"I just want the company," Zev said with pure innocence.

"No, really. What's going on in that Talmudic mind of yours? What are you cooking?"

"Nothing, Father Joe. Nothing at all."

Joe stared at him. Damn it all if his interest wasn't piqued. What was Zev up to? And what the Hell? Why not go? He had nothing better to do.

"All right, Zev. You win. I'll come back to Lakewood with you. But just for today. Just to keep you company. And I'm not going anywhere near St. Anthony's, okay? Understood?"

"Understood, Joe. Perfectly understood."

"Good. Now wipe that smile off your face and we'll get something to eat."

Under the climbing sun they walked south along the deserted beach, barefooting through the wet sand at the edge of the surf. Zev had never done this. He liked the feel of the sand between his toes, the coolness of the water as it sloshed over his ankles.

"Know what day it is?" Father Joe said. He had his sneakers slung over his shoulder. "Believe it or not, it's the Fourth of July."

"Oh, yes. Your Independence Day. We never made much of secular holidays. Too many religious ones to observe. Why should I not believe it's this date?"

Father Joe shook his head in dismay. "This is Manasquan Beach. You know what this place used to look like on the Fourth before the vampires took over? Wall-to-wall bodies."

"Really? I guess maybe sun-bathing is not the fad it used to be."

"Ah, Zev! Still the master of the understatement. I'll say one thing, though: The beach is cleaner than I've ever seen it. No beer cans or hypodermics." He pointed ahead. "But what's that up there?"

As they approached the spot, Zev saw a pair of naked bodies stretched out on the sand, one male, one female, both young and short-haired.

Their skin was bronzed and glistened in the sun. The man lifted his head and stared at them. A blue crucifix was tattooed in the center of his forehead. He reached into the knapsack beside him and withdrew a huge, gleaming, nickel-plated revolver.

"Just keep walking," he said.

"Will do," Father Joe said. "Just passing through."

As they passed the couple, Zev noticed a similar tattoo on the girl's forehead. He noticed the rest of her too. He felt an almost-forgotten stirring deep inside him.

"A very popular tattoo," he said.

"Clever idea. That's one cross you can't drop or lose. Probably won't help you in the dark, but if there's a light on it might give you an edge."

They turned west and made their way inland, finding Route 70 and following it into Ocean County via the Brielle Bridge.

"I remember nightmare traffic jams right here every summer," Father Joe said as they trod the bridge's empty span. "Never thought I'd miss traffic jams."

They cut over to Route 88 and followed it all the way into Lakewood. Along the way they found a few people out and about in Bricktown and picking berries in Ocean County Park, but in the heart of Lakewood . . .

"A real ghost town," the priest said as they walked Forest Avenue's deserted length.

"Ghosts," Zev said, nodding sadly. It had been a long walk and he was tired. "Yes. Full of ghosts."

In his mind's eye he saw the shades of his fallen brother rabbis and all the yeshiva students, beards, black suits, black hats, crisscrossing back and forth at a determined pace on weekdays, strolling with their wives on Shabbes, their children trailing behind like ducklings.

Gone. All gone. Victims of the vampires. Vampires themselves now, most of them. It made him sick at heart to think of those good, gentle men, women, and children curled up in their basements now to avoid the light of day, venturing out in the dark to feed on others, spreading the disease . . .

He fingered the cross slung from his neck. *If only they had listened!*

"I know a place near St. Anthony's where we can hide," he told the priest.

"You've traveled enough today, Reb. And I told you, I don't care about St. Anthony's."

"Stay the night, Joe," Zev said, gripping the young priest's arm. He'd coaxed him this far; he couldn't let him get away now. "See what Father Palmeri's done."

"If he's one of them he's not a priest anymore. Don't call him Father."

"*They* still call him Father."

"Who?"

"The vampires."

Zev watched Father Joe's jaw muscles bunch.

Joe said, "Maybe I'll just take a quick trip over to St. Anthony's myself —"

"No. It's different here. The area is thick with them — maybe twenty times as many as in Spring Lake. They'll get you if your timing isn't just right. I'll take you."

"You need rest, pal."

Father Joe's expression showed genuine concern. Zev was detecting increasingly softer emotions in the man since their reunion last night. A good sign perhaps?

"And rest I'll get when we get to where I'm taking you."

Father Joe Cahill watched the moon rise over his old church and wondered at the wisdom of coming back. The casual decision made this morning in the full light of day seemed reckless and foolhardy now at the approach of midnight.

But there was no turning back. He'd followed Zev to the second floor of this two-story office building across the street from St. Anthony's, and here they'd waited for dark. Must have been a law office once. The place had been vandalized, the windows broken, the furniture trashed, but there was an old Temple University Law School degree on the wall, and the couch was still in one piece. So while Zev caught some Z's, Joe sat and sipped a little of his scotch and did some heavy thinking.

Mostly he thought about his drinking. He'd done too much of that lately, he knew; so much so that he was afraid to stop cold. So he was taking just a touch now, barely enough to take the edge off. He'd finish the rest later, after he came back from that church over there.

He'd stared at St. Anthony's since they'd arrived. It too had been extensively vandalized. Once it had been a beautiful little stone church, a miniature cathedral, really; very Gothic with all its pointed arches, steep roofs, crocketed spires, and multifoil stained glass windows. Now the windows were smashed, the crosses which had topped the steeple and each gable were gone, and anything resembling a cross in its granite exterior had been defaced beyond recognition.

As he'd known it would, the sight of St. Anthony's brought back memories of Gloria Sullivan, the young, pretty church volunteer whose husband worked for United Chemical International in New York, commuting in every day and trekking off overseas a little too often. Joe and Gloria had seen a lot of each other around the church offices and had become good friends. But Gloria had somehow got the idea that what they had went beyond friendship, so she showed up at the rectory one night when Joe was there alone. He tried to explain that as attractive as she was, she was not for him. He had taken certain vows and meant to stick by them. He did his best to let her down easy but she'd been hurt. And angry.

That might have been that, but then her six-year-old son Kevin had come home from altar boy practice with a story about a priest making him pull down his pants and touching him. Kevin was never clear on who the priest had been, but Gloria Sullivan was. Obviously it had been Father Cahill — any man who could turn down the heartfelt offer of her love and her body had to be either a queer or worse. And a child molester was worse.

She took it to the police and to the papers.

Joe groaned softly at the memory of how swiftly his life had become Hell. But he had been determined to weather the storm, sure that the real culprit eventually would be revealed. He had no proof — still didn't — but if one of the priests at St. Anthony's was a pederast, he knew it wasn't him. That left Father Alberto Palmeri, St. Anthony's fifty-five-year-old pastor. Before Joe could get to the truth, however, Father Palmeri requested that Father Cahill be removed from the parish, and the bishop complied. Joe had left under a cloud that had followed him to the retreat house in the next county and hovered over him till this day. The only place he'd found even brief respite from the impotent anger and bitterness that roiled under his skin and soured his gut every minute of every day was in the bottle — and that was sure as Hell a dead end.

So why had he agreed to come back here? To torture himself? Or to get a look at Palmeri and see how low he had sunk?

Maybe that was it. Maybe seeing Palmeri wallowing in his true element would give him the impetus to put the whole St. Anthony's incident behind him and rejoin what was left of the human race — which needed him now more than ever.

And maybe it wouldn't.

Getting back on track was a nice thought, but over the past few months Joe had found it increasingly difficult to give much of a damn about anyone or anything.

Except maybe Zev. He'd stuck by him through the worst of it, defending him to anyone who would listen. But an endorsement from an Orthodox rabbi had meant diddly in St. Anthony's. And yesterday Zev had biked all the way to Spring Lake to see him. Old Zev was all right.

And he'd been right about the number of vampires here too. Lakewood was *crawling* with the things. Fascinated and repelled, Joe had watched the streets fill with them shortly after sundown.

But what had disturbed him more were the creatures who'd come out *before* sundown.

The humans. Live ones.

The collaborators.

If there was anything lower, anything that deserved true death more than the vampires themselves, it was the still-living humans who worked for them.

Someone touched his shoulder and he jumped. It was Zev. He was holding something out to him. Joe took it and held it up in the moonlight: a tiny crescent moon dangling from a chain on a ring.

"What's this?"

"An earring. The local Vichy wear them."

"Vichy? Like the Vichy French?"

"Yes. Very good. I'm glad to see that you're not as culturally illiterate as the rest of your generation. Vichy humans — that's what I call the collaborators. These earrings identify them to the local nest of vampires. They are spared."

"Where'd you get them?"

Zev's face was hidden in the shadows. "Their previous owners . . . lost them. Put it on."

"My ear's not pierced."

A gnarled hand moved into the moonlight. Joe saw a long needle clasped between the thumb and index finger.

"That I can fix," Zev said.

"Maybe you shouldn't see this," Zev whispered as they crouched in the deep shadows on St. Anthony's western flank.

Joe squinted at him in the darkness, puzzled.

"You lay a guilt trip on me to get me here, now you're having second thoughts?"

"It is horrible like I can't tell you."

Joe thought about that. There was enough horror in the world outside St. Anthony's. What purpose did it serve to see what was going inside?

Because it used to be my church.

Even though he'd only been an associate pastor, never fully in charge, and even though he'd been unceremoniously yanked from the post, St. Anthony's had been his first parish. He was here. He might as well know what they were doing inside.

"Show me."

Zev led him to a pile of rubble under a smashed stained glass window. He pointed up to where faint light flickered from inside.

"Look in there."

"You're not coming?"

"Once was enough, thank you."

Joe climbed as carefully, as quietly as he could, all the while becoming increasingly aware of a growing stench like putrid, rotting meat. It was coming from inside, wafting through the broken window. Steeling himself, he straightened up and peered over the sill.

For a moment he was disoriented, like someone peering out the window of a city apartment and seeing the rolling hills of a Kansas farm. This could not be the interior of St. Anthony's.

In the flickering light of hundreds of sacramental candles he saw that the walls were bare, stripped of all their ornaments, of the plaques for the stations of the cross; the dark wood along the wall was scarred and gouged wherever there had been anything remotely resembling a cross. The floor too was mostly bare, the pews ripped from their neat rows and hacked to pieces, their splintered remains piled high at the rear under the choir balcony.

And the giant crucifix that had dominated the space behind the altar — only a portion it remained. The cross-pieces on each side had been sawed off and so now an armless, life-size Christ hung upside down against the rear wall of the sanctuary.

Joe took in all that in a flash, then his attention was drawn to the unholy congregation that peopled St. Anthony's this night. The collaborators — the Vichy humans, as Zev called them — made up the periphery of the group. They looked like normal, everyday people but each was wearing a crescent moon earring.

But the others, the group gathered in the sanctuary — Joe felt his hackles rise at the sight of them. They surrounded the altar in a tight knot. Their pale, bestial faces, bereft of the slightest trace of human warmth, compassion, or decency, were turned upward. His gorge rose when he saw the object of their rapt attention.

A naked teenage boy, his hands tied behind his back, was suspended over the altar by his ankles. He was sobbing and choking, his eyes wide and vacant with shock, his mind all but gone. The skin had been flayed from his forehead — apparently the Vichy had found an expedient solution to the cross tattoo — and blood ran in a slow stream across his abdomen and chest from his freshly truncated genitals. And beside him, standing atop the altar, a bloody-mouthed creature dressed in a long cassock. Joe recognized the thin shoulders, the graying hair trailing from the balding crown, but was shocked at the crimson vulpine grin he flashed to the things clustered below him.

"Now," said the creature in a lightly accented voice Joe had heard hundreds of times from St. Anthony's pulpit.

Father Alberto Palmeri.

And from the group a hand reached up with a straight razor and drew it across the boy's throat. As the blood flowed down over his face, those below squeezed and struggled forward like hatchling vultures to catch the falling drops and scarlet trickles in their open mouths.

Joe fell away from the window and vomited. He felt Zev grab his arm and lead him away. He was vaguely aware of crossing the street and heading toward the ruined legal office.

"**W**hy in God's name did you want me to see that?"

Zev looked across the office toward the source of the word. He could see a vague outline where Father Joe sat on the floor, his back against the wall, the open bottle of scotch in his hand. The priest had taken one drink since

their return, no more.

"I thought you should know what they were doing to your church."

"So you've said. But what's the reason behind that one?"

Zev shrugged in the darkness. "I'd heard you weren't doing well, that even before everything else began falling apart, you had already fallen apart. So when I felt it safe to get away, I came to see you. Just as I expected, I found a man who was angry at everything and letting it eat up his *guderim*. I thought maybe it would be good to give that man something very specific to be angry at."

"You bastard!" Father Joe whispered. "Who gave you the right?"

"Friendship gave me the right, Joe. I should hear that you are rotting away and do nothing? I have no congregation of my own anymore so I turned my attention on you. Always I was a somewhat meddlesome rabbi."

"Still are. Out to save my soul, ay?"

"We rabbis don't save souls. Guide them maybe, hopefully give them direction. But only you can save your soul, Joe."

Silence hung in the air for awhile. Suddenly, the crescent-moon earring Zev had given Father Joe landed in the puddle of moonlight on the floor between them.

"Why do they do it?" the priest said. "The Vichy — why do they collaborate?"

"The first were quite unwilling, believe me. They cooperated because their wives and children were held hostage by the vampires. But before too long the dregs of humanity began to slither out from under their rocks and offer their services in exchange for the immortality of vampirism."

"Why bother working for them? Why not just bare your throat to the nearest bloodsucker?"

"That's what I thought at first," Zev said. "But as I witnessed the Lakewood holocaust I detected the vampires' pattern. They can choose who joins their ranks, so after they've fully infiltrated a population, they change their tactics. You see, they don't want too many of their kind concentrated in one area. It's like too many carnivores in one forest — when the herds of prey are wiped out, the predators starve. So they start to employ a different style of killing. For only when the vampire draws the life's blood from the throat with its fangs does

the victim become one of them. Anyone drained as in the manner of that boy in the church tonight dies a true death. He's as dead now as someone run over by a truck. He will not rise tomorrow night."

"I get it," Father Joe said. "The Vichy trade their daylight services and dirty work to the vampires now for immortality later on."

"Correct."

There was no humor in the soft laugh the echoed across the room from Father Joe.

"Swell. I never cease to be amazed at our fellow human beings. Their capacity for good is exceeded only by their ability to debase themselves."

"Hopelessness does strange things, Joe. The vampires know that. So they rob us of hope. That's how they beat us. They transform our friends and neighbors and leaders into their own, leaving us feeling alone, completely cut off. Some of us can't take the despair and kill themselves."

"Hopelessness," Joe said. "A potent weapon."

After a long silence, Zev said, "So what are you going to do now, Father Joe?"

Another bitter laugh from across the room.

"I suppose this is the place where I declare that I've found new purpose in life and will now go forth into the world as a fearless vampire killer."

"Such a thing would be nice."

"Well screw that. I'm only going as far as across the street."

"To St. Anthony's?"

Zev saw Father Joe take a swig from the scotch bottle and then screw the cap on tight.

"Yeah. To see if there's anything I can do over there."

"Father Palmeri and his nest might not like that."

"I told you, don't call him Father. And screw *him*. Nobody can do what he's done and get away with it. I'm taking my church back."

In the dark, behind his beard, Zev smiled.

Joe stayed up the rest of the night and let Zev sleep. The old guy needed his rest. Sleep would have been impossible for Joe anyway. He was too wired. He sat up and watched St. Anthony's.

They left before first light, dark shapes

drifting out the front doors and down the stone steps like parishioners leaving a predawn service. Joe felt his back teeth grind as he scanned the group for Palmeri, but he couldn't make him out in the dimness. By the time the sun began to peek over the rooftops and through the trees to the east, the street outside was deserted.

He woke Zev and together they approached the church. The heavy oak and iron front doors, each forming half of a pointed arch, were closed. He pulled them open and fastened the hooks to keep them open. Then he walked through the vestibule and into the nave.

Even though he was ready for it, the stench backed him up a few steps. When his stomach settled, he forced himself ahead, treading a path between the two piles of shattered and splintered pews. Zev walked beside him, a handkerchief pressed over his mouth.

Last night he had thought the place a shambles. He saw now that it was worse. The light of day poked into all the corners, revealing everything that had been hidden by the warm glow of the candles. Half a dozen rotting corpses hung from the ceiling — he hadn't noticed them last night — and others were sprawled on the floor against the walls. Some of the bodies were in pieces. Behind the chancel rail a headless female torso was draped over the front of the pulpit. To the left stood the statue of Mary. Someone had fitted her with foam rubber breasts and a huge dildo. And at the rear of the sanctuary was the armless Christ hanging head down on the upright of his cross.

"My church," he whispered as he moved along the path that had once been the center aisle, the aisle that brides used to walk down with their fathers. "Look what they've done to my church!"

Joe approached the huge block of the altar. Once it had been backed against the far wall of the sanctuary, but he'd had it moved to the front so that he could celebrate Mass facing his parishioners. Solid Carrara marble, but you'd never know it now. So caked with dried blood, semen, and feces it could have been made of styrofoam.

His revulsion was fading, melting away in the growing heat of his rage, drawing the nausea with it. He had intended to clean up the place but there was so much to be done, too much for two men. It was hopeless.

"Fadda Joe?"

He spun at the sound of the strange voice. A thin figure stood uncertainly in the open doorway. A man of about fifty edged forward timidly.

"Fadda Joe, izat you?"

Joe recognized him now. Carl Edwards. A twitchy little man who used to help pass the collection basket at 10:30 Mass on Sundays. A transplantee from Jersey City — hardly anyone around here was originally from around here. His face was sunken, his eyes feverish as he stared at Joe.

"Yes, Carl. It's me."

"Oh, tank God!" He ran forward and dropped to his knees before Joe. He began to sob. "You come back! Tank God, you come back!"

Joe pulled him to his feet.

"Come on now, Carl. Get a grip."

"You come back ta save us, ain'tcha? God sent ya here to punish him, din't He?"

"Punish whom?"

"Fadda Palmeri! He's one a dem! He's da woist a alla dem! He —"

"I know," Joe said. "I know."

"Oh, it's so good to have ya back, Fadda Joe! We ain't knowed what to do since da suckers took ova. We been prayin fa someone like youse an now ya here. It's a freakin' miracle!"

Joe wanted to ask Carl where he and all these people who seemed to think they needed him now had been when he was being railroaded out of the parish. But that was ancient history.

"Not a miracle, Carl," Joe said, glancing at Zev. "Rabbi Wolpin brought me back." As Carl and Zev shook hands, Joe said, "And I'm just passing through."

"Passing t'rough? No. Dat can't be! Ya gotta stay!"

Joe saw the light of hope fading in the little man's eyes. Something twisted within him, tugging him.

"What can I do here, Carl? I'm just one man."

"I'll help! I'll do whatever ya want! Jes tell me!"

"Will you help me clean up?"

Carl looked around and seemed to see the cadavers for the first time. He cringed and turned a few shades paler.

"Yeah . . . sure. Anyting."

Joe looked at Zev. "Well? What do you think?"

Zev shrugged. "I should tell you what to do? My parish it's not."

"Not mine either."

Zev jutted his beard at Carl. "I think maybe he'd tell you differently."

Joe did a slow turn. The vaulted nave was utterly silent except for the buzzing of the flies around the cadavers. A massive clean-up job. But if they worked all day they could make a decent dent in it. And then —

And then what?

Joe didn't know. He was playing this by ear. He'd wait and see what the night brought.

"Can you get us some food, Carl? I'd sell my soul for a cup of coffee."

Carl gave him a strange look.

"Just a figure of speech, Carl. We'll need some food if we're going to keep working."

The man's eyes lit again.

"Dat means ya staying?"

"For a while."

"I'll getcha some food," he said excitedly as he ran for the door. "An' coffee. I know someone who's still got coffee. She'll part wit' some of it for Fadda Joe." He stopped at the door and turned. "Ay, an' Fadda, I neva believed any a dem tings dat was said aboutcha. Neva."

Joe tried but he couldn't hold it back.

"It would have meant a lot to have heard that from you last year, Carl."

The man lowered his eyes. "Yeah. I guess it woulda. But I'll make it up ya, Fadda. I will. You can take dat to da bank."

Then he was out the door and gone. Joe turned to Zev and saw the old man rolling up his sleeves.

"*Nu?*" Zev said. "The bodies. Before we do anything else, I think maybe we should move the bodies."

By early afternoon, Zev was exhausted. The heat and the heavy work had taken their toll. He had to stop and rest. He sat on the chancel rail and looked around. Nearly eight hours work and they'd barely scratched the surface. But the place did look and smell better.

Removing the flyblown corpses and scattered body parts had been the worst of it. A foul, gut-roiling task that had taken most of

the morning. They'd carried the corpses out to the small graveyard behind the church and left them there. Those people deserved a decent burial but there was no time for it today.

Once the corpses were gone, Father Joe had torn the defilements from the statue of Mary and then they'd turned their attention to the huge crucifix. It took a while but they finally found Christ's plaster arms in the pile of ruined pews. They'd been still nailed to the sawn-off cross-piece of the crucifix. While Zev and Father Joe worked at jury-rigging a series of braces to reattach the arms, Carl found a mop and bucket and began the long, slow process of washing the fouled floor of the nave.

Now the crucifix was intact again — the life-size plaster Jesus had his arms reattached and was once again nailed to his refurbished cross. Father Joe and Carl had restored him to his former position of dominance. The poor man was upright again, hanging over the center of the sanctuary in all his tortured splendor.

A grisly sight. Zev could never understand the Catholic attachment to these gruesome statues. But if the vampires loathed them, then Zev was for them all the way.

His stomach rumbled with hunger. At least they'd had a good breakfast. Carl had returned from his food run this morning with bread, cheese, and two thermoses of hot coffee. He wished now they'd saved some. Maybe there was a crust of bread left in the sack. He headed back to the vestibule to check and found an aluminum pot and a paper bag sitting by the door. The pot was full of beef stew and the sack contained three cans of Pepsi.

He poked his head out the doors but no one was in sight on the street outside. It had been that way all day — he'd spy a figure or two peeking in the front doors; they'd hover there for a moment as if to confirm that what they had heard was true, then they'd scurry away. He looked at the meal that had been left. A group of the locals must have donated from their hoard of canned stew and precious soft drinks to fix this. Zev was touched.

He called Father Joe and Carl.

"Tastes like Dinty Moore," Father Joe said around a mouthful of the stew.

"It is," Carl said. "I recognize da little potatoes. Da ladies of the parish must really be excited about youse comin' back to break inta deir canned goods like dis."

They were feasting in the sacristy, the small room off the sanctuary where the priests had kept their vestments — a clerical Green Room, so to speak. Zev found the stew palatable but much too salty. He wasn't about to complain, though.

"I don't believe I've ever had anything like this before."

"I'd be real surprised if you had," said Father Joe. "I doubt very much that something that calls itself Dinty Moore is kosher."

Zev smiled but inside he was suddenly filled with a great sadness. Kosher . . . how meaningless now seemed all the observances which he had allowed to rule and circumscribe his life. Such a fierce proponent of strict dietary laws he'd been in the days before the Lakewood holocaust. But those days were gone, just as the Lakewood community was gone. And Zev was a changed man. If he hadn't changed, if he were still observing, he couldn't sit here and sup with these two men. He'd have to be elsewhere, eating special classes of specially prepared foods off separate sets of dishes. But really, wasn't division what holding to the dietary laws in modern times was all about? They served a purpose beyond mere observance of tradition. They placed another wall between observant Jews and outsiders, keeping them separate even from other Jews who didn't observe.

Zev forced himself to take a big bite of the stew. Time to break down all the walls between people . . . while there was still enough time and people left alive to make it matter.

"You okay, Zev?" Father Joe asked.

Zev nodded silently, afraid to speak for fear of sobbing. Despite all its anachronisms, he missed his life in the good old days of last year. Gone. It was all gone. The rich traditions, the culture, the friends, the prayers. He felt adrift — in time and in space. Nowhere was home.

"You sure?" The young priest seemed genuinely concerned.

"Yes, I'm okay. As okay as you could expect me to feel after spending the better part of the day repairing a crucifix and eating non-kosher food. And let me tell you, that's not so okay."

He put his bowl aside and straightened from his chair.

"Come on, already. Let's get back to work.

There's much yet to do."

"Sun's almost down," Carl said.

Joe straightened from scrubbing the altar and stared west through one of the smashed windows. The sun was out of sight behind the houses there.

"You can go now, Carl," he said to the little man. "Thanks for your help."

"Where youse gonna go, Fadda?"

"I'll be staying right here."

Carl's prominent Adam's apple bobbed convulsively as he swallowed.

"Yeah? Well den, I'm staying too. I tol' ya I'd make it up ta ya, din't I? An besides, I don't tink the suckas'll like da new, improved St. Ant'ny's too much when dey come back tonight, d'you? I don't even tink dey'll get t'rough da doors."

Joe smiled at the man and looked around. Luckily it was July and the days were long. They'd had time to make a difference here. The floors were clean, the crucifix was restored and back in its proper position, as were most of the Stations of the Cross plaques. Zev had found them under the pews and had taken the ones not shattered beyond recognition and rehung them on the walls. Lots of new crosses littered those walls. Carl had found a hammer and nails and had made dozens of them from the remains of the pews.

"No. I don't think they'll like the new decor one bit. But there's something you can get us if you can, Carl. Guns. Pistols, rifles, shotguns, anything that shoots."

Carl nodded slowly. "I know a few guys who can help in dat department."

"And some wine. A little red wine if anybody's saved some."

"You got it."

He hurried off.

"You're planning Custer's last stand, maybe?" Zev said from where he was tacking the last of Carl's crude crosses to the east wall.

"More like the Alamo."

"Same result," Zev said with one of his shrugs.

Joe turned back to scrubbing the altar. He'd been at it for over an hour now. He was drenched with sweat and knew he smelled like a bear, but he couldn't stop until it was clean.

An hour later he was forced to give up. No use. It wouldn't come clean. The vampires must have done something to the blood and foulness to make the mixture seep into the surface of the marble like it had.

He sat on the floor with his back against the altar and rested. He didn't like resting because it gave him time to think. And when he started to think he realized that the odds were pretty high against his seeing tomorrow morning.

At least he'd die well fed. Their secret supplier had left them a dinner of fresh fried chicken by the front doors. Even the memory of it made his mouth water. Apparently someone was *really* glad he was back.

To tell the truth, though, as miserable as he'd been, he wasn't ready to die. Not tonight, not any night. He wasn't looking for an Alamo or a Little Big Horn. All he wanted to do was hold off the vampires till dawn. Keep them out of St. Anthony's for one night. That was all. That would be a statement — *his* statement. If he found an opportunity to ram a stake through Palmeri's rotten heart, so much the better, but he wasn't counting on that. One night. Just to let them know they couldn't have their way everywhere with everybody whenever they felt like it. He had surprise on his side tonight, so maybe it would work. One night. Then he'd be on his way.

"What the fuck have you *done?*"

Joe looked up at the shout. A burly, long-haired man in jeans and a flannel shirt stood in the vestibule staring at the partially restored nave. As he approached, Joe noticed his crescent moon earring.

A Vichy.

Joe balled his fists but didn't move.

"Hey, I'm talking to you, mister. Are you responsible for this?"

When all he got from Joe was a cold stare, he turned to Zev.

"Hey, you! Jew! What the Hell do you think *you're* doing?" He started toward Zev. "You get those fucking crosses off —"

"Touch him and I'll break you in half," Joe said in a low voice.

The Vichy skidded to a halt and stared at him.

"Hey, asshole! Are you crazy? Do you know what Father Palmeri will do to you when he arrives?"

"*Father* Palmeri? Why do you still call him that?"

"It's what he wants to be called. And he's

going to call you *dog meat* when he gets here!"

Joe pulled himself to his feet and looked down at the Vichy. The man took two steps back. Suddenly he didn't seem so sure of himself.

"Tell him I'll be waiting. Tell him Father Cahill is back."

"You're a priest? You don't look like one."

"Shut up and listen. Tell him Father Joe Cahill is back — and he's pissed. Tell him that. Now get out of here while you still can."

The man turned and hurried out into the growing darkness. Joe turned to Zev and found him grinning through his beard.

"'Father Joe Cahill is back — and he's pissed.' I like that."

"We'll make it into a bumper sticker. Meanwhile let's close those doors. The criminal element is starting to wander in. I'll see if we can find some more candles. It's getting dark in here."

He wore the night like a tuxedo.

Dressed in a fresh cassock, Father Alberto Palmeri turned off County Line Road and strolled toward St. Anthony's. The night was lovely, especially when you owned it. And he owned the night in this area of Lakewood now. He loved the night. He felt at one with it, attuned to its harmonies and its discords. The darkness made him feel so alive. Strange to have to lose your life before you could really feel alive. But this was it. He'd found his niche, his métier.

Such a shame it had taken him so long. All those years trying to deny his appetites, trying to be a member of the other side, cursing himself when he allowed his appetites to win, as he had with increasing frequency toward the end of his mortal life. He should have given in to them completely long ago.

It had taken undeath to free him.

And to think he had been afraid of undeath, had cowered in fear each night in the cellar of the church, surrounded by crosses. Fortunately he had not been as safe as he'd thought and one of the beings he now called brother was able to slip in on him in the dark while he dozed. He saw now that he had lost nothing but his blood by that encounter.

And in trade he'd gained a world.

For now it was his world, at least this little

corner of it, one in which he was completely free to indulge himself in any way he wished. Except for the blood. He had no choice about the blood. That was a new appetite, stronger than all the rest, one that would not be denied. But he did not mind the new appetite in the least. He'd found interesting ways to sate it.

Up ahead he spotted dear, defiled St. Anthony's. He wondered what his servants had prepared for him tonight. They were quite imaginative. They'd yet to bore him.

But as he drew nearer the church, Palmeri slowed. His skin prickled. The building had changed. Something was very wrong there, wrong inside. Something amiss with the light that beamed from the windows. This wasn't the old familiar candlelight, this was something else, something more. Something that made his insides tremble.

Figures raced up the street toward him. Live ones. His night vision picked out the earrings and familiar faces of some of his servants. As they neared he sensed the warmth of the blood coursing just beneath their skins. The hunger rose in him and he fought the urge to rip into one of their throats. He couldn't allow himself that pleasure. He had to keep the servants dangling, keep them working for him and the nest. They needed the services of the indentured living to remove whatever obstacles the cattle might put in their way.

"Father! Father!" they cried.

He loved it when they called him Father, loved being one of the undead and dressing like one of the enemy.

"Yes, my children. What sort of victim do you have for us tonight?"

"No victim, father — trouble!"

The edges of Palmeri's vision darkened with rage as he heard of the young priest and the Jew who had dared to try to turn St. Anthony's into a holy place again. When he heard the name of the priest, he nearly exploded.

"Cahill? Joseph Cahill is back in my church?"

"He was cleaning the altar!" one of the servants said.

Palmeri strode toward the church with the servants trailing behind. He knew that neither Cahill nor the Pope himself could clean that altar. Palmeri had desecrated it himself; he had learned how to do that when he became nest leader. But what else had the young pup dared to do?

Whatever it was, it would be undone. *Now!*

Palmeri strode up the steps and pulled the right door open —

— and screamed in agony.

The light! The *light!* The LIGHT! White agony lanced through Palmeri's eyes and seared his brain like two hot pokers. He retched and threw his arms across his face as he staggered back into the cool, comforting darkness.

It took a few minutes for the pain to drain off, for the nausea to pass, for vision to return.

He'd never understand it. He'd spent his entire life in the presence of crosses and crucifixes, surrounded by them. And yet as soon as he'd become undead, he was unable to bear the sight of one. As a matter of fact, since he'd become undead, he'd never even *seen* one. A cross was no longer an object. It was a light, a light so excruciatingly bright, so blazingly white that it was sheer agony to look at it. As a child in Naples he'd been told by his mother not to look at the sun, but when there'd been talk of an eclipse, he'd stared directly into its eye. The pain of looking at a cross was a hundred, no, a thousand times worse than that. And the bigger the cross or crucifix, the worse the pain.

He'd experienced monumental pain upon looking into St. Anthony's tonight. That could only mean that Joseph, that young bastard, had refurbished the giant crucifix. It was the only possible explanation.

He swung on his servants.

"Get in there! Get that crucifix down!"

"They've got guns!"

"Then get help. But get it *down!*"

"We'll get guns too! We can —"

"No! I want him! I want that priest alive! I want him for myself! Anyone who kills him will suffer a very painful, very long and lingering true death! Is that clear?"

It was clear. They scurried away without answering.

Palmeri went to gather the other members of the nest.

Dressed in a cassock and a surplice, Joe came out of the sacristy and approached the altar. He noticed Zev keeping watch at one of the windows. He didn't tell him how ridiculous he looked carrying the shotgun Carl had brought back. He held it so gingerly, like it was full of nitroglycerine and would explode if he jiggled it.

Zev turned, and smiled when he saw him.

"*Now* you look like the old Father Joe we all used to know."

Joe gave him a little bow and proceeded toward the altar.

All right: He had everything he needed. He had the Missal they'd found in among the pew debris earlier today. He had the wine; Carl had brought back about four ounces of sour red babarone. He'd found a smudged surplice and a dusty cassock on the floor of one of the closets in the sacristy, and he wore them now. No hosts, though. A crust of bread left over from breakfast would have to do. No chalice, either. If he'd known he was going to be saying Mass he'd have come prepared. As a last resort he'd used the can opener in the rectory to remove the top from one of the Pepsi cans from lunch. Quite a stretch from the gold chalice he'd used since his ordination, but probably more in line with what Jesus had used at that first Mass — the Last Supper.

He was uncomfortable with the idea of weapons in St. Anthony's but he saw no alternative. He and Zev knew nothing about guns, and Carl knew little more; they'd probably do more damage to themselves than to the Vichy if they tried to use them. But maybe the sight of them would make the Vichy hesitate, slow them down. All he needed was a little time here, enough to get to the consecration.

This is going to be the most unusual Mass in history, he thought.

But he was going to get through it if it killed him. And that was a real possibility. This might well be his last Mass. But he wasn't afraid. He was too excited to be afraid. He'd had a slug of the scotch — just enough to ward off the DTs — but it had done nothing to quell the buzz of the adrenalin humming along every nerve in his body.

He spread everything out on the white tablecloth he'd taken from the rectory and used to cover the filthy altar. He looked at Carl.

"Ready?"

Carl nodded and stuck the .38 caliber pistol he'd been examining into his belt.

"Been a while, Fadda. We did it in Latin when I was a kid, but I tink I can swing it."

"Just do your best and don't worry about any mistakes."

Some Mass. A defiled altar, a crust for a host, a Pepsi can for a chalice, a fifty-year-old, pistol-packing altar boy, and a congregation consisting of a lone, shotgun-carrying Orthodox Jew.

Joe looked heavenward.

You do understand, don't you, Lord, that this was arranged on short notice?

Time to begin.

He read the Gospel but dispensed with the homily. He tried to remember the Mass as it used to be said, to fit in better with Carl's outdated responses. As he was starting the Offertory the front doors flew open and a group of men entered — ten of them, all with crescent moons dangling from their ears. Out of the corner of his eye he saw Zev move away from the window toward the altar, pointing his shotgun at them.

As soon as they entered the nave and got past the broken pews, the Vichy fanned out toward the sides. They began pulling down the Stations of the Cross, ripping Carl's makeshift crosses from the walls and tearing them apart. Carl looked up at Joe from where he knelt, his eyes questioning, his hand reaching for the pistol in his belt.

Joe shook his head and kept up with the Offertory.

When all the little crosses were down, the Vichy swarmed behind the altar. Joe chanced a quick glance over his shoulder and saw them begin their attack on the newly repaired crucifix.

"Zev!" Carl said in a low voice, cocking his head toward the Vichy. "Stop 'em!"

Zev worked the pump on the shotgun. The sound echoed through the church. Joe heard the activity behind him come to a sudden halt. He braced himself for the shot. . . .

But it never came.

He looked at Zev. The old man met his gaze and sadly shook his head. He couldn't do it. To the accompaniment of the sound of renewed activity and derisive laughter behind him, Joe gave Zev a tiny nod of reassurance and understanding, then hurried the Mass toward the Consecration.

As he held the crust of bread aloft, he started at the sound of the life-sized crucifix crashing to the floor, cringed as he heard the freshly buttressed arms and crosspiece being torn away again.

As he held the wine aloft in the Pepsi can, the swaggering, grinning Vichy surrounded the altar and brazenly tore the cross from around his neck. Zev and Carl put up a struggle to keep theirs but were overpowered.

And then Joe's skin began to crawl as a new group entered the nave. There had to be at least forty of them, all of them vampires.

And Palmeri was leading them.

Palmeri hid his hesitancy as he approached the altar. The crucifix and its intolerable whiteness were gone, yet something was not right. Something repellent here, something that urged him to flee. What?

Perhaps it was just the residual effect of the crucifix and all the crosses they had used to line the walls. That had to be it. The unsettling aftertaste would fade as the night wore one. Oh, yes. His nightbrothers and sisters from the nest would see to that.

He focused his attention on the man behind the altar and laughed when he realized what he held in his hands.

"Pepsi, Joseph? You're trying to consecrate Pepsi?" He turned to his nest siblings. "Do you see this, my brothers and sisters? Is this the man we are to fear? And look who he has with him! An old Jew and a parish hanger-on!"

He heard their hissing laughter as they fanned out around him, sweeping toward the altar in a wide phalanx. The Jew and Carl — he recognized Carl and wondered how he'd avoided capture for so long — retreated to the other side of the altar where they flanked Joseph. And Joseph . . . Joseph's handsome Irish face so pale and drawn, his mouth drawn into such a tight, grim line. He looked scared to death. And well he should be.

Palmeri put down his rage at Joseph's audacity. He was glad he had returned. He'd always hated the young priest for his easy manner with people, for the way the parishioners had flocked to him with their problems despite the fact that he had nowhere near the experience of their older and wiser pastor. But that was over now. That world was gone, replaced by a nightworld — Palmeri's world. And no one would be flocking to Father Joe for anything

when Palmeri was through with him. "Father Joe" — how he'd hated it when way the parishioners had started calling him that. Well, their Father Joe would provide superior entertainment tonight. This was going to be *fun*.

"Joseph, Joseph, Joseph," he said as he stopped and smiled at the young priest across the altar. "This futile gesture is so typical of your arrogance."

But Joseph only stared back at him, his expression a mixture of defiance and repugnance. And that only fueled Palmeri's rage.

"Do I repel you, Joseph? Does my new form offend your precious shanty-Irish sensibilities? Does my undeath disgust you?"

"You managed to do all that while you were still alive, Alberto."

Palmeri allowed himself to smile. Joseph probably thought he was putting on a brave front, but the tremor in his voice betrayed his fear.

"Always good with the quick retort, weren't you, Joseph. Always thinking you were better than me, always putting yourself above me."

"Not much of a climb where a child molester is concerned."

Palmeri's anger mounted.

"So superior. So self-righteous. What about *your* appetites, Joseph? The secret ones? What are they? Do you always hold them in check? Are you so far above the rest of us that you never give in to an improper impulse? I'll bet you think that even if we made you one of us you could resist the blood hunger."

He saw by the startled look in Joseph's face that he had struck a nerve. He stepped closer, almost touching the altar.

"You do, don't you? You really think you could resist it! Well, we shall see about that, Joseph. By dawn you'll be drained — we'll each take a turn at you — and when the sun rises you'll have to hide from its light. When the night comes you'll be one of us. And then all the rules will be off. The night will be yours. You'll be able to do anything and everything you've ever wanted. But the blood hunger will be on you too. You won't be sipping your god's blood, as you've done so often, but *human* blood. You'll thirst for hot, human blood, Joseph. And you'll have to sate that thirst. There'll be no choice. And I want to be there when you do, Joseph. I want to be there to laugh in your face as you suck up the crimson nectar, and keep on laughing every night as the red hunger lures you into infinity."

And it *would* happen. Palmeri knew it as sure as he felt his own thirst. He hungered for the moment when he could rub dear Joseph's face in the muck of his own despair.

"I was about to finish saying Mass," Joseph said coolly. "Do you mind if I finish?"

Palmeri couldn't help laughing this time.

"Did you really think this charade would work? Did you really think you could celebrate Mass on *this*?"

He reached out and snatched the tablecloth from the altar, sending the Missal and the piece of bread to the floor and exposing the fouled surface of the marble.

"Did you really think you could effect the Transubstantiation here? Do you really believe any of that garbage? That the bread and wine actually take on the substance of —" He tried to say the name but it wouldn't form. "— the Son's body and blood?"

One of nest brothers, Frederick, stepped forward and leaned over the altar, smiling.

"Transubstantiation?" he said in his most unctuous voice, pulling the Pepsi can from Joseph's hands. "Does that mean that this is the blood of the Son?"

A whisper of warning slithered through Palmeri's mind. Something about the can, something about the way he found it difficult to bring its outline into focus . . .

"Brother Frederick, maybe you should —"

Frederick's grin broadened. "I've always wanted to sup on the blood of a deity."

The nest members hissed their laughter as Frederick raised the can and drank.

Palmeri was jolted by the explosion of intolerable brightness that burst from Frederick's mouth. The inside of his skull glowed beneath his scalp and shafts of pure white light shot from his ears, nose, eyes — every orifice in his head. The glow spread as it flowed down through his throat and chest and into his abdominal cavity, silhouetting his ribs before melting through his skin. Frederick was liquefying where he stood, his flesh steaming, softening, running like glowing molten lava.

No! This couldn't be happening! Not now when he had Joseph in his grasp!

Then the can fell from Frederick's dissolving fingers and landed on the altar top. Its contents splashed across the fouled surface releasing another detonation of brilliance, this one more devastating than the first. The glare spread rapidly, extending over the upper surface and running down the sides, moving like a living thing, engulfing the entire altar, making it glow like a corpuscle of fire torn from the heart of the sun itself.

And with the light came blast-furnace heat that drove Palmeri back, back, back until he he had to turn and follow the rest of his nest in a mad, headlong rush from St. Anthony's into the cool, welcoming safety of the outer darkness.

As the vampires fled into the night, their Vichy toadies behind them, Zev stared in horrid fascination at the puddle of putrescence that was all that remained of the vampire Palmeri had called Frederick. He glanced at Carl and caught the look of dazed wonderment on his face. Zev touched the top of the altar — clean, shiny, every whorl of the marble surface clearly visible.

There was fearsome power here. Incalculable power. But instead of elating him, the realization only depressed him. How long had this been going on? Did it happen at every Mass? Why had he spent his entire life ignorant of this?

He turned to Father Joe.

"What happened?"

"I — I don't know."

"A miracle!" Carl said, running his palm over the altar top.

"A miracle and a meltdown," Father Joe said. He picked up the empty Pepsi can and looked into it. "You know, you go through the seminary, through your ordination, through countless Masses *believing* in the Transubstantiation. But after all these years . . . to actually *know* . . ."

Zev saw him rub his finger along the inside of the can and taste it. He grimaced.

"What's wrong?" Zev asked.

"Still tastes like sour barbarone . . . with a hint of Pepsi."

"Doesn't matter what it tastes like. As far as Palmeri and his friends are concerned, it's the real thing."

"No," said the priest with a small smile. "That's Coke."

And then they started laughing. It wasn't

that funny, but Zev found himself roaring along with the other two. It was more a release of tension than anything else. His sides hurt. He had to lean against the altar to support himself.

It took the return of the Vichy to cure the laughter. They charged in carrying a heavy fire blanket. This time Father Joe did not stand by passively as they invaded his church. He stepped around the altar and met them head on.

He was great and terrible as he confronted them. His giant stature and raised fists cowed them for a few heartbeats. But then they must have remembered that they outnumbered him twelve to one and charged him. He swung a massive fist and caught the lead Vichy square on the jaw. The blow lifted him off his feet and he landed against another. Both went down.

Zev dropped to one knee and reached for the shotgun. He would use it this time, he would shoot these vermin, he swore it!

But then someone landed on his back and drove him to the floor. As he tried to get up he saw Father Joe, surrounded, swinging his fists, laying the Vichy out every time he connected. But there were too many. As the priest went down under the press of them, a heavy boot thudded against the side of Zev's head. He sank into darkness.

A throbbing in his head, stinging pain in his cheek, and a voice, sibilant yet harsh . . .

". . . now, Joseph. Come on. Wake up. I don't want you to miss this!"

Palmeri's sallow features swam into view, hovering over him, grinning like a skull. Joe tried to move but found his wrists and arms tied. His right hand throbbed, felt twice its normal size; he must have broken it on a Vichy jaw. He lifted his head and saw that he was tied spread-eagle on the altar, and that the altar had been covered with the fire blanket.

"Melodramatic, I admit," Palmeri said, "but fitting, don't you think? I mean, you and I used to sacrifice our god symbolically here every weekday and multiple times on Sundays, so why shouldn't this serve as *your* sacrificial altar?"

Joe shut his eyes against a wave of nausea. This couldn't be happening.

"Thought you'd won, didn't you?" When Joe wouldn't answer him, Palmeri went on. "And even if you'd chased me out of here for good, what would you have accomplished? The world is ours now, Joseph. Feeders and cattle — that is the hierarchy. We are the feeders. And tonight you'll join us. But *he* won't. *Voilà!*"

He stepped aside and made a flourish toward the balcony. Joe searched the dim, candlelit space of the nave, not sure what he was supposed to see. Then he picked out Zev's form and he groaned. The old man's feet were lashed to the balcony rail; he hung upside down, his reddened face and frightened eyes turned his way. Joe fell back and strained at the ropes but they wouldn't budge.

"Let him go!"

"What? And let all that good rich Jewish blood go to waste? Why, these people are the Chosen of God! They're a delicacy!"

"Bastard!"

If he could just get his hands on Palmeri, just for a minute.

"Tut-tut, Joseph. Not in the house of the Lord. The Jew should have been smart and run away like Carl."

Carl got away? Good. The poor guy would probably hate himself, call himself a coward the rest of his life, but he'd done what he could. Better to live on than get strung up like Zev.

We're even, Carl.

"But don't worry about your rabbi. None of us will lay a fang on him. He hasn't earned the right to join us. We'll use the razor to bleed him. And when he's dead, he'll be dead for keeps. But not you, Joseph. Oh no, not you." His smile broadened. "You're mine."

Joe wanted to spit in Palmeri's face — not so much as an act of defiance as to hide the waves of terror surging through him — but there was no saliva to be had in his parched mouth. The thought of being undead made him weak. To spend eternity like . . . he looked at the rapt faces of Palmeri's fellow vampires as they clustered under Zev's suspended form . . . like *them?*

He *wouldn't* be like them! He would not allow it!

But what if there was no choice? What if becoming undead toppled a lifetime's worth of moral constraints, cut all the tethers on his human hungers, negated all his mortal concepts of how a life should be lived? Honor, justice, integrity, truth, decency, fairness, love — what if they became meaningless words

instead of the footings for his life?

A thought struck him.

"A deal, Alberto," he said.

"You're hardly in a bargaining position, Joseph."

"I'm not? Answer me this: Do the undead ever kill each other? I mean, has one of them ever driven a stake through another's heart?"

"No. Of course not."

"Are you sure? You'd better be sure before you go through with your plans tonight. Because if I'm forced to become one of you, I'll be crossing over with just one thought in mind: To find you. And when I do I won't stake your heart, I'll stake your arms and legs to the pilings of the Point Pleasant boardwalk where you can watch the sun rise and feel it slowly crisp your skin to charcoal."

Palmeri's smile wavered. "Impossible. You'll be different. You'll want to thank me. You'll wonder why you ever resisted."

"You'd better sure of that, Alberto . . . for your sake. Because I'll have all eternity to track you down. And I'll find you, Alberto. I swear it on my own grave. Think on that."

"Do you think an empty threat is going to cow me?"

"We'll find out how empty it is, won't we? But here's the deal: Let Zev go and I'll let you be."

"You care that much for an old Jew?"

"He's something you never knew in life, and never will know: He's a friend." *And he gave me back my soul.*

Palmeri leaned closer. His foul, nauseous breath wafted against Joe's face.

"A friend? How can you be friends with a dead man?" With that he straightened and turned toward the balcony. "Do him! *Now!*"

As Joe shouted out frantic pleas and protests, one of the vampires climbed up the rubble toward Zev. Zev did not struggle. Joe saw him close his eyes, waiting. As the vampire reached out with the straight razor, Joe bit back a sob of grief and rage and helplessness. He was about to squeeze his own eyes shut when he saw a flame arc through the air from one of the windows. It struck the floor with a crash of glass and a *wooomp!* of exploding flame.

Joe had only heard of such things, but he immediately realized that he had just seen his first Molotov cocktail in action. The splattering gasoline caught the clothes of a nearby vampire who began running in circles, screaming as it beat at its flaming clothes. But its cries were drowned by the roar of other voices, a hundred or more. Joe looked around and saw people — men, women, teenagers — climbing in the windows, charging through the front doors. The women held crosses on high while the men wielded long wooden pikes — broom, rake, and shovel handles whittled to sharp points. Joe recognized most of the faces from the Sunday Masses he had said here for years.

St. Anthony's parishioners were back to reclaim their church.

"Yes!" he shouted, not sure whether to laugh or cry. But when he saw the rage in Palmeri's face, he laughed. "Too bad, Alberto!"

Palmeri made a lunge at his throat but cringed away as a woman with an upheld crucifix and a man with a pike charged the altar — Carl and a woman Joe recognized as Mary O'Hare.

"Told ya I wun't letcha down, din't I, Fadda?" Carl said, grinning and pulling out a red Swiss Army knife. He began sawing at the rope around Joe's right wrist. "Din't I?"

"That you did, Carl. I don't think I've ever been so glad to see anyone in my entire life. But how —?"

"I told 'em. I run t'rough da parish, goin' house ta house. I told 'em dat Fadda Joe was in trouble an' dat we let him down before but we shoun't let him down again. He come back fa us, now we gotta go back fa him. Simple as dat. And den *dey* started runnin' house ta house, an' afore ya knowed it, we had ourselfs a little army. We come ta kick ass, Fadda, if you'll excuse da expression."

"Kick all the ass you can, Carl."

Joe glanced at Mary O'Hare's terror-glazed eyes as she swiveled around, looking this way and that; he saw how the crucifix trembled in her hand. She wasn't going to kick too much ass in her state, but she was *here,* dear God, she was here for him and for St. Anthony's despite the terror that so obviously filled her. His heart swelled with love for the these people and pride in their courage.

As soon as his arms were free, Joe sat up and took the knife from Carl. As he sawed at his leg ropes, he looked around the church.

The oldest and youngest members of the parishioner army were stationed at the windows and doors where they held crosses aloft,

cutting off the vampires' escape, while all across the nave — chaos. Screams, cries, and an occasional shot echoed through St. Anthony's. The vampires were outnumbered three to one and seemed blinded and confused by all the crosses around them. Despite their superhuman strength, it appeared that some were indeed getting their asses kicked. A number were already writhing on the floor, impaled on pikes. As Joe watched, he saw a pair of the women, crucifixes held before them, backing a vampire into a corner. As it cowered there with its arms across its face, one of the men charged in with a sharpened rake handle held like a lance and ran it through.

But a number of parishioners lay in inert, bloody heaps on the floor, proof that the vampires and the Vichy were claiming their share of victims too.

Joe freed his feet and hopped off the altar. He looked around for Palmeri — he *wanted* Palmeri — but the vampire priest had lost himself in the melee. Joe glanced up at the balcony and saw that Zev was still hanging there, struggling to free himself. He started across the nave to help him.

Zev hated that he should be hung up here like a salami in a deli window. He tried again to pull his upper body up far enough to reach his leg ropes but he couldn't get close. He had never been one for exercise; doing a sit-up flat on the floor would have been difficult, so what made him think he could do the equivalent maneuver hanging upside down by his feet? He dropped back, exhausted, and felt the blood rush to his head again. His vision swam, his ears pounded, he felt like his skin of his face was going to burst open. Much more of this and he'd have a stroke or worse maybe.

He watched the upside-down battle below and was glad to see the vampires getting the worst of it. These people — seeing Carl among them, Zev assumed they were part of St. Anthony's parish — were ferocious, almost savage in their attacks on the vampires. Months' worth of pent-up rage and fear was being released upon their tormentors in a single burst. It was almost frightening.

Suddenly he felt a hand on his foot. Someone was untying his knots. Thank you, Lord. Soon he would be on his feet again. As the cords came loose he decided he should at least attempt to participate in his own rescue.

Once more, Zev thought. *Once more I'll try.*

With a grunt he levered himself up, straining, stretching to grasp something, anything. A hand came out of the darkness and he reached for it. But Zev's relief turned to horror when he felt the cold clamminess of the thing that clutched him, that pulled him up and over the balcony rail with inhuman strength. His bowels threatened to evacuate when Palmeri's grinning face loomed not six inches from his own.

"It's not over yet, Jew," he said softly, his foul breath clogging Zev's nose and throat. "Not by a long shot!"

He felt Palmeri's free hand ram into his belly and grip his belt at the buckle, then the other hand grab a handful of his shirt at the neck. Before he could struggle or cry out, he was lifted free of the floor and hoisted over the balcony rail.

And the demon's voice was in his ear.

"Joseph called you a friend, Jew. Let's see if he really meant it."

J oe was half way across the floor of the nave when he heard Palmeri's voice echo above the madness.

"Stop them, Joseph! Stop them now or I drop your friend!"

Joe looked up and froze. Palmeri stood at the balcony rail, leaning over it, his eyes averted from the nave and all its newly arrived crosses. At the end of his outstretched arms was Zev, suspended in mid-air over the splintered remains of the pews, over a particularly large and ragged spire of wood that pointed directly at the middle of Zev's back. Zev's frightened eyes were flashing between Joe and the giant spike below.

Around him Joe heard the sounds of the melee drop a notch, then drop another as all eyes were drawn to the tableau on the balcony.

"A human can die impaled on a wooden stake just as well as a vampire!" Palmeri cried. "And just as quickly if it goes through his heart. But it can take hours of agony if it rips through his gut."

St. Anthony's grew silent as the fighting stopped and each faction backed away to a different side of the church, leaving Joe alone in the middle.

"What do you want, Alberto?"

"First I want all those crosses put away so that I can see!"

Joe looked to his right where his parishioners stood.

"Put them away," he told them. When a murmur of dissent arose, he added, "Don't put them down, just out of sight. Please."

Slowly, one by one at first, then in groups, the crosses and crucifixes were placed behind backs or tucked out of sight within coats.

To his left, the vampires hissed their relief and the Vichy cheered. The sound was like hot needles being forced under Joe's fingernails. Above, Palmeri turned his face to Joe and smiled.

"That's better."

"What do you want?" Joe asked, knowing with a sick crawling in his gut exactly what the answer would be.

"A trade," Palmeri said.

"Me for him, I suppose?" Joe said.

Palmeri's smile widened. "Of course."

"No, Joe!" Zev cried.

Palmeri shook the old man roughly. Joe heard him say, "Quiet, Jew, or I'll snap your spine!" Then he looked down at Joe again. "The other thing is to tell your rabble to let my people go." He laughed and shook Zev again. "Hear that, Jew? A Biblical reference — Old Testament, no less!"

"All right," Joe said without hesitation.

The parishioners on his right gasped as one and cries of "No!" and "You can't!" filled St. Anthony's. A particularly loud voice nearby shouted, "He's only a lousy kike!"

Joe wheeled on the man and recognized Gene Harrington, a carpenter. He jerked a thumb back over his shoulder at the vampires and their servants.

"You sound like you'd be more at home with them, Gene."

Harrington backed up a step and looked at his feet.

"Sorry, Father," he said in a voice that hovered on the verge of a sob. "But we just got you back!"

"I'll be all right," Joe said softly.

And he meant it. Deep inside he had a feeling that he would come through this, that if he could trade himself for Zev and face Palmeri one-on-one, he could come out the victor, or at least battle him to a draw. Now that he was no longer tied up like some sacrificial lamb, now that he was free, with full use of his arms and legs again, he could not imagine dying at the hands of the likes of Palmeri.

Besides, one of the parishioners had given him a tiny crucifix. He had it closed in the palm of his hand.

But he had to get Zev out of danger first. That above all else. He looked up at Palmeri.

"All right, Alberto. I'm on my way up."

"Wait!" Palmeri said. "Someone search him."

Joe gritted his teeth as one of the Vichy, a blubbery, unwashed slob, came forward and searched his pockets. Joe thought he might get away with the crucifix but at the last moment he was made to open his hands. The Vichy grinned in Joe's face as he snatched the tiny cross from his palm and shoved it into his pocket.

"He's clean now!" the slob said and gave Joe a shove toward the vestibule.

Joe hesitated. He was walking into the snake pit unarmed. A glance at his parishioners told him he couldn't very well turn back now.

He continued on his way, clenching and unclenching his tense, sweaty fists as he walked. He still had a chance of coming out of this alive. He was too angry to die. He prayed that when he got within reach of the ex-priest the smoldering rage at how he had framed him when he'd been pastor, at what he'd done to St. Anthony's since then would explode and give him the strength to tear Palmeri to pieces.

"No!" Zev shouted from above. "Forget about me! You've started something here and you've got to see it through!"

Joe ignored his friend.

"Coming, Alberto."

Father Joe's coming, Alberto. And he's pissed. Royally pissed.

Zev craned his neck around, watching Father Joe disappear beneath the balcony.

"Joe! Come back!"

Palmeri shook him again.

"Give it up, old Jew. Joseph never listened to anyone and he's not listening to you. He still believes in faith and virtue and honesty, in the power of goodness and truth over what he perceives as evil. He'll come up here ready to

sacrifice himself for you, yet sure in his heart that he's going to win in the end. But he's wrong."

"No!" Zev said.

But in his heart he knew that Palmeri was right. How could Joe stand up against a creature with Palmeri's strength, who could hold Zev in the air like this for so long? Didn't his arms ever tire?

"Yes!" Palmeri hissed. "He's going to lose and we're going to win. We'll win for the same reason we'll always win. We don't let anything as silly and transient as sentiment stand in our way. If we'd been winning below and situations were reversed — if Joseph were holding one of my nest brothers over that wooden spike below — do you think I'd pause for a moment? For a second? Never! That's why this whole exercise by Joseph and these people is futile."

Futile . . . Zev thought. Like much of his life, it seemed. Like all of his future. Joe would die tonight and Zev would live on, a cross-wearing Jew, with the traditions of his past sacked and in flames, and nothing in his future but a vast, empty, limitless plain to wander alone.

There was a sound on the balcony stairs and Palmeri turned his head.

"Ah, Joseph," he said.

Zev couldn't see the priest but he shouted anyway.

"Go back Joe! Don't let him trick you!"

"Speaking of tricks," Palmeri said, leaning further over the balcony rail as an extra warning to Joe, "I hope you're not going to try anything foolish."

"No," said Joe's tired voice from somewhere behind Palmeri. "No tricks. Pull him in and let him go."

Zev could not let this happen. And suddenly he knew what he had to do. He twisted his body and grabbed the front of Palmeri's cassock while bringing his legs up and bracing his feet against one of the uprights of the brass balcony rail. As Palmeri turned his startled face toward him, Zev put all his strength into his legs for one convulsive backwards push against the railing, pulling Palmeri with him. The vampire priest was overbalanced. Even his enormous strength could not help him once his feet came free of the floor. Zev saw his undead eyes widen with terror as his lower body slipped over the railing. As they fell free, Zev wrapped his arms around Palmeri and clutched his cold and

surprisingly thin body tight against him.

"What goes through this old Jew goes through you!" he shouted into the vampire's ear.

For an instant he saw Joe's horrified face appear over the balcony's receding edge, heard Joe's faraway shout of *"No!"* mingle with Palmeri's nearer scream of the same word, then there was a spine-cracking jar and a tearing, wrenching pain beyond all comprehension in his chest. In an eyeblink he felt the sharp spire of wood rip through him and into Palmeri.

And then he felt no more.

As roaring blackness closed in he wondered if he'd done it, if this last desperate, foolish act had succeeded. He didn't want to die without finding out. He wanted to know —

But then he knew no more.

Joe shouted incoherently as he hung over the rail and watched Zev's fall, gagged as he saw the bloody point of the pew remnant burst through the back of Palmeri's cassock directly below him. He saw Palmeri squirm and flop around like a speared fish, then go limp atop Zev's already inert form.

As cheers mixed with cries of horror and the sounds of renewed battle rose from the nave, Joe turned away from the balcony rail and dropped to his knees.

"Zev!" he cried aloud. "Good God, Zev!"

Forcing himself to his feet, he stumbled down the back stairs, through the vestibule, and into the nave. The vampires and the Vichy were on the run, as cowed and demoralized by their leader's death as the parishioners were buoyed by it.

Slowly, steadily, they were falling before the relentless onslaught. But Joe paid them scant attention. He fought his way to where Zev lay impaled beneath Palmeri's already rotting corpse. He looked for a sign of life in his old friend's glazing eyes, a hint of a pulse in his throat under his beard, but there was nothing.

"Oh, Zev, you shouldn't have. You shouldn't have."

Suddenly he was surrounded by a cheering throng of St. Anthony's parishioners.

"We did it, Fadda Joe!" Carl cried, his face and hands splattered with blood. "We killed 'em all! We got our church back!"

"Thanks to this man here," Joe said, pointing to Zev.

"No!" someone shouted. "Thanks to *you!*"

Amid the cheers, Joe shook his head and said nothing.

Let them celebrate. They deserved it. They'd reclaimed a small piece of the planet as their own, a toehold and nothing more.

A small victory of minimal significance in the war, but a victory nonetheless.

They had their church back, at least for tonight. And they intended to keep it.

Good.

But there would be one change. If they wanted their Father Joe to stick around they were going to have to agree to rename the church.

St. Zev's.

Joe liked the sound of that.   Ω

MIRROR, MIRROR

by Tina & Tony Rath

When Nievis Bianca was seventeen her old man married again, for the fourth, or maybe it was the fifth time, as he certainly hadn't bothered to keep count and no-one else had either. And the lady he married was a real Queen of the Witches. Well, she was heavily into the occult anyway, and she certainly looked the part. She had long, long, night black hair, that Nievis thought must be a dye job because she never would go in swimming, even on the hottest day, and a pale skin that owed a whole lot to heavy foundation and light green face powder. Now this may have been the cause of the trouble between them, because Nievis was by nature exactly what her step-mother aspired to be by art. She had a skin like white rose petals, because she knew all about the bad effects of sun-bathing and never went out without her broad-brimmed hat. And she too had long, long hair like black satin, but she got that from her own mama, who had been Spanish as you might guess from the name she gave her baby daughter. She had also been Old Man Bianca's One True Love as he was apt to tell everyone when he'd been drinking, which was most days, and this did not help things between Nievis and her step-mother either.

Now, the day after the wedding the new Mrs Bianca took a long look at her step-daughter, as if she was measuring her for a shroud, and then she enrolled herself at a gym which offered aerobics and beauty therapy and all the aids a rich man's wife could ever ask to get her into top condition. And they gave her a diet sheet and an exercise programme, and they massaged her and depilated her and exfoliated her and gave her mud baths and vapour baths, and they brushed herbal jells into her long black hair, and when they had finished they started in and did it over again. Well, at last she decided she was ready for the final test. So she went into her bedroom and closed the shutters and locked the door. Then she lit three black candles and opened a locked drawer in her dressing table, and she took out a little tarnished square of glass. And holding it in her palm she intoned:

"Mirror, mirror in my hand
Who's the fairest in the land?"

And the mirror wrinkled as if it was shrugging its shoulders and replied: "Well, you're not bad for your age, baby, but let's face it, you'll never be eighteen again."

"You mean, like Nievis?" she gritted.

"You said it, snookums, not me," said the mirror.

She swung back her arm as if to throw the glass against the wall, but it only sniggered and said: "OK, go ahead honey, get yourself seven years bad luck, but remember it's the real double whammy if you break a magic mirror." So the new Mrs Bianca, who was naturally rather superstitious, dared not take out her bad temper on the mirror, but turned it on Nievis instead. Unfortunately Nievis was as good as she was beautiful. She responded to her step-mother's jealous rages by saying that she understood that she (Mrs Bianca) was going through a difficult time of life, and suggesting holistic remedies, or psychotherapy, which, for some reason, made her step-mother angrier than ever.

One evening, after a conversation with Nievis about the marvellous effects of the oil of evening primrose on the health and temper of the menopausal woman, the new Mrs Bianca locked herself in her bedroom again. But this time she consulted the telephone directory instead of her magic mirror. Now, in the course of his business, Mr Bianca had made a wide range of acquaintances, and some (well, practically all, really) were from the criminal classes. One of them in particular was a hitman who happened to admire Mrs Bianca very much, so much indeed that he had once rashly told her that if she ever wanted anyone removed from her circle of friends in a perfectly private and genteel style, she had only to ask. That evening she did ask; and the person scheduled for removal was, of course, the beautiful Nievis.

The hitman was very sorry to hear such a

request from Mrs Bianca but he had given his word, and he felt honour-bound to do as she asked. So he waited outside Nievis's high school and prepared to do what he had promised. But when he saw her tripping blithely down the steps, swinging her school-books in her hand, she reminded him so sharply of his own baby sister that instead of shooting her he took her to a drug store, and over a chocolate soda he told her just what her step-mother had asked him to do.

"But," he said, "now I have seen you, I know I cannot do any such thing. I will go back and tell your step-mother that I have reformed my life and I will never shoot people for money again."

Now Nievis was good and beautiful, but she was by no means a bimbo. So she said to the hitman, "Don't do that, because she will only find someone else, who has fewer scruples, or no baby sister, who will shoot me instead. Go and tell her you have done the dreadful deed, and take my locket as proof. But first please drive me to somewhere where I will be safe from her."

So, following her directions he drove her over seven rivers, through seven forests, and over seven mountains until — very late at night — they came to a little ranch-style house in the middle of nowhere. And Nievis pushed open the door and went in. The hitman went back to her step-mother and showed her the locket. He was so convincing that as soon as he had gone Mrs Bianca went to her room, lit her candles, picked up her mirror, and demanded:

"Mirror, mirror in my hand
Who's *now* the fairest in the land?"

But the mirror said: "Like I said, sugar, you're OK for your age, but your step-daughter, Nievis, currently living in a ranch-style bungalow with the seven dwarves, is still better-looking."

"She's doing what!" shrieked the Witch Queen.

"You heard, angel-pie. So what do you expect? You get into the occult, find yourself a magic mirror, and marry a man called Bianca, who has a daughter named Nievis, which makes her Snow White in plain American English, and you don't expect the seven dwarves to turn up somewhere? Now you have to disguise yourself as an Avon lady and make with the poisoned apples."

But the Witch Queen said: "No way!"

"What do you mean 'No way'," the mirror demanded shrilly. "You can't fly in the face of tradition."

"Just watch me," said Mrs Bianca, who was beginning to remember the rest of the story. "You really think I'm schlepping across seven mountains, to say nothing of the forests and the rivers just to poison some ungrateful girl who'll only be revived by a handsome prince, and marry him, while I get to dance at her reception in centrally heated shoes? If she wants to play house with seven short persons, let her! If her poor father ever finds out it will kill him, that's all."

And she flounced off to tell him.

However, Mr Bianca accepted the news philosophically. After all, Nievis would have been leaving home to go to college quite soon and, all things considered, there was probably less to worry about if she was living in the middle of nowhere chaperoned by seven dwarves than if she was at a college, however respectable, exposed to the triple evils of Drugs, Feminism, and College Athletes. So he was not unhappy. But others were.

To begin with, there were the dwarves. They had accepted custody of Nievis in the belief that she would shortly succumb to her step-mother's poisoned apple and spend the rest of her stay in a trance, until her prince arrived to take her away. They certainly had not expected an open-ended contract, with no prospect of release from the regimen of low-fat, whole-food vegetarian meals she inflicted on them, to say nothing of the music that blared from her little radio cassette player morning, noon, and night. They began to picket the Bianca residence, and it was not long before other interested groups joined them. A number of Writers' Guilds and Groups objected to Snow White's story being deprived of its traditional happy ending. Romantic novelists were especially concerned, as they said it undermined all they stood for. When the lady novelists and the dwarves were joined by a delegation of English actors representing the pantomime interest, the Biancas' front lawn began to resemble a three-ring circus. The dispute escalated. Questions were asked in Congress, and all the participants appeared on most of the major chat shows.

Mrs Bianca had some supporters. An anonymous but encouraging note arrived from a Big Bad Wolf trying to start a new life as a vegetarian chef in San Francisco, and a group calling itself Woman In Total Charge of Herself (Eastern Section) mounted a counter-picket. But even if the whole world had been against her, she announced, she still had no intention of relenting and poisoning her step-daughter.

The deadlock was broken by someone that almost everyone else had forgotten about. One day the reformed hitman got in his car and travelled over seven mountains, across seven rivers, and through seven forests until he found Nievis sitting by the fake wishing well that the dwarves had set up on their front lawn. He went down on one knee and said: "Snow White, you should marry the handsomest prince in the world. But he could not love you more than I do. I was a hitman and to tell you the truth, not much of a one at that: it was mostly talk with me. Now I am only a poor salesman. But if you will marry me I promise we will live happily ever after."

And Nievis smiled and got into his car, and they drove off into the sunset. They were married very quietly, and all that danced at their wedding were their hearts.

The years passed. The ex-hitman never did make a lot of money, but he and Nievis had many beautiful children, and they were very happy. And Mrs Bianca? Well, she was very happy too. She watched as Nievis — as women with low incomes and large families will — grew fat. Nievis cut off her long black hair because it was just too much trouble, and she forgot to wear her broad-brimmed hat, and her skin coarsened. To her husband she was always the beautiful Snow White he had first married; but often, after her step-daughter and her family had visited with her father at Christmas or Thanksgiving, Mrs Bianca would go to her bedroom and look into the little tarnished mirror with the gold frame she now kept on her bedroom wall, and she would say:

"Mirror, mirror on the wall
Cosmetic surgery beats them all."

And the mirror would chuckle and reply:

"You said it, honey-pie, you said it."   Ω

SIRENS

by Steve Rasnic Tem

As a child, Mary had often fantasized about running away from home. But that was the Fifties, and running away was something boys did, or at least that was what she had thought at the time. She'd known a couple of boys who'd done it, one for an afternoon, the other for almost two days. But the amount of time apparently didn't matter — both had come back bragging of adventures, and even though all the other children knew they were mostly lying they didn't seem to mind the embellishments. Mary had envied those boys terribly. She never forgot.

A hundred miles from home, driving through pouring rain, it occurred to her that this did not seem like such a wonderful adventure after all. She thought about her two small girls left with her parents, told that Mommy was just going on an overnight business trip, and began to cry, feeling like a hag, a witch in one of their fairy story books. She might have turned around right there, but told herself her girls were better off without a lying monster for a mother.

Colin would have never understood. But if Colin had lived she wouldn't be doing this. Cancer was something she'd never believed in; she couldn't picture it so it had never made much sense to her. It was a cruel fairytale told by a terrible mother to her children. He'd rotted away like an old discarded doll, like some *object*. His death had been more like an evil enchantment than something that should happen to normal people.

The passing cars whined and shimmied beneath the rain's assault. Water crashed in sheets across the silvered roadway. Every now and then she peered upward through the windshield, half-expecting to find herself on a collision course with a gigantic wall of water, the ocean having left its banks to walk across the land. A small sea-side town lay a few hours away according to the markers. She'd rest there for the night.

It was a serious day; the weather meant business. She could hear the siren wail of ambulances in the foggy distance. Someone was having a very serious day indeed. For the next several hours she couldn't help thinking about those sirens, the rise and fall of them, the approach and the going away. Living in the city, she heard sirens almost every day, but until now she'd purposefully ignored them. She guessed that most people did. Otherwise you'd always be wondering if one of these days the sirens would be coming for you.

Perhaps once you really focused on them, you'd feel compelled to follow, to find out what they wanted. She knew there were people who followed every siren, voyeurs to disasters both public and private. You'd see them in the newsphotos, staring as if mesmerized. Watching someone else die, someone else break down. Just as long as you and yours were safe. Getting as close as possible to death without actually involving yourself. There had been people like that the final days of Colin's life: neighbors and distant relatives, a few casual friends, who'd dropped by unannounced as if they could hear death's footsteps approaching, low trumpet sounds, the sirens' beautiful lament.

The motel was right on the beach. From her balcony she could see distant ships in the bay, and now and then she could hear a plane take off or land at the airport a few miles away. And above their roar, the sirens' wail, asking her to come higher, to go even farther away from her girls and the life she had had before.

After Colin died the girls had become too much for her. She had grown impatient with them, and worried obsessively over every little cut or scrape. For the first time since childhood she'd felt trapped, and began to worry that she was going to explode some day, and that she might do something truly awful to her girls.

A hot bath began to melt the fatigue out of her, but under the rush of the tap she could still hear the sirens.

The sirens followed, muffled in the rug beneath her padding feet, and jangled about in the tangle of hangers as she tried to get dressed.

She thought about putting on the new white outfit, but suddenly she was thinking of a straitjacket, long white corridors and a uniformed attendant leading her to a sea of white beds. And the sirens whispering their song from the shadows.

Mary slipped on an old dress, green and nondescript, and went out to find a bar. She walked unsteadily, listing toward any unidentifiable sound. She walked several miles that way down the shore road before she finally found an establishment she felt safe to go into.

The bar was noisy, full of loud talk and the impact of glass against glass, wood against wood. Enough clamor to drown out the most persistent melody. Even the amateurish rock band up on the tiny stage had a difficult time being heard above the din. She perched on a stool at one end of the bar, sipping beer after beer, more than the usual for her, seeking a comfortable numbness.

She began to wonder what her parents were telling her girls right now, what they'd be forced, eventually, to tell them. Nothing was worth that. A nap for a couple of hours, then an all-night drive, and she could be there when they woke up in the morning. She lifted the glass to finish off her drink. She felt the rim of the glass vibrating against her fingertips.

All along the bar top, beer and liquor glasses were singing. She looked around her. Sloe-eyed women had their mouths open, and the song was growing louder.

She could go back for her babies, but then who was going to take care of her? Whisper to her. Hold her.

At the other end of the bar a man stepped out of the shadows. He had almond eyes and dark, bushy brows. The rough hide of his face shone brightly with sweat. His smell, and even that far away she knew it was his smell, made her light-headed. His head, she suddenly realized, was massive. Bull-like.

Mary pushed her way down the back corridor of the saloon. The back door was heavy, and the music behind her — from the glasses, from the drunken men and women, from the rock band which had suddenly turned expert and melodic — was a heaviness that combined with the alcohol she'd consumed, making it difficult for her to move. But she leaned forward blindly and pushed, and then she was out in the cold sea air, all sound locked away on the other side of the door behind her.

She walked down the damp alleyway and turned into another. Here there was standing water, an inch or so above the paving stones. A dark wetness lapped over the tips of her shoes. She started to turn around but couldn't find the exit. She splashed through the water, eventually finding another turn, another alley. But here the water was deeper still. And deep with beautiful music as well.

Mary stood ankle-deep in brine, living through every note. Ahead of her the darkness took shape: she could see all the places she might go, all the dark men to make love to, with no one to answer to, no one who depended on her for so much. She pushed her way through floating garbage, deeper into the water, closer to the darkness. The figure in the darkness sang to her, drawing her closer for an embrace. Then, reaching out, she saw the face with no eyes and a wide, toothless mouth, the two huge fish tails sprawled out in the filthy water as if to gather her in, the naked female torso spotted with disease.

Her song is so beautiful because it's so sad, she thought.

The siren opened her mouth wider as if to devour Mary with the song, but Mary had already stopped her eyes and ears with memories: her daughter Amy wrapping her small arms around her for hide-and-seek, her daughter Bridgett kissing each of her mother's ears because she knew she'd said something hurtful.

The song died away. Mary opened her eyes. The siren's face slowly turned to dark stone. Mary gazed at her and knew. The thing could never bear children, nor nurture them. All it had was its beautiful, sad songs of loss.

Mary reached out and stroked the damp weed of its hair, then turned to find her way out of the alley. In a few more hours, her girls would be awake.   Ω

WEIRD TALES TALKS WITH F. PAUL WILSON

by Darrell Schweitzer

Weird Tales: As of this writing, your most recent book is *Black Wind*. Is that right?

Wilson: The most recent book is *Sibs*. *Black Wind* came out in 1988. Before that there was *Reprisal*, then *Reborn*. Probably as this issue of *Weird Tales* ® is coming out there will be *Night World*, which ties up the dark fantasy or horror universe I've been working in. I've tied up six books into a single cycle. It's taken eleven years to write. It's amazed me that I could do it. I didn't intend them to be linked together when I started out.

WT: The point about *Black Wind* is that many readers are no doubt wondering whether you're following the trend in the horror field away from supernaturalism into straight thrillers and crime/psychological fiction.

Wilson: No. *Black Wind* was just the next book that was ready to be done at that time, and frankly it didn't do that well. I think that Tor certainly got enough copies out into the stores, but an awful lot of them came back. The timing was bad because it was sort of a pro-Japanese novel and there is growing anti-Japanese sentiment in the country. But, while I would still like to stay with supernatural fiction, I don't want to repeat myself. That becomes a problem, doing the same book over and over again, or slightly different clones of the same book. I don't know. At this point I have taken off much of the summer and fall and am just looking around for which direction I do want to go in, and I haven't decided yet.

WT: You'll notice that most of the great supernatural writers of the past — Machen or E.F. Benson or Blackwood — didn't have *careers* as supernatural writers the way publishers want writers to now. They didn't just turn out one horror novel and then another and another throughout the whole of their writing lives. A contemporary horror novelist, beginning in his late twenties, might well be expected to write forty or fifty horror novels by the time he's 75. I'm not sure that's possible.

Wilson: I agree. I suppose you can just keep on writing the same book over and over again. Certainly we know science-fiction authors who have done that and gotten away with it, but, unfortunately, I haven't had a plan in my career so far. I think it shows. Some publishers have even told me that I don't write the same stuff often enough. In other words I may stop and I may write a science-fiction novel, and then I may do something like *Sibs,* which is much more street-level and has a very small weird element to it. (Or I should say it has a very large weird element, but a very small hint of the supernatural. You're not sure if there's anything supernatural going on or not.) I've talked to a few publishers, or batted a few ideas off a few publishers recently, and anything that doesn't sound like what I've done before is met with coolness.

So I think that all of us who have had any sort of sales record have run up against that. You are expected to do what you did before.

WT: I should think that sooner or later you will become unable to do what you did before, and will end up writing increasingly ineffective pastiches of your former work. Possibly some mystery writers, Agatha Christie or John Creasey for example, could write the same books forever, but since horror is a matter of mood and emotion rather than an intellectual construct, once the sincere feeling is dulled through repetition, the books won't scare anybody anymore.

Wilson: True. You lose the freshness. I just finished Ed McBain's *Tricks,* which is his umpteenth 87th Precinct novel, all of which have the same formula. There are all these multiple storylines weaving in and out until finally everything comes to a conclusion. He can do those *ad infinitum,* and they still remain

49

interesting. But in a horror novel, with that single focus and emotional intensity that you have to maintain, it can wear you out. You find that even with the most visceral material, you become repetitive in how you describe it. You have to be careful about that. So horror seems to be a much more wearing type of genre than, say, science fiction, which I've written too. I could see going on and doing more of that much more easily than the intense supernatural horror that I have been working with.

WT: Perhaps the reason for this is that what is currently marketable as horror is very narrow in its focus. You know, ordinary people in a contemporary American frame of reference, as opposed to, say, a horror novel set in 12th century Greece. I gather that non-contemporary settings are a bit of a taboo in this business.

Wilson: I imagine that it is, although I've gotten away with a lot. *The Keep* is set in World War II. *The Tomb* shuttled back and forth between the Raj in India, the Sepoy Rebellion of that time, and modern-day Manhattan. So I've been able to mix genres and toy with history. *Black Wind,* which is nominally a horror novel but is really a historical novel, started in 1926 and went up through World War II. I have gotten to stretch in that sense, but, again, they want me to do more historical horror novels. It's just that my interests are in certain periods, and once I've tapped them out, I don't necessarily want to go back to them.

WT: You're a victim of your own success then.

Wilson: That's very true. When you run up against an instance where the sales figures of the new book aren't as good as for the previous one, you can feel the publishers turning on you. I've gotten to see now that in this current climate the publishers tend to look at your past sales figures and *then* read the book. If those figures aren't what they want to see, it really doesn't matter what this current book is. They have to make a decision then not to buy it. Fortunately I have good sales figures, but I know other writers whose sales have slacked off, and they've seen doors slammed in their faces. They are good writers and are still doing good work. But past performance seems to count more than what you're submitting.

WT: Does the writer then end up at another house with a smaller advance, or does he become unable to publish at this point?

Wilson: In this market, he's becoming unable to publish. There are already plenty of other writers at the other house with the smaller advance. Your timing has to be right. You have to be there firstest with the mostest. I think this is temporary. I think it will turn around, but a lot of editors are looking over their corporate shoulders. They're feeling the chill wind of the Recession and no one is going to stick his or her neck out.

WT: This suggests that a new writer might be better off under some circumstances with less money. If you get a $500,000 advance for your first book, then all your subsequent books must sell well enough to meet such a figure. But if you started off at $20,000, chances are you can always meet expectations.

Wilson: That's very true. In a sense you feel very sorry for the writer who gets a large amount on his first novel, because he has to live up to that, right away. The publisher will demand something similar and just as strong. You are much better with a smaller starting advance, both internally and externally, externally so you can build on those smaller successes, and internally it can mess up your head to get that kind of initial success without really having earned it or felt you have paid your dues. Getting a lot of rejections on the way up toughens you. When you finally do make a score, you feel you've earned it.

WT: Let's imagine that right now Stephen King suddenly writes a fluffy, romantic comedy, something as innocent as *Mary Poppins*. Assume it's very good, a masterpiece of its type. What would King's publishers *do?* Wouldn't they be on a spot?

Wilson: Well, they would publish it and put a nice price-tag on it, and I think it would go the way of *My Pretty Pony,* which I have just seen selling for half-price.

WT: I'm not sure that's a good example, because the regular edition of *My Pretty Pony* was badly-produced, poorly-illustrated, over-priced, and "limited" to something like twenty-five thousand copies. At $50.00 a copy, it wouldn't move. At $15.00, it might have.

Wilson: That's what I'm saying. There is a limit to what people will buy because King's name is on it. But if you're talking about King, you're talking about a pop-cultural phenomenon. If you'd said Dean Koontz or Peter Straub, you'd get a totally different answer, because while they do sell in very high figures and Koontz reaches number one on the bestseller lists, neither of these writers is an icon like King. If the book was good, I think King could carry it off.

WT: Surely when the writer is actually writing the book, he can't afford to think too much about these sorts of marketing considerations, or he'll go nuts —

Wilson: You have to be true to the book. But again, you can't ignore your market. Those are the realities. If you write to be read, and obviously if you are sending your work out to a publisher you intend to be read, you have to give some thought to the people who are going to read you. If you have an established readership in a certain genre, I think you have to somehow take them into account.

When I switched from science fiction and did *The Keep,* I didn't have to worry about that. I was leaving behind my entire readership and going into new territory where I would be selling to people who had never heard of me. It was a nice, free feeling that I was not carrying a burden from my own past. I think that whenever you write in a genre you do carry a certain burden from other writers, but I had no baggage of my own to bring along, and the publishers had no baggage that they brought to the manuscript in what they expected. Now, whatever I do, somebody's expecting another *Keep,* or looking for it and hoping for it.

WT: It seems to me that you have two advantages, the first being that if things got really bad in horror, you could go back to science fiction where you would be welcomed with open arms; and the other is that you're probably not economically dependent on writing since you're also a full-time physician.

Wilson: True. If I never sold another book, my mortgage would be paid. My children's education is assured. But writing becomes a part of your identity after a while. Whether it's an economic necessity for me or not, it's also a part of who I am and what I do and how I spend a good part of my life. Having that taken away from me, not so much given up but taken away in the sense that I could no longer sell and no one wanted to buy my books, would be equally as crushing as if it were a financial catastrophe.

WT: At what point in your life did you start writing? Was it before or after you became a doctor?

Wilson: I actually started writing at around age six or seven, in the first grade. I wrote little stories then. My first story was a haunted house story. I wrote stories off and on through high school. In college, I was pre-med when I decided I really wanted to sell something. The idea then was to sell one story. Then I would be a published author and I could get on with my medical career.

It took me years, and I finally sold a story to John W. Campbell at *Analog* in 1970, and by that time, after all those years of trying, I became hooked. So I was actually a published author before I was a doctor. I was in medical school then. I didn't get my degree for a few more years. During my internship I didn't get a chance to write a word. You are working twelve hours a day, twelve days a week . . . no, I should say you work twelve days in a row, then get two days off. There was no time for writing then, but once I got into group practice some time did free up and I did *Healer.* From then on it has just been balancing the two careers, making time, and just trying to enjoy both and do both well.

WT: Has your medical career influenced your writing career other than by competing for time?

Wilson: Being in family practice, I am in contact with people on an intimate basis four or five days a week, and it's a wide variety of people. So my contact with the human species and its variations is pretty broad and, as I said, pretty intimate. It helps with an ongoing appreciation of people. I certainly do pick and choose little pieces of them for characters. I'm not a terribly social person, so if I was a full-time writer, I might see very few people on a day-to-day basis. So it helps keep the humanity in my work.

WT: It also gives you convincing details. Your story "Soft," for instance, displays a lot of sound medical speculation.

Wilson: Strangely enough, I showed it to Shawna McCarthy and she picked up on an anatomical error right away. I had this person turn into a blob of flesh lying on a bed, and he was still breathing. Shawna said, "His ribs are gone. How could he breathe?" I thought about it for a second, and I said to myself, *Damn it. She's right.* So I went back and put in a few ribs and bones left to hang his diaphragm on so he could still have something to pull against. But, to use another example, in *The Keep*, Dr. Kousis suffers from scleroderma. I've seen scleroderma patients. I know how it affects their personality, what it does to them. It also gave me a lot of good little bits to do with this character. In that sense, certainly, that extra knowledge, that dimension of how human physiology works certainly works. But I'm not interested in writing medical thrillers and I'm not interested in writing about doctors, *per se*. I did it once in *The Touch*, and that was fun, but otherwise my writing is my golf game. It gets me away from my practice. I don't really want to write about diseases.

WT: You are writing more about the region you live in, though. I can't think of too many people writing horror about the New Jersey Pine Barrens.

Wilson: Someone does have a book out called *The Pines*. [by Robert Dunbar — D.S.] That took place in the Barrens. But I've used the setting in a number of stories, in "Pelts," in "The Barrens," and I also used it in the upcoming *Freak Show*, which ends up in the Pine Barrens. But it's a fascinating place with an enormous amount of history, and truly Lovecraftian in the sense that you have enclaves of people who have probably not seen civilization, and who do inbreed. It's much more overstated in some of the stories about the place than really happens, but there really are, definitely, people you can look at and say, "Well, somebody's brother and sister got together on that one."

WT: I'd think that with that sort of inbreeding, the result would just be an exaggeration of whatever was running in the family, longer noses or whatever.

Wilson: It's probably overstated, but there are some really strange-looking characters out there in the pines. And they're truly living off the land in every respect. They eat what grows wild and they kill what runs wild. Their contact with civilization is coming out to get kerosene or gasoline and buying some clothes and boots. Then they high-tail it back into the Barrens.

WT: Can they be that isolated in a state as small as New Jersey? Surely they watch the same TV, shop in the same malls, etc., as the rest of the population.

Wilson: No. No electricity. They have kerosene stoves. They wouldn't have TVs without the electricity. Some of the more sophisticated ones may have a generator and perhaps a battery-operated radio, but there are places, they say, which a human eye has yet to see, out in the Pine Barrens. It's that unexplored. There's nothing in there and really no one wants to go in there anymore. The only people who ever were in there were chased in there, except the ones who were hired to work the iron industries and the glass industries. They almost deforested a large part of it, and then the industries collapsed just because of overcutting of the wood.

WT: How much personal exploration of the area have you done and how much contact have you had with people like the ones depicted in your story, "The Barrens"? Are these your neighbors and patients, or are they people you have to seek out?

Wilson: I've seen some of them, and I've done some driving through the Barrens, but a lot of stories I've picked up from descriptions, like the Pine Lights. I know hunters who swear they have been out there in the night and have seen the lights going through the sky, going from treetop to treetop. And I know hunters who have run into the people out there, and they say they're pretty scary, in the sense that they're very suspicious. They seem quite hostile and they do not welcome company out there. What was that Lovecraft family . . .?

WT: The Whateleys?

Wilson: The Whateleys.

WT: To be specific, the degenerate side of the Whateley family.

Wilson: I could see the Whateleys out there and even some people from Innsmouth, coming up the Bass River from the ocean. I haven't actually spoken to any of the wild Pineys. Now there are Pineys who are definitely civilized, but they still live in the Pines. The ones who live in the small towns, they have electricity, they watch TV; they're somewhat homogenized like the rest of us, but they've got nephews or distant relatives in the backwoods and the off-roads that they don't necessarily speak about, but they know they're back there, and they're living their own lives.

WT: What sort of supernatural legends comes out of this region, other than the Pine Lights and, of course, the Jersey Devil?

Wilson: I went into some of it in "The

Barrens." Virtually any of the stories I told were true, in the sense I didn't make them up: the Witch of the Pines and things like that. Mostly I take stories that are available and give them a little twist, or take off from them and use them as a springboard. But the lore of the Pines is not so much supernatural as it has to do with robbers and thieves and Tories and some of the old Lenape Indians.

WT: Could you get as much material out of this as Manly Wade Wellman did out of the southern Appalachians?

Wilson: I don't think so. I guess there is a richer culture in the Appalachians. The pine culture isn't as extensive. They have their applejack and they have their stories of the Jersey Devil and stuff, but a lot of them are isolated and there isn't that deep a vein to mine, at least not to my mind.

WT: Do you travel around while researching novels? Did you, for instance, go to Rumania for *The Keep*?

Wilson: No. For *Black Wind* I did. I went to San Francisco and I bit the bullet and went to Hawaii and researched Honolulu and Pearl Harbor and places like that. Most of my research in *The Keep* was done from people who had been to Rumania or who used to live there, and from books. I guess I used a lot of what I'd learned in science fiction to try to give it a patina of reality. I guess I succeeded when the movie company was looking for a location, and they came to me and asked where was the Dainu Pass, which was a fictional location near the Transylvanian Alps where I had set the story. They actually believed there was such a place, which of course there wasn't.

WT: The movie version of *The Keep* was not notably successful. Any comments on why?

Wilson: I've been over this a lot and I get crazy whenever I start talking about it; but Michael Mann, who seems to have a great visual sense, had no sense at all of this type of story and how to tell it. He doesn't seem to have much sense of how a story is constructed. He just wanted to do what he wanted to do, and he did not want any mention of a vampire in the movie. Even though a vampire is just a red herring in the book, he wanted no mention of it at all. So if you do that, you take away the very reason that the book is set in the Transylvanian Alps, which is to highlight this red herring. Then, things start to crumble. He did

not build character. He did not tell a coherent story. When I read the script, I wrote to him and I pointed out all of this to him in a very gentle, non-ego-trampling way, I thought. But he ignored me, and when I did make a visit to the set, he was very cool. I don't know if he felt threatened, or what, but he wanted no input at all from anyone. It was to be a Michael Mann picture. As a matter of fact, in some of the pre-release publicity, he never mentioned that it was based on a previously existing novel. If you didn't know otherwise, you would think that he had invented the whole story himself. Of course this backfired on him terribly when the movie came out and flopped miserably. It opened in eight hundred theaters and the grosses were terrible, and they went down steadily and swiftly, which indicated bad word-of-mouth. So, in the sense that he wanted all the credit for it, he wound up taking all the blame. But he landed on his feet. He wound up in television producing *Miami Vice*, which got him back in the good graces of the money people.

WT: Has there been movie interest in any of your other works?

Wilson: Yes. *The Tomb* has been optioned twice. New World Pictures had it for a long time, but they couldn't get a good script. Then they found that somebody else had come out with another movie called *The Tomb* — it was a real dog of a movie, but they couldn't get the title then of *The Tomb*, which they wanted. So they let it drop. *The Touch* has been optioned twice, once by Stephen J. Kinnell Productions for a Movie of the Week. Now, as we speak, *Sibs* has had some good reviews in *Publishers Weekly*, and there have been maybe twenty calls from production companies or studios for copies. So we'll see what happens on that. I would like to have more control next time.

WT: What do you find to be necessary for a successful horror story, either on film or in a book?

Wilson: Every time I try to put this type of thing into words, I read it later and say, well, no, that's wrong. It's one of those things where I know it when I see it, and I know it when it's missing. The obvious thing to say is the human element. There has to be something to latch onto, something human to touch and to draw you along into the story. I think that without that humanity, *any* story will fail. In horror fiction, where you are stressing your characters to the extreme and you're stressing the reader as well as the characters, you need that anchor of humanity to keep the reader emotionally involved. Otherwise the gore, the violence, or whatever loses its human meaning and becomes some sort of recitation.

Also, the thing that I demand in something that I'm reading, and also in something I'm writing, is a sense of wonder. That's usually applied to science fiction, but I think it adds an extra dimension to horror fiction, that there is something else going on, there is something wondrous out there. Even if it's horrible, it's wondrous, not mundane and tacky. That to me makes the horror, in a sense. It gives it a greater scope.

WT: You are describing something close to Lovecraft's theories of "cosmic horror." He definitely wanted a broader sense of the extra-mundane. But he didn't think that the individual characters were very important, because in the cosmic scheme of things, all individuals are dwarfed. But this seems to be the rationale for *supernatural horror,* as opposed to, say, serial-killer books.

Wilson: Exactly. I think that's why Lovecraft works better in small doses than he does in large doses, because of his lack of emphasis on the human element. I find his novels tedious, but his short stories are very effective. When there is less time to develop character, you will excuse a more perfunctory or superficial job. But when you're given a lot of elbow room, the reader does expect more depth. Obviously I've been influenced by the Lovecraftian cosmic horror. I've always been impressed by the way he threw out the Judeo-Christian mythology without even saying he was throwing it out. He just dismissed it and introduced his own, which, even as a young teenager — a thirteen-year-old when I started reading him — I found very impressive. But the cosmic horror is a definite sense of wonder that gives Lovecraft, for me, a dimension that makes him readable, even later on. I have recently gone back and reread a few of his things.

WT: It sounds like he was an important influence on you, but couldn't be correctly described as one of your current favorites.

Wilson: I rarely reread anybody, so the fact that I reread him at all is a testimony to his importance. I was doing an essay on "The

Thing on the Doorstep" for a British magazine, and I really enjoyed rereading it. The other thing that occurred to me as I did was that *Sibs* knocks off some of the plot elements of "The Thing on the Doorstep," and I hadn't read it since 1959. But I realized that I had stolen a few things from the story. It shook me up a little because I thought I had been so wonderfully original with *Sibs,* and here I was finding out that I had already read part of it.

WT: We've all had that experience to some extent. The readers of *Weird Tales* ® know this. In issue number 296, there is a story by one Darrell Schweitzer entitled "Soft," which of course sounds remarkably like "Soft" by F. Paul Wilson, which was published a couple of years earlier. And some while after my story had been published, I was looking through a copy of *Masques* and I thought, *Oh, shit . . .* Both stories have to do with people getting squishy, too, although mine achieved this in a very different manner and for very different reasons. But the title was *right.* My story made no attempt at medical realism, for instance. I couldn't very well have entitled it "Squishy," though. But I had read yours. I had even reviewed the book it appeared in, and still managed to forget that title, and there we were.

Wilson: There are things I have consciously swiped through the years. When I was starting out, I swiped little things from Niven and Heinlein when doing science fiction, concepts or little twists. Most writers start off by imitating. But you do forget, and I'm sure you file away things you like into some part of the morass in the center of your brain. Then it'll pop up in another part and you think it's all your own. But as long as it's not too blatant, I don't think anybody really minds.

WT: Have you always been widely read in classic horror fiction? You could then be consciously or unconsciously digging into Robert W. Chambers or Arthur Machen, or whoever. Lovecraft, for instance, had read virtually everything, and therefore was open to the influence of an enormous range of writers.

Wilson: No. I was more influenced by writers from Lovecraft onward. Those were the ones I read when I could find the material. In the 1950s, if you were a fan of horror fiction, it was damn hard to find anything unless you knew somebody who had old magazines, because you had a Matheson collection now and then, the old Bradbury stuff, though he had basically stopped writing horror fiction by 1950 or so. You found a Charles Beaumont or a Dennis Wheatley, and besides the reprints — like *The Macabre Reader* or the Avon anthology, *Brrr!* — you couldn't find it. There was a big hunger for it. *Famous Monsters of Filmland* could take you just so far. So, the old Gothic folks like Machen or LeFanu weren't really there. Sure I read *Dracula* and *Frankenstein,* but the others I tried I found almost unreadable. They had no influence on me at all. I was much more influenced by the old *Weird Tales* crowd, and Matheson's *Shock* books. Some of his earlier stories like "Third from the Sun" just blew me away. I can still get a chill when I reread "The Distributor." "Born of Man and Woman" still gives my heart a little tug when I reread it.

WT: But you didn't find all the classic, fat ghost-story anthologies like the Fraser and Wise *Great Tales of the Supernatural* or Boris Karloff's *And the Darkness Falls.*

Wilson: I never saw them, I guess, although I did make a trip to Bermuda when I was sixteen and I came across the *Not At Night* paperbacks, from Arrow, I think, with the neat, lurid covers. They were still old tales. George Fielding Eliot's "The Copper Bowl" was something that really grossed me out as a kid. Of course there were things like *The Graveyard Reader* and Basil Davenport's anthologies for Ballantine. But all of them, even *Zacherley's Midnight Snacks* and *Vulture Stew,* were from *Weird Tales* and *Unknown Worlds.* So there was nothing new happening, even in the '60s, until *Rosemary's Baby.*

WT: There was nothing happening in horror when you started writing? Was that what caused you to start in science fiction initially, because there wasn't a horror market?

Wilson: Yes. I read both. I read science fiction as a substitute for the horror fiction I couldn't find. I think I got into science fiction because I read the old Ray Bradbury, *The October Country,* and I liked it so much that I picked up the next Ray Bradbury book I saw and it was *The Martian Chronicles.* So I would start to move into science fiction. The other thing was that when I was seven years old, the two things I liked the most in the world were rocketships and dinosaurs. Dinosaurs were more representative of the horror end of

things, and rocketships were the science fiction. I started trying to sell a story at the height of the New Wave. Where could you sell a horror story? I tried to sell them to Jessica Salmonson's *Fantasy and Terror.* I tried selling to Joseph Payne Brennan's *Macabre.* I got turned down by both.

WT: Did you try the various digests edited by Robert A.W. Lowndes?

Wilson: I finally sold a semi-horror, semi-science fiction story to *Startling Mystery Stories* for the final issue. But, basically if you wanted to write something with imagination, science fiction was the only place to do it. But as soon as the horror market started opening up, I made the switch. There was no place I could actually sell something like *The Keep,* which had been brewing for quite some time. It was something that I wanted to write. I had pretty much said what I had to say in science fiction. I figured I could just go on repeating myself, so I showed a few story ideas to my agent, and he said, "Why don't we go with this castle in Rumania here and see what you can do with that?" So that's how it began.

WT: Have you ever personally had a horrific experience which could be fodder for this sort of story?

Wilson: No. I lead a very mundane existence and I'm a hard-bound realist. I really do not believe in the supernatural at all, but I do love it as a storytelling medium, and I love to tell stories. I love to be scared. Of course my mother used to tell me stories which gave me a chill. She always had an aunt or someone who had seen something strange. She was rural Irish from the Berkshire area of Massachusetts, and she'd tell stories about how her aunt would see this glowing hand with a knife in it go floating down the hall past her door and continue down the hall every night. So finally she followed it into her brother's room and it stabbed him in the belly. Two days later he had appendicitis and had his appendix removed. So those types of things used to give me the willies. But I always used to say, "Have you got any more stories like that?" I never used them. I may use that sometime, but I haven't yet.

WT: It seems that for the horror reader, the approach to this sort of material is an ambiguous mix of "If only" and "I'm glad it's not."

Wilson: Yes. In science fiction it's "If only"

and "I wish it were" and definitely in horror fiction you're glad it's not. It's a safe kind of thrill in the sense that you have more control over it even than you do with the movies. With the movie you can close your eyes, but you still hear it, or even if you put your hands over your ears, the movie is running. With a book, you have that safety limit. *Any time I want, I can close this book, and I'll be okay. I won't have to see what's going on there*. But, I think, to get past that, the writer has to somehow get beneath the skin of the reader. I've always said that the splatter you can wash off, but somehow if you can get beneath the skin and have it linger with the reader even after he or she closes the book, then I think you have really done your job. You've disturbed the readers on a deeper level. You've reached them. You've made contact. I think that's what we're all trying to do.

I remember the first story I ever wrote. I only half wrote it. I was in, I think, the first or second grade. We had a reading group and we took turns reading things. I told the teacher I had written a story myself. She was very happy and she said, "Well, do you want to read it to us?" I had only written half of it. It was a ghost story. So I read the part I had written, and then I started ad-libbing. Within a few sentences it became obvious that I hadn't finished. The teacher was very nice, and she said, "Well Paul, when you finish it, you can come back and read the rest of it to us." I was a little embarrassed that I'd gotten caught, but as we were putting our chairs away from the reading circle, a couple of the kids came up to me and said, "Well what happened? What happened next?" I didn't say so in as many words, but somewhere, something inside of me clicked and said, *You've got them*. I really liked that. I think it somehow stuck with me. I'd made contact. They were mine. They really wanted to know. They would have sat down right there and listened to the rest of the story. That's what we're all after. Maybe to other people it means nothing, but to me it was a wonderful feeling. I just wanted to do it again.

WT: Thanks, Paul.   Ω

MONSTERS

There were monsters in the olden days,
and people who believed in them. Ghouls,
vampires, werewolves, witches, warlocks
        played
with people's minds and bodies. Sucked their
        souls
right out and hurled them down to Satan's
        Hell!
We did have Satan then, too, which made
the stakes a little higher. When the knell
sounded, well, you could wind up a shade
condemned for all eternity to roam
the earth — perhaps with wings and fangs or
        fur
and teeth: blood suck, flesh rend . . . send
        home
to Hell some innocent, or make a spectre
    of some poor mortal, who for his moral
        stains
    is doomed to roam forever stooped in chains.

But look around. It's not as if we see
no monsters here and now. The fearsome
        beasts
are secular, are human, but their feasts
of blood are worse for their humanity.

Forget drive-bys, muggings, murders for
        fee. . . .
The serial beast who butchers dozens, at least
we can call insane, call in the priests
of law, of social work, psychiatry,

to deal with him. Say he isn't one
of us — by insanity forgiven.
But . . . to have his mythic counterpart:
the mouldy casket opened to the sun,
then the sharpened wooden spike that's
        driven
with a righteous anger through the heart . . .
                              — Joe Haldeman

F. PAUL WILSON: BIBLIOGRAPHY

(as of October 1, 1991)

FICTION

"The Cleaning Machine" (ss)
  in *Startling Mystery Stories* #18 (3/71)
  in *Strange Galaxies* #11 (8/71) (unauthorized reprint)
  collected in **Soft & Others** (Tor 1989)

"Higher Centers" (ss)
  in *Analog Science Fiction* (4/71)

"The Man with the Anteater" (ss)
  in *Analog* (7/71)

"The Sound of Wings" (comic script)
  in *Eerie* #34 (8/71)

"Ratman" (ss)
  in *Analog* (8/71)
  collected in **Soft & Others** (Tor 1989)

"Wheels Within Wheels" (novelette)
  in *Analog* (9/71)

"With Silver Bells and Cockle Shells . . ."
  (comic script)
  in *Creepy* #44 (3/72)

"Pard" (novelette)
  in *Analog* (12/72)
  reprinted with **The Tery** (Baen 1/90)

"He Shall Be John" (ss)
  in *Fiction* #4 (1973)

Healer (novel) (includes "Pard")
  (elected to the Prometheus Hall of Fame 1990)
  Doubleday 6/76
  Dell 1977
  Sidgwick & Jackson (GB)
    reg. trade: 1977
    SF Special #28: 1978
  Hamlyn (GB) pb: 1979
  Ediciones Martines Roca (Spain) 1980 (as **El Curandero**)
  Bastei Lubbe (Ger.) 1982 (as **Der Heiler**)
  Berkley 1984

"Lipidleggin' " (ss)
  in *Isaac Asimov's Science Fiction Magazine*
  (5–6/78)
  in **Asimov's Choice: Dark Stars & Dragons** (Dale 1978)
  in **The Survival of Freedom** (Fawcett 1981)
  collected in **Soft & Others** (Tor 1989)

Wheels Within Wheels (novel) (expanded/replotted from novelette)
  (winner of first Prometheus Award: 7.5 oz. gold)
  Doubleday 10/78
  Dell 1979
  Sidgwick & Jackson (GB) 1980
  Mondadori (Italy) 7/1/79 (in *Urania* #790 as "Intrigo Interstellare")
  Bastei Lubbe (Ger.) 1983 (as **Mein Vater Starb auf Jebinos**)
  Berkley 1985

"To Fill The Sea and Air" (ss)
  in **Asimov's SFM** (2/79) (cover story)
  in **Asimov's SF Anthology** #2 (1979)
  in **Asimov's Marvels of SF** Vol. 2 (Dial 1979)
  collected in **Soft & Others** (Tor 1989)

"The Tery" (novella) (expanded from "He Shall Be John")
  in **Binary Star #2** (Dell 2/79)
  Bastei Lubbe (Ger.) 1982 (as **Der Tery**)

"Demonsong" (ss)
  in **Heroic Fantasy** (DAW #334 1979) ed. by Gerald W. Page
  in **Fata Morgana** (Netherlands) (Meulenhoff 1980)
  in **Necon Stories** (Necon X – 1990)

An Enemy of the State (novel)
  Doubleday 1980
  Bastei Lubbe (Ger.) 1982 (as **Der Staatsfeind**)
  Berkley (1984)

"Green Winter" (ss)
  in *Analog* 1/5/81 ("Biolog" in same issue)
  collected in **Soft & Others** (Tor 1989)

The Keep (novel)
  William Morrow 8/81
  Science Fiction Digest (excerpt) 1–2/82
  Berkley
    Reg. mass market edition 10/82
      (N.Y. *Times* Bestseller List)
    Movie tie-in edition 12/83
    8 Berkley printings thru 9/85
      (1,000,000+ copies)
  Jove: First printing 10/86
  New English Library (GB)
    trade: 1982; pb: 1983
  Editions Presses de la Cité (Fr.) 1982 (as **Le Donjon**)
  ECI (Netherlands) 1983 (as **De Vesting**)
  Edivision Diana (Mexico) 1983 (as **La Fortaleza**)
  Eder (Italy)
  Editions A. Simossi (Greece)
  Kelebek Yayinlari (Turkey)
  Books On Tape 1983
  Mayfair Games (12/83) rôle-playing board game
  Paramount Pictures (theatrical film released 12/16/83)
  Kadokawa Shoten, Ltd. (Japan)
  Distribudoria Record (Brazil) (as **O Fortim**)
  Wilhelm Goldmann Verlag (Germany) (**Das Kastell**) (1990)
  Amber (Poland)
  Mondadori (Italy) **La Fortezza** (8/91)

"Be Fruitful and Multiply" (ss)
  in **Perpetual Light** (pb: Warner 1982; hc: SFBC 1983)
  collected in **Soft & Others** (Tor 1989)

The Tomb (novel)
  Winner: Porgie Award from *The West Coast Review of Books*: "Best Paperback Original Novel of 1985"
  Whispers Press 10/84 (limited hardcover first edition)
  Berkley 11/84 (N.Y. *Times* Bestseller List)
  Jove 10/86, 2/89
  New Worlds Pictures – theatrical film option (12/84)
  New English Library
    hc: 1985
    pb: 1986
  Sankei Shuppan (Japan) 1988; new edition 1991
  Distribudora Record (Brazil) 1987 (**O Sepulcro**)

First Street Productions — theatrical film option (5/88)
Wilhelm Goldman Verlag (Germany) 1989 (**Die Gruft**)
CIA Books (Poland)

"Soft" (ss)
  in **Masques** (Maclay 1984)
  in **Best of Masques** (Berkley 1988)
  collected in **Soft & Others** (Tor 1989)

"The Last ONE MO' ONCE GOLDEN OLDIES REVIVAL" (ss)
  in **Whispers V** (hc: Doubleday 1985; pb: Jove, 1988)
  in *The Twilight Zone Magazine* 2/86
  collected in **Soft & Others** (Tor 1989)

"Dydeetown Girl" (novella) (Nebula Award finalist)
  in **Far Frontiers IV** (1/86)
  in (*Author's Choice Monthly* #13) (Pulphouse 10/90)

The Touch (novel)
  Putnam (6/86)
  Doubleday Book Club
  The Mystery Guild
  The Literary Guild
  The Science Fiction Book Club
  Jove 10/86, 4/89
  New English Library
    hc: 7/86
    pb: 4/88
  Books On Tape 1987
  Editions Garranciere (France)
  Distribudoria Record (Brazil) (as **O Toque Magico**)
  Hayakawa (Japan)
  Stephen J. Cannell Prod. – Movie-of- the-Week option (7/87)
  Wilhelm Goldman Verlag (Germany) 1989 (as **Die Gabe**)
  CIA Books (Poland)

"Dat-Tay-Vao" (ss) (Bram Stoker Award finalist)
  in *Amazing Stories* (3/87)
  collected in **Soft & Others** (Tor 1989)

"Traps" (ss) (Bram Stoker award finalist)
  in *Night Cry* (Summer 1987)
  collected in **Soft & Others** (Tor 1989)
  in *Author's Choice Monthly* #13 (Pulphouse 10/90)

"The Years the Music Died" (ss)
  in *Whispers VI* (hc: Doubleday 1987; pb: Jove 1989)
  collected in *Soft & Others* (Tor 1989)

"The Death of Balajuro" (ss) (excerpt from *Black Wind*)
  in *Footsteps* VII (11/87)

"Ménage à Trois" (novelette)
  in *Weird Tales* #290 (Spring 1988) (publ. 10/87)
  revised for *Hot Blood* (Pocket Books, 1989)
  collected in *Soft & Others* (Tor 1989)

"Doc Johnson" (ss)
  in *Doom City (Greystone Bay II)* (Tor 1987)
  collected in *Soft & Others* (Tor 1989)

"Cuts" (ss)
  in *Silver Scream* (hc: Dark Harvest 4/88; pb: Tor 11/88)
    (Tokyo Sogan sha Ltd. 1991)
  collected in *Soft & Others* (Tor 1989)
  in *Author's Choice Monthly* #13 (Pulphouse 10/90)

"Wires" (novella)
  in *New Destinies IV* (Baen 5/88)

"Muscles" (ss)
  in *The Magazine of Fantasy & Science Fiction* (6/88)
  collected in *Soft & Others* (Tor 1989)

Black Wind (novel) (Bram Stoker Award finalist)
  Tor 9/88; pb 8/89
  Michael Joseph (GB) 1/89
  Bastei Lubbe (Germany, 1989) (as *Der Schwarze Wind*)
  Sphere (GB) 1/90
  Distribudoria Record (Brazil) 1991 (as *Vento Negro*)
  Fusosha (Japan)

"Faces" (novelette)
  in *Night Visions VI* (Dark Harvest 1988)
  in *The Year's Best Fantasy* (2nd) (St. Martin's 1989)
  in *Under the Gun: Mystery Scene Presents the Best Mystery and Suspense — First Annual Collection* (NAL/Plume 3/90)
  in *The Bone Yard* (Berkley 5/91)
  in *Dark Crimes* (Carroll & Graf 6/91)

"Tenants" (novelette)
  in *Night Visions VI* (Dark Harvest 1988)
  in *The Bone Yard* (Berkley 5/91)

"Feelings" (novelette)
  in *Night Visions VI* (Dark Harvest 1988)
  in *The Bone Yard* (Berkley 5/91)

"Kids" (novella)
  in *New Destinies VII* (Baen 4/89)

Soft & Others (collection) (Bram Stoker Award finalist)
  Tor hc 5/89; pb: 7/90

"Buckets" (ss)
  first published in *Soft & Others* (Tor 1989)
  in *The Year's Best Horror Stories: Series XVIII* (DAW 10/90)
  in *The Mammoth Book of Terror* (Robinson(GB)/Carroll & Graf 1/91)
  as Short Story Paperback #36 (Pulphouse) 11/91

Dydeetown World (novel) (novelization of "Dydeetown Girl," "Wires," and "Kids")
  on ALA's list of "Best Books for Young Adults"
  in NY Public Library's "Books for the Teen Age"
  Easton Press (leatherbound signed first edition) (7/89)
  Baen (7/89)
  Bastei Lubbe (Germany)
  Ultramar Editores (Spain)
  CIA Books (Poland)

"The Tenth Toe" (ss)
  in *Razored Saddles* (Dark Harvest 1989; Avon 9/90)

"A Day in the Life" (novelette)
  in *Stalkers* (Dark Harvest 1989; NAL/ROC tp 12/90; Mystery Guild 5/91)
  in *Stalkers* (audio version)

The Tery (novel) (expanded from the novella)
  Baen (1/90)

"Definitive Therapy" (ss)
  in *The Further Adventures of the Joker* (Bantam 2/90)

Reborn (novel)
  Dark Harvest (3/90)
  option for theatrical film by Agincourt Ventures Ltd. (5/90)
  Jove 6/90

Reborn (continued)
NEL (hc 9/90; pb 7/91)
Distribudoria Record (Brazil)
Mondadori (Italy)
Amber (Poland)

"Biosphere" (comic script)
in *Open Space* #2 (Marvel 4/90)

"Rumors" (drabble)
in **Double Century (the Drabble Project II)** (4/90)

"Rockabilly" (ss)
in **Dick Tracy: The Secret Files** (Tor 6/90)

"The Last Rakosh" (ss)
in **The World Fantasy Convention 1990 Program Book** (11/90)

"The Barrens" (novella)
in **Lovecraft's Legacy** (Tor 1990)
(Hayakawa 1992)
Wildside Press, ltd. ed. 1991

"Midnight Mass" (novella)
as **Midnight Mass** (as Axolotl Press #16) (Pulphouse) (10/90)
Hardcover (limited to 75 leather + 300 cloth)
Softcover (limited to 525)
in *Weird Tales* #305 (Fall 1992) (publ. 5/92)
in **The Mammoth Book of Vampires** 1992
in **Blood Is the Life** (Marboro 1992)

Author's Choice Monthly #13: "Ad Statum Perspicuum" (collection)
collects "Dydeetown Girl," "Traps," and "Cuts" with title essay.
Pulphouse (10/90)
Hardcover (limited to 350)
Softcover (trade)

"Pelts" (ss)
Footsteps Press chapbook (12/90)
in **Best New Horror 2** (1991)

"Topsy" (ss)
in **Obsessions** (Dark Harvest 2/91)
"preview publication" in *Summer/Fall Preview: 1990* for the ABA (Dark Harvest 6/90)
"An Evening in the Park" (ss)
in *Mystery Scene* #29 (Spring 1991)

"Home Repairs" (ss)
in **Cold Blood** (Zeising 6/91)

Reprisal (novel)
Dark Harvest 7/91
NEL (hc 8/91)
Jove 3/92
Distribudoria Record (Brazil)

"Memoirs of the Effster" (ss)
in *Mystery Scene* #30 (8/91)

"Dreams" (ss)
in **The Ultimate Frankenstein** (Dell/BPVP) 10/91

Sibs (novel)
Dark Harvest 10/91

"The Long Way Home" (ss)
for **Dark at Heart** (Dark Harvest 1991)

"The November Game" (ss)
in **The Bradbury Chronicles** (Penguin/ROC 10/91)

"Please Don't Hurt Me" (ss)
in **Masques IV** (Maclay/Pulphouse 1991)

"Foet" (ss)
in **Borderlands 2** (Borderlands Press 1991)

"Bob Dylan, Toby Jonson, and the Speed Queen" (ss)
in **Shock Rock** (Pocket Books, 1992)

"When He Was Fab" (ss)
in *Weird Tales* #305 (Fall 1992) (publ. 5/92)

Nightworld (novel)
Dark Harvest 1992
NEL 1992
Jove 1992

"Slasher" (ss)
in **Stalkers II** (NAL 1992)

"Hunters" (ss)
in **50 Very SF Stories II** (Niekas Publications)

"Bugs" (novelette)
in *Fantasy &Science Fiction* 1992

The LaNague Chronicles
omnibus edition of **Healer, Wheels Within Wheels, An Enemy of the State** (Baen, 1992)

F. PAUL WILSON: BIBLIOGRAPHY

DRAMA

"Glim-Glim" (original 30-min. teleplay)
to Laurel-EFX for the TV series *Monsters*
First airing: Week of Jan. 30, 1989

NON-FICTION

"Lamont Cranston is NOT The Shadow!"
(semi-fiction article)
in *Reminiscing Time* (organ of the Nostalgia Book Club) 1969

"Requiem for a Giant" (an appreciation of
John W. Campbell, Jr.)
in *Reason* (12/73)

"And Now, from the People Who Brought You
Viet Nam and Watergate . . ."
in *Analog* as a guest editorial (4/75)
in *Social Education* (vol. 40, #2; 2/76)

"Literary Darwinism"
in *Patchin Review* #4 (Spring, 1982)

"Of Gold, Weed, and Lenny" (transcript of remarks at the Prometheus Awards, 1983)
in *Prometheus* #4 (Fall, 1983)

"Look What They've Done To My Song, Ma"
in *Science Fiction Review* (Summer, 1984)

"TZ Terror" (semi-fiction)
in *The Twilight Zone Magazine* (12/85)

"*The Exorcist*" (essay)
in *Horror: The 100 Best Books* (1988)

"Dydeetown World" (essay)
in *Mystery Scene* #21 (5–6/89)

"Twenty Years with *Reborn*" (essay)
in *Mystery Scene* #25 (3–4/90)

Introduction to "No Flies on Frank" by John
Lennon
in *Dark Voices* (Pan 4/90)

"Ad Statum Perspicuum" (essay)
intro to *Author's Choice Monthly* #13 (1990)

"*Red Dragon*" (essay)
in *Scream Factory* #7 (7/91)

"Re: *Reprisal*" (essay)
in *From the Tunnel* (7/91)

Introduction to *Sandman: Preludes & Nocturnes* (DC Comics) 9/91

Foreword to *Dead End: City Limits* (St. Martin's) 10/91

Introduction to *Night Visions IX* Dark Harvest 10/91

INTERVIEWS

Starfix (Fr.) (4/84)
Fangoria #36 (5/84)
Physician's Management (4/85)
Science Fiction Review #60 (Fall/86)
Footsteps VII (11/87)
Asbury Park *Press* (8/12/90)

BOOK REVIEWS

"BEMs and Such" (column)
in *Invictus* (4-5/73) (6/73)
Sundry reviews in:
Reason (12/79, 12/80, 10/82)
Science Fiction Review #29 (1–2/79)
SF & Fantasy Book Review (9/79, 10/79, 11/79, 12/79)
The Intergalactic Reporter (5/83)
Yucsnuc #4 (10/83) four movie reviews
Asbury Park *Press* (1/10/88; 9/4/88)
"That Comic Book Stuff" (column) in *Short Form* Vol. I, #1, #2

MISCELLANEOUS

Two recipes in *Liberated Cooking* (1987)
"Jill Bauman" — an appreciation for the
I-CON IX Program Book (1990)
"F. Paul Wilson: Bibliography"
in *Weird Tales*® #305 (Fall 1992)

Ω

WINTER

A most silent thing:
The sound a spirit makes
When dancing on fresh snow.

— **Kathleen Youmans**

YELLOW ROME,
OR, VERGIL AND THE VESTAL VIRGIN

by Avram Davidson

In Rome — Yellow Rome! Yellow Rome! — a man was being led to public execution. Aristocrats might be quietly done-in in dungeons; this was no aristocrat. Some common thug, a street-robber by night, or a house-breaker; thick and shambling, ill-made and ill-looking, he had killed a cobbler's apprentice for a stiver — the smallest coin. The lictor went first, carrying the bundle of rods which might be used to flog the criminal (but wouldn't) wrapped around the single-edged axe which might be used to cut off his head (but wouldn't). It was a symbol only, and the lictor looked bored and disdainful. Then, arms bound behind him at the elbows, legs hobbled with ropes, the felon followed between two files of soldiers. Grasping him fast by a noose round his neck came the common hangman: one might have had them change clothes and places and scarcely told them apart.

"Well, 'one Vergil, a natural of Rome, and no mere denizen,' do they have anything to do with this in Naples . . . I say nothing of the Bail of Brundisy . . . ?" The wauling in my ear was Quint's, to be heard above the clamor of the throng. There was in his voice some light and affectionate taunt that I had not been born in the City itself but in a fœderate town in the Italies' south, well within the Empery, but nearer to where I now lived by the great Voe of Naples than to Yellow Rome itself. The so-well-paved Appian Way went straight and strait between Yellow Rome and Brundisy, but there branched off a branch of it for Naples. A young mage, not yet very well-established in his profession (or in public fame) did well to travel now and then to the Imperial capital, and gently press the thought that there was one (myself) useful to be friend of a friend (Quint) with a friend (the rich Etruscan) to the Court Imperial, to the Oliphaunt Throne . . . not to be lightly named: whosoever sate upon it.

I pressed my bearded lips to Quint's smooth ear-hole, said loud and sharp, that we had throngs and thugs, all right: but neither one was anything to this particular display.

The throng howled, as the throng always would.

"Chin up, cock! Brave it out!"

"They'll stretch that short neck!"

"Hang the hangman! A louse for the hangman!"

"You'll scrag no more widdies nor prentices!"

"Up tails all!"

"Die! For a lousy stiver? *Die!*"

The wretch's face changed expression, but it changed slowly: now he had the sly look of a pig who had broken into a pea-patch, now he was pleased at the attention, now he scowled as some thick and gross insult struck home, now he looked desperately from side to side; always the hangy forced him on, as close to him as the butcher to the ox. All this passed before me and before Quint, and we stood and looked on; I was his guest, and he was the guest of Someone Important in Yellow Rome. Even a wizard, even if he did not want wealth, was willing to draw near to wealth, if he were young and new and scarcely known. And near to power, even if that sort of power he did not much want. Soon enough this procession would pass by, and then we would cross, cross safely on foot, for in Rome (and in Rome alone) no wheeled vehicle might pass through the streets in the day time.

In that case, in a sudden silence, what hooves were those, and what wheels? Quint, I saw, that Roman of Romans, knew at once: and would tell me soon enough . . . if I did not ask. The mob broke into noise again, its inalienable right, and though it was still shouting, it seemed to be shouting the same something, though not all at the same time. Half the yammering throng faced the nice little wagonette and its nice little mule, and the woman,

half-veiled, who was in it. Her small slave-girl holding the sea-silk sunshade or ombello was beginning to be inattentive a bit and a bit the sunshade slipped.

And half the vulgus faced the procession and shouted and gestured, pointing, pointing —

The lictor had strode on, eyes down; and in fact by then he had gotten ahead of the procession and seemed rather to have forgotten it: lictors, too, have their secret private thoughts.

The soldiery slogged along in its fixed rhythms, paying no attention at all to the *thing* its ranks confined; probably thinking of the evening's rations: bread, salt, garlic, parsley, wine, perhaps a bit of dried meat or a bit of dried fish — tunny harpooned in the bloody trapping pens, for instance — and the anticipated meal with its, perhaps, treat, meant far more to them than any execution of a sentence of death (death, to an old soldier, was more boring than exciting).

The hangman, whose attention was so suddenly besought by many cries and movements, pressed on. I noticed that the hangman pressed on.

What Quint, with his pale thin face and dark thin hair, noticed, was not known to me.

Who made up the mob rabbling and howling? The meanest class of citizenry, whose leather badges with **S P Q R** stamped in gilt served to prove citizenship, made up the largest part. They had no money to buy anything and no mind to read anything, so a procession to the gibbet was an absolute gift for them.

Men, too, from all the peoples of the Empery were there: Franks with long hair and Celts with short and Ægyptians with none; pale Berbars from the Solitudes of Syrtica and of As'hara, sand as high as mountains and hills of solid stone pierced with holes where the Troglodytes live; dark Numidians who had seen the Sphynges flying in their thousands to drink of the waters at the sources of the Nile — of all other waters drink they not, of the Waters of Ægypt drink they not — and Gauls with their bearded chops, the wailing of whose dead fills the islands and the highlands of the misty great green darkling Sea of Atlantis between shore to shore of whose vasty waters might no bird fly; and Æthiops with emeraulds in their ears. Many indeed could I see (though not *so* many) were aliens from outside the Empery, and even

the Œconomium.

I was indifferent at seeing or smelling the so-called Foul or Infamous Crafts such as the knackers and the carriers of dogs'-dung for the tanneries, for I still had the muck of the farmyards and the fernbrooks on my legs and feet, and the odors of dead beasts and dungheaps was fresher to my nose-holes than those of ambergrise and nard.

And here and there, as so often of late (and some said, more and more often, and they darkly mumbled their gums about laws graven on the Twelve Iron Tablets about the artificial production of monsters and other omens . . . no one of course was ever able to find such laws) here and there through the mass went wandering a satyr or a centaur of, say, the size of a goat-kid. There were no weanling Lapiths to be seen, however; and who would know one, had there been? memory of one Cluco, a night-soilman little wittier than a wittold, in my homehamlet in the Bail of Brundisy, who used to stop anyone too purblind to avoid him, and confide, "My granddam, now, she seen a Laypith, she seen 'un with a horn in the muddle o' his forrid: which be the reason, she bein' six months gorn wi' child, that I has six finger on my left 'and." What the logical, or even illogical connection between the two things were, no one was ever able to conjecture; certainly all local priests denied that ever there had been stories — "myths," you might call them — of monoceroid Lapiths; and neither was anyone, lay or cleric, able to credit Cluco's being able to invent such a story. But, however invented, tell it he did, decade after decade, to whoever could not trot faster than he could, and who — usually — was glad or let us say willing enough to avoid the presence of Cluco, polydactylous or not (for *rhododactylos* I assure you he wasn't, and neither was he rosy-scented) with the dole of a very small coin or a not-quite-so-small chunk of bread: at which see Cluco become unseen; this may or may not have been more profitable than the night-soil business, but was certainly much easier.

When I mention the size of a goat-kid I refer to the centaurs, for the satyrs were man-sized (as I could have told anyone), and very near each creature was someone (invariably a shill) mentioning confidentially the name of the thaumaturge who'd made it, in some such words as, "That 'un's the work of that same

Septimus as keeps his crib atween Apollo's Court and the Steps of Woe." —why would anyone *want* a confected satyr or centaur? perhaps one of those newly-rich who kept a baby elephant in his atrium might want one, and for the same reason: show.

Thieves were there, in the vulgus; as they could not steal the golden spikes from the ridge-poles of the temples and the other public buildings, they cut the thongs of purses with their knives so much sharper than razors; sellers of snacks were there, for many a man had neither cook nor kitchen to dress a meal of victuals, and if he turned aside into a cheap eating-place he might miss something: but whether a rabbleman stewed hog-palates in vinegar or cut the thongs of purses or did, as was the right of citizens, nothing at all, something there had now changed and perhaps everything had changed. But the hangman wished to behave as though nothing had happened. The lictor, whose attention was now besought by many cries and movements, strode on, eyes down, and in fact by now he had gotten ahead of the procession. The hangman pressed on. A bit the woman's sunshade slipped and a bit the veil, revealing to me a face of such extraordinary loveliness and purity that my breath was stopped.

The word coming up from the populus now was *pardon:* the hangman would not stop for it; why should he? He received the deadman's clothes as a perquisite: even if they were rags (and they were not always rags) they had their value and their price as ingredients of the Black Rite; he got to receive everything which was, or at the time of prisonment had been, on the body of the dead-man-to-be; and he also received his fee for making the liveman's body dead by pushing it off the ladder at the gibbet and at once leaping onto his shoulders and jumping up and down on them — thus assuring that the caitiff's neck must break if it had not already been broken by the drop. Of these benefits the hangman would receive none at all in case of *pardon,* so why should he stop for it? and lastly, it would deprive him of all the pleasure of the death scene: the hangman, howl the mob as it would, would not stop. And who might stop him?

(The lictor, fasces bundled into his arms, was by now rather far ahead, stooped, aloof, deep in thought: of what, who could say? Perhaps that *time there was, ere Roma's woes began . . .* perhaps not.)

Who else? Himself, the August Caesar? Where was *he?* not *here.* From what other place, then, did the musty multitude seem to think that help might arise? The woman in the wagonette commenced to rise, in a slow and flowing motion like a hieratical dancer: though, perhaps actually not: only . . . somehow . . . it seemed so. The brute would not see her. I caught her eye, and again, that ambiguous impression, that impression deep yet perhaps false. Had I caught her eye at all? Erect, like a statue of the golden age, she seemed.

The lictor, perhaps grown somewhat aware of the hideous shriek and hum from that mass of men — here and there some women: not trulls alone: vendors of fragrant citrons, of pickled samphire for relish, of sieves and baskets in many sizes, fishwives going down to the river to renew supplies of mullet and sardines and dogfish with double-lobed livers; others — the lictor at once saw all. Quint, keenly enjoying everything, was telling me nothing; scarcely he raised a thin and hairy hand to brush the ever-deliquescent ointment from his bleary eyes — his physicians were generally agreed 'twas from an excess of some humor, but they never yet agreed on which humor, though there were not many, but prescribed this salve or that; they might as well, I thought, have told him to graze grass like an ox . . . whoever saw a blear-eyed ox? And, "Ow!" shouted the throng, and "Yow!" shouted the throng. "*Pardon! Pardon!*" it howled. And ever and again, "Up-tails, all!" and "A louse for the hangman!"

The hangman may or may not have gotten a louse (close-pressed in that stinking swarm, it would have been no surprise if he had) but what he very quickly got was the lictor at his side; and the lictor said to him, more in astonishment than anger, "Where are you *going,* turd of a toad? Don't you *see* the high-born Virgin lady? *Stop!* — Or I'll let the populus have you, and may they eat your liver!"

The Vestal, meanwhile, remained standing in her wagon all but motionless, the very image of aristocratic calm. Silence took a while. When things were almost silent, the felon seemed to emerge from his daze. One could almost read — no, one *could* read — the play of thoughts coursing over across his sword-slashed and much-confused face. Where *was* he? What was *hap*pening? Why had they *stop*ped? Why was everything *quiet?* Answer: they were arrived and halted at the place of execution; any minute now he might have a small and ill-tasting coin thrust into his mouth and feel nothing beneath his feet, and a sharp brief pain in his neck. With a sound like the lowing of a yearling ox he spread his hobbled legs, and pissed.

The swarm went wild with laughter. Only the lictor's leather face, the vestal's marmoreal countenance, did not change, for all that her little maid, hand hiding mouth, seemed to whisper in her ear. At length silence was again achieved, and in that silence — though the punks and pogues still rolled their painted eyes and smirked at potential clients — the Vestal rose completely to attention, put out her white arm and hand and in a lovely ringing tone declared, *"I pardon that man."* No one word more. And sat down. It had been a completely legal formula, sans emotion. "I divorce you; herewith your dower-fund." "Slave, thou art henceforth free." "Bear witness: I sell this horse-stud for six solids." *I pardon that man.* No one word more. And sat down.

The crowd went wild again. A soldier in a swift second slashed the bonds about the elbows; another slightly stooped and severed those around the ankles. For a second more the thug gaped. Then he started to run at a stumbling trot. Many hands caught at him: he fought against them. Many cries of, "Not yet, man!"

"Not yet! *Thank* the holy lady! Go and kiss the Virgin's foot! Thank her for your life!"

But one might as well have spoken to a pig escaped from the shambles; *loose,* was he? Then he meant to stay loose. And this meant to flee. For a full minute (so I guessed) the absurd scene continued, the pardoned man butting furiously against the arms and bodies which would have had him first do his duty by giving thanks for that pardon; the crowd all of one mind now (the whores most of all: could it have been they fancied a slight upon that one quality which they universally lacked, and lacked, one might say, almost by definition?), the crowd's sense of amour propre was seriously offended; while the lictor covered his grim face with his free hand and gazed through his spread and ringless fingers as though he could not believe his eyes — And then herself the Vestal: some-

thing which might have been a mere flicker of rueful amusement passed over her fine face and was in an instant gone (more than Caesar's wife must a Vestal Virgin be above suspicion, she must be above suspicion of vulgar emotion). She raised her hand at an angle to her wrist, slightly pushed it away from her; the other hand fluttered the colored leathers on the mule's neck. The crowd released the fool felon and laughed to hear his running feet; at once made way for the Vestal's wee carriage, and saluted her with the utmost respect. Did the little maid murmur something, something, anything, with well-practised and almost motionless lips? did the sea-silk sunshade dip for a second a fraction of an inch in a particular direction? this was not certain.

Certain it was that a mule was not a horse, all horses were hysterical more or less, the most placid old cob was likely to behave like a northish bear-shirt if — if, whatever; this would differ from cob to cob — horse to horse. But mules were mysterious creatures, that this one was a small mule did not make its potential mystery any smaller; probably it had been bred for the service it now performed out of a pony-mare by one of the jack-donkeys of the northern lands, lighter in build and in size than the asses of the south, brought to Rome or its countryside for just this purpose. And in view of what was about to happen it was necessary to consider also the probable history of the street-bed. Quint might know just when the street had last been paved, I not. But in some short moment I envisioned the scene — a man engaged in ramming the gravel turning aside for a moment to go piss or to get a drink of water, another workman not waiting for his return or not even considering the matter of had the gravel been rammed sufficiently — and it had not — the second workman perhaps, then, mechanically setting down the pavestone; the first workman returning and, likely even without so much as a shrug, picking up his implement and moving on a few feet to commence the work of ramming a bit further on. And then the passing of the years, the rains, many years of rains, the not-fully-packed gravel shifting, moving; then perhaps the fall of a heavier stone from an improperly-laded wagon passing by in the torchlight: the paving stone sustaining a crack not observed in the night, more years passing, the incessant traffic at last splitting the pavestone. Somehow the inspectors had missed it . . . or, their reports ignored . . . the night-traffic cared nothing for any bad spot which their heavy wagons could lurch across . . . had, anyway, the drivers and teamsters, no time to spend on complaints: into the city by nightfall, in-cargo laded-off, out-cargo laded-on, out of the city by nightrise: so.

A horse, had it felt a sunken spot behind it . . . *if* it felt it . . . would either have strained forward or strained backward. An ass would have stopped. And stayed. Time to put something under the wheel. But the mule, even the small, supposedly sophisticated mule, reacted entirely differently. The mule was, after all, the Symbol of Unbridled Lust — though why this should be so when the mule was sterile, was hard to say: the mule (this particular one) had somehow missed the sunken spot. Now it somehow backed up a trifle. Now it felt it. *The wheel not right! The wheel sinking!* The entire universe of a sudden gone awry! The mule at once went insane: the mule screamed, rolled back its eyes, laid down its ears, made as if to stand on its hind legs — on its forelegs — to lie down and roll over — it was at once evident that there was nothing the mule might not do.

In a second the little slave girl had jumped out of the car to safety, held up her wrists, thin as carrots, at an absolutely useless angle for the Vestal to lean upon. The crowd gave a great groan. It was no slight thing to witness the fall of a Vestal Virgin. Should she be killed, for a space of time at least there would be only *five* "sisters" to hold safe the hearths of Rome . . . who knew what might happen during such an interregnum. Many in the crowd believed that seeing such a sight obliged one to fast: many even believed that whoso saw such would — must! — within the year surely die. From the crowd a great groan. Many rushed forward . . . I amongst them . . . some seized the mule . . . some seized the car . . . some seized hold of their knives, such as each man wore at his belt, or was no man: to cut reins, traces . . . one man alone seized the Vestal by the arm . . . by the upper and the lower arm . . . it lasted a second. The mule was suddenly calm and collected: panic? what panic? The car was suddenly steady and safe. The knives were all suddenly back in their belts, absit omen lest any delator or informer should occasion to ask, *How didst thou dare to bare thy knife unto the high-born*

Virgin Lady? a man might well be well-dead before an explanation were forthcoming. A man might receive a most pressing intimation to slip the short sword between any twain ribs he preferred, thus to prevent his family from attainder and his property from escheatal. Might. Might not. A man might receive a silver pottle or an ember-scuttle enchased with gold, as reward. Might. Might not.

It was all so very suddenly done. So very suddenly her arm was free from my steadying hands. In a second's time; less than it took a drop of water to fall from the clock — And in that second, while a flame of fire seemed to run up both my hands and arms and through my heart and thence into my manly parts (Touched a Vestal! Touched the Virgin's naked arm!); in that second our eyes chanced to meet — then her eyes were gone — then she was gone herself — and three thoughts like three bolts of lightning, so swift that before one fades away the other flashes, passed across my mind.

What color are her eyes?

It is death, *by the Tarpaean Rock, to have carnal congress with a Vestal.*

Her virgin's vows expire in her forty-fifth year.

The woman's age then, I did not know. How old was I then, I will not say.

She was gone at once, long enough had she tarried at the sordid scene beneath the walls of saffron-colored stone, sallow where long suns had beat upon them; not swiftly yet very steadily the small carriage departed, the mule's ears aprick, heading back towards the Temple of Vesta up there beneath the Palatine. It might be that her six-hour watch approached, of guarding and tending the sacred fire. Or it might be that she sought rest and refreshment after the noise and dust and glare. Where had she been? Secluded though they generally were, the Vestals were allowed to take the air at intervals: perhaps to worship at another temple, perhaps to pray before two-faced Janus, he *with red mouth straining and with face all grim,* as the Oracles of Maro had it. Scraps of thought flitted through my mind. Only a Vestal Virgin might drive a wheeled vehicle through day-time Rome (but ah gods! the hideous rumbling noisy nights!). Should she be accused of inchastity, two defenses were open to her: she might draw off a ship foundered on some shoal in the Tiber . . . using only a single thread. The Tiber at Rome was full of shoals, but as this knowledge was elementary and universal, ships (as distinct from bumboats) seldom came as high as Rome. Or . . . she might instead carry water in a sieve. A brave option; small wonder they were seldom accused. Only a Vestal might pardon a man on the way to execution. No one might pardon a vestal caught in flagrant delight, or convicted after trial — Meherc! that a priestess of fire should be tried by water! — she was buried alive in a tomb at once sealed shut and a grim byword pointed out her last and only choice: starve while the lamp burned, or drink the oil and live a while longer in the dark. Whichever, the glory of the world would soon enough pass, and with it, too: the beauty, the damps, the chills, the plots, the pests, the fevers, and the fleas, of eternal Rome. Of Yellow Rome. Yellow Rome.

As the great fire of the First Year of the Emperor Julius I was destined to occur, *dixit David cum Sybilla* (whoever "David" is), it was fortunate that it occurred whilst the Roy was completing the conquest of Gaul the Sur, for when word of the extent of the conflagration reached Himself the August Caesar as he was entering the great Port called Marsayle, he ordered that it never be fired but that every building faced with marble be taken apart and the facing be sent by galley-drawn barges to the Ost Port of Rome and thence by oxen-courted shallow-draft vessels up the Tiber. This nonpareil stayne was at once named the *Gallo Antico*, the Ancient Gaul; some take it from *giallo antico*, the old gayle, as one says, *the blaunche fever and the gayle*: or in that poetic line, *his face as gayle as Winter grass, sello beneath the snae.* Soon enow came marbe of tother hues, *rosso antico*, and the green one green as the pistuquim-nut; the maid-pale-white, the black-as-night, the mottled and the creamy brown; other yet. Well might the Julio exult, *A hamlet of wooden huts and hovels so I found, and one of marmol structoes I am to leave behind.* As this was in effect the first great quantity of marmorstone seen in Mamma Roma, its popular name was quickly given and ever been left so.

"Good fortune to that man," I said, shaking my head as though to dispel the flimsies of bad dreams.

Quint made a scoffing sound, such as only the tutelage of the costliest of rhetors could have produced. "Did you *see* that animal face? He will be caught for another dirty crime and condemned again and this time surely hanged for it within the year — if not, indeed, the week — and should he encounter another vestal?"

I asked if the Vestals always set the felon free. Quint considered. "First you must meet your felon face to face," he said, shrugging. Quint was a great shrugger. "Then — of the current Six, you mean?" Instantly it occurred to him that I would scarcely have meant the Six current in the reign of Tarquin the Proud or Judah King of the Jews, and he went on to capitulate them. "Clothilda pardons everyone. Volumnia pardons no one. Honoria, would you believe it, gravely casts dice to decide. Carries them with her in a monopede's shoe — a *monopede's* shoe!" (There would be no gain in asking how he knew it was the shoe of a monopede, for he might have given me some such answer as, "Everybody knows it," or, "Because there is only one" — in which case my respect for him would be diminished.)

"Aurelia pardons now and then. — the dice? They are the most ordinary dice; sort of spoils the story, doesn't it? Stories are often spoiled like that: tiresome." My respect for him increased. "Lenora, they say, never drives that way, so as not to have to choose." He quirked his mouth, hunched his shoulders, flung out his hand and fluttered his fingers, with what might just be perceived as a very slight emphasis of the digit of infamy. "Soft-hearted Lenora, eh? — but they are all brutes, these fellows. Kindness to them is cruelty to others."

And he told a recent report, not even to be designated as a rumor, that the man just freed had once been a provincial gladiator of the lowest sort, probably expelled for incompetence. "I shouldn't wonder," he said. "You saw that sword-scarred face. No brow. No chin. Some ancestral taint, I'd venture. They sell very good bread with opium seed over there."

My question almost burst forth. "But which one was *she*?" She was only one of six sacred women in the service of Vesta, the goddess of the hearth, without whom there could really be no home, and hence, no Rome: but which one was she? The bread *did* smell good; they say there is at least one bake-shop in the capital for every province in the Empery. One does not doubt.

Quint turned to me, immediately (he) a man

of the most scornful urban world. "But my dear
fellow, you know *nothing!* — mage though you
are — Well . . . how could you, there in Naples?
She is Claudia."

"And does she often spare?"

Quint started again his rigmarole, stopped.
Sincerely he seemed in doubt. Then, somewhat
surprised, said that he did not know. That the
matter had never — in his presence — come up
before. Then he fell silent, merely gestured to
his important friend's litters (only two of many,
of course) which were waiting for us: quite in
the Roman fashion: not *too* very far from the
appointed place. He certainly did not ask,
"Handsome woman, is she not?" or "What did
you think of her?" or, "Do you fancy her?" One
simply never asked such questions about a
Vestal Virgin. It was a long way up to the
Tarpaean Rock when you had to climb.

But it was only a short way down when you
were pushed.

There were nights when I slept like a farmer,
and nights when I could not sleep, or slept but
ill. That night I fell soon into slumber, for
thank the gods, in that very quiet — and very,
very rich — quarter of Rome, where Quint's
Etruscan friend had one of his villas, there was
neither wagon traffic nor roistering. Whence,
then, came that noise, a mere murmur at first,
then tumult and clamor? I must have left my
bed the better to observe and to hearken —
what, then a horrid shock, to realize that my
arms were bound behind me at the elbows and
my feet confined by straps or ropes so that I
might take no very long steps and certainly
could not run. I turned to ask my terrified
question of the man nearest to me, an intent
and stinking fellow in a dirty tunicle; but this
one held, looped around his hands and arms, a
rope: and the rope was noosed round my neck!
It did not choke me, not so long as I kept up
with my keeper. "But what then?" I begged the
fellow. "But what then?" The shunsoap made
no answer, but steadily led me along, as a
nacker leads the nag before stopping him,
stunning him, stabbing him, skinning him, and
then cutting him up: hooves, hide, and pizzle to
the glue-maker, and the other parts to —
Suddenly the sound of the vulgus ceased, then
resumed in another note and another register.

Then ceased again.

A woman's voice, strong and level and chill.

"I pardon that man." Our gazes met. She
showed her shock. Her eyes were blue and clear.

It was yet dark when I woke, but Rome
generally awoke in the yet dark; a few lamps
had already been kindled in the corridor; I
noticed this abstractedly as I rushed to Quint:
but Quint was already rushing to me. We met
in the lesser atrium with the dull red walls
where a few servants passed hither and thither
like wraiths, thin vapors rising from the vessels
in their hands. The heavy master of the household had either not yet aroused, or was occupied elsewhere; had he been present, our own
respective business, however much it agitated
us, must needs wait: but present he was not. At
first our confrontation was in silence, there
were sighs and moanings inarticulate, but not
words. Then Quint said, and his voice trembled,
"I have had such a dream!"

"And I —"

"Dreams are best kept silent, except to a
qualified interpreter — or to a closemost
friend —"

"Yes. . . ."

"I am older, let me speak first," said
Quint. I staying silent, he went on to speak
his words, clutching my arm, my arms, as
though he would draw me to him. "Did you
notice?" he asked. "Did you notice that old
pedlar-dame in yesterday's mob? selling baskets and sieves? She passed through my
dream at an angle and then I saw the
woman, I mean *the* woman . . . the real
woman . . . I saw the woman holding the
sieve . . . Claudia it was . . . it was Claudia
. . . she held the sieve — *you know what that
means* — and my heart went chill and
swollen and I peered to see if the sieve did
indeed hold the water, or if it had merely let
it slip through and the mesh still wet. But
she held it upside-down, she held it upside-
down! What does *that* mean? And she looked
at me and I saw that her eyes were very blue
and very clear," his own eyes, I saw in the
increasing light of early day, were very red,
and quite without salve or ointment; "and
she looked past *me* and she looked at *you*
and her eyes went wide and I remarked her
voice, I shall always remember her voice: it
was level and strong and clear, and she
pointed her hand at you and she said, *'Thou
art the man!'* And what *that* means, I dare

not think: but I would that you would leave our Yellow Rome at once."

After I had spoken in turn, Quint leaned closer to me, and almost, somehow, I expected to see a thin cold breath from his mouth, like that from the basins of hot water for a quick early morning wash even now hurried past us by a few diligent slaves: but slavery makes for diligence . . . and makes it, much. Quint asked, "What is the meaning of this two-part dream? Does one part come from the Gate of Ivory and is false? does one part issue from the Gate of Horn and is it true? Is the whole dream one of evil omen? or of good? If we say, *Good,* in that she pardons you? of some sentence of death, it is sure, for if it were merely a matter of a fine . . . prison . . . the dungeon . . . or the scourge —" here I shuddered, he went on — "how many men yearly die beneath the lash, merely, the lash? how many in the dungeon, where even a reflection of a reflection of the light of the sun or the moon never shines? . . . let alone in the mere prison? where sometimes a gleam of sunlight creeps as it were uncertainly amongst the filthy littered rushes or the trampled straw . . . or now and then a beam of moonlight is reflected by a burnished mazer or a pewter plate polished like a mirror? For that matter," he babbled, as we stood, crouched, in the atrium, close together; "for that matter," he went on, "when a mere fine, merely the matter of a fine has broke a man's bench, his *bancus* become *ruptus,* his lands his fields his house his yards his loft his laboratory all his goods his gear his tools his attire and even the very dead embers of his hearth for potash, and even the broken pisspot in the corner of his house of office: all, all, sold to pay the fine — eh? — how many, sinking beneath shame and broken spirit, the fine like blazing fire consumes all means of earning food?"

Quint, beside himself, was now unwittingly imitating the gestures, the very vocal tricks, of any advocate seen and heard in Apollo's Court. He swept the air with his hands, he bulged his eyes, he stood on his tip-toes, he touched his ear-lobe with a finger. "But all of these *minor penalties,*" this was a new Quint to me and no longer the sophisticate, the man-about-Rome, the cynical; "and if the enemy of the enemies of mine enemy does not die of the stinking-pox, then let him live . . . let him live under these minor penalties; And these, allegedly the lesser of evils, the Vestal Virgin may not pardon: not a farthing, not a fig: not the theft of enough crushed walnut paste to cover the toenail of an infant child: *none!*"

To sum up: I, Vergil, once with brief: an advocate: 'twas very brief: eh? if the Vestal Virgin in this probably vatic dream — and every dream in one way or another must be vatic, must be prophetic, else why is a dream dreamed? if I, Vergil, am he whom the Vestal pardons, she can be pardoning me only from sentence of death. Not from charge of a crime meriting death, no, from *sentence* of death. And what can I, Vergil, have done or what would I *do,* to merit?

Dared I, would I dare? to love her —?

And as for the other dream, and her cry of, *"Thou art the man!"* if this was not accusative, then what was it? *Could* it be exculpatory? all things were, some barely, possible: but . . . he would believe that this the Virgin's exclamation was exculpatory? then he would believe anything . . . let him, if he would, believe —

But let him first flee. And if not to the end of the Empery, then at least from Yellow Rome. To be, at least, a while more, safe.

Where would he safest be? from the accusations of the vatic voice in a state of dream —? whither flees the frightened child? he flees to home.

And now and for a long time: *Naples was home.*

. . . whence he might, if he would, if he need, having taken stock, flee again . . .

But why *at once* . . . ? Why, because there was no set time indicated in these dreams. Who knows but what even now delators and informants were bespeaking those who bespoke the soldiery, *He laid his hands upon the Virgin's naked flesh,* and, *Act quickly, he may soon escape and flee . . .*

Also, *did* I wait, tarry? . . . opportunity . . . temptation . . . lust . . .

Thus: *at once.*

It is tiresome to say what everyone knows, in this case that some things are more quickly said than done. There was no ship at a wharf behind a signboard reading **HOME, AT ONCE.** We had to wait until Quint's friend, our host, was willing to see us. Then it was needful (he,

Quint, thought) that I should leave the City by a round-about way and not by any of the broader streets, and essential (I thought) that Quint should not be seen with me; and I was a long time persuading him of this, and even I had a chore preventing him of this, and even I had a chore preventing him that he might not even, as he put it, "put bread in my wallet" for the journey, in my old doe-skin budget, *bread:* had I yielded at all, we would likely have wandered over half of Rome to find some particular bake-shop. With or without opium seed. Even, yes indeed! he might bethink him, *bread is not enough!* and insist he obtain me *cheese,* and *salame-sausage!* — at which, by the sod and staff! might I give myself up for lost —

I was therefore long in leaving, and I neither drew rein of my borrowed horse, a gentle stalwart grey with dappled haunches; his name alas I never learned, I called him *Thee* (the Etruscan . . . a bit mysterious, like most his kind; and like most his kind: rich . . . had many horses, asked no questions) nor looked back till I had reached the rise by the third milestone.

Then I halted, and turned. No pursuit? None . . . though I was uneasy in recalling that a dream, like a curse, might sometimes wait as much as seven years for fulfillment. No sign of pursuit, nor yet I was not easy. Ease is not always to the wise; was I wise? Some knowledge had I gained, but had I gained wisdom?

And lifting my eyes from the Appian Road I saw in the setting sun the cloud of dust raised by the hooves of the beasts being driven into the city to be slaughtered early next morning for sale in the markets, and the dust was faintly yellow. I saw in the suddenly visible middle distance the gold-spiked roofs, and stonework in marble the color of the hair of a fair-haired woman, brickwork the shade of straw, tiles a tint between that of the lemon of Sicily and a bright marigold blowing in the wind. I saw the glittering roofs and glowing golden buildings of Rome. By the yellow Tiber in the yellow dust of the yellow dusk I saw the city of Yellow Rome . . . of Yellow Rome. . . .

Yellow Rome.

I turned and urged on my horse. It was a long way to Naples.   Ω

CONAN POSTMORTEM

Higgledy-piggledy
Robert E. Howard's great
Swordswinging hero out-
Lived him a while

Conquered the screen, Mr.
Universe starring . . . in
Heaven somewhere there's a
Big Texas smile.

— **Ann K. Schwader**

AURALINCUBI

with a nod to Joe Haldeman*

Astrogenic beings call daily,
eavesdropping forever: ghosts
hectoring incessantly, jabberwocks keening
loudly, morning, noon, or post-meridiem.
Quit ranting! Stop tirades! Ululating viragos,
whining Xantippes, yammering zillions!

Always be cheerful.
Dying ends further grotesque hounding,
instills jubilant knowledge. Life means nothing!
Only painful quibblers remain,
saying this: "Unmerciful villains
will xysterize your zombie!"

* Joe suggested this manic form on GEnie. The 26 words in each stanza are in alphabetical order!

— **Keith Allen Daniels**

WHEN HE WAS FAB

by F. Paul Wilson

Floor drains.

Sheesh. Doug hated them.

Being super of this old rat-trap building wasn't a bad job. The hours could play hell with you sometimes, but he got a free room, he got his utilities, and he got a salary — if you wanted to call that piddly amount in his weekly check a salary. But you couldn't knock the deal too hard. Long as he stayed on the job, he had shelter, warmth, and enough money for food, enough time to work out with his weights. Wasn't glamorous, but a guy with his education — like, none to speak of besides seventh grade and post-grad courses in the school of hard knocks — couldn't ask for a whole helluva lot more.

'Cept maybe for drains that worked.

The basement floor drain was a royal pain. He hovered over it now in his rubber boots, squatting ankle deep in the big stinky puddle that covered it. Around him the tenants' junk was stacked up on the high ground against the walls like a silent crowd around a drowning victim. Third time this month the damn thing had clogged up. Course there'd been a lot of rain this month, and that was part of the problem, but still, the drain shoulda been working better than this.

Now or never, he thought, unfolding his rubber gloves. He wished he had more light than that naked 60-watter hanging from the beam overhead. Would have loved one of those big babies they used at night games up at Yankee Stadium.

Jeez, but he hated this part of the job. Last week the drain had clogged and he'd reached down like he was about to do now and had come up with a dead rat.

He shuddered now with just the memory of it. A monster Brooklyn brown rat. Big, tough mother that could've easily held its own with the ones down on the docks. Didn't know how it had got in this drain, but the grate had been pushed aside, and when he'd reached down, there it was, wedged into the pipe. So soft, at first he'd thought it was a plastic bag or something. Then he'd felt the tail. And the feet. He'd worked it loose and pulled it free.

Just about blew lunch when he'd looked at it, all soft, puffy, pulpy, and drippy, the eyes milk white, the sharp yellow buck teeth bared, the matted hair falling off in clumps. And God, it stunk. He'd dumped it in his plastic bucket, scooped up enough of the rapidly draining water to cover it, and run like hell for the dumpster.

"Whatta y'got for me this week, you sonuvabitch?" he said aloud.

He didn't usually talk to floor drains, but his skin was crawling with the thought of what might've got stuck down there this time. And if he ever grabbed something that was still moving . . . forget about it.

He pulled the heavy rubber gloves up to his elbows, took a deep breath, and plunged his right hand into the water.

"What the hell?"

The grate was still in place. So what was blocking it?

Underwater, he poked his fingers through the slots and pulled the grate free, then worked his hand down the funnel and into the pipe.

"What now, you mother? What *now*?"

Nothing. The water felt kind of thick down there, almost like jello, but the pipe was empty as far as his fingers could reach. Probably something caught in the trap. Which meant he'd have to use the snake. And dammit to Hell, he'd left it upstairs.

Maybe if he squeezed his fingers down just a little further he'd find something. Just a little —

Doug reached down too far. Water sloshed over the top of his glove and ran down the inside to his fingers. It had a strange, warm, *thick* feel to it.

"Damn it all!"

But when he went to pull back, his hand wouldn't come. It was stuck in the hole and all his twisting and pulling only served to let more

of the cloudy water run into his glove.

And then Doug noticed that the water was no longer running down his arm — it was running *up*.

He stared, sick dread twisting in his gut, as the thick, warm fluid moved up past his elbow — *crawled* was more like it. After a frozen moment, he attacked it with his free hand, batting at it, wiping it off. But it wouldn't wipe. It seemed to be traveling *in* his skin, becoming part of it, migrating up his arm like water spreading through blotter paper.

And it was *hot* where it moved. The heat spread up under the half sleeve of his work shirt. He tore at the buttons but before he could get them undone, the heat had spread across his chest, up his shoulder to his neck.

Doug lost it then. He began whimpering and crying, clawing at himself as he splashed and scrambled and flopped about like an animal caught in a trap, trying to yank his right hand free from the drain. He felt the heat on his face now, moving toward his mouth. He clamped his lips shut but it ran into his nostrils and through his nose to his throat. He opened his mouth to scream, but no sound would come out. A film covered his eyes, and against his will his muscles began to relax, lowering him into the water, letting it soak into him, all through him. He felt as if he were melting, dissolving into the puddle . . .

Marc hopped out of the cab in front of the Graf Spee's entrance, paid the driver with his patented flourish, and strolled past the velvet cords that roped off the waiting dorks.

Bruno was on the door tonight. A burly lump of muscle with feet; at thirty-five he was maybe ten years older than Marc; his hair was a brown similar to Marc's but there the resemblance stopped. As Marc approached the canopied entrance, he wondered what Bruno had looked like as an infant, or if perhaps the doorman's mother had been prescient. Because Bruno had grown up to be the epitome of Bruno-ness.

"Ay, Mister Chevignon," Bruno said with a wide grin and a little bow. "How ya doon anight?"

"Fine, Bruno. Just fine."

Keeping his hands jammed deep into the pockets of his Geoffrey Beene tweed slacks, and trapping his open, ankle-length Moschino black leather coat behind his elbows while

WHEN HE WAS FAB

exposing his collarless white Armani shirt, buttoned to the throat, Marc swiveled and surveyed the line of hopefuls awaiting the privilege of admission to the Spee.

"Real buncha loooosuhs tonight, Mister C."

Marc let his eyes roam the queue, taking in all the well-off and the trying-to-look-it, all dressed in their absolute best or their most fashionably tacky ensembles, trying to look so cool, so with-it, so very-very, but unable to hide the avid look in their eyes, that hunger to be where it was most in to be, to dance on the rotating floor of the Spee and search for the famous faces that would be on the "Star Tracks" page of next week's *People*.

"Have they been good little aspirants, Bruno?"

"Yeah. No wise guys so far."

"Then let's make someone's day, shall we?"

"Whatever you say, Mister C."

He sauntered along outside the cords, watching them stare his way and whisper without taking their eyes off him. *Who's he? . . . You ever seen him before? . . . Looks like Johnny Depp . . . Nah, his shoulders is too big . . . Gawd, he's gawgeous! . . . Well, if he ain't somebody, how come he's getting in ahead of us? . . . I dunno, but I seen him around here before.*

Right you are, sweetheart, he thought.

The last speaker was a bony, brittle, bottle blonde with a white hemline up to here and a black neckline down to there. Knobby knees knocking in the breeze, spiky hair, a mouth full of gum, three different shades of eye shadow going half way up her forehead, and wearing so many studs and dangles her ears had to be swiss-cheese when her jewelry was off.

Perfect.

"What's your name, honey?"

She batted her lashes. "Darlene."

"Who you with?"

"My sister Marlene." She reached back and pulled forward an identically dressed clone of herself. "Who wants t'know?"

"Twins," he said, smiling. "More than perfect." He lifted the velvet cord. "Come on, girls. You don't have to wait any longer."

After exchanging wide-eyed glances, they ducked the velvet and followed him to the canopy. Some of the dorks grumbled but a few of them clapped. Soon they were all clapping.

He ushered them to the door where Bruno stepped aside and passed the giggling twins

through into the hallowed inner spaces of the Graf Spee.

"You're a prince, Mister C," Bruno said, grinning.

"How true," he replied, passing him.

He slowed, almost tripped. What a lame remark. Surely he could have come up with something better than that.

Bruno stepped into the dark passageway and touched his arm.

"You feelin' okay, Mister C.?"

"Of course. Why?"

"You look a little pale, is all. Need anyting?"

"No, Bruno. Thanks, but I'm fine."

"Okay. But you need anyting, you lemme know an' it's done. Know what I'm sayin'?"

Marc clapped Bruno on the shoulder and nodded. As he walked down the narrow black corridor that led past the coat check room he wondered what Bruno had meant. Did he look pale? He didn't *feel* pale. He felt fine.

The twins were hovering near the coat check window, looking lost. They'd finally achieved their dream: They'd made it to the swirling innards of the Spee, and they weren't sure what to do about it. So they stood and numbly watched the peristalsis. One of them turned to Marc as he approached.

"Thanks a million, mister. It was like really great of you to get us in and like if, you know, you like want to get together later, you know, we'd like really be glad to show our appreciation, know what I mean?"

The second twin batted her eyes over the other's shoulder.

"Yeah. We really would. But do you mind if I, like, ask, uh . . . are you someone?"

Just as he was thinking how pathetic they were, he reminded himself that once he'd had to wait in line like them. That had been years ago, back in the days when King Kong had been THE place. But after he'd been let in once, he'd never stood on line again. He'd taken his chance and he'd capitalized on it. And as time had passed and his status had risen, he'd developed the nightly ritual of picking one or two of the *hoi polloi* for admission to the inner sanctum of whatever club he was gracing with his presence that night.

"Everyone is someone," he said. "I happen to be Marc."

"Which is your table?" said Twin One.

"They're all my tables."

Twin Two's eyes bulged. "You *own* this place?"

He laughed. "No. Of course not. That would be too much trouble." And besides, he thought, these places stay hot for something like the lifespan of a housefly. "I just go where the action is. And tonight the action is here. So you two wiggle in there and enjoy yourselves."

"All *right!*" said Twin One.

She turned to her sister and they raised their fists and gave each other an Arsenio Hall salute.

Marc shuddered as he watched them hurry toward the main floor. They might be just vulgar enough to amuse someone. He opened the door marked **PRIVATE** and took the narrow stairway up to the gallery. Gunnar, Bruno's Aryan soul-mate, was on duty at the top of the steps. He waved Marc into the sanctum sanctorum of alcoved tables overlooking the dance floor.

The Manhattan In-Crowd was out in force tonight, with various Left Coast luminaries salted among them. Madonna looked up from her table and waved as she whispered something in a pert brunette's ear. Marc stuck his tongue out and kept moving. Bobby DeNiro and Marty Scorcese nodded, Bianca blew him a kiss, and on and on . . .

This was what it was all about. This was what he lived for now, the nightlife that made the drudgery of his daylife bearable. Knowing people, important people, *being* known, acknowledged, sought out for a brush with that legendary Marc Chevignon wit. It was that wit, that incisive, urbane flippancy that had got him here and changed his nightlife. Soon it would be changing his daylife. Everything was falling into place, beautifully, flawlessly, almost as if he'd planned it this way.

And he hadn't.

All he'd wanted was a little excitement, to watch the watchables, to be where the action was. He'd never even considered the possibility of being *in* the play, he'd simply hoped for a chance to sit on the sidelines and perhaps catch a hint of breeze from its hem as the action swirled by.

But when lightning struck and he got through the door of the Kong a couple of years ago, things began to happen. He'd sat at the bar and fallen into conversation with a few of the lower-level regulars and the quips had begun to flow. He hadn't the faintest where they'd come from, they simply popped out. The cracks stretched to diatribes using Buckley-level vocabulary elevated by P.J. O'Rourke-caliber wit, but bitchy. *Very* bitchy. The bar-hangers lapped it up. The laughter drew attention, and some mid-level regulars joined the crowd. He was invited back to an after-hours party at the Palladium, and the following night when he showed up at King Kong with a few of the regulars, he was passed right through the door.

A few nights and *he* was a regular. Soon he was nobbing with the celebs. They all wanted him at their tables. Marc C. made things happen. He woke people up, got them talking and laughing. Wherever he sat there was noise and joviality. He could turn just-another-night-at-the-new-now-club into an event. If you wanted to draw the people who mattered to your table, you needed Marc Chevignon.

And his wit didn't pass unnoticed by the select few who recognized obscure references and knew high-level quick-draw quippery when they heard it. Franny Lebowitz said he could be the next Tom Wolfe. And LuAnn agreed.

He stopped at LuAnn's table.

"Hiya, Marky," she said, reaching for his hand.

Her touch sent a wave of heat through him. He and LuAnn were an *item* these days. They had a *thing* going. He spent three or four nights a week at her place. Always at her place. Never at his. No one saw his place. Ever.

That, he knew, was part of his attraction for these people. They'd taken the measure of his quality and found it acceptable, even desirable. But he was an unknown quantity. Where he came from, who he came from, where he lived, what he did in the day were all carefully guarded secrets. Marc Chevignon, the cagey, canny mystery man, the acid-tongued enigma.

He suspected that LuAnn genuinely cared for him, but it was hard to tell. She tended to let down her panties a lot quicker than her guard. She'd been around the scene so much longer than he, seemed to have had so many lovers — Christ, when he walked her into some of the private after-hours parties he could be pretty sure she'd screwed half the guys there, maybe some of the women too — but she really seemed interested in him. At least now. At least for the moment.

She was the one who'd been pressing him to write down his more incisive observations so she could show them to a few editors she knew — and she knew all the important ones. She was sure she could land him a regular spot in the *Voice*, and maybe *Esquire*, if not both.

Thus the tape recorder in his pocket. During the day he never could remember a thing he'd said the night before. So he'd decided to record himself in action and transcribe the best stuff the next morning.

Nothing so far tonight worth writing down. Hadn't really come up with anything last night either. No inspiration, he guessed.

But it would come. Because it was happening. *He* was happening. Everything coming his way. *Esquire*, the *Voice*, maybe an occasional freelance piece for *GQ* later on. He wasn't going to be a mere hanger-on anymore, someone who merely knew Somebodies. He was going to *be* one of those Somebodies.

But the best part of it all was having LuAnn. LuAnn . . . twenty-eight with the moon-white skin of a teenager who'd never been to the beach, night-dark hair, pale blue, aventurine eyes, and the trademark ruby lipstick. All day long he ached for the sight of her. He couldn't tell her that, of course. Had to play it cool because Marc C. was cool, but sometimes it was hard to hide. *Most* times it was hard to hide. Most times he wanted to fall at her feet professing his undying love and begging her never to leave him.

Sure, it scanned like a third-rate Tin Pan Alley ditty, but that was how he felt.

"Ms. Lu," he said, bending and kissing her. God, he loved the soft, glossy touch of her lips.

She jerked back.

"What's wrong, Lu?"

"Your lips. They feel . . . different."

"Same ones I wore last night." He tugged at them. "I don't remember changing them."

LuAnn gave him a patient smile and pulled him down next to her. He waved and nodded hellos in the dimness to the LuAnn-table regulars, then turned his attention to the lady herself. Her eyes sparkled with excitement as she leaned toward him and whispered close in his ear; the caress of her warm breath raised gooseflesh down his left side.

"I hear you gave Liz's guy the slip last night."

"Liz's guy?"

"Don't be coy, Marc. I heard it earlier this afternoon. Liz had one of her people tail you home from my place last night — or at least *try* to tail you home."

Any warmth he'd been drawing from her vanished in a chilly draft of unease. She could only mean Liz Smith, the columnist who'd been trying to get the scoop on him for months now. He guessed she was tired of tagging him with the "mystery man" line when she did a piece on the club scene. Other people had tried to tail him before but he'd spotted them easily. Whoever this guy was must have been good. Marc hadn't had the slightest suspicion. . . .

"He said you ducked into an old apartment house in Brooklyn and never came out."

"Oh, yes . . ." Marc said carefully. "I spotted him shortly after I left your place. He was good. I couldn't lose him in the usual manner so I led him all the way into Bay Ridge and used the key I have from the owner of this dump there — in the front door and out the back. I always do that when I think I'm being followed." He rubbed his chin, Bogart style. "So he was one of Liz's boys. That's interesting."

More than interesting — terrifying.

"Yeah, she's determined to track you down," LuAnn said, snuggling closer. "But she's not going to be first, is she, Marky? You're going to take me to your place firstest, aren't you?"

"Sure, Lu. You'll be the first. But I warn you, you'll be disappointed when the day comes."

"No I won't."

Yes, you will. I guarantee it.

He sat next to her and tried to keep from shaking. God, that had been close! He'd been right on the edge of having his cover blown and hadn't had an inkling. Suddenly Marc didn't feel so good.

"Excuse me a moment," he said, rising. "I need to make a pit stop." He winked. "It's a long ride from Bay Ridge."

LuAnn laughed. "Hurry back!"

Feeling worse by the minute, he headed straight for the men's room. As he pushed into the bright fluorescent interior, he saw Karl Peaks turning away from the sink, licking a trace of white powder from his index finger.

"Marc?" Peaks said, sniffing and gawking. "Is that you, man?"

"No. It's Enrico Caruso." *Enrico Caruso? Where the hell did that come from?*

"It's your face, man. What's happened to it?"

Alarmed, Marc stepped over the mirror. His knees almost buckled when he saw himself.

My face!

His skin was sallow, leaching into yellow under the harsh light. And the left side was drooping, the corners of his mouth and left eye sagging toward his chin.

My God! he thought. *What's happening?*

He couldn't stay here, couldn't let anyone see him like this. Because it wasn't going to get better. Somehow he knew that the longer he waited the worse it would sag.

He spun and fled past Peaks, turned a hard right and went down the back steps, through the kitchen, and out into the rear alley.

It was raining now. He slunk through the puddles like a rat until he found an intersecting alley that took him out to West Houston. He flagged a cab and huddled in the protective darkness of the rear seat as it carried him through the downpour, over the Williamsburg Bridge to Brooklyn. Home.

Doug watched Marc flow back into the bucket, sliding down his arm, over his wrist and hand, to ooze off his fingertips like clear, warm wallpaper paste. A part of Doug was furious with Marc for letting him down tonight, but another part of him knew that something was seriously wrong. He'd half-sensed it during the last time they'd been together. And tonight he was sure. Marc wasn't acting right.

Marc . . . Christ, why did he call this pile of goo Marc? It was *goo*. A nameless *it*. Marc Chevignon was someone who existed only when Doug was wearing the goo. He'd picked the name Marc because it sounded classy, like Marc Antony, that Roman guy in the Cleopatra movie. And Chevignon? He'd borrowed that from the label inside some fancy leather coat he'd seen in a men's shop.

Somewhere along the way he had started thinking of the goo as a friend . . . a friend named Marc.

"What's the matter, Marc?" he whispered into the bucket when the goo had all run off him. "What's goin' on, man?"

Marc didn't answer. He just sat in his bucket under the harsh light of the white-tiled bathroom. Marc never answered. At least not from the bucket. Marc only spoke when he was riding Doug. Marc was brilliant when he was riding Doug. At least he had been up till now.

Doug remembered the first time Marc climbed on him, down in the basement, when he'd reached into the plugged drain . . . remembered the heat, the suffocating feeling. He'd been so scared then, afraid he'd been caught in some real-life replay of *The Blob*, absolutely sure he was going to die. But he hadn't died. After blacking out for a minute or so, he'd come to on the basement floor, half in, half out of the shrinking puddle. He'd scrambled to his feet, looked at his hands, felt his neck, his face. The goo was gone — not a trace of it left on him. Everything seemed almost normal.

Almost. His skin didn't feel quite right. Not slimy or nothing, just . . . different. He ran upstairs to his place, the super's apartment on the first floor. He seemed to be moving a little different, his steps quicker, surer. You could almost say he was like graceful. He got to the bathroom and stared in the mirror.

He'd changed. He looked the same, but then again he didn't. His normally wavy brown hair was darker, straighter, maybe because it was wet and slicked back. But even his eyebrows looked a little darker. His eyes were still blue but they seemed more intense, more alive.

And he felt different *inside*. Usually when he finished a day's work he liked to get a six-pack, flip on the tube, and mellow out for the night. Now he wanted to *move*. He felt like going places, doing things, making things happen instead of letting them happen to him.

He stared at the reflection for a long time, telling himself over and over he wasn't crazy. He'd just had some sort of daymare or something. Or maybe fumes — yeah, some sort of fumes bubbling up from the drain had screwed up his head for a little bit. But he was okay now. Really.

Finally, when he sort of believed it, he staggered back to the basement. Still had to do something with that water.

But the water was gone. The drain had unclogged and all that was left of the stinking puddle was a big round glistening wet spot. Relieved that he didn't have to stick his arm down that pipe again, Doug collected his gloves and junk and headed back upstairs.

In the hall he ran into Theresa Coffee, the busty blonde graduate student in 308. He gave her his usual smile — at least he thought it was his usual smile — and expected her usual curt nod in return. She'd caught him staring at her underwear down in the laundry room once too often and had been giving him the cold shoulder ever since. Treated him like a pervo. Which he wasn't. But her underwear, man — looked like it came straight out of a Victoria's Secret catalog. Whoa.

But this time she actually stopped and talked to him. And he actually talked back to her. Like intelligently. He actually sounded like he had a brain in his head. Like a guy who'd finished high school. College even. He didn't have the faintest idea where all that talk came from, all he knew was that for the first time in his life he sounded brainy. She seemed to think so too. She even invited him up to her place. And before too long she was modeling all that underwear for him.

Much later, when he left her, he didn't go back to his apartment to sack out. He went back to change into his best clothes — which weren't much then, for sure — and headed for Manhattan. For the King Kong.

The rest was history.

History . . . the celebrity friends, the notoriety, the promised writing career, LuAnn, a way *up* and *out* . . . history.

Yeah. History. Only right now history seemed to be coming to an end.

Doug stared down at the two-gallon bucketful of goo. *Cloudy* goo. Marc used to be clear. Crystal clear. Like Perrier. What kind of game was it trying to run?

"C'mon, guy," Doug said, rolling up his sleeve. "One more time."

He slipped his right hand up to his wrist in the goo. He noticed how Marc was cooler than usual. In the past there'd always been a near-body-temperature warmth to it. Slowly it began to slide up his forearm.

"There y'go!"

But it only made a few inches before it started to slide back into the bucket.

"You bastard!"

Doug couldn't help being mad. He knew he owed a lot to Marc — everything, in fact — but he couldn't help feel that he'd been teased along and now he was being dumped. He wanted to kick the bucket over. Or better yet, up-end it over the toilet and flush it down to the sewers. See if Marc liked it down there in the dark with the crocodiles.

"So what's up, here, Marc? What's doin'? You gonna put me through the wringer? Gonna

make me crawl? Is that it? Well it won't work. Because I don't need you, Marc. I owe you, I'll give you that. But if you think I can't live without you, f'get about it, okay?"

For Doug had arrived at the conclusion that he didn't need Marc any more. Marc hadn't really done nothing. Marc just was like the Wizard in *The Wizard of Oz.* How'd that song go? "Oz never did give nothing to the Tin Man, that he didn't already have." Right. And Doug was the Tin Man. All that sharp wit and grooviness had been hiding within him all along. All Marc had done was bring it to the surface — and take credit for it. Well, Marc wasn't going to take credit any more. *Doug* was taking the wheel now. He knew he had it in him. All the doors were already open to him. All he had to do was walk through and make this city his oyster.

"Okay," he said, rising and heading for the door. "If that's the way you want it, fine. You make plans for the sewer, I'll head for the Spee."

He should have felt great, free, lighter than air. So how come he felt like he'd just lost his best friend?

"Yo, Bruno," Doug said as he stepped under the canopy and headed toward the entrance of the Graf Spee. "I'm back."

Bruno straightened his arm and stopped Doug with a palm against his chest. It was like thumping against a piling.

"Glad to hear it," Bruno said, dead pan. "Now get back in line."

Doug smiled. "Bruno, it's me. Marc."

"Sure. And I'm David Bowie."

"Bruno —"

"Ay! Fun's fun, guy, an' I 'preciate a good scam much as the next fella, but don't wear it out, huh? When the real Mr. Chevignon comes out, maybe I'll introduce you. He'll get a kick outta you. Maybe even pass you in. He's good like dat."

"I snuck out the back, Bruno. Now I'm —"

The piling became a pile driver, thumping Doug out from under the canopy and back into the rain. Bruno was speaking through his teeth now.

"I'm startin' to get pissed. You may dress like him, you may comb your hair like him, you may even look sompin' like him, but you ain't Marc Chevignon. I know Marc Chevignon, and you ain't no Marc Chevignon." Bruno's face broke into a grin. "Ay. I sound like a presidential debater, don't I? I'll have to tell Mr. Chevignon — the *real* one — when he comes out."

"At least let me get, like, a message to LuAnn. Please, Bruno."

Bruno's grin vanished like a pulse from one of the strobes winking over the Spee's dance floor. "Ms. Lu's gone home. The real Marc Chevignon would know where dat is. Now lose yourself before I kick your butt down to Chinatown."

Doug stumbled away through the rain in shocked disbelief. What was happening here? Why didn't Bruno recognize him?

He stopped and checked himself out in the darkened grimy window of a plumbing supply place. He couldn't see himself too well, but he knew he looked right. He'd checked himself out in the mirror before leaving his apartment. The same tweed slacks, same leather coat, same white shirt. What was wrong?

At first he'd thought it was because Bruno hadn't seen him leave, but there was more to it than that. They'd stood within a foot of each other and *Bruno thought he was somebody else.*

LuAnn! He had to see LuAnn. Bruno had said she'd gone home. Early for her, but maybe she was looking for Marc.

Well, okay. She was going to find him.

Doug flagged down a cruising cab and rode it up to the West Eighties. LuAnn's condo was in a refurbished old apartment house with high-tech security. Doug knew the routine. He rang her bell in the building's foyer and waited under operating-room floodlights while the camera ogled him from its high corner perch.

"*Marc!*" her voice squawked from the speaker. "*Great! Come on up!*"

On the eighth floor the elevator opened onto a three-door atrium. The middle was LuAnn's. She must have heard the elevator because her door opened before Doug reached it.

Her smile was bright, welcoming. "Marky! Where on earth did you disappear to? I was —"

And then the smile was gone and she was backing away.

"Hey! What *is* this? You're not Marc!"

As she turned and started to close the door, Doug leapt forward. He wasn't going to be shut out twice tonight. He had to convince her he was Marc.

"No! LuAnn, wait!" He jammed his foot against the closing door. "It's me! Marc! Don't do this to me!"

"I don't know what your game is, buddy, but I'm going to start screaming bloody murder in a minute if you don't back off right now!"

Doug could see how scared she was. Her lips were white and she was puffing like a locomotive. He had to calm her down.

"Look, Lu," he said softly. "I don't unnerstand what's come over you, but if I, like, step back, will you, like, leave the door open just a crack so we can talk and I can prove I'm Marc? Okay. Ain't that fair?"

Without waiting for a reply, he pulled his foot free of the door, took the promised step back, and held his hands up, under-arrest style. When he saw LuAnn relax, he started talking. In a low voice, he described how they'd made it last night, the positions they'd used, the hardcore videos she'd insisted on running, even the yellow rose tattooed on her left cheek. But instead of wonder and recognition in her eyes, he saw growing disdain. She was looking at him like he might look at a sink one of the tenants had tried to fix on his own.

"I don't know what your game is, clown, and I don't know what Marc's up to, but you can tell him LuAnn's not amused."

"But I *am* Marc."

"You don't even come close. And get some diction lessons before you try to pull this off again, okay?"

With that she slammed the door. Doug pounded on it.

"LuAnn! Please!"

"I'm calling security right now," she said through the door. "Beat it!"

Doug beat it. He didn't want no police problems. No way.

And when he got outside to the street, he felt awfully small, while the city looked awfully, awfully big. It didn't seem the least little bit like an oyster.

Something awful occurred to Doug on his way home. What if Marc was sick? Or worse yet — dying?

The thought was a sucker punch to the gut.

"What d'ya need, Marc?" he said softly over the bucket once he was home and back in the bathroom. "Just lemme me know an' I'll get it for you. Anything. Anything at all."

Doug shoved his hand and forearm into the

bucket again, deep, all the way to the bottom. He noticed how the goo was even cooler than before. Another bad sign.

"Come on, Marc. Make me say what you need. I'll hear it and then I'll get it for you. What d'ya need?"

Nothing. Doug's lips remained slack, forming not even a syllable. Frustration bubbling into anger, Doug yanked his arm free, rose to his feet, and smashed his moist fist into the mirror. The glass spider-webbed, slicing up his reflection. His knuckles stung . . . and bled.

He stared at the crimson puddles forming between his knuckles and dripping into the sink. He turned to look at the bucket.

And had an idea.

"This what y'want?" he said. "Blood? You want my blood? Awright. I'll give it to you."

So saying, he jammed his fist back into the bucket and let the blood flow into the goo. When the bottom of the bucket turned red, he withdrew his hand and looked at it. The cuts had stopped bleeding and were almost healed.

Doug tried to stand but felt a little woozy, so he sat on the toilet seat cover and stared into the reddened goo.

Marc wanted blood — *needed* blood. That had to be it. Maybe the goo was some sort of vampire or something. Didn't matter. If Marc wanted blood, Doug would find it for him. He'd said he'd get anything Marc needed, hadn't he? Well, he meant it. Problem was . . . where?

As he watched the goo that was Marc he noticed the red of his blood begin to swirl and coalesce in its depths, flowing to a central point until all the red was concentrated in a single golf-ball-sized globule. And then the globule began to rise. As it approached the surface it angled toward the edge of the bucket. It broke the surface next to the lip and spilled its contents over the side. The rejected blood ran down over the metal and puddled stark red against the white bathroom tiles.

"All right," Doug said, a cold bleakness setting in. "So you don't want no blood. What *do* you want, man?"

Marc lay silent in his galvanized metal quarters.

"You're sick, aren't you? Well, who the hell do I take you to? A vet?"

And then it hit him: Maybe Marc wanted to go home.

Slowly, reluctantly, Doug lifted the bucket by

its handle and trudged through his apartment, out into the hall, and down to the basement. Wet down here again, but the floor drain wasn't backed up. Not yet, anyway. He knelt by the drain, lifted the bucket —

And paused. This was pretty radical. Pouring Marc down the drain . . . there was no coming back from that. Once he was back down there it was pretty good odds he was gone for good.

Or maybe not. Maybe he'd come back. Who knew? What choice did Doug have anyway? Maybe Marc just needed to get back to the drain to recharge his batteries. Maybe he had friends or family down there. Might as well put him back where he came from because he didn't look like he was gonna last too much longer up here.

Doug lifted the grate and tipped the bucket. The goo almost leapt over the side, diving for the opening. It slid down the pipe and splashed when it hit the water in the trap below. Then it was gone.

Doug sat down and waited, wishing, hoping, praying for Marc to come bubbling back up the drain and crawl onto his arm again. He didn't know how long it would take, maybe days, maybe weeks, but he'd keep waiting. What else could he do? Without Marc he'd have to be Doug all the time.

And he didn't want to be Doug anymore. Ω

THE UNIQUE MAGAZINE
Spring 1993

ISSN 0898-5073
Art by Nicholas Jainschigg

FICTION

THE PULSE OF THE MACHINE . . . . Nina Kiriki Hoffman 10
FOUR BY LORD DUNSANY:
    THE RATIONS OF MURDOCH FINUCAN, A MODERN PORTRAIT,
    ECHOING DREAM, & HELPING THE FAIRIES . . . Lord Dunsany 21
A SÉANCE . . . . Nina Kiriki Hoffman 29
RIDI BOBO . . . . Robert Deveraux 32
ROGUE WAVE . . . . Gary David Johnson 38
WHERE THE SUN STAYS FOR WINTER . . . . . . Nina Kiriki Hoffman 41
VALENTINES . . . . Nina Kiriki Hoffman 43
CECILEY AT THE SUPERMARKET . . . . Nina Kiriki Hoffman 44
SKINNED . . . . Jimm Gordon 46
BUCK, GLORY RAE,
    & THE THREE LITTLE PIGS . . . . John Gregory Betancourt 52
ANTONIUS BEQUEATHED . . . . Tanith Lee 54
THE SWITCH-BACK . . . . R. Chetwynd-Hayes 65

VERSE

THE SPIRIT'S LAMENT by John S. Davis: 20.   THE DEVIL AND THE
MODERN MAN by Darrell Schweitzer: 28.   THE DANCE OF THE CORPSES
by Jason J. Marchi: 37.   THE SHARK by Margo Skinner: 43.   WHATEVER IT
IS by Stanley McNail: 51.   PRISONERS OF THE ROYAL WEATHER by
Bruce Boston: 82.

FEATURES

THE EYRIE 4
THE DEN . . . . Gahan Wilson 8
WEIRDISM: NECROMANCY . . . . Jason Van Hollander 27
WEIRD TALES TALKS WITH
    NINA KIRIKI HOFFMAN . . . . Darrell Schweitzer 60

Weird Tales® is published 4 times a year by Terminus Publishing Co., Inc., PO Box 13418, Philadelphia PA 19101-3418 (4426 Larchwood Ave., Philadelphia PA 19104-3916). 2nd Class Postage paid at Philadelphia PA & additional mailing offices. Single copies, $4.95. Subscriptions: 4 issues (one year) $16.00 in U.S.A. & possessions; $22.00 elsewhere, in U.S. funds. Postmaster: send address changes to *Weird Tales*®, PO Box 13418, Philadelphia PA 19101-3418. Copyright © 1993 by Terminus Publishing Co., Inc.; all rights reserved; reproduction prohibited without prior permission. Typeset, printed, & bound in the United States of America. *Weird Tales*® is a registered trademark owned by Weird Tales, Limited.

THE EYRIE

Welcome to *Weird Tales*® #306, our second issue in the new format.

We hope you have noticed some improvement. While we don't normally go on at length about production details, there was enough dissatisfaction with the appearance of our previous issue, #305, by both our readers and ourselves, that we should explain what went wrong.

Briefly, the change to what magazine distributors call the "B" format, about 8.5 by 11 inches, exceeded the capability of our in-house typesetting equipment. We managed to get the issue out at the cost of several unfortunate compromises. This issue, in contrast, is being typeset on equipment owned by John Betancourt. As a result, the type size and the spacing between lines return to that used in issues #290 through 304, and the type itself is far less grainy.

(The only things we are satisfied about last issue are the quality of the artwork — we are very proud of Bob Eggleton's Cthulhu and gave it, literally, larger play than expected — and the quality of the writing.)

Issue #305, then, was an awkward transition. *This* issue, #306, begins the "new look" of *Weird Tales*®, with *20% more words* than #305 with no increase in cover price. Now the type and page format are properly adjusted for the new size. Starting *next* issue, our artwork will be drawn for the new size as well. (And, by the way, we are pleased to announce the return of Jason Van Hollander's "Weirdism" feature.)

We thank you all for your patience (and your comments). We certainly hope you'll like the results.

The World Fantasy Convention for 1992 was held over Halloween weekend at Calloway Gardens in scenic (and we do not use the term frivolously) Pine Mountain, Georgia. It was more lightly attended by the professional community than usual, more because of fear of cost than actual cost. This incredibly exclusive, beautifully landscaped resort area an hour south of Atlanta must be impossible to get to, right? Actually your editor and managing editor bought airline tickets during a price war, rented a car, used the rented car to commute from much cheaper accommodations ten miles away, and did the whole trip for about $400 apiece.

The result was a much quieter, lower-key convention than World Fantasy Conventions usually are, with a higher ratio of fans to professionals in attendance, but still, we hasten to add, very interesting fans we enjoyed talking to. There was certainly enough to keep us busy all weekend, so that we had to force the time for the one outside activity a lot of conventioneers managed to indulge in: a tour of the beautiful Gardens themselves with a stop at the Butterfly Pavilion, a large greenhouse (it felt like walking into a humidifier) populated by exotic tropical butterflies and other alien life forms.

But a World Fantasy Convention otherwise consists of a series of parties and panel discussions, where readers can meet or hear many of their favorites. There is a spectacular art show. Enough publishing professionals attend WFC that this is where the artists want to be *seen*. (At one point an outsider, what fans call a "mundane," wandered through the art show and was overheard muttering, "This is the work of the Devil!") Want to get a book autographed? Some authors are just too much in demand for impromptu signings in hallways, because if they signed one book, they'd have to sign another, and another, and get stuck there for hours. (A problem none of us have ever faced, we admit . . .) Well, the World Fantasy Convention provides for this Friday night with a massive "Autographathon" (as we call it, anyway) wherein all the authors present sit behind tables along the walls in a large auditorium, and autograph-seeking is not only allowed, but encouraged.

Among the hundred or so authors in attendance were Michael Bishop, Anne McCaffrey, Marion Zimmer Bradley, John Farris, F. Paul Wilson, Fred Chappell, S.P. Somtow, Orson Scott Card, Jane Yolen, and L. Sprague de Camp. The climax of the weekend was the World Fantasy Awards Banquet on Sunday at which — we can restrain ourselves no longer — **we won!!**

Yes, a Special Professional Award went to George Scithers and Darrell Schweitzer for *Weird Tales*®, which was gratefully accepted by Darrell Schweitzer, who took the opportunity to thank several people also responsible for *Weird Tales*® being here: John Betancourt, who helped us start, and Carol

4

Adams, who manages to keep things running coherently.

Darrell Schweitzer's novella from issue #303, "To Become a Sorcerer," was on the final ballot but did not win. Nevertheless, our table at the banquet came to resemble an Easter Island hillside as we accumulated three of Gahan Wilson's distinctive pewter busts of H.P. Lovecraft: one for Darrell, one for George, and one for our good friend W. Paul Ganley, editor and publisher of *Weirdbook*. (Paul always said that someone at his table always wins, so we decided to make sure and sat next to him. Apparently his talent for attracting awards worked very well this year.)

The final award results were:

Best novel: *Boy's Life* by Robert R. McCammon.

Best novella: "The Ragthorn" by Robert Holdstock and Gary Kilworth.

Best short story: "The Somewhere Doors" by Fred Chappell.

Best collection: *The Ends of the Earth* by Lucius Shepard.

Best anthology: *The Year's Best Fantasy and Horror: Fourth Annual Collection* edited by Ellen Datlow and Terri Windling.

Special Award, Professional: George Scithers and Darrell Schweitzer, for *Weird Tales®*.

Special Award, Non-professional: W. Paul Ganley, for *Weirdbook* and Weirdbook Press.

Best artist: Tim Hildebrandt.

Life Achievement Award: Edd Cartier.

The only sad note of the weekend was news of the death of *Weird Tales®* contributor **Robert Sampson,** who was, by the way, one of this year's World Fantasy Award judges, but did not live long enough to see the awards given out. We never met him; and when he sent us his "Magician in the Dark," which appeared in issue #293, we thought we had discovered a terrific new writer. We soon learned that he had published fiction widely, if sparingly, in the science fiction, detective, and horror fields. His first story appeared in *Planet Stories* in 1954. He was an expert on pulp magazines, and wrote several excellent volumes on their history. He was not particularly old and had, as one of his friends told us at the convention, "a lot of writing left to do." Now, tragically, it will never get done. A second Sampson story ran in issue #299 and a third will appear in these pages soon.

Next year's convention is in Minneapolis. See you on Halloween.

Weird Tales® welcomes its oldest contributor to these pages, if we're allowed to stretch a point slightly. **Lord Dunsany,** Edward John Moreton Drax Plunkett, 18th Baron Dunsany (1878–1957) was this century's premier fantasy writer, the author of such unparalleled classics as *The Gods of Pegāna, A Dreamer's Tales,* and *The King of Elfland's Daughter.* About him, H.P. Lovecraft wrote, " . . . no amount of mere description can convey more than a fraction of Lord Dunsany's pervasive charm. His prismatic cities and un-heard-of-rites are touched with a sureness which only mastery can engender . . . . To the truly imaginative he is a talisman and a key unlocking rich storehouses of dream and fragmentary memory; so that we may think of him not only as a poet, but as one who makes each reader a poet as well."

Your editor and the distinguished Lovecraft scholar, S.T. Joshi, have been working on a bibliography of Dunsany's work for the last ten years; it will be published soon by Scarecrow Press. In the course of this they discovered yet another "rich storehouse of dream": *nearly 400* hitherto unknown and uncollected Dunsany pieces, including roughly 150 short stories. Three of them, reprinted from English magazines of the '40s and '50s, never before published in the United States, appear this issue, including one adventure of Dunsany's famous clubman and liar, Jorkens. Five volumes of Jorkens stories appeared in the author's lifetime. They were enormously influential. Virtually all fantasy and science fiction "told-in-a-bar" stories (such as Spider Robinson's Callahan series and Arthur C. Clarke's *Tales from the White*

Publisher: George H. Scithers.   Editor: Darrell Schweitzer.   Managing Editor: Carol Adams
Art Director: Michael W. Betancourt.   Assistant Editors: Leslie Smith, Dainis Bisenieks,
Diane Weinstein, Don Keller, & Nicholas Beauchamp
Circulation Manager: Tina Hoffman.   Computer Consultant: David J. Williams III.
Of Counsel: Matthew Wolfe
Typesetters: Wildside Press and Campus Copy Center
Printer & Soft-Cover Binder: The Sheridan Press   Hard-Cover Binder: Hoster Bindery, Inc.

Manuscript Submissions:

Yes; we read unsolicited submissions — but **only** if they are in standard manuscript format. To survive, all editors insist on a few Rules: each submission must be in proper format and must include a return envelope addressed to you with enough postage affixed to bring the manuscript back to you. If you want us to discard the manuscript if not bought, tell us so, but include a business-letter-size envelope with postage affixed, addressed to you, so we can send you our comments. No loose stamps, please!

Proper manuscript format is discussed in many reference works. Some of us have even written one: *On Writing Science Fiction: the Editors Strike Back!* by Scithers, Schweitzer, & John M. Ford; $19.50 in hardcovers, from Owlswick Press, P.O. Box 8243, Philadelphia PA 19101-8243. Another excellent work from the same publisher is Barry B. Longyear's *Science-Fiction Writer's Workshop*: $9.50 in trade paperback. These prices include shipping and handling; in Pennsylvania, please include 6% sales tax.

We are not responsible for manuscripts in our hands or in transit. You **must** keep a copy of every manuscript you send out. You **must** put your name and address on the first page of every manuscript. Please: **no** binders, folders, or padded envelopes; and especially: **no** registered or certified mail for which we would have to stand in line at the post office!

Hart) are direct literary descendants of Jorkens.

We hope to feature more of the unknown Dunsany in the next few issues of *Weird Tales®*.

Glenn Whidden, like many readers, wrote to express initial reservations over the format change, then, happily, was won over by the contents of #305:

"Midnight Mass" was incredible. My friends have been trying to get me to read F. Paul Wilson for years, but I never quite got around to it. My loss. Now I'm going to have to play catch up (thanks for the handy bibliography). Mr. Wilson was right to stress "the human element" in your interview. Knowing or being able to surmise what is going on behind the eyes of those experiencing the horror is what makes the most fantastical of events terribly (or wonderfully) believable. The author's talent with characterization was displayed in "When He Was Fab." Doug was made a real person, not just some stock "blob" victim. The depth of artistry can be seen in seemingly small touches, the kinds of analogies the character makes. When Doug reaches for an analogy, it is not with a Buckley-level vocabulary or references to dead opera stars. When not with Marc, his level of "wit and grooviness" is that of the lowest common denominator, so the best he can do is think in terms of movies he has seen on TV (e.g. *The Blob, The Wizard of Oz*). This way the analogy performs double duty: its usual descriptive function and a reiteration of the nature of the character.

The rest of the issue was very good indeed. "Mirror, Mirror," for example, was very clever. I was less impressed, however, with "Yellow Rome." The difficult thing about historical fiction is that for most readers the setting is as truly alien as Barsoom or Middle Earth. For this reason it becomes necessary to drop great lumps of exposition into a very small space. While much of this is of the lovely "It was a long way up to the Tarpeian Rock when you had to climb. But it was a short way down when you were pushed" variety, too much was in the more obvious style of, "She was only one of six sacred women in the service of Vesta, the goddess of the hearth, without whom there really could be no home, and hence, no Rome." A delicate balance this exposition stuff, and I think just barely missed.

But that is part of the reason I'm going to keep reading *Weird Tales®*. Where else am I going to find a fictive meditation on that aspect of Roman culture that viewed the supernatural as a normal, if wonderful, part of daily life? Few other magazines would even have the guts to make the effort. If the format change is the economic compromise that had to be made in order to continue this work, then it's a good deal by me.

Elaine Weaver inquires, in a scholarly frame of mind:

People keep coming over to visit, and they look at my copy of #305 and say, "What's that awful *thing* on the cover?" I tell them that the "thing" is Cthulhu, the original boogeyman, but I'm not sure if I'm pronouncing his name right. Can you help?

As great Cthulhu's creator, H.P. Lovecraft, carefully explained, the names of the Old Ones were never intended for human speech organs, so any pronunciation of "Cthulhu" can only be an approximation. According to one source, HPL himself pronounced it something like "Klootl-klootl," with a kind of grunting or whistling (or ichor-gurgling) sound implied (though this may be just a dialectal variant prevalent among the amoeboid shoggoths); but if all such are indeed approximations limited by the inadequacy of available vocal equipment, we don't see why the more common "CUTH-oo-loo" shouldn't be as valid as any other.

On another scholarly note, distinguished author **Gerald Pearce** offers:

. . . congratulations to the uncredited writer of #304's "Eyrie" for remarking that the movie industry seems to think that Egypt is an imaginary country — just as English language writers seem to think that Arabic is an imaginary language. *Vide* John Brunner's HPL pastiche in the same issue 304. I know it's not his fault, and he's only building on ancient screw-ups of writers long past . . . but as the name of an Arab writer, "Abdul al-Hazred" is about as Arabic as Fu Manchu, Lazarus Long, or Mr. Micawber. There is no such Arab name as "Abdul." What some tin-eared Westerners have heard as "Abdul" is actually one word, "abd," meaning slave or servitor, and the definite article, "al" (sometimes transliterated as "el"); a name is formed by the completion of a phrase by adding another word describing an attribute of the Deity — resulting in names like Abd al-Rahim, slave or servitor of the Merciful, Abd al-Malik, slave or servitor of the King, and so on. Believe it or not, "Abdul al-Hazred" seems to be some tin-eared European's idea of 'Abd al-Azhar. (That apostrophe, by the way, stands for an Arabic letter that I have seen described as a voiced pharyngial fricative, and perhaps less scientifically as a vomitic gag.)

"Abdul al-Hazred" (or Alhazred, as it is often spelled) was the invention of the seven-year-old H.P. Lovecraft in his *Arabian Nights* phase (possibly derived from the old and decidedly English family name, Hazzard). As an adult, he put this name to literary use, as the author of the imaginary *Necronomicon*. In his introduction to the Owlswick Press "facsimile" edition of *Al Azif* (1973), L. Sprague de Camp playfully speculated that the name, "a corruption of a lost original, which passed through several languages before it reached its present form . . . may have been Abdallah Zahr-ad-Din, or Servant-of-God Flower-of-the-Faith."

Michael L. Hansen is seriously irate:

This letter is in reply to your statements on Satanism in *Weird Tales®* #305.

First, you are correct in stating that all *beliefs* are protected by the Bill of Rights. Satanism, however, is the organized *practice* of certain beliefs. Nowhere does the U.S. Bill of Rights protect the "right" of *anyone* to ritually murder and torture, or sexually molest children, animals, etc., as is the practice of Satanic cults.

If you cannot bring yourself to forthrightly condemn such abominable and obscene practices, you may consider my subscription *cancelled* and may promptly refund the balance due.

Furthermore, your refusal to condemn Satanism only plays into the hands of Fundamentalist morons who *already* equate, not only fantastic literature, but *anything* to do with the occult, such as astrology, tarot divination, psychic phenomena, etc. with Satanic cultism.

I ask you, therefore, to reconsider your incorrect stance on this issue.

Or non-issue as the case may be. *Of course* we do not approve such abominable practices as murder, child-abuse, animal-torture, etc.; but these are adequately covered by the criminal codes. They're all against the law, whether motivated by cult beliefs or not.

What we would like to suggest is that the standard hooded, chanting, candle-holding, baby-sacrificing "Satanic cult" is more a creation of the fevered imaginations of the aforementioned Fundamentalist morons and those latterday descendents of Matthew Hopkins, the professional "experts," than anything which actually exists. *The Skeptical Inquirer* recently took a long hard look at claims of "Satanic cult activity," which turn out to be as dubious as UFO abductions. Yes, there is a self-proclaimed Church of Satan which has at least one member, Anton Szandor LaVey, but we suspect this is really a promotional scheme to sell copies of Mr. LaVey's *The Satanic Bible*, a work which we also find difficult to take seriously.

So the comment, "Satanism is protected by the constitution. What are you? Un-American?" was mere flippancy.

Michael Johnson takes us to task for suggesting in #305 that all Christians are censors and the enemies of art, in which case "Michaelangelo was extremely self abusive." Actually, we did not say that. Indeed, many authors and fantasy writers are professed Christians. We could run out a long list. But there *are* fundamentalists, the people who leave those strange pamphlets lying around train stations, who explicitly believe that *all* imaginative literature is the work of Satan, including, just as explicitly (named in one of the pamphlets) C.S. Lewis (a noted Christian apologist) and J.R.R. Tolkien (a Catholic). Of course these people represent only a tiny percentage of Christians, their beliefs are a ludicrous caricature of mainstream Christianity, but they are loud, and they can do damage (particularly in the schools) unless just as loudly opposed and openly ridiculed. Actually our culture's best hope against lunatic Fundamentalists may be opposition from the major Christian sects, the Catholics, the Lutherans, etc., who seem to have learned something from Europe's several centuries of witch-burning and heretic-hunting.

G.W. Young is a very long-time reader of *Weird Tales®*, who does not like our new format (but we had a choice, this or no magazine at all), disapproves of the amount of space devoted to one author in #305 (admittedly unbalanced, something that happened when we suddenly reformatted the issue), suggests we could save money by cutting down the number of people listed on our masthead (What makes you think all these people get *paid?*), and asks "Why should authors take a flippant, smart-aleck attitude toward their work?" He then, puzzlingly to us, finds Steve Rasnic Tem's "Sirens" (which we thought a serious, moody story) and Tina and Tony Rath's "Mirror, Mirror" (an overt parody) "so much alike in style and attitude toward subject matter." All we can say is that we didn't find them alike at all, and we will continue to publish an occasional humorous story to keep the magazine unpredictable: having the hero *always* be eaten (or worse) can be just as boring as having him *always* live happily ever after (or even longer). We hope that, despite everything, Mr. Young will stay with us and find #306 more to his liking. Finally **James C. Tibbetts** demands we 'fess up and admit that F. Paul Wilson's "Midnight Mass" was a "reprint." Why are we resorting to reprints, he wants to know. Certainly not to save money, since we pay as much for such "reprints" as we do for totally unpublished stories. As the Wilson bibliography in #305 makes no effort to conceal, "Midnight Mass" was indeed first published as a small book by Axolotl Press, a limited edition of fewer than a thousand copies, not available in most stores, aimed strictly at the (high-priced) collectors' market. We still regarded the story as unlikely to be familiar to most of our readers. On occasion we do reprint from obscure sources, either from overseas or from the limited-editions market. Some of the Gene Wolfe stories in #290, for instance, had previously been published by Cheap Street in editions of less than two hundred.

The Most Popular Story in issue #305 was overwhelmingly F. Paul Wilson's "Midnight Mass." Second place went to "Mirror, Mirror" by Tina and Tony Rath. Voting was sparse, most correspondents were more concerned with the new format and what it portended than with the specific contents. We hope things will be back to normal next issue. Do let us hear from you.   Ω

To you may befall a horror even more frightening than stories and art in each issue of The Unique Magazine: the awful *Curse of the Undelivered Subscription*. But — there *is* a way to avoid that Curse: whenever you move from one lair to another — you *gotta* tell us! And well beforehand, if at all possible!! We need your old address (with Zip or postal code) and your new address (again, with Zip or postal code; if you can give us your full, 9-digit Zip code, so much the better).

THE DEN

by Gahan Wilson

I have, through an increasingly long life, always tended to gravitate to the disreputable in literature and the arts.

Poe, for example, despite sincere if sporadic attempts to update and uplift my preferences, stubbornly remains my truly favorite author. I was an insatiable devourer of comic books (was creepy enough to arrange a subscription so that *Captain Marvel* would be delivered to me at Summer camp!); went through (and still miss) the old Hearst Sunday Supplements which featured gaudily-illustrated articles explaining that Rasputin yet lived and exposing spirit mediums that made your dead Aunt Nellie out of phosphorescent cheesecloth; moved on to the glories of pulps, first the bug-eyed delights of '40s science fiction and then — I'm sure you've guessed — *Weird Tales*®; moved to hard-cover books of equal, if not worse, dubiosity; and there, very largely, I seem to have remained stuck.

A thing I have noticed throughout the passing decades is that, one by one, all these above-mentioned areas (save for the Hearst Supplements, which have cleverly transformed themselves into TV shock-shows) appear to be, more and more, receiving increasingly serious attention of various kinds.

The prices of comic books are now openly discussed in *The Wall Street Journal* and their contents become the subject of notably humorless critical essays; science fiction is solemnly and routinely referred to as the final authority by TV anchor people whenever some new evidence of our increasingly obvious dystopia hits the headlines; the authors of the pulps have achieved an autumnal dignity which has taken the ones I've talked to very much by surprise; and a whole new industry has sprung up which delivers at least one new Eddie Poe hard-cover biography — favorably reviewed by the *New York Times* — per year.

Time was if you were interested in the spooky, odd-ball sort of stuff that occupies the pages of this magazine and wanted

to read *about* it, you had to be a browser in strange bookstores and make yourself privy to the secret information grapevine formed by oddballs such as yourself. The literature was so extremely hard to locate that it almost had the air of the illegal, and if you were rash enough to ask the wrong dealer whether he carried such things you risked being treated with scorn and might even be favored with a sneer of outright contempt.

There *was* good material available, however; and it's still worth the tracking down. A few of the more valiant gatherers and publishers in those antique days — obviously the books mentioned here and hereafter will be only a tiny part of the whole, a mere hit-or-miss, eccentric hinting — would include August Derleth and Donald Wandrei of Arkham House, whose *Arkham Sampler* quarterly set a permanently challenging high level for any later comers, and whose hard-cover collections of essays on and about Lovecraft (interest in HPL seems ever and always to have been a basic kick-starter in the field), starting with *Something About Cats,* form a cherished core to many a reader's trove. George T. Wetzel's seven-volume *The Lovecraft Collector's Library* remains an absolutely invaluable source of information on the old gent; Gerry de la Ree's *The Occult Lovecraft* was one of the more interesting early demonstrations that there were many odd and unusual ways to skin the critical cat; L. Sprague de Camp's collection of Grandpa's essays, *To Quebec and the Stars,* was — and is — a particularly outstanding example of locating and then kindly sharing valuable material which had been heretofore hidden away in this or that dark corner; and Willis Conover's brilliantly-produced *Lovecraft at Last* has shown the way to a whole new style of loving revelation, which has yet to be even closely approached by any following effort.

Other major pioneers were Jack L. Chalker of the Mirage Press, which produced heroic amounts of material on a wide variety of authors (e.g., *H.P. Lovecraft, a Portrait* by *W. Paul Cook,* and *The Conan Reader* and *The Conan Grimoire* by L. Sprague de Camp); Dennis Rickard *(The Fantastic Work of Clark Ashton Smith* is my own personal favorite); Robert Weinberg (he may have exhumed more bad but wonderful pulp shockers than any other living human, and his *The Weird Tales Story* is possibly the best overall survey on its subject); Jack Sullivan (author of an excellent survey of the English ghost story: *Elegant Nightmares,* and editor of the handsome and invaluable *Penguin Encyclopedia of Horror and the Supernatural);* and Donald Sidney-Fryer (whose bibliography, *Emperor of Dreams,* is indispensable if you hope to be a serious student of Clark Ashton Smith).

The output of worthwhile material on both Lovecraft (once again serving to open the fray) and the weird field in general took on an absolutely glorious velocity at the start of the '80s when Marc A. Michaud created *Lovecraft Studies,* a very serious and ambitious critical quarterly magazine which gives a regular podium for essayists as varied as Peter Cannon, Will Murray, Steven Mariconda, Donald Burleson, Stanley Wiater, *Weird Tales*'s very own Darrell Schweitzer, and the apparently inexhaustible S.T. Joshi, plus providing proper and well-deserved showcasing for the works of two really brilliant macabre artists: Jason Eckhardt and Robert H. Knox.

The occasionally high-falutin tone of *Studies* was responded to by Robert M. Price when he brought out *Crypt of Cthulhu,* which is described on the masthead of the latest (82nd) issue as "A Polyp Thriller and Theological Journal." Price is living proof that being pastor of the First Baptist Church in no way prevents one from being a wild and crazy guy, and if *Crypt* sometimes acts a little like a Shriners' convention which has gotten a touch out of hand in the hotel lobby, the quality of its essays is right up there with *Studies* (not surprising, since the magazines share most of their authors), and Price does not hesitate to take deadly serious and highly effective aim at those who stray from what he feels is the righteous path.

As a reader of both these publications (I await the arrival of new issues *almost* as eagerly as I did those of *Captain Marvel),* I can attest that some of their most endearing aspects are the really excellent brawls which reliably occur between their various critics, both individually and in schools. It is great fun and most stimulating to curl up in one's armchair by the fire and follow their bloody and remorseless battles blow by bone-shaking blow as they slug it out over Deconstruction or whether or not Derleth was all wet about the Mythos. Among my favorite features in both magazines are their letter columns because therein not only do the aforementioned critics seem inspired to rise to new levels of vituperation, but offended (and not uncommonly offensive) authors get to respond to real or imagined hurts they've received from those critics, whilst the general brouhaha is enthusiastically spurred on from the sidelines by well-aimed missives from the ever-raucous readership.

Both Michaud and Price have created other magazines (the oddest and most genuinely eccentric doubtless being Price's *CHURCHYARD: an Anthology of Christian Weird Tales),* but Michaud has proven the more successful publisher; and his Necronomicon Press now prints not only *Crypt* (thus freeing

Price to devote more time to his possibly jumpy parishioners) but a number of other worthwhile magazines, including *The Dark Man: the Journal of Robert E. Howard Studies,* which is ably edited by Rusty Burke, and *The Dark Eidolon: the Journal of Smith Studies,* edited by Steve Behrends, a first-rate Smith scholar, who has labored bravely to correct the general indifference which that brilliant author has so far received from the reading public. Behrends has also, via Necronomicon Press, produced a highly valuable series of books called *The Unexpurgated Clark Ashton Smith,* which form a body of restored manuscripts not on any account to be missed by any lover of Clark Ashton Smith. The Press has produced and continues to produce the most useful and informative sort of stuff, ranging from the more-or-less expected — such as three *H.P.Lovecraft Uncollected Prose and Poetry* collections — all the way to various items truly surprising, such as a really, really weird bit of Lovecraftian [Lovecrafty?] ghost writing which he did for his ex-wife Sonia Green. It's a strange dream-travelogue called *European Glimpses* that lovingly — and with heart-breaking naïveté — describes a trip to those old places abroad he loved so much and which I am sure he knew, deep, deep inside, he would always be too poor to visit.

Nowadays the doors have been flung open so wide that "horror" has actually become a genre — God help us! — like mysteries or even Westerns, and huge chain stores in the vast malls across this glorious land of ours are always careful to devote a full, very clearly labeled bookshelf or two to the stuff.

This has been a mixed blessing, of course, as blessings tend to be, but the wise will take the good with the bad — since there really isn't any choice in the matter, is there? — even if now and then it strikes one that there *does* seem to be rather an awful lot of bad.

Without this new expansion of the field we probably wouldn't be reading this magazine, for instance; nor would we have so many lavish and well-produced books available about our favorite sort of writing — so many that it now and then seems impossible to get around to reading them all, or even list them.

I must admit it *was* fun being the devotee of a shunned form of art; a sneaker into second-hand bookshops lurking in shabby areas, owning shady reputations; a browser in their cobwebbier shelves. I liked — I confess it — the sneakiness of it all. I miss the startled pauses in polite conversations when I brought the matter up.

But it's so much easier now; so much more relaxed. It's damned pleasant to have all this stuff available, even too much of it! I confess I sometimes stand in front of the genre shelves rubbing my hands together, quietly gloating and grinning, softly cackling, probably scaring an innocent child or two as I contentedly mull over how well all that lovely, scary stuff has done.

And those other books over there — the pretty ones with thousands of pictures, both in nostalgic black-and-white and in Technicolor, about all those gorgeous horror movies and how they got that way, not to mention the TV cassettes which do more of the same.

Ah . . . but that's another column.

Ω

THE PULSE OF THE MACHINE

by Nina Kiriki Hoffman

for Jay Sheckley, who knows where to cut

Pool balls click against each other like the rattle of dried bones. Cigarette smoke hazes the air, mixing with the less-visible scents of pizza, nachos, lime, alcohol, and humanity. I hear the distant trills and warbles of video games, like the territorial cries of birds. Heat outlines the people in the bar. Their emotion-scent hangs below the ceiling with the smoke. Mostly it is a battling mix of relief, joy, sexual excitation, relaxation; but there is a constant undercurrent of fear and worry because of the Slasher. On the Friday before spring break, all the college students who haven't left Paradise, Idaho for the week are crowded into the Side Pocket. They feel safe in the bar, but they know that later they will leave this haven and go out into darkness.

I tilt my glass and touch my tongue to the liquid. It bites me, a playful nip, then vanishes before I can taste it back. A cue stick clicks against a ball, then a cascade of clicks, and the muffled thunk of balls hitting cushions, dropping into pockets. I look across the table at Anitra, my best human friend, and say, "Did you play with bones as a child?"

"How do you play with bones?" She sounds distracted. She has ditched her boyfriend Philip tonight and I am happy about that. I don't like him. Maybe she no longer likes him either. Our table stands behind a railing on a platform. We sit in darkness, the pool tables green islands of light to one side, the bar dim glimmers of curved light on bottles to the other. In a back corner a large-screen television shows big people in helmets clashing on too-green grass. The bartenders, faces lit from below by worklights under the lip of the bar, build drinks and murmur to customers. Anitra focuses on the people with the sticks who lean under the lights and tap jewel-colored balls.

I play tag with my drink again and more of it creeps inside me. It is my third drink. I have never tasted alcohol before. The heat in my throat, the flush that raises the hair on my arms, these things remind me of change. I didn't know humans knew what that felt like. I smile at Anitra. "You want to crunch the bones up and lick the marrow out, but some bones are just too big."

She glances at me, her eyebrows up. People behind us cheer because of something they see on television.

"It's the little ones, though, that are fun to play with. My brother Emelya and I had our favorites. We gave the big ones to the younger litter to teach them prey scent, but the little ones . . ."

"You're making me sick," says Anitra.

I laugh. I lift my glass to toast the memory of my brother, then finish my drink. "My grandmother tosses the little vertebrae and tells fortunes from how they fall."

"You're drunk," says Anitra, reaching for my empty glass.

I consider extending a claw to protect my property, but my territorial imperatives have relaxed with my inhibitions. I let her wrest the glass from me. I lean back, enjoying the chair's cushioned curves, and turn my concentration inward, trying to understand my new transformation. It is like no other I have known. I glare at my hand. It is human. The form has not changed while I was facing away from a mirror. But inside . . .

"Terry, I better take you home," Anitra says. "You should have told me you got this way."

"What way?" Can she see the change? I should feel alarm, but I don't.

"Loopy," she says.

I frown. I have heard this term before. People don't apply it to creatures they consider dangerous, so I believe I am all right.

"I didn't know I got that way. I have never tried to drink this before. It smells like poison, but I watched and no one drinking it died. Is this a change that other people don't make?"

"No, a lot of people get loopy when they drink. But you've got your landlady to consider." My landlady is Mormon. I forgot: I promised her I would not drink, though I didn't realize she meant not drink Tom Collinses. I just thought she was saying she didn't want to see me drinking liquid. And I don't, not in front of her.

"Coffee could help," said Anitra. "Come on home with me. I'll make you some." She rises and grasps my wrists, pulling me out of my chair. She is smaller than I am, but determined. I laugh as she pulls my arm across her shoulder. "Try walking," she says.

Balance has fled; up and down are not definite any longer. The bones in my legs have turned liquid.

"One foot in front of the other," she says. We stagger between people and out the door.

The cool night air, with its rich freight of scents, wakes me a little. But I do not wake to my normal knowing. Instead I am aware of a delirious freedom from accustomed restraints. I am not sure why I don't have to think twice about everything I say and do. It is as if the secret part of me walks about without clothes, enjoying the touch of air on its skin. I laugh. Anitra is a blaze of warmth against my side, within my arm, and she smells like wild plants and peppermint and musk. She smells like one of my relatives after a spring run through the forest. Even though these scents are mixed with the nose-stopping, tongue-coating smell of soap, I feel happy to be with her.

She supports me around a corner, into the alley where her tiny yellow car is parked. A sudden wash across my heat sensors, from a nearby shadow: in human form, I am less aware than in lynx form, but I am never heat blind. And I always recognize this scent, a sweat that comes from humans in stalk mode. Everything brightens and amplifies. I hear the breath brushing against damp membranes as it slides in and out of me, Anitra, and the person in the shadow. My arm tightens around Anitra's shoulders before she can shrug me off. Her keys drop from her hand to the pavement. "Terry," she begins, a scolding edge in her voice. A growl spins in my throat as I glance toward the shadow, trying to sharpen focus with eyes that don't respond. I hold out my free hand and watch the buried claws unsheathe.

"Terry," says Anitra, a rich thread of terror in her voice. The pulse in her rises, as the heat seeps away; her muscles lock, and her scent strengthens with fear. Suddenly she becomes prey.

The other person steps out of the shadow, and I force myself to shift attention. I release Anitra, turn toward the other.

It is larger than I. The hair on the back of my neck rises. I hunch toward it, my legs tight with restrained pounce. I growl.

It runs, past Anitra's car, on down the alley, brushing against dumpsters and piles of soiled boxes.

The power, the flux, shudders just beneath my skin; it threads through all my muscles. I draw in breath, calming all systems that govern change. I retract my claws and silence my growl, then turn to face Anitra, remembering why I am always careful in company. The glowing mist that fogged my thoughts has gone.

She crouches, her hand closing around the dropped keys on the pavement. "What happened? What was that?" Her words come out on short puffs of breath. She still surrounds herself with the sharp stink of fear.

"I think it was a person," I say, glancing down the alley where the stalker disappeared.

She rises, flattens against the car. "Not that. Your hand. What happened to it?" Keys poke out between the fingers of her fisted hand.

"I think I'm all right to go home now," I say. "I'll walk. It's not far."

"With the Slasher loose in town?" She straightens, leans forward just a little to look into my face. "I drove you here and I'll drive you home." Then she leans back. "Oh, Terry. Oh, Terry." Her keys fall from her fingers again. "Are you the Slasher?"

"No," I say. Inside me a battle begins: she knows something, but not much; she is the best friend I have made since I came down out of the mountains in search of education; no one outside our family must know, ever, ever, ever again. What am I to do with her? To her? About her?

If I kill her, I know I can stay.

"You're sure? You're sure you're not the Slasher?" She steps away from the car. Her systems begin to settle, pulse slowing.

"I'm not." There have been seven murders in our small town over the past year, and I only committed the first one. It satisfied me in some way I do not understand. My brother Emelya died at the hands of humans, but my anger over that has cooled, the appetite it awoke in me satisfied. My landlady feeds me well enough. I don't have to forage.

Anitra takes two more steps toward me. She holds out her hands. Confused, I hold out mine. She grips and examines them, turning them back and forth, touching the narrow nails. I feel calm, human, and cold.

"Come on," she says. Releasing my hands, she fetches her keys, unlocks the passenger's door and holds it open.

I don't want to get into her car. The proximity will force a decision on me. I will have to think about whether she lives or dies. If she will leave without me, I can shrug and say, oh, well, too late, she might forget about it in the morning. If I go with her, she will not leave it alone. She will make it into a memory.

"Please, Terry. Please come."

I untense and go to her car. I climb in and close the door.

She starts the car, raising a low thrum that permeates the car's structure. It was hibernating. We sit snug inside it like two meals. It judders into motion.

"All that about bones — that was true, wasn't it?"

I say nothing.

"I thought I knew you so well. The accent, the walk, the smaller sense of personal space. I saw people like you in Europe during the two years when I was traveling. Terry, who are you?"

I lean against the door, letting the car's pulse go through me. I can smell its metallic breath. Things go by quickly outside, scentless and unreal. She is not taking me to my landlady's place. "You should let me out," I say.

"I should never have let you get drunk. It was just the grades. A's in chemistry, Terry. I was so happy."

"I was, too." Tests are fresh phenomena to me, but Anitra's excitement was contagious. I mimicked it, because I don't know how to feel yet. I watch a lot of people. Anitra is my favorite model human.

I don't want to kill her.

"Terry. Please. We're friends, aren't we?"

"Yes."

"Talk to me. I swear I won't tell anybody. I'd like to analyze you."

Though she's majoring in history, Anitra is taking psychology courses. She often tells me about human behavior. I am fascinated. I plan to take classes next semester.

The car's steady purr slows, then stops. She removes the keys and slides out, locking the door.

I sit. Perhaps I can stay in the car.

She opens my door. "Terry?"

I emerge.

I have been to her place before. She lives in half a duplex on the edge of town. I can smell horses and new green wheat and ditch water, cattails, cattle, dust, and a breath of daffodils on the breeze.

She climbs the two cement steps and turns toward me. The porch light splashes yellow on her dark hair and shoulders, leaving her face in shadow. "Terry. Come on."

I walk toward her, feeling again the shimmer of power under my skin. The change is near the surface. Sometimes it comes without volition — a sound, a scent will trigger it. Tonight it waits. "Do you have anything to drink?" I ask.

"Tequila — and orange juice, I guess. You want to get drunk again?"

"I don't know."

She turns, unlocks the front door, walks into darkness. She flicks a switch, and a hanging wicker lamp gives her living room a speckled yellow glow. "Come in," she says, going to the television and switching it on.

I curl among cushions on the couch, watching colored blurs and listening to the low voices of unwed teenage mothers. The unscented flatness of the small screen confuses my perception. Anitra comes from the kitchen with tall orange drinks which smell of citrus and poison. She hands one to me. I drink it, trying to reach a stage of inner transformation where I don't have to care about secrets.

Presently I feel the laughter invade me. "Spring is coming," I tell Anitra. She sits in a wicker chair across from me, her drink on a table near her. "The earth is moist, cool under your pads; the grass hasn't toughened yet, and the winter bark sloughs off under your claws. Can you smell it?"

"No," says Anitra.

"It gets in your blood. It feels like this." I lick my glass.

"Terry, who are you?"

I run my tongue over my teeth. The human mouth is equipped to deal with vegetation: nippers and grinders. I can make all these smooth-backed teeth retract and change.

I hold out my glass to her. She brings me another drink, waits while I finish it. For a while I feel too tense, too conscious of my restraints, but at last the barriers melt. I stare at Anitra, who sits, throned in a spicy-scented wicker chair with a large round back that haloes her upper body. She has her feet tucked up underneath her, so that the whitened knees of her jeans stick out. Her arms rest on the chair's arms, her hands lax, not clenched. Her dark hair curls about her head like little drifts of duck down. She has her own wild scent, part herbs, part peppermint, part sweat.

"Talk to me," she says.

The young voices murmur from the television, speaking of school, babies, diapers. Children who have children, the interviewer calls these girls. Do they regret it? If they could go back and start over, would they have done something different?

"Curiosity kills cats," I say. I have heard this phrase. I am not sure I completely understand it.

"It gets teenage girls pregnant."

"Can you live with the consequences of your actions?"

"What consequences? What actions?"

I am not thinking clearly. I want to talk; I want to stop talking. "You ask questions. The answers might kill you."

She grins. "Oh, no, I don't think so. I've seen a lot of weird things. I've known you for a year now, and I know some important things about you. Whoever else you are — I don't think that will change how I feel about you and our friendship."

"I am a shapeshifter."

She cocks her head, frowning so that lines show in her forehead. She blinks. "What?"

"I change from one creature into another."

Heat flushes her, and her heart beats faster. Her pupils dilate. I feel tense, tuned to her slightest shift of movement. Even without her fear-scent to make her attractive, she has become prey again.

I usually don't feel like this in human form.

She sips her drink, swallows. "See? That didn't hurt. What do you turn into?"

"A human."

She shakes her head, smiling, almost laughing. "So what are you in real life?"

"A forest creature. A carnivore. And I must protect myself and my family."

"What do you mean?" She loses her smile, sets her drink aside. She clenches her hands in her lap. "Protect them against me? I won't tell anyone."

"You probably think this is a grand delusion anyway."

She takes a deep breath, lets it out slowly. The drink she set aside, her first, is only half empty. She doesn't smell loose, the way I still feel; I feel relaxed and tense at once. "No," she murmurs. "No. I saw your claws." And then, a whisper, "I did. I saw them." She sips from her glass again, looks at it, at me. "I can believe anything if I think I'm dreaming or drunk at the time. None of this makes any sense, of course." She takes a large swallow of her drink. "Would you show me your claws again?"

"No," I say. I lift my hand, then let it drop, limp, on the couch beside me. I know this is a serious discussion, but somehow I am losing focus. I look at Anitra and she slowly smiles at me.

"Do you kill things?" she asks after a moment.

"Of course."

"And play with their bones. It doesn't bother you?"

I remember the run of the hunt, paws striking ground, nose seeking scent, pushing through bushes, all muscles working together, all abilities directed toward a single goal; the strike and the struggle, the taste; the hot feast at the finish that strengthens me for the next hunt. And then, the start, the stalking . . . "Bother me? It's when I know I'm alive."

In a hushed voice, she says, "Do you kill humans to feel alive?"

"No," I say, and laugh. "They don't know how to run away or fight back, and I don't like the way they taste."

"How do you know?"

"I did kill one. I killed one a year ago. A person who was going to kill other people. A person who had already killed other people. A person like the one who killed my brother. Once was enough."

She stares at me. She cocks her head sideways, like a bird examining something it wants to eat, not sure whether it is string or a worm.

After a moment, she says, "You would consider killing me? To protect yourself."

I watch her. "I don't want to. And it wouldn't be the kind of hunt I like. But how can I trust you?"

She frowns again. Her brows draw together. She finishes her drink. "Let's see. If I was you, would I trust me?" She wrestles with it for a while, until I can no longer restrain my chuckles. I imagine Anitra turning into me. I imagine her turning into a black lynx. I have never seen a black lynx, but with her hair color . . . my own is frosted silver. Setting my glass on the carpet, I collapse among the cushions, feeling drowsy in an unfamiliar way, as if sleep will pounce on me and take me by force.

The teenagers murmur on. I feel warm inside and out, and my chuckles change to purr. "I think I'd trust me," Anitra says. "Can't you tell by the way I smell? How do you make that sound?"

I close my eyes.

I wake with a hiss. An unknown sound alerts me, and the scents and resonance of the space are all wrong. I claw my way free of something binding, and of a blanket that smells of somebody else, and land on my hands and knees on a carpet unlike the braided rag rug beside my own bed. My mouth tastes like I licked a puddle of oil. Blood throbs in my head. The room tries to whirl past my eyes, but I recognize Anitra's living room. Her scent marks everything here.

My stomach has gone on a journey of its own. I hope it doesn't come back.

A knock sounds at the door, the same sound that woke me. "Anitra!" someone yells. I rise on my hind legs, clutching my head.

"Anitra!"

"Oh, God, Philip, what is it?" she yells from another room. I hear her steps, and the movement of smooth fabric against itself. She enters the living room. Her hair sticks out all over her head except it is flattened on one side, and she wears a jewel-blue bathrobe made of something other than animal hair or plant fibers. She notices me, and freezes. Her gaze flicks to the couch, then back to me. I turn and look behind me, see the tatters of a blanket mixed with snippets of rope. She must have tried to confine me while I slept.

"Anitra! I need you!" the voice calls from outside the front door.

Daylight prints a slanted image of the window on the thick green curtain. Anitra stares at me. She smells sour, the way I feel; also a little afraid, but more surprised. I smile and shrug.

She goes to the door. "Philip, go away. I can't see you just now."

"Anitra!" He pounds on the door. I hear his body lean against it, slide down the splintery surface. His shoes clatter on the cement steps. He begins to sob.

"We killed that bottle of tequila last night," Anitra tells me softly. Her voice wobbles. "Have you made up your mind what you're going to do about me?"

For a moment I don't know what she's talking about. I have awakened in a strange place and determined it is not immediately dangerous; I am waiting for more information. Then memory of last night creeps into me, and dark dread follows its trail. "Anitra . . ."

She stands quietly, hugging herself and looking at me. Her eyes are bloodshot.

"I don't want to move," I say.

"What does that mean?"

"I want to get my degree in wildlife and range science here. I can't do that if you talk about me."

"I won't talk about you. I promise."

I test the scents, the heat, her heartbeat. She

believes what she says — for now. But do any of them know what they feel, say what they mean, do what they say? Well . . . Anitra does more than most. She is my friend. "All right," I say. What if I'm wrong? What if the information gets away? Can I stop it from traveling? That other time, when we lived in the mountains to the east, there was no stopping the information. Attempting to stop it made everything worse. We had to disappear. It is one of the stories my grandmother tells over and over. She numbers our ancient dead on her crooked fingers. When she speaks of the battles, her claws emerge.

Anitra watches me a moment after I speak, smiles wide, then goes to the door and opens it. A sobbing body collapses inward. "Philip," says Anitra. "You promised not to do this again."

"Anitra," he says, clutching the edge of her robe.

She prods him with a bare toe. "I've got company."

He looks at me and his sobs cease. He is half heat, and smells of Brut, hair oil, sweat, stale coffee, staler wine, tears, and unclean synthetic fibers. He sits up, raising his hand to rake his pale oiled hair into some sort of order, then smooths his mustache. "You could have told me," he says. He slaps dust off his jacket.

"Oh, so now it's my fault you're making an ass of yourself?" She jerks her bathrobe free of him and turns away. "Want some coffee, Terry?"

"Something to clear my mouth," I say. I look down at my self. Somehow my olive coverall has survived unclawed and unspilled-on. I am almost presentable. As Anitra heads for the kitchen, I head for her bathroom. Philip moves around behind me, but I don't turn to look. Lately, every time she learns about a new mental disorder in psychology class she weighs it against her image of Philip and tells me the verdict.

The fan and the light flick on together in the bathroom, where mint toothpaste scent mingles with the odors of sandalwood and soap. I lean toward the mirror. My silver-gilt hair, cropped close to my head, takes only a few licks with a wet comb to settle. I don't know what to do about the red veins in my eyes. I have never seen them there before. Anitra has told me about aspirin. She has a bottle in her cabinet, and I eat two.

In the living room, Anitra hands me a mug with half coffee, half milk in it. She raises her eyebrows and tilts her chin up. I nod, sniff the coffee, and discover she has left the sugar out, which I appreciate. Philip sits on the couch where I slept. He sifts through tatters. "Rope?" he says. "Anitra, what have you been doing?" His pale eyes look from me to Anitra and back.

"I've been telling you and telling you I'm not what you think I am, Philip," says Anitra. She has not offered him coffee. She sits down beside me on the wicker loveseat and leans against me, taking my free hand and lacing her fingers through mine. I can feel the small cold thrill that shakes her, and the hot pulse point at her inner wrist flutters. Her warm thumb traces the creases in my palm. I swallow coffee to drown the purr, an involuntary response I make to being stroked.

"You're disgusting!" cries Philip, leaping up, scattering bits of blanket and rope.

"I've been telling you that, too," says Anitra. She turns her face so that her lips touch my throat, at the base of my jugular. I can feel my claws tense within my fingers and the tips of my ears tingle with nascent ear-tufts. Passion is for lynx form. Anitra doesn't know what she's doing.

Philip's eyes opaque. His heartbeat strengthens. Breath hisses in and out through his clenched teeth. He storms out, slamming the door behind him.

Anitra straightens, moving away from me, and my purr erupts, full-bodied bass, much lower than my speaking voice. She untangles our hands and stares at me. My purr stutters and dies.

She bites her lower lip and glances toward the door. "I'm sorry," she says, and rubs her eyes. "I kept thinking I was the only thing holding him together. Every time I tried to break it off, he'd cry, and beg, and stop taking care of himself. I woke up a couple weeks ago with the words 'I am not his mother' in my head. But I haven't been able to convince him I'm not going to take care of him anymore. . . . Terry, did last night happen?"

"Suppose I said no?"

She rises, walks to the television, flicks it on. Live coverage of a rape trial. She turns it off, then wanders to the couch and picks up shredded rope. "What did this? Not scissors. I do remember tying you up." She takes a piece of rope with her to the wicker chair, sits facing me. "Terry?"

"What?"

"Can you talk about it without being drunk?"

"I don't know. I never have before. The defenses are very deep."

"Let's try." Her hands finger the rope. She is calm, with no fear scent. "Where did you come from?"

I sip coffee. So many systems in revolt; aspirin and coffee and milk make a strange breakfast. I am not comfortable inside my self, not the way I was last night. My automatic evasions have switched on. But after a moment, I answer. "My family came from what is now Czechoslovakia in the 1800s. Most ended up in Canada, but a few of us live in the Idaho outback. It's not far from here, but you can't get there by road."

"Then you're — you're — oh, this sounds so stupid. An Earth creature?" One side of her mouth smiles. Her gaze drops. She twists the rope and closes her eyes.

I have been to the movies, though I don't process them like most humans do. Sound and sight without scent don't carry enough weight to convince me what I'm seeing is real enough to fall into. Still, I know what she is talking about. Aliens. Extraterrestrials. I laugh, surprising myself.

She peeks up at me, looks down again, sighs. She stares down at her hands. "Last night you told me you killed one person. You're not the Slasher? I mean, what do I expect? You wouldn't tell me if you were, would you? But — "

I pull my knees up on the loveseat and hug my legs. "You asked me if I would trust you, and I have trusted you. Do you trust me?" I offer her a quick grin. "Can't you tell by how I smell?"

"No," she says, laughing, then stops, startled, putting a hand over her mouth.

"You told me you know me."

She looks at me. Her lips pinch shut. Then she says, "Yes. I did. I didn't know a lot of things about you, but I think the things I did know, I still believe. So yes, I trust you. Okay. You're not the Slasher." She frowns down at the rope in her hands, then tosses it on the floor. "Six other people have died by violence — by claws — in the last year. Is there another . . . shapeshifter in town?"

"I don't think so. Not one of my family; I would have gotten a letter. But I haven't taken time to investigate. Now, with spring break . . ." On most of the long breaks I go back to the mountains. This time I had planned to stay in town, see what it's like with most of the student population gone. From observing my landfamily, I know that the people who live here but aren't connected to the university have a whole other kind of life, and I have wanted to study it ever since I arrived. Like all human things, it fascinates me.

Anitra nips her lower lip, then says: "There's a murderer in town. If you found that person, what would you do?"

I reach for my response, and in my mind see two creatures fleeing, too far away for me to catch. I know that one creature is my old response, what my family would do: fight the competition if I feel it is hunting my prey in my territory, or just watch its technique if it doesn't threaten my supply. The other creature is the response I would make if I understood — if I understood my human half. During the night, something in me has changed; I have moved several steps away from the self I knew. "What would you do?" I ask Anitra.

"Tell the police."

"Why didn't you call the police last night?"

"I believed I could trust you. I thought I could control you. Besides, what could I tell them? That you have claws and growl? Anyway, you're my friend."

I remember when I first noticed Anitra. Not in first semester chemistry, though we both took the same section. There were two hundred people in that class, filling the air with so many different breaths I became confused and drowsy. I noticed Anitra in algebra. We both sat in the back row. She asked the best questions. And she talked to me when everyone else was still trying to decide who or what I was. I hadn't learned to copy the walk, to drop my eyes and dodge glances, to meet eyes at the right moments. I always stood too close, trying to sense the shifts in skin temperature, scent, and hair arousal, information I consider vital. Anitra decided I was from another country. She gave me lessons in interactions. She taught me to trust visual and aural clues, to stand farther away, to live in a world of more limited information; and people stopped backing away from me.

I look at her. Something has changed. I know I can never kill her, no matter how necessary it might become. "You're my friend," I say. The word means something new to me, different from anything I thought it meant when I heard it or read it. I hold out my hand. She looks at it, then places her hand in mine. She watches as I raise her hand to sniff it, then copies my action. She offers me a shaky smile and says: "What do you eat? I could make toast."

"Thought you'd already left on vacation," says Mrs. Henderson, my landlady.

"I was sick last night, and stayed at a friend's."

"Celebrating, huh?" She gives me a little grin as I kneel to hug Lionel, the German shepherd. Mrs. Henderson wasn't always Mormon. She had two children and Mr. Henderson had one when they met and married and she converted. Mr. Henderson isn't a strict church-goer either, sleeps Sundays away in the recliner, awakening just long enough to smoke a forbidden cigarette and catch a few instant replays. The Hendersons live with the constant company of the TV. The two high school boys still at home, one his, one hers, argue over what to watch until Mr. Henderson takes the remote control away from them.

"I didn't think you'd like it," I tell Mrs. Henderson.

"Shh." She holds an index finger before her smile. "Just don't tell the old man. He'd want to go with you."

The moon has been up two hours when I lean out my upstairs window toward the big oak. I have never climbed down it in human form before, but it proves simple, now that I have had time to get comfortable inside my self again. Cows low in the pasture behind the house, and I can smell distant rain, raspberry canes, asphalt and a trace of hyacinth. I drop quietly to the ground. Spring has almost chased the frost away; soon the Henderson boys will bring out their buckets and flashlights and hunt night-crawlers in the front lawn, spotting, stooping and pulling like large midnight robins. I'll have to cut back on my activities then.

Loose gravel on the asphalt slips beneath my moccasins as I trot along the road. I round a curve and spy Anitra's car, dark and silent between two farm driveways that lead over spring-wheat-furred hills and away. The ticking of the engine glows with heat, and the thumbprint of Anitra's heat signature, though muted by the car, is still strong. I approach and rap on the window. She lifts a dark shawl to look up at me, then unlocks the passenger door.

As I round the car, I notice another car up the road, also parked. Its engine, too, retains a faint blur of heat. I study it, then climb into Anitra's car.

"You don't think we're going to find anything, do you?" she asks as she starts the car.

"I don't know if I want to," I say. "It's a nice night for a hunt." The air is rich with spring damp and new green smells. I roll my window down a little as Anitra drives west, the moon throwing the car's shadow ahead of us. The car up the hill starts and follows.

"We're safe, aren't we? The murderer doesn't use a gun. There are two of us, and one of us is you."

I answer with a drowsy purr, matching the car's purr. Emelya and I used to stalk together, and not always to kill. Sometimes the spring or fall just infected us, tracks clear in the moist earth. Sometimes the tingle of the air after summer thundershowers triggered change and stung us into forest-wide runs that ended in mock-fights. I touch a thin white welt on

the back of my left hand. Emelya had been a few minutes younger than I. I had teased him that he didn't have as good control of his claws.

Anitra is not Emelya; she does not have even one scent in common with him. But she wishes to hunt with me. I have longed to hunt with someone.

The vagrants who drift through town stay mostly close to the train tracks. At the place where men load the grain cars, there are sheltered overhangs. I scouted the area when I first came to town. The murderer killed someone there. The murderer strikes at the helpless, almost as if the murderer is hunting for food; the victims are clawed, but not eaten.

Anitra wants to start looking where the grain cars are loaded.

"Someone is following us," I say.

Anitra glances in her rearview mirror. Reflected headlight glare touches her eyes, pinches her pupils. She flips the mirror to night mode. "Damn," she says. "Can't see it."

"I saw it, but I don't know cars. It was parked behind you near my place."

"Did it have a big front? Was it white?"

"I think so."

"Oh, it's Philip. He has a white Corvette." Her lips tighten. "What a nuisance. What do we do now?"

"What do you think he thinks we're doing?"

She glances at me, then at the road. A chuckle escapes her. "We're going someplace kinky, maybe to do things with other kinky people." She laughs. She looks in the now-muted mirror, then squints at our surroundings. We have passed the supermarket-drug-store complex. We are now on the one-way couplet heading south; to our left lurks a string of closed-for-the-evening, fast food places. On the right, acres of harvesters and combines loom, blades upraised, like giant metal insects waiting their season to emerge from hibernation. Anitra pulls over and parks next to the field. "People come here to neck — there's no night watchman, just a light, and it's easy to find shadows," she says, "but doesn't it look like the perfect place for a Satanic rite?"

No one could walk away with these machines. Their enormity renders them safe from thievery. They stand twice as tall as I, their window-cased cabs riding like bubbles on top of them. Streetlights give their upraised ranks of disks and harrows long, spidery shadows.

"He pulled over," Anitra says, watching the rearview mirror. "Let's get out."

I hesitate. I can smell the chill, dewed metal, and the weeds that try to grow, stunted and sunless, beneath the machines. These metal forests have always disturbed me.

"Come on, Terry," Anitra says, climbing out. She wears what she probably considers a hunting outfit — jeans, black turtleneck, a jean jacket, and heavy-soled hiking boots. She has twisted her dark hair into a knot at the nape of her neck. Things clink in her pockets as she moves.

I get out. I am wearing a loose, cheap coverall, in case change overtakes me and I have to rip free of it.

Somehow, with moonlight snagging on the edges of the machines, change feels distant.

With a careless glance toward Philip's car, Anitra takes my hand and pulls me in among the farm machinery. Heat sense does me little good among things colder than trees, rocks, and earth. Anitra leads me farther in, wending away so that my sense of the street as a broad open space behind me fades. Trucks rumble by, shifting the block-laid concrete, so I don't lose the direction.

Anitra ducks down next to the shoulder-high rear wheel of a combine. She tugs me down beside her. We listen to our breathing. Then to Philip's footsteps, each set with the furtive care of an inept stalker. I can see the edge of Anitra's grin, sense the building excitement in her spectrum. Philip's heat signature approaches. Anitra's hand tightens on mine. I hear another, slithery noise not connected with Philip . . .

Anitra leaps up as Philip rounds a machine. "Boo!" she yells, and he jumps, all muscles loose, then tense.

"Great suffering God," Philip yells. "Are you out of your mind, Anitra?" He has been eating onion soup.

"Why are you following us?" Anitra asks.

"I won't give up on you. I know there's something in you worth saving. I can't just stand by and watch you —"

It moves up over the machinery pressing silent rubber linings to steel surfaces, brushing past paint. It is drawn by our heat and noise. My hand grips Anitra's shoulder. I stare, waiting for a sight by moonlight and vagrant streetlight of what I can already sense. It is down-breeze of us — it is a true hunter — but its heat signature comes, dead calm, none of the feverish excitement I usually sense in humans who have broken their conditioning against killing.

" — throw your life away," Philip finishes. "It's not too late."

Anitra glances at me, then looks where I look. "What is it?"

"It's coming." My voice sounds thin to me. I search my self for the power of change, but I don't feel powerful. I don't feel the animal in me, waiting for a cue to take over. Instead I feel something unknown, a creeping paralysis. The thing's heat signature is so odd. Its position is so advantageous.

"What's the matter, Terry?" Anitra asks, glancing at me.

"I'm scared."

Anitra's eyes widen, pupils swallowing irises. She shudders, her spectrum flaring. Then she faces forward. "Philip, get out of here. You can't save me, and Lord knows, I don't want to try to save you anymore. Go home. Look for someone nice who'll appreciate you."

"But Anitra —"

Her shoulder muscles shift under my hand as she rummages in a pocket. She pulls out a Buck knife and opens it. "Go away," she says, her voice shrill. She waves the knife.

"Anitra . . ."

"Can't you see I'm someone else now?" she cries.

It pauses, hidden, on the machine across from us. It is listening. I can't even hear it breathe.

"Anitra," Philip says. He sighs. "Maybe tomorrow. Please don't do anything tonight you'll regret later." He turns and walks away.

Anitra whirls to face me. "You can't be scared," she says, showing her teeth with each word. "Where do you come from?"

"The mountains."

"What do you do with the — the bones of your — your prey?"

"Play with them."

She takes my hand, holds it up. "What's hidden inside here?"

"Claws," I say, then glance at the knife in her other hand. Her grip tightens on it. Her face looks fierce. I can feel knowledge of my self reawakening. Anitra has an animal inside her and so do I. The power of choice slips back, fortifying me. She lets go of my hand.

I look up toward where it waits. Anitra looks too. Her heart beats faster, and a light masking of sweat adds to her hair and body, soap and Bounce scents.

It rises from behind a sheet of metal.

"Can you see it?" I ask Anitra.

"That? It's some college football player, Terry. Some young frat rat." She steps forward. "Hey, you!" she yells.

"No," I whisper, coming up behind her. Now that she has described him, I can almost see him through the haze of strange sense impressions he makes. He is like nothing I have ever sensed.

He raises a hand. His fist clenches around a bar that supports a row of claws poised over his knuckles, metal like the harrows on the machinery around us.

"The Slasher," Anitra whispers.

He smiles.

The breeze shifts, and I scent him, and suddenly know: despite his odd heat signature, he is just another animal, not some strange machine. He is a large, graceful, well-clawed animal, but he is just another animal. Power fills me. Systems wait for my signal. I am ready.

"Go call the police," I tell Anitra. "I'll try not to hurt him."

She touches my cheek, then runs toward the street.

His glance tracks her, then comes back to me. "I'll get you," he says. His voice is low and smooth. "Then I'll get her. Maybe even the boy."

I raise my hands and unsheathe my claws.

He gasps. I can sense the heat blossoming in him, as his signature shifts a little closer to the temperature of life. "You," he whispers. "I saw your work. You did that first one, didn't you? I saw it in the morgue. I thought about it a lot. How it feels to sculpt a human to death. To make a whole town run scared. I made these claws." He brandishes them. He wears them on both hands.

I drift nearer to him. The body is just another animal. The mind is some sort of human; Anitra has probably read a case history. I ought to be able to jump him, especially if he keeps talking.

"I dreamed about you. Not the way you look. Those kids who saw you kill him said you looked like a white lion. I dreamed you came to me, and initiated me into the mysteries of the kill."

A truck rumbles by. I stand just below him. A car slows on the street. Since the Slasher murders the police have increased night patrols.

"Every living body pumps blood," he says, his voice gaining volume, "and I can make that machine run faster, or break it open and watch the blood spill out. I can control the machines because I know fear motivates them. I keep them inside at night, or if they come out, I play with them. I learned that from you." He kneels on his height, lowering his face.

My teeth have changed. The shifts have started, slowly.

"Teach me more," he whispers.

I stare at him. My ears tingle.

"It's not enough anymore. The good feeling from the kill goes away too fast. What's the next mystery?"

Footsteps behind me.

"I thought maybe younger victims," he said. "When it's just bums and rummies it's not like it makes a dent in anybody else's life. You get some kid and people really get upset. I was looking for kids necking tonight."

I lift my hands. Just another animal. I grasp his shoulders. What's the next mystery?

"Hey! What are you doing?"

I pull him down off the combine, and we roll together on the hard-packed earth. His claws rake my ribs, as he awakens from his strange passive killing trance and begins to struggle. I hold one half of him in my upper arms and kick with my feet at the other half, baring my teeth, growling. This is the spine-breaker move, and inside the heat of change and pulse and fight, I realize this and restrain myself. I taste blood and recognize the rust in it. I am not a machine. People are not interchangeable parts. Even though he has tried to become me, I am not him.

"Terry!" Anitra cries, and I sense the others, two of them, as they close in on us. I am human. Humans don't growl or have claws. People are pulling him away from me. I can feel the cool air across the bleeding scratches on my ribs. I hold my hands above me where I can see them. They are wholly human.

The Slasher struggles and growls in the arms of the police. He still wears his claws. "Are you all right?" Anitra asks, kneeling beside me.

"I think so," I say. I sit up, resist the impulse to lick my wounds. It's physically impossible this form, anyway. "I feel confused."

In Idaho, hard liquor is sold in state stores, which close at seven P.M. The bars close at one in the morning.

Anitra gives me coffee with lots of milk.

The visit to the police station raised my hackles. They had someone bandage my scratches. Strangers should not touch me. They fingerprinted me, because the Slasher kept saying I was guilty. I can't remember if any of my family got caught this way before, locked into records.

They asked questions: What were Anitra and I doing out there?

Playing a practical joke on a friend.

Didn't we know it was dangerous?

"We were only going to be there a minute," Anitra said, sounding injured.

Anitra gave them her phone number. I had to give them my address, but I dind't want them waking up my Hendersons, so I told them I'd spend the night at Anitra's.

She closes her hands around her mug of coffee and watches me sip mine. "What happened?"

"I want to go home."

"Why?"

"I don't understand it myself. After you left, he talked to me. He saw my human kill, and he — he turned it into a religion. At home, there are things you like to do and things you don't like, but you do them; they're just part of the day, that's all. At home I understand what everyone does and why. But he — but he — the death took over his life. How could he take something *I* did and make it his reason for . . . I don't feel safe here. I don't understand why you people do things. I — " I look at my human hand and it seems alien. I want to see faces furred and whiskered, ears pointed and tufted. I want to speak in scents.

"That guy is psychotic. Christ, Terry, don't leave because of him. I'd miss you. And I don't even know you yet."

Her face is smooth. She has hands and sits upright. I stare at her for a while and finally she looks like a normal creature.

"There are more like him out here?" I ask.

"Yes," she says. She looks upset. "They're not very common, but they're here." After a minute she says, "He looked different to you, didn't he? When I thought he was just some normal guy, you saw something else."

"Yes," I said. "He was half-dead but still moving."

"So you can tell when you meet them. You don't have to live in ignorance like the rest of us."

I look away from her, at the dark television screen. They live with only sound and color. Anitra is right: I still don't understand why they do things, but I can understand things about them they don't know themselves. Face to face, I have an advantage. "But," I say, "I did something, and then he — he wanted to be me. I don't want people to want to be me."

She blows a breath out through her nose. "Didn't you ever have a relative who did something you admired?"

"Of course, all the time."

"Didn't you try to get them to teach you what they were doing?"

"Of course."

"So?" She holds her hands out, palms up.

I push back against the couch, squashing into the cushions. I feel frustrated. She is right. Still, I just want to run away.

She sighs. "If you leave, you'll never understand us," she says.

I sip coffee. I remember something else. "Anitra, in the metal forest — "

"Yes?" She gives me a fleeting smile.

"When I was scared, you said things to me. I remembered who I was. How did you know what to say to me?"

"I think I understand you — a little, anyway." She leans toward me, her eyes bright. "If you stay till the end of the semester, I'll teach you as much as I can about human behavior."

She has always been my best teacher.

"Just another three months," she says. "After that you can decide again."

And besides, she is my friend, and I haven't figured out what that means yet.

She says: "We can go on field trips. I could take you to Seattle."

"Oh, no. No. Paradise has enough people for me." She is my friend, and we went hunting together, the way Emelya and I used to. I wonder if this is what I came down out of the mountains to find. "All right," I say.

She grins very wide, holds out her mug. I click mine against it, like the rattle of bones.

Ω

THE SPIRIT'S LAMENT

I have spent years denying afterlife.
It seemed the thoughtful, rational thing to do.
When others said (especially my wife)
They'd seen a ghost or maybe even two,
I took it with a grain of salt, for few
Were ever documented to my taste,
And Occam's Razor said that ghosts were too
Irregular. These feelings were misplaced.
We argued, she and I, and fin'lly faced
The fact that no agreement could be made.
I learned, too, as she moved with all due haste,
That other hands than Occam's own a blade.

I've changed. I do believe (now that I'm dead)
In ghosts and afterlife. But where's my head?

— John S. Davis

FOUR
BY LORD DUNSANY

THE RATIONS OF MURDOCH FINUCAN

Sergeant Macinerny walked up to the whitewashed porch of Mick Heraghty's house and knocked, and Mrs. Heraghty came to the door. It was an ordinary enough Irish farm-house in front, with a kitchen to the left as you entered and a little parlour to the right, with a large mahogany table in the middle, and a photograph on the wall of Mr. and Mrs. Heraghty on their wedding-day, and a holy picture and a print of one by Landseer. But leading out of the kitchen was a door that opened upon a spiral staircase of stone that wound up a tower many centuries old, that was all covered with ivy. There was only one room in the tower, now used as a store-room. There had been three other towers once, it was said, but this was the only one that remained of a castle of bygone days, whose story was still remembered, a story that, true or not, was somewhat bloodcurdling. The tower rose up behind the house and loomed strangely above it.

"I was wondering, Mam," said Sergeant Macinerny, "would himself be indoors at present."

"Sure, he's after coming in," said Mrs. Heraghty. "Didn't you see him?"

"Sure, I saw somebody entering," said the sergeant. "But I couldn't be sure it was Mr. Heraghty."

"It was so," said Mrs. Heraghty. "Won't you come in?"

"Ah, it's very kind of you," said Macinerny. "Sure, I will, if it's not troubling you."

"Sure, it's no trouble at all," said Mrs. Heraghty.

So the sergeant went in, and there was Mick Heraghty sitting by the big fireplace in the kitchen. They shook hands. "Won't you sit down?" said Heraghty.

"It's very kind of you," said the sergeant.

"Was there anything you were wanting?" asked Heraghty.

"Ah, nothing at all," said the sergeant; "sure, nothing at all. There was only one thing I wanted, but it will do any time."

"And what was that?" asked Heraghty.

"It was only that I wanted to see Murdoch Finucan, to speak a few words with him about his ration-card."

"Sure, you can do that any time," replied Heraghty, "any time that he comes to my old tower."

"I know," said the sergeant, "I know. But maybe, as it's only a little formality about his ration-card that they were asking about in Dublin, I might have a word with him before that."

"Sure, you might," said the farmer. "I'd go and call him for you now, if I knew where he was."

"I know you would," said Sergeant Macinerny. "But maybe you could tell me about it yourself, without putting Mr. Finucan to any trouble."

"I'd be glad to help you," said Heraghty. "What was

it you wanted to know?"

"Hasn't Murdoch Finucan been dead three hundred years?" asked the sergeant.

"He's been *buried* three hundred years," corrected Heraghty.

"Isn't it the same thing?" asked the sergeant.

"Not in the case of Murdoch Finucan," replied Heraghty.

"Maybe not," said the sergeant, "and I'm not saying it is. But what I was getting at is — does a man want a ration-card when he's been buried all that time?"

"Sure, I got the card for him from Sergeant O'Phelan before you came here," said Heraghty.

"Maybe you did," said Macinerny. "But Sergeant O'Phelan has left the Force, and he was too easy-going any way."

"Sure, it was only for the tea and sugar I wanted it. I wouldn't give a damn for the rest," said the farmer.

"I know," said Sergeant Macinerny. "But the point I was making was — what good would that be to a man who's been dead three hundred years?"

"Buried," said Heraghty.

"Well, buried, then," said the sergeant.

"Ah, would you grudge a cup of tea to a ghost?" complained Heraghty.

"They might in Dublin," said Sergeant Macinerny.

"Ah, what do they know in Dublin of the way things should be done?" asked Heraghty. "Or in any town, for that matter. Sure, they're out of touch with things there. They know nothing."

"Maybe," said the sergeant. "But they're very sharp with us if we don't keep to their rules. And what they are asking now is — Who signed Murdoch Finucan's ration-card?"

"Sure, he signed it by proxy," said Heraghty.

"I understand all that," said the sergeant. "But there's ways and ways of signing by proxy. And did he do it in a way that would satisfy them in Dublin?"

"Maybe he didn't," said Heraghty. "But wasn't Murdoch Finucan a terrible man anyway?"

"Sure, he was, by all accounts," said the sergeant.

"Was he the sort of man you're wishing to pick a quarrel with?" asked Heraghty.

"Maybe one mightn't believe in him at all," said the sergeant.

"Don't the people believe in him?" asked Heraghty.

"Sure, they do, seemingly," said the sergeant.

"And are you going to set yourself against the people?" said Heraghty. "Sure, you'll never go down here if that's what you do."

"I only wanted to see Murdoch Finucan," said the sergeant, "and to ask him about his ration-card."

"Then you may come to my old tower at the full of the

moon," said Heraghty, "and you may say to his face the things that you have been saying to me about him. And tell him to his face, his white face in the moonlight, that you grudge him a cup of tea. And you may tell the people what you've done."

"Ah, sure, I wouldn't go to those lengths," said the sergeant. "Sure I don't want to annoy you. I'll tell them in Dublin that Murdoch Finucan signed by proxy; and that he'll look in on them and verify it the next time that he is in Dublin. Won't that be the best way?"

"Sure, that will do grand," said Heraghty.

Ω

A MODERN PORTRAIT

Going to see an exhibition of pictures the other day, I went straight up to one of them, ignoring a hundred and forty-two, for the rather inadequate reason that I had heard several people talking about it. Well, it would not have been an inadequate reason if they had greatly praised it; but, as it was, they had all been doing the opposite. And I am glad I went, for I might otherwise have accepted their hasty opinions. I must say that, at first sight, I agreed with them, and the picture seemed to me to be all they had said of it. It was a picture of a woman, if you could call her such, standing in a very smooth fawn-colored landscape, that went right to a pale-green sky, beside a thin ruined tower full of odd angles. Looking at it close, the picture seemed quite impossible, so I stepped back four or five paces and sat on a bench to look at it, so as to give it every chance, and I was just about to decide that it could be no likeness of anybody on earth when I glanced at a lady who was sitting on the same bench. Then I saw how wrong I had been. The likeness was astonishing, and she was obviously sitting in front of her own portrait. So perfectly had the artist got her likeness that I could not help turning away from her portrait to gaze at her. This of course she saw, but did not resent, as she showed by saying at once, "Do you think it is like me?"

"It is marvellous," I said. "A speaking likeness. How did you come to be like that?"

My last remark sounds so rude that I should like to take up a little space in explaining it. To begin with, it was wrung from me by surprise — the surprise of finding myself so completely wrong, and all my friends wrong who had told me about this picture, believing it to be unnatural; and there she was beside me, with the same long Victorian dress right to the ground that there was in the picture, the same forehead of steel, or bright metal, with a wisp of rusted iron above it in the form of a query mark, and one of those small horns sometimes carried on bicycles, in place of a nose, with one eye just below it. And I noticed that one of her hands was a lobster's pair of claws, while the other one was a spanner, with a gold wedding-ring on one of the horns of the implement, neat and well-fitting as it was in the picture. Her only other ornament was an oval brooch in gold, framing a miniature of a gentleman wearing whiskers, and a few jet buttons down the front of the black dress. As I have said, my words were wrung from me. But she took no exception to them, and answered at once. "My mother was a late-Victorian lady," she said, "and my father was a bicycle; a lady's bicycle, you know."

I glanced at her again and saw it all in a flash, the long dress, the cameo, and then the bright drops of rain on her metal forehead, and a few faint stains of rust, marking some earlier drops.

"Yes, yes, of course," I said. And I could not at first think of anything more to say to her, till I remembered something that had puzzled me, at first sight, over the tower. "That tower," I said, "the one you were standing by. Was it quite safe? I was wondering if it might not have fallen."

"But why?" she asked.

And all I could find to say was "The force of gravity."

"Oh, that's quite superseded now," she said.

"And again I said, "Yes, of course."

And with her next remark we luckily got away from modern science, of which I really know nothing; for she looked up at her portrait again, and said to me: "Do you think I take more after my mother?"

But, as I was beginning to get a little bit bewildered, I hurriedly spoke of the artist, instead of answering her question, and said what a wonderful likeness he had got. And this could not be denied, and somehow left little to talk about; so little that she soon got up from the bench and hurried away. And it was not till I saw the swift gliding movement with which she went down the gallery, that I noticed, what her long skirts had prevented my seeing before, that she had wheels instead of feet. One snort through the bicycle-horn may have been some sort of farewell.

It only shows that one should not say of any portrait that it is like nothing on earth, as a good many people are too ready to do, until one is quite sure.

Ω

ECHOING DREAM

In the course of a year or so I think that most topics have their turn at our club; and one day we were discussing the feasibility of possession by evil spirits, and in spite of all examples quoted, the weight of the opinion of the Billiards Club appeared to be against it, when Jorkens joined in with the remark, "I should say it was quite possible."

"Ever seen a case of it?" asked Terbut.

And for a while Jorkens was silent. And then he said, "No."

"Then what makes you think it is possible?" said Terbut.

"Well," said Jorkens, "it is a long story." And Terbut uttered a sigh and Jorkens began.

It was in a southern country and a long way to the west, a land of earthquake-rumpled hills, and the hospitality of hearts warmed by that southern sun. My kind host had a Caribbean cook and a Guatemalan gardener, who seemed to understand the gorgeous flowers that bordered all the lawns, and for whom they seemed to thrive. And he employed an odd man as a mechanic, to look after all the machinery that he had in his house and grounds, and to attend to anything that went by electricity, and to see that it did, and in addition to that, he did every job that the Guatemalan and Caribbean neglected to do.

So he was really a very industrious man, though where he learnt industry I have no idea; that land was too warm to have taught him, and he came from some sunny shore of Andalusia that would not have taught him, either. He was just a freak, a throwback perhaps to some old conquering horseman left behind by the Moors.

And another odd thing about him, besides his industry in that warm land, was what my host told me about him as we sat in his garden, when the heat of the day was beginning to cool, and the sun that had gone from the white walls was brightening the red of the tiles and the tops of palms and making the oranges flame, and the odd man walked past us along a row of hibiscus.

My host also came from southern Spain, but long generations ago, a forbear of his having been a conquistador by profession, who had left his Spanish towers to carry religion after the setting sun and to plant it far in the west, where he had possessed himself of lands as wide as a good-sized county, and the King of Spain had made him Count of the Golden Mountains, for there was a range on the lands of his conquest which had been thought to be gold. And these lands his family had held for ages till the curse of modernism, as my friend put it, had left him with no more than a grand old house — built under the influence that was the pagan Moors' rather than of the religion for which his sires had fought — and some spacious and lovely gardens shadowed by cypresses.

And as his odd man now walked under orange trees and past a blaze of hibiscus, Mr. Sierradoro, which is the name in use today by that old line of conquistadors, told me this of his odd man.

He had asked him, he said, when he first employed him, if he ever took dope, and the man said no; and he had asked him if he drank, and he said only seldom, but that he was sometimes possessed by an angel. And my host had asked him if that happened to him often, and he had said no. And so he had decided to chance it.

"I judge a man," Sierradoro said, "by the amount of work he gets through in a year. I never dismiss a man because he gets incapacitated on a feast day or a holiday and for most of the day after. I judge by his total output. This man gets through a wonderful amount of work in the year, both his own and other people's, and I shouldn't dream of parting with him just because he may go off for a whole day and not quite know what he is doing."

"What kind of things does he do?" I asked.

"Well, for instance," he said, "one day a queer look came into his face and he said he was possessed by his angel, and I could see by his eyes that something of the sort had occurred."

"What sort of thing?" I asked.

"You never can tell," said Sierradoro. "But he said he must play some music, and he set off down the road to look for a violin, and I saw it was no use stopping him."

"Did he find a violin?" I asked.

"I don't know," he said. "But the trouble was that all the girls that he met as he went down that road followed him, and some children too. I think he did get hold of a violin, because I heard some rather queer music in the distance, and from complaints that I heard later it seemed that it was a long time before any of the girls came back, and all the children who followed him were out late.

"It only happened once, but he won't promise that it will not happen again. He is a good man and I shouldn't dream of dismissing him. But I have told him that if he does get like that again and feels that he must play music, he had better come in here and play on my organ. That will prevent any more trouble outside, and I have promised the neighbours, that there shall not be."

Sierradoro had a very fine organ; not in a central place on any wall, but rather as an incidental feature of the great room.

I was about to ask what abilities he had with an organ, when the handy man turned and came back along the flowers, facing us as he came, and I saw that he was of a quite illiterate type and that, whatever he could do with machinery and whatever he knew about flowers, he would never be able to handle such an instrument as an organ.

I stayed some time in that house of a bygone day, entertained by Sierradoro with such courtesies as, I fear, may almost be called bygone too. And then, one afternoon, I heard my host say in a low voice to his wife, "I am afraid that man Huan is possessed again today."

"Why?" she exclaimed at once.

"There is that look again," he said.

"Are you sure?" she asked.

"I think so," he said.

"Then get him indoors at once," she said. "We cannot have him making all that trouble again."

And Sierradoro went to look for his odd man, while the Señora and I stayed in the long room in which the organ was built into a wall.

She wore a long mantilla of fine black lace, whether because she herself was Spanish, or because of the lineage of her husband, I did not know, but she certainly wore it with a natural grace that seemed to show she was born to it.

She was troubled about Huan, for she did not estimate him, as her husband did, by the amount of work he accomplished so much as by the risks that his strange seizures, as she named them, entailed.

"But is there any harm in him?" I asked.

"There is always harm in a drunken man," she said.

"What do you think he will do?" I asked.

"There is no telling with drink," she replied.

"But is it drink?" I asked.

"There are only two things," she said, "that will make a man act like that."

"Drink and love?" I suggested.

"Sí," she said.

"And you think it is drink in his case?" I asked.

"But certainly," she replied. "One cannot miss a woman. And I have watched. Bottles are so much smaller that they are more easily hidden."

And then Huan came in with that look in his eyes. I don't know where Sierradoro had found him; probably doing some useful job that the gardener had neglected, but with that look in his eyes. I saw it the moment he entered: a look as far from us as we were from heaven. He was dressed in a thin shirt, open all down the front, for it was a warm day, and a pair of trousers, and shoes that were more like sandals. He wore no socks.

As soon as Huan saw the organ an awed look came into his face, and he almost ran to it. His fingers were stained with the dark oil of some machine at which he had been working; he spread them upon the keys as he sat down, and then he began to play.

The music rose up from under his hands at once. It was like torrents coming down the faces of brazen mountains which rang with them as they fell; torrents full of river-nymphs in the gold of the dawn, singing, as they swam by, their songs to a quiet land turning from sleep below, to the sound of sheep-bells and pipes of awakening shepherds. There was lark-song in it and the sound of trumpets, and it seemed full of old memories of all melodious things ever heard long ago.

It set me somehow thinking about my childhood and my earliest pictures of heaven, but that music seemed to brighten them, making them more like visions. And it made me think of acres of may in bloom, and they somehow seemed to be singing, singing of things long gone, but brought back by that music.

Before our eyes as we looked out of the window, Sierradoro and the Señora and I, were the flowers of that warm land shining in the late sunlight, and from a lily-pond in the garden came the roaring boom of the bullfrogs; but we did not seem to see or notice these things, or anything but the music, as it flowed over deep soft carpets and filled the room to the rafters, and lingered among old memories brought back to our day and enchanted. That's how it seemed to me as he played, and a great deal more that I can never describe, for words limp far behind music.

The Señora was looking past me out of the window, as though to something very far away, and Sierradoro had his gaze fixed on something else — one couldn't tell what — and he seemed to be puzzled by it, whatever it

was. Huan's back was towards us so that I could not see his face, but his head was lifted upward, away from the keys on which he seemed to play with the ease of a butterfly's dances. I wondered if he was conscious of what he was playing. The Señora, motionless under her black mantilla, seemed hardly to hear the music, so absorbed were her dark eyes with the vision the music had shown them. Nor did Sierradoro appear to be within years of what was happening here.

Horns from a far country seemed to be luring and calling, as those hands flashed over the keys like shadows of birds migrating; birds of paradise, as I fancied, on a flight from their distant home. I wondered who had taught this miraculous art to the peasant from Andalusia. And then I suddenly saw it was as he had said, and that what you were talking about just now was possible, and that he was possessed by an angel.

The music flowed on with that astounding ease and that clear call to Sierradoro and his wife and to me, but all to different dreams. And in the great flood of that music, all heaven seemed to be smiling, and the earth and its common things to be glowing in that smile's radiance. The large leaves of bananas in the garden outside, slowly swaying, seemed lit by that smile, and the shadows of leaves of an olive on a white wall seemed to rest with an infinite rest, and in that rest there seemed to be living again old memories of the simple things of our world, and I thought I could hear bells chiming in valleys of lost summer evenings.

Then the spirit that played that organ seemed growing weary of earth, for there came a longing into the music more wistful than any of ours, as the sadness of all earth's sorrows weighed more and more on his wings, and he seemed to be yearning now for his far home and to sigh for the glories of heaven that he had left. And then he suddenly ended on one great note, like a thunderbolt falling upon mountains of bronze and setting their peaks a- ringing, and a window of heaven seemed to have been thrown open, and I thought I heard its choirs singing their answer with the sound of a far rejoicing, or was it but the sound of Huan's music coming back from heaven's walls?

I could not tell. But I thought at the time that all the others were calling him with their unearthly musical voices, and — was it possible — me too, who was so far from heaven and did not know the way.

And the boom of the bullfrogs came back, and the Señora withdrew her gaze from that far past where it had wandered, and I left all that I left in far-away days, and Sierradoro came back with me to the present, and Huan rose up and brushed his hands together, as a man leaving a job that has been forced on him, and walked out of the house, and I heard the smack of his spit hitting the paved path as he hurried back to his work, the plain peasant again.

And outside the window I saw the evening light reflected upwards from ripples that the bullfrogs made in the lily-pond, pale gold on the under side of the leaves of a lemon tree; and, something causing me to lift my gaze, I looked on and slanting upwards, with gold light shining on large leaves, on and on, till my eyes met golden clouds which parted asunder as though making a pathway all the way to the lily-pond, till it was almost lost in the radiance to which it led. And into that radiance I saw, just as it passed from sight, what may have been a flock of white herons or anything else, but which looked like two great wings with which a spirit departed. And up that golden vista it seemed to right into heaven.

I would have followed, I would have followed indeed, for I felt I could. I don't know how, but I felt I could have walked up that shining pathway into heaven. But just at that moment, just as I would have gone, I heard a door slamming, the door of the engine-shed, actually, in which that fellow worked; and the gates of heaven closed.

Ω

HELPING THE FAIRIES

The young journalist from London on holiday at Rathgeel was feeling lonely for want of news. There was plenty of fishing and shooting, but no news; for nothing in Rathgeel ever seemed to happen. The weather may have changed a bit at times in Rathgeel, but not while he was there; the wind blew warm and damp from the south-west all the time, and all the thorn trees sloped the same way, as though that one wind had been blowing for ever.

And the odd thing was, as it seemed to Draffin, the young journalist I have mentioned, nobody seemed to want anything new to happen; they complained a bit while they were talking of the weather and the crops, the price of cattle and one or two other things, but they never seemed in their hearts to want anything new. And Draffin was lonely and homesick for want of news, good as the fishing was, and the shooting too.

And then one day a man called William Smith was found lying dead in a narrow old sunken lane, where nobody went but an odd tramp, and he had been lying there nearly a week when they found him, and there were some bullet-holes in him.

This was like dawn to Draffin after a long night. News at last! And he ran round, with his notebook open in his hand, to all the acquaintances that he had made during his holiday, to get the details of it. And nothing could he get.

"I thought the Irish were a talkative people," he said to one of them at last, a tall, dark, thin man called Michael Heggarty.

"And so we are," said Heggarty.

"I think you are the dumbest people in the whole world," said Draffin. "And that's not excepting the people in deaf-and-dumb asylums."

"Is that so?" said Heggarty.

"I am sure it is," replied Draffin.

"Maybe that's because you don't use the right key," said Heggarty. "You would not say there was no money in the Bank of England because you couldn't open the vaults. But there's a key to them."

"What's the key here?" asked Draffin.

"Sure, it's whisky," said Heggarty, "if you can find the right man for it."

"And who's the right man?" asked Draffin.

"Ah, I'd not like to be telling you," said Heggarty.

"Well, one must make a beginning," said Draffin, "so I'll begin by trying you, if you wouldn't mind coming in here."

For they were standing outside the white wall of Jimmy Doyle's public-house, under its dark thatch.

And they went inside and whisky was ordered by Draffin and drunk by them both, sitting together at a table, and the heavy silence continued. And Draffin paid for more whisky, and that was drunk too. And in the few minutes that went by after that the little room seemed to grow darker in the autumn afternoon, but a light was growing in the eyes of Heggarty. And then Draffin said half to himself and half to the far wall at which he was gazing, "I wonder what happened to William Smith."

"I'll tell you," said Heggarty. "It was like this. He comes over here from England, or from some place where they must be very ignorant, about a year ago, and he buys a bit of land to do some farming, and he settles down all alone in the farmhouse on it. I wouldn't say he didn't understand farming. but he was terrible ignorant of the land and all the ways of it. And there was a lone thorn in a field that he wanted to plough, an old thorn, what was left of it by the ages, and he said it would get in the way of the plough.

"There was no harm in ploughing the field, but it stands to reason he could have run a plough round the tree, and by bending his head a bit he could have got under the branches, and the horse too, for a horse would have had more sense than what he had. But he couldn't see that, and he must cut down the tree, a lone thorn of the fairies, one that the Little People had danced round for ages.

"Well, he asks several young men to cut it, but none of them would do anything so foolish and made various excuses. So what does he do but he gets an axe and he cuts it down himself. And nobody says a word at first. We was all too horrified. And then some of us goes to old Timmy Maguire to hear what he will say. And we tells him what William Smith has done, and he had heard already, and old Timmy Maguire says, 'No matter. You only have to wait. Watch him and wait and see what the Little People will do. For I never knew anybody do anything agin them without they being revenged on him; never yet, and I've lived to be ninety.'

"Well, that satisfied all of us, except one young fellow who must always be asking questions.

" 'What'll they do to him?' he says.

" 'You have only to watch,' says old Timmy Maguire. 'They will take his luck away. Watch his luck and see what happens to it. I never knew the Little People leave a man's luck when he had offended them, not a shred of it. I never saw them do that in ninety years.'

" 'And did you often see them at it?' asks the young fellow.

" 'Begob,' says old Timmy Maguire, 'many's the time I seen them take all a man's luck right away to the mountains, nor I never seen it come back.'

" 'Sure, that's terrible,' says one of us.

" 'It's what they do,' says old Timmy Maguire.

"Well, we all decides to do what old Timmy Maguire says, and to watch the luck of William Smith and to see what happens to it; and what happens is this: it's the most extraordinary part of my story, but it's the truth I'm telling you. William Smith puts five pounds on a horse a few days later that's running at a hundred to one. Well, that's tempting your luck to leave you; no horse is going to win at a hundred to one, and it's throwing five pounds away, and a man who begins like that will throw everything away. But this horse wins and the bookie pays and we all says, 'What about the Little People?'

"And that isn't all. There's a competition next week to guess the number of rabbits that there are in County Meath, with a motor-car for a prize for the man whose guess is nearest. And William Smith guesses the right number within three, and he gets the motor-car. And the Little People says nothing.

"And it doesn't stop there. For a few days later he sells a horse for a thousand pounds what he had bought out of a cart for twenty-five pounds, either knowing something about a horse or finding a man that thought he did; but it was luck either way. Ay, out of a cart, and he sells it for a thousand pounds. And that wasn't all, nor nearly all, but I won't weary you with telling you all of it, and maybe you wouldn't believe me if I did; but he had a run of luck such as no one ever saw, and it went on week after week, and was an insult to those that dance under the moon.

"And we goes to old Timmy Maguire and says, 'What about it now?' And he says, 'Only wait.' And that man Smith's run of luck went on and on. And then he backs another horse in a race and it was three to one on, and he puts on six hundred pounds to win two hundred; and he could afford to do that when he knew that he couldn't lose. And it was just the same as the horse at a hundred to one, and he gets two hundred pounds.

"Well, that was the limit, and something had to be done. It was no use asking old Timmy Maguire, who would say nothing but 'Wait' or 'Watch him.' We had to do something ourselves. I had nothing to do with it myself, because I have always kept away from religion and politics and all them kind of things, and I says to the rest of the boys, 'I'll have no hand in it'; and they says, 'Sure, we all respect your principles. At the same time the Little People are being insulted by this man's luck, as though they didn't exist, or as though there were nothing sacred in their old thorns, and we can't allow that kind of thing in a place like Rathgeel.' And

I had to agree that that was so: what else could I say? Though I took no part in it myself.

"Well, when the boys was gone I goes once more to old Timmy Maguire to tell him that the young lads is getting impatient. 'Sure, they needn't be,' says he. 'For I never knew any man to hold his luck against that people, and they'll be avenged for their thorn.'

"It was no use telling him of all the good luck that was continually coming to William Smith, for he wouldn't listen, but only says to me, 'Wait.'

"Well, the young lads goes that night to the house of William Smith, and they finds him sitting at a table totting up the figures of all the money that had been coming his way ever since he cut down the old thorn; and there was little smiles on his face. That is what the boys told me afterwards, and I only tell you what they told me, but I can't say exactly what happened when I wasn't there myself, but was at home with my poor old mother who had a cold and wanted me to look after her.

"But the young lads came to William Smith and say to him, 'Rathgeel was always a quiet place, where no one takes any part in religion or politics and never interferes with anyone, whatever his religion is. At the same time,' they says, 'if anyone thinks that they can come here from England and buy a farm and insult those that dance round the thorn, and make money that many a man would be glad of with an old mother to support, as though his luck hadn't changed and the Little People didn't exist, is greatly mistaken, as you'll soon find out if you don't give up all the money you've made since you desecrated the thorn, and a great deal more besides, till you've given up to fellows that will know how to use it properly, as much as you would have lost if your luck had turned against you weeks ago, as it should; if you know what we mean, and if you don't it's a bullet you'll get, which may help to teach you.'

"That's what the young lads told me they said to him. And William Smith says nothing, and they sees he is in two minds what to do; and Rathgeel being a quiet place, as I told you and as you've seen for yourself, where no trouble of any sort ever occurred, and they not wanting its name to become a byword from having a man there that was insulting the Little People and growing fat on it, and interfering with their dancing at night, for a lone thorn is their ballroom, they asks him to step outside with them, before he can make up his mind for fear he would make it up wrong. And they takes him to that bohereen where the body was found, and what happened there they none of them told me, so there's no knowing, and it's no use any man saying there is.

"But they goes to old Timmy Maguire and tells him that William Smith is dead, and what ought they to do now? And old Timmy Maguire says, 'Sure, there's nothing more for anybody to do. Didn't I tell you that all you had to do was wait?' "

Ω

Weirdisms

NECROMANCY: The sorcerous practice of animating corpses, and then directing their actions ... whether for material gain, for arcane knowledge, or for other reasons less easily described ... is regarded as the most depraved of the Black Arts.

"...woe to those Unnatural Unmakers who disrupt the dreamless slumbers of the Dead – Woe to those Heaven-Hating Adepts who undo the Stillness of the Fallen."

        – The Canticles of Hell

THE DEVIL
AND THE MODERN MAN

I.

"Come with me," the Tempter said,
in the darkness of my dream,
*"I'll show you all the kingdoms of the Earth,
and treasures that the hills conceal."*

So I rose up in the night,
and journeyed through the storms.
The demon laughed when lightning flashed;
he howled amid the winds.

I saw his ragged wings spread wide;
I saw his cloven hooves;
and I saw his iron hands reach out
and part a starry screen.

He showed me mighty works of Man,
the gleaming cities of the plain,
and hidden caverns filled with gold,
where long ago the dragons slept.

*"All this and more I'll give to thee,
if you'll but give your soul."*
I merely turned my back on him
and slowly walked away.

And awoke within my chamber
in the clean light of day,
where nothing lurked in shadows,
and all was as before.

II.

"Come with me," the Tempter said
in the silence of the night,
*"and you shall hear the secret songs,
the songs we devils know,*

*"the chants infernal, the beauteous dread
which drives the seeker mad,
and whispers of the Lamiae
which dwell in ancient tombs."*

So I rose and walked the endless path,
through the country of the dead,
and learned the necromantic truths
which ghosts alone can teach.

And, yes, I heard the secret songs,
and viewed the gaping gulf
of stars and worlds and dust and time,
through which my demon swam.

But then I slowly turned my back
and slowly walked away,
and woke again within my room,
in the twilight of the morn.

III.

"Now tell to me," the Tempter said,
in the rattling afternoon;
we ran to catch the subway,
then stood amid the crowd.

The demon nearly lost his grip,
the subway lurched and turned.
His eyes met mine; he seemed afraid;
I caught hold of his arm.

"Tell to me," he gasped again,
wheezing out his breath,
*"what man are you, what sage, what saint,
that turns away from me?*

*"Many men would kill and more
to see what you have seen,
and many more would gladly die
and give to me their souls."*

"Alas, I am a modern man,
and not a saint or sage.
I believe ten wonders every morn,
but none by afternoon.

"I am a thing of labelled parts,
of chemistry and cells.
My thoughts are mere electric sparks.
My words are so much noise.

"Statistics bound my daily life;
I fill out lots of forms.
I pay my bills, then watch TV;
then sleep, then rise, then work.

"It's hardly relevant for me
to dwell on secret sins,
or know dark spells from ages past,
or hear the sirens sing."

"What price? What price!" the Tempter cried,
"What price wouldst have from me?"
"No price, no deal, a modern man
has simply got no soul!"

—Darrell Schweitzer

A SÉANCE

by
Nina
Kiriki
Hoffman

"I brought this. I thought it might help," said the girl. She reached into her purse, a turquoise sack large enough to hold a picnic lunch for four, and fished out an urn. "Uncle Fred," she said, offering the urn to Natasha Clayton.

"What an odd idea, my dear," said Natasha. She took the urn and surveyed the girl, who — aside from her purse — looked like a new-minted sorority girl, from the feathery brown hair that curled away from her face to her teetery slim-heeled shoes. She wore the requisite floating-heart pendant, short ski jacket, and name-brand jeans, as well as a dusting of makeup and a synthetic birthstone high-school ring.

"Well, you know, a séance," said the girl. She twitched her shoulders like a person who used to play horse and hadn't grown out of it. "I've had Uncle Fred on my dresser for years. He doesn't get many opportunities to go out."

"I see," said Natasha. The urn was heavy; it made her hands cold. "Well," she said, "won't you come this way? And what is your name, dear?"

"Buffy," said the girl. She followed the old lady through some dark velvet curtains, and they emerged in the séance room. A pall of incense lay just under the ceiling. All the walls were obscured by dark curtains. In the center of the room stood a round table with a black surface, surrounded by ladder-back chairs. In front of the one odd chair — a short, well-padded one with arms — a crystal ball nested in a swatch of black velvet, and two silver candlesticks supported white candles.

"We'll just put Uncle Fred here," said Natasha, placing the urn in the center of the table. She flexed her fingers, trying to get the circulation going.

"Gee, it looks kind of spooky," said Buffy, glancing uncertainly at the room's sole light fixture, a wagon-wheel chandelier with five lamp chimneys shielding flame-shaped light bulbs from a nonexistent wind.

Natasha looked up too. "I quite agree. That horrid thing came with the house. I haven't gotten around to replacing it yet, but we'll turn it off when we get down to business."

"I didn't mean —"

"That's fine, dear. Choose any seat but mine." She pointed to the padded chair. "I've got to trot out and greet a few more guests."

Buffy watched her push out between the curtains. Natasha glanced back, her black eyes brighter than the masses of jet beads encrusting the front of her black dress. When she had gone, silence dropped over the room, heavy as six feet of earth. The air was remarkably stuffy. Stooping, Buffy peered under the table, searching for strings and hidden devices. She went around to the medium's chair and checked it for buttons or loose pieces. She was peering behind the dusty black curtains and had discovered some yellowing wallpaper with a pattern of beribboned Easter baskets on it when she heard voices. Natasha came in, escorting a couple who looked the same age as Buffy's parents. Buffy dropped the curtain.

"We've tried everything, Mrs. Clayton, everything. I just know my little Lisbeth is a restless spirit. The wind keeps blowing her bedroom door shut, even when there's not a window open in the house. Lizzie used to hate to have that door shut. She was so afraid of the dark. I think she's trying to tell us something."

"You may very well be right, Mrs. Griffin. If you are, I'm sure we'll find out tonight. Won't you take a seat? Oh, Buffy, this is Mr. and Mrs. Griffin."

Buffy came forward and grasped Mr. Griffin's large, work-roughened hand. He held his hat in his other hand. The twinkle in his eye seemed to indicate he didn't believe in this séance business any more than Buffy did. She grinned and held out her hand to Mrs. Griffin, who shook it, but seemed preoccupied and sad. "That's my Uncle Fred on the table," said Buffy, twitching a shoulder toward the urn.

A heavy-browed girl, her black hair loose about her shoulders, came through the curtains. Her white dress, an Alice-in-Wonderland number, seemed out of place on her; she looked too rough-and-tumble for it.

"Oh, Tanya, glad you could make it," said Natasha. "I do so detest even numbers. Tanya, Mr. and Mrs. Griffin and Buffy. Shall we be seated?"

"Do we pay now or later?" asked Mr. Griffin.

"You understand that the money goes to the Rutherford Elementary School lunch fund?" Natasha asked.

"Yep," he said. "The article in the paper said you were the school's principal. Is that true?"

"Perfectly true. Please pay in advance. No guarantees."

Buffy fished her wallet out of her purse and handed Natasha a twenty-dollar bill, then took a seat to the medium's right. Mr. Griffin took his wallet out of his back pocket and flipped out forty dollars. "This will help," said Natasha. She tucked the money away and lit the candles, adding the clean scent of wax to the odor of stale incense. "Tanya, dear, will you turn out the light?"

The sullen-mouthed girl reached in among the curtains near the door. There was a click and then darkness. Buffy waited for her eyes to adjust to the candle light. Tanya, a white wraith, came silently to the table and sat down on Buffy's right.

"Oh, Tanya, that's Buffy's Uncle Fred in the urn. Who shall we start with, Lisbeth or Uncle Fred?"

"Lisbeth," said Buffy. "Are you going to use the crystal ball?"

"Oh, no, that's just a prop. Please, everyone, place your hands on the table. You may feel more comfortable if you touch the hands of those next to you." She put her own hands flat on the table. Buffy touched hands with Natasha on her left and Tanya on her right. Tanya had a warm, dry hand. Across the table, Mr. and Mrs. Griffin established contact. Natasha leaned her head back and closed her eyes. "Lisbeth Griffin, are you there?"

They waited. Buffy's nose itched. She wiggled it. Finally a small voice spoke. "I'm here. Mama, I'm here."

Buffy glanced at Natasha, but didn't see her lips move.

"Lisbeth!" cried Mrs. Griffin, her head turning back and forth as she searched for her daughter. "Lizzie, honey, are you shutting the door to your room?"

"Yes," said the voice. It seemed to come from above. Buffy wondered if there was a loudspeaker hidden in the wagon wheel.

Mr. Griffin cleared his throat. "Why?" he said. He sounded a little hoarse.

"Shut the door, Mama. Shut the door on me. I'm done with my earthly days as Lisbeth. Let me go, Mama. You got to stop mourning me. It keeps me here."

"Is it good on the other side, baby?" said Mrs. Griffin.

"Mama, I don't know yet. You don't let me go. I see the light up ahead. I long for it. But you keep me here. Remember me, Mama, but don't mourn me any more."

"Lisbeth," said Mrs. Griffin. Buffy heard tears in her voice.

"Say good-by to me now. You've got to get on with your life, Mama. Let me go."

"Good-by, Lizzie," said Mrs. Griffin, her voice faint.

"Papa, you get Mama back out there in the garden, get her working on her begonias, okay?"

"Yes, Lizzie," said Mr. Griffin, hesitating. He looked around the room without seeming to focus on it. He cleared his throat again. Then he nodded again. "Yes."

"I love you, Papa. Say good-by to me?"

"Good-by," he whispered.

"The light is getting clearer. I'm almost there. I love you, Mama." The childish voice faded away.

Mrs. Griffin rubbed her eyes. "She was right," she murmured. "I have to stop clinging to her."

Natasha rolled her head and opened her eyes. "Did we finish with Lisbeth?" she asked.

"Yes, we did," said Mr. Griffin, with a touch of gentle irony.

"Well, now. Shall we try to contact Uncle Fred, Buffy?"

"Sure," said Buffy. But she was not really sure. When she arrived, she had imagined large headlines (maybe even boxcar letters) on the front page of the college newspaper she worked for:

GIRL REPORTER EXPOSES MYSTIC FRAUD

and in smaller print:

LITTLE OLD LADY TAKES MONEY OUT OF THE MOUTHS OF SCHOOLCHILDREN

But what she had witnessed felt genuine, if a bit prissy. One would expect a medium to say all the standard things about how good life was on the Other Side, and how Lisbeth wanted her parents to see Natasha Clayton on a regular basis (bring money). Instead, she had pretty much cut herself off from further contact.

What would Natasha make of Uncle Fred?

Too late for hesitations now.

Natasha pulled the urn toward her. Then she grimaced and shook her hands. She sat down and gripped Buffy's hand, then said, "Everyone, hang on tight for this one." Her eyes closed. "I address the urn. If the spirit to whom these remains once belonged is still nearby, please manifest yourself."

The air in the room grew cold. For an instant Buffy felt as if she had been dipped in ice water, but that passed. She could feel the warmth of Tanya's strong hand in hers.

"Don't clutch, Buff," said a gruff little voice, the first words she had heard from the white wraith.

An evil laugh started near the ceiling and spiralled down around the room.

"Uh — Uncle Fred?" said Buffy, her voice wavering. But of course she had never had an Uncle Fred. She had had a friend who worked for the local mortuary smuggle her out some unclaimed cremains, thinking the ultimate test of a medium would be to supply one with false information.

"I am Silas Caulder," boomed the voice. "Sixty years I been waiting for one of my kin to fetch my last remains and take them to a good place, and now along comes this puffy-headed critter, no kith nor kin to me, and takes me away from what I'm starting to look on as my final resting place, and puts me in her *purse!*" He began screeching. Buffy wanted to put her hands over her ears, but she was afraid of letting go of Tanya's and Natasha's hands.

"Quiet," said Natasha, and Silas shut up. The ensuing silence seemed full of surprise. "Silas Caulder, you are a restless spirit. What action needs to be taken to put you to rest?"

The voice began muttering, its words indistinct. At last it said, "I had nine children, and they littered like kittens. Where's my family tree? Why did all of 'em leave my remains in the funeral home instead of taking me someplace better to wait for the Last Trump?"

"Mr. Caulder, do you believe we are all children of Adam?" Natasha asked.

"It's in the Bible."

"Can you accept Buffy as your kin?"

"That puffy-headed featherbrain?"

"I suspect there's more to her than meets the eye," said Natasha.

Buffy winced. She didn't like the direction this was taking.

"What is so terrible about a ride in her purse?" continued the medium. "At least she took you somewhere. She says she has a dresser you could stay on."

"Better 'n nothing," said Silas's voice.

"Maybe she can discover where your children went and get you back to them. Until then, you could stay with her."

"I accept," said Silas Caulder's voice. "Howdy, niece."

Buffy managed an almost-bright smile. "Hi, Uncle Silas."

Tanya began to giggle.   Ω

RIDI BOBO

by Robert Devereaux

At first little things niggled at Bobo's mind: the forced quality of Kiki's mimed chuckle when he went into his daily pratfall getting out of bed; the great care she began to take painting in the teardrop below her left eye; the way she idly fingered a pink puffball halfway down her shiny green suit. Then more blatant signals: the creases in her crimson frown, a sign, he knew, of real discontent; the bored arcs her floppy shoes described when she walked the ruff-necked piglets; a wistful shake of the head when he brought out their favorite set of shiny steel rings and invited her, with the artful pleas of his expressive white gloves, to juggle with him.

But Bobo knew it was time to seek professional help when he whipped out his rubber chicken and held it aloft in a stranglehold — its eyes X'd shut in fake death, its pitiful head lolled against the back of his glove — and all Kiki could offer was a soundless yawn, a fatigued cock of her conical nightcap, and the curve of her back, one lazy hand waving bye-bye before collapsing languidly beside her head on the pillow. No honker would be brought forth that evening from her deep hip pocket, though he could discern its outline there beneath the cloth, a coy maddening shape that almost made him hop from toe to toe on his own. But he stopped himself, stared forlornly at the flaccid fowl in his hand, and shoved it back inside his trousers.

He went to check on the twins, their little gloved hands hugging the blankets to their chins, their perfect snowflake-white faces vacant with sleep. People said they looked more like Kiki than him, with their lime-green hair and the markings around their eyes. Beautiful boys, Jojo and Juju. He kissed their warm round red noses and softly closed the door.

In the morning, Bobo, wearing a tangerine apron over his bright blue suit, watched Kiki drive off in their new rattletrap Weezo, thick puffs of exhaust exploding out its tailpipe. Back in the kitchen, he reached for the Buy-Me Pages. Nervously rubbing his pate with his left palm, he slalomed his right index finger down the Snooper listings. Lots of flashy razz-ma-tazz ads, lots of zingers to catch a poor clown's attention. He needed simple. He needed quick. Ah! His finger thocked the entry short and solid as a raindrop on a roof; he noted the address and slammed the book shut.

Bobo hesitated, his fingers on his apron bow. For a moment the energy drained from him and he saw his beloved Kiki as she'd been when he married her, honker out bold as brass, doing toe hops in tandem with him, the shuff-shuff-shuff of her shiny green pants legs, the ecstatic ripples that passed through his rubber chicken as he moved it in and out of her honker and she bulbed honks around it. He longed to mimic sobbing, but the inspiration drained from him. His shoulders rose and fell once only; his sweep of orange hair canted to one side like a smart hat.

Then he whipped the apron off in a tangerine flurry, checked that the boys were okay playing with the piglets in the backyard, and was out the front door, floppy shoes flapping toward downtown.

Momo the Dick had droopy eyes, baggy pants, a shuffle to his walk, and an office filled to brimming with towers of blank paper, precariously tilted — like gaunt placarded and stilted clowns come to dine — over his splintered desk. Momo wore a battered old derby and mock-sighed a lot, like a bloodhound waiting to die.

He'd been decades in the business and had the dust to prove it. As soon as Bobo walked in, the tramp-wise clown seated behind the desk glanced once at him, peeled off his derby, twirled it, and very slowly very deliberately moved a stiffened fist in and out of it. Then his hand opened — red nails, white fingers thrust out of burst gloves — as if to say, Am I right?

Bobo just hung his head. His clownish hands drooped like weights at the ends of his arms.

The detective set his hat back on, made sympathetic weepy movements — one hand fisted to his eye — and motioned Bobo over. An unoiled drawer squealed open, and out of it came a puff of moths and a bulging old scrapbook. As Momo turned its pages, Bobo saw lots of illicit toe hops, lots of swollen honkers, lots of rubber chickens poking where they had no business poking. There were a whole series of pictures for each case, starting with a photo of his mopey client, progressing to the flagrante delicto evidence, and ending, almost without exception, in one of two shots: a judge with a shock of pink hair and a huge gavel thrusting a paper reading **DIVORCE** toward the adulterated couple, the third party handcuffed to a Kop with a tall blue hat and a big silver star on his chest; or two corpses, their floppy shoes pointing up like warped surfboards, the triumphant spouse grinning like weak tea and holding up a big pistol with a **BANG!** flag out its barrel, and Momo, a hand on the spouse's shoulder, looking sad as always and not a little shocked at having closed another case with such finality.

When Bobo broke down and mock-wept, Momo pulled out one end of a checkered hanky and offered it. Bobo cried long and hard, pretending to dampen yard upon yard of the unending cloth. When he was done, Momo reached into his desk drawer, took out a sheet with the word **CONTRACT** at the top and two X'd lines for signatures, and dipped a goose-quill pen into a large bottle of ink. Bobo made no move to take it but the old detective just kept holding it out, the picture of patience, and drops of black ink fell to the desktop between them.

Momo tracked his client's wife to a seedy Three-Ring Motel off the beaten path. She hadn't been easy to tail. A sudden rain had come up and the pennies that pinged off his windshield had reduced visibility by half, which made the eager Weezo hard to keep up with. But Momo managed it. Finally, with a sharp right and a screech of tires, she turned into the motel parking lot. Momo slowed to a stop, eying her from behind the brim of his sly bowler. She parked, climbed up out of the tiny car like a souffle rising, and rapped on the door of Room Five, halfway down from the office.

She jiggled as she waited. It didn't surprise Momo, who'd seen lots of wives jiggle in his time. This one had a pleasingly sexy jiggle to her, as if she were shaking a cocktail with her whole body. He imagined the bulb of her honker slowly expanding, its bell beginning to flare open in anticipation of her little tryst. Momo felt his bird stir in his pants, but a soothing pat or two to his pocket and a few deep sighs put it back to sleep. There was work afoot. No time nor need for the wild flights of his long-de-parted youth.

After a quick reconnoiter, Momo went back to the van for his equipment. The wooden tripod lay heavy across his shoulder and the black boxy camera swayed like the head of a willing widow as he walked. The rest — unexposed plates, flash powder, squeezebulb — Momo carried in a carpetbag in his free hand. His down-drawn mouth puffed silently from the exertion, and he cursed the manufacturers for refusing to scale down their product, it made it so hard on him in the inevitable chase.

They had the blinds down but the lights up full. It made sense. Illicit lovers liked to watch themselves act naughty, in Momo's experience, their misdoings fascinated them so. He was in luck. One wayward blind, about chest high, strayed leftward, leaving a rectangle big enough for his lens. Miming stealth, he set up the tripod, put in a plate, and sprinkled huge amounts of glittery black powder along his flashbar. He didn't need the flashbar, he knew that, and it caused all manner of problem for him, but he had his pride in the aesthetics of picture-taking, and he was willing to blow his cover for the sake of that pride. When the flash went off, you knew you'd taken a picture; a quick bulb squeeze in the dark was a cheat and not at all in keeping with his code of ethics.

So the flash flared, and the smoke billowed through the loud report it made, and the peppery sting whipped up into Momo's nostrils on the inhale. Then came the hurried slap of shoes on carpet and a big slatted eyelid opened in the blinds, out of which glared a raging clownface. Momo had time to register that this was one hefty punchinello, with muscle-bound eyes and lime-green hair that hung like a writhe of caterpillars about his face. And he saw the woman, Bobo's wife, honker out, looking like the naughty fornicator she was but with an overlay of uh-oh beginning to sheen her eyes.

The old adrenaline kicked in. The usually poky Momo hugged up his tripod and made a mad dash for the van, his carpetbag shoved under one arm, his free hand pushing the derby down on his head. It was touch and go for a while, but Momo had the escape down to a science, and the beefy clown he now clouded over with a blanket of exhaust — big lumbering palooka caught off-guard in the act of chicken stuffing — proved no match for the wily Momo.

Bobo took the envelope and motioned Momo to come in, but Momo declined with a hopeless shake of the head. He tipped his bowler and went his way, sorrow slumped like a mantle about his shoulders. With calm deliberation Bobo closed the door, thinking of Jojo and Juju fast asleep in their beds. Precious boys, flesh of his flesh, energetic prank-sters, they deserved better than this.

He unzipped the envelope and pulled out the photo. Some clown suited in scarlet was engaged in hugger-mugger toe hops with Kiki. His rubber chicken, unsanctified by papa church, was stiff-necked as a rubber chicken can get and stuffed deep inside the bell of Kiki's honker. Bobo leaned back against the door, his shoes levering off the rug like slapsticks. He'd never seen Kiki's pink rubber bulb swell up so grandly. He'd never seen her hand close so tightly around it nor squeeze with such ardency. He'd never *ever* seen the happiness that danced so brightly in her eyes, turning her painted tear to a tear of joy.

He let the photo flutter to the floor. Blessedly it fell facedown. With his right hand he reached deep into his pocket and pulled out his rubber chicken, sad purple-yellow bird, a male's burden in this world. The sight of it brought back memories of their wedding. They'd had it performed by Father Beppo in the center ring of the Church of Saint Canio. It had been a beautiful day, balloons so thick the air felt close under the bigtop. Father Beppo had laid one hand on Bobo's rubber chicken, one on Kiki's honker, inserting hen into honker for the first time as he lifted his long-lashed eyes to the heavens, wrinkle lines appearing on his meringue-white forehead. He'd looked to Kiki, then to Bobo, for their solemn nods toward fidelity.

And now she'd broken that vow, thrown it to the wind, made a mockery of their marriage.

Bobo slid to the floor, put his hands to his face,

and wept. Real wet tears this time, and that astonished him, though not enough — no, not nearly enough — to divert his thoughts from Kiki's treachery. His gloves grew soggy with weeping. When the flood subsided, he reached down and turned the photo over once more, scrutinizing the face of his wife's lover. And then the details came together — the ears, the mouth, the chin; oh God no, the hair and the eyes — and he knew Kiki and this bulbous-nosed bastard had been carrying on for a long time, a very long time indeed. Once more he inventoried the photo, frantic with the hope that his fears were playing magic tricks with the truth.

But the bald conclusion held.

At last, mulling things over, growing outwardly calm and composed, Bobo tumbled his eyes down the length of the flamingo-pink carpet, across the spun cotton-candy pattern of the kitchen floor, and up the cabinets to the Jojo-and-Juju-proofed top drawer.

Bobo sat at his wife's vanity, his face close to the mirror. Perfume atomizers jutted up like minarets, thin rubber tubing hanging down from them and ending in pretty pink squeezebulbs Bobo did his best to ignore.

He'd strangled the piglets first, squealing the life out of them, his large hands thrust beneath their ruffs. Patty Petunia had pistoned her trotters against his chest more vigorously and for a longer time than had Pepper, to Bobo's surprise; she'd always seemed so much the frailer of the two. When they lay still, he took up his carving knife and sliced open their bellies, fixed on retrieving the archaic instruments of comedy. Just as his tears had shocked him, so too did the deftness of his hands — guided by instinct he'd long supposed atrophied — as they removed the bladders, cleansed them in the water trough, tied them off, inflated them, secured each one to a long thin bendy dowel. He'd left Kiki's dead pets sprawled in the muck of their pen, flies growing ever more interested in them.

Sixty-watt lights puffed out around the perimeter of the mirror like yellow honker bulbs. Bobo opened Kiki's cosmetics box and took out three squat shallow cylinders of color. The paint seemed like miniature seas, choppy and wet, when he unscrewed and removed the lids.

He'd taken a tin of black paint into the boys' room — that and the carving knife. He sat beside Jojo in a sharp jag of moonlight, listening to the card-in-bike-spoke duet of their snores, watching their fat wide lips flutter like stuck bees. Bobo dolloped one white finger with darkness, leaning in to **X** a cross over Jojo's right eyelid. If only they'd stayed asleep. But they woke. And Bobo could not help seeing them in new light. They sat up in mock-stun, living outcroppings of Kiki's cruelty, and Bobo could not stop himself from finger-scooping thick gobs of paint and smearing their faces entirely in black. But even that was not enough for his distracted mind, which spiraled upward into bloody revenge,

even though it meant carving his way through innocence. By the time he plunged the blade into the sapphire silk of his first victim's suit, jagging open downward a bloody furrow, he no longer knew which child he murdered. The other one led him a merry chase through the house, but Bobo scruffed him under the cellar stairs, his shoes windmilling helplessly as Bobo hoisted him up and sank the knife into him just below the second puffball. He'd tucked them snug beneath their covers, Kiki's brood; then he'd tied their rubber chickens together at the neck and nailed them smackdab in the center of the heartshaped headboard.

Bobo dipped a brush into the cobalt blue, outlined a tear under his left eye, filled it in. It wasn't perfect but it would do.

As horsehair taught paint how to cry, he surveyed in his mind's eye the lay of the living room. Everything was in readiness: the bucket of crimson confetti poised above the front door; the exploding cigar he would light and jam into the gape of her mouth; the tangerine apron he'd throw in her face, the same apron that hung loose now about his neck, its strings snipped off and spilling out of its big frilly kangaroo pouch; the Deluxe Husband-Tamer Slapstick he'd paddle her bottom with, as they did the traditional high-stepping divorce chase around the house; and the twin bladders to buffet her about the ears with, just to show her how serious things were with him. But he knew, nearly for a certainty, that none of these would stanch his blood lust, that it would grow with each antic act, not assuaged by any of them, not peaking until he plunged his hand into the elephant's-foot umbrella stand in the hallway and drew forth the carving knife hidden among the parasols — whose handles shot up like cocktail toothpicks out of a ripple of pink chiffon — drew it out and used it to plumb Kiki's unfathomable depths.

Another tear, a twin of the first, he painted under his right eye. He paused to survey his right cheekbone, planning where precisely to paint the third.

Bobo heard, at the front door, the rattle of Kiki's key in the lock.

Momo watched aghast.

He'd brushed off with a dove-white handkerchief his collapsible stool in the bushes, slumped hopelessly into it, given a mock-sigh, and found the bent slat he needed for a splendid view of the front hallway and much of the living room, given the odd neck swivel. On the off-chance that their spat might end in reconciliation, Momo'd also positioned a tall rickety stepladder beside Bobo's bedroom window. It was perilous to climb and a balancing act and a half not to fall off of, but a more leisurely glimpse of Kiki's lovely honker in action was, he decided, well worth the risk.

What he could see of the confrontation pleased him. These were clowns in their prime, and every swoop, every duck, every tumble, tuck, and turn, was carried out with consummate skill. For all the heartache Momo had to deal with, he liked his work. His clients quite often afforded him a front row seat at the grandest entertainments ever staged: spills, chills, and thrills, high passion and low comedy, inflated bozos pin-punctured and deflated ones puffed up with triumph. Momo took deep delight — though his forlorn face cracked nary a smile — in the confetti, the exploding cigar, what he could see and hear of their slapstick chase. Even the bladder-buffeting Bobo visited upon his wife strained upward at the down-droop of Momo's mouth, he took such fond joy in the old ways, wishing with deep soundless sighs that more clowns these days would re-embrace them.

His first thought when the carving knife flashed in Bobo's hand was that it was rubber, or retractable. But there was no drawn-out scene played, no mock-death here; the blow came swift, the blood could not be mistaken for ketchup or karo syrup, and Momo learned more about clown anatomy than he cared to know — the gizmos, the coils, the springs that kept them ticking; the organs, more piglike than clownlike, that bled and squirted; the obscure voids glimmering within, filled with giggle power and something deeper. And above it all, Bobo's plunging arm and Kiki's crimped eyes and open arch of a mouth, wide with pain and drawn down at the corners by the weight of her dying.

Momo drew back from the window, shaking his head. He vanned the stool, he vanned the ladder. There would be no honker action tonight. None, anyway, he cared to witness. He reached deep into the darkness of the van, losing his balance and bellyflopping so that his legs flew up in the night air and his white shanks were exposed from ankle to knee. Righting himself, he sniffed at the red carnation in his lapel, took the inevitable faceful of water, and shouldered the pushbroom he'd retrieved.

The neighborhood was quiet. Rooftops, curved in high hyperbolas, were silvered in moonlight. So too the paved road and the cobbled walkways that led up to the homes on Bobo's side of the street. As Momo made his way without hurry to the front door, his shadow eased back and forth, covering and uncovering the brightly lit house as if it were the dark wing of the Death Clown flapping casually, silently, overhead. He hoped Bobo would not yank open the door, knife still dripping, and fix him in the red swirl of his crazed eyes. Yet maybe that would be for the best. It occurred to Momo that a world which contained horrors like these might happily be left behind. Indeed, from one rare glimpse at rogue-clown behavior in his youth, as well as from gruesome tales mimed by other dicks, Momo thought it likely that Bobo, by now, had had the same idea and had brought his knife-blade home.

This case had turned dark indeed. He'd have lots of shrugging and moping, much groveling and kowtowing to do, before this was over. But that came, Momo knew, with the territory.

Leaning his tired bones into the pushbroom, he swept a swatch of moonlight off the front stoop onto the grass. It was his duty, as a citizen and especially as a practitioner of the law, to call in the Kops. A few more sweeps and the stoop was moonless; the lawn to either side shone with shattered shards of light. He would finish the walkway, then broom away a spill of light from the road in front of Bobo's house, before firing the obligatory flare into the sky.

Time enough then to endure the noises that would tear open the night, the clamorous bell of the mismatch-wheeled, pony-drawn firetruck, the screaming whistles in the bright red mouths of the Kops clinging to the Kop Kar as it raced into the neighborhood, hands to their domed blue hats, the bass drums booming as Bobo's friends and neighbors marched out of their houses, spouses and kids, poodles and ponies and piglets highstepping in perfect columns behind.

For now, it was enough to sweep moonlight from Bobo's cobbled walkway, to darken the wayward clown's doorway, to take in the scent of a fall evening and gaze up wistfully at the aching gaping moon.   Ω

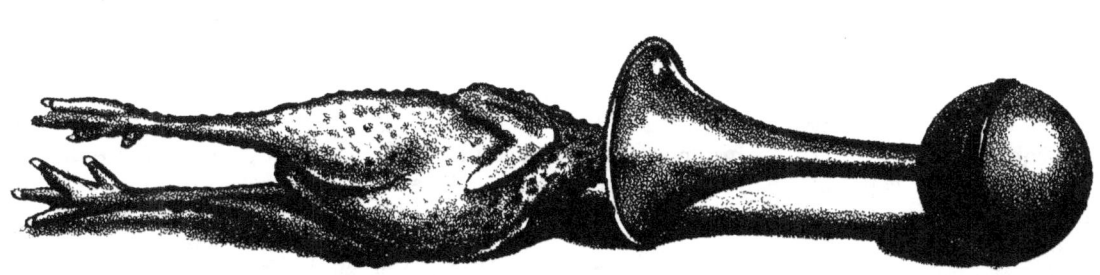

THE DANCE OF THE CORPSES

In cemeteries across the world
A great waltz ensues.
Husbands next to wives
Lovers and the loved
Shrink and dry together
In the great black ballroom.
Earth's pale melodies
Are slow, soft and slight,
The gaunt midnight dancers
Waltzing away to bone.
The rigor mortis fingers
Of lean drawn men
Reach out to ashen cheeked girls
Yet they never reach, never touch.
Each waltz is solitary,
Each dancer alone in his corner,
Yet together.

In one corner, side by side,
As a worm through the soil,
His last living thought,
Now embalmed, reaches for her.
(He died at 20, she at 80.)
And she has newly arrived on the
  dance floor,
Her dress fresh, sweet and pink.
And here he has waited,
In his dusty blue suit, practicing.
No longer apart
The ballroom is theirs.
Now, finally, they carrion together,
In the dance of the corpses.

— **Jason J. Marchi**

ROGUE WAVE

by Gary David Johnson

Now would I give a thousand furlongs
of sea, for an acre of barren ground.
— Wm. Shakespeare

Suddenly, incredibly, impossibly, it was there. Rising, above the deck, above the crow's-nest, finally above the top of the mast itself — and still rising. A towering, menacing black wall of water at first fifty, then seventy, then an uncountable number of feet up into the dark sky, its crest — if even there was one — seemingly lost in the stormclouds above the terrified boy.

"Wh . . . what *is it?*" he choked out, his wide eyes held in thrall by the majestic, dreadful vision.

"It's a rogue! It's a Goddamn rogue!" yelled the old sailor, and he grabbed the boy and threw him none too gently against the nearby capstan. "Kneel down an' put your arms around it," he screamed, "like you was huggin' your mama!"

The boy obeyed instantly, thrusting his arms as far around the cylinder as he could. The old man knelt opposite him and gripped the boy's arms above the elbows. The boy winced but said nothing.

"Now grab my arms, tight as y'can!" the man ordered, and the boy dug his fingers as best he could into the old sailor's sinewy forearms.

The bow of the ship started to rise, with alarming speed and at an even more alarming cant. The boy's stomach seemed to be pushing its way down into his pelvis. The Skipper had taken him into Frisco once, where they had gone up a very steep hill in a very small carriage. It had felt much like this. **Whooosh!** He had been ashamed, then, because he wasn't very sure of himself on land. And he was suddenly ashamed of himself now.

"What do we do now?" he screamed into the wind, trying to sound . . . not unconcerned, certainly, but at least not panicked.

"Nuthin'!" the other voice croaked back. "Just hang on an' pray! As long as we're not broachin', an' if the wave don't break, we still got a chance!"

The ship continued its dizzying ascent up the impossible slope. The boy knew that the other members of the crew must be somewhere near, all gaping at the . . . *thing* which had risen from the sea in front of them. But he was unaware of them. He was alone with the old sailor, attached to the squat capstan like gargoyles on some medieval bell tower. And just as useless.

The boy looked back, astern, into the trough from which they had risen. It was an appalling distance back down into that void. But when he looked forward

again, he was awed to see that it was at least that far again to the top of this monstrosity. He had never seen anything like it in all his years as a cabin boy. And he somehow realized that he would never see anything like it again. In fact, he realized, he just might not see *anything* again.

The ship suddenly pitched forward and down. No, not down. *Flat.* And as the boy looked around, he could see only the clouds and the dark sky beneath. They had crested.

And now the ship began its descent, down the backside of the wave, at an even more dizzying speed than before. The boy braced himself for what he felt must inevitably come next, when, amazingly, the old sailor loosed his grip and stood up.

"Made it," he said, almost too quietly to hear. "Hot damn. Made it again."

The boy was surprised, but he accepted what his elders said and, presumably, believed. So he also stood, noting thankfully that his legs were still capable of propping him up.

The boy went to the rail and looked forward, but there were no new horrors looming before them. The sea was the same sea they had been churning through before that . . . thing had reared up before them so long ago. So long ago? He felt a bit foolish as he realized that the whole experience with what the old sailor called a "rogue" had probably lasted no more than three or four minutes.

It had been a rough sea, but he had seen rougher — far rougher. So what had happened? *What was it?*

He turned his gaze astern and felt, for a moment, as if the ship were rising again, but quickly determined that the sea behind him was sinking. He had turned in time to witness a mountain falling, submerging, back into the sea. Then he felt rough arms grab him, turn him around, and press him hard against a familiar peacoat. Just as quickly, they released him.

"So," the Skipper bellowed, in more than his usual heartiness, "how did you like *that* hill, eh, boy? Better than Frisco, eh?"

Other members of the crew had materialized on the afterdeck, talking loudly and rapidly, and the boy noticed that they spoke with the same odd sort of relieved nervousness he had detected in the Skipper's greeting.

"I didn't much like it at all, sir," answered the boy, and he was puzzled when this response was met with a sudden burst of hilarity by the seamen around him.

"What . . . what was it, sir?" he finally asked after the laughter had subsided.

The Skipper waved his arm in dismissal. "That? Oh, that's what they call a freak wave. It's not a tidal wave, or a storm surge. It's just a . . . freak. It happens every once in a while. No one knows why, it just happens. Now *that* one . . ." he nodded astern, "that one was . . ." He turned back and smiled. "Well, let's just say that everyone gets an extra tot tonight."

A cheer erupted from the gathered crew. They had beaten the wave — or at least survived it — and they obviously agreed that extra whiskey was in order.

The Skipper walked over to the old sailor, who had remained strangely silent.

"You," he said quietly, putting his hand on the old man's shoulder, "you can have as much as you like."

The boy had noticed that the old sailor had not joined in the general merriment resulting from their mutual survival. And even now, with the promise of unlimited access to precious liquor supplies, he still seemed nervous and distracted.

And long, long after the rogue had subsided, had sunk back into the bosom of its mother sea — after the crew had left the deck for their victory celebration and the sea had returned to some semblance of calm (if only in contrast to the monster it had so recently spawned) — the old sailor, with only the boy for silent company, remained at the taffrail, gazing out over the waves as if looking, perhaps waiting, for something.

The entire crew — "Every man-jack of them," as the Skipper might have put it — was still in the main cabin when the old sailor and the boy finally entered. The Skipper had ordered all sails shortened, and now they simply drifted while awaiting first light to assess whatever damages there might be. The Skipper himself had volunteered to keep watch.

The whiskey — what the Skipper quaintly insisted on calling their "tot" — had already done its work. The nervousness so evident on the afterdeck had all but disappeared. But these rough, simple men were honest enough to acknowledge the naked terror they had felt so recently, and so deeply. The talk had never strayed too far from the topic of rogue waves.

The Swede thrust a small cup into the boy's hand ("You deserve one tonight, boy!"), and the old sailor received an entire bottle of his own ("Captain's orders"). He took it gratefully. The Swede then continued his story:

"It was off the southeast coast of Africa. Yah, *there's* treacherous waters if there *ever* was. The Agulhas current, they call it. But that night, the sea was eight to ten foot, if that. And then suddenly, out of nowhere, here's this seventy-footer off to port. Too far away to do any harm, but there it was. I saw it, I tell you. And no reason in the world for it to be there."

"I don't doubt you," said another, a Limey. "I 'ad a mate on the *Princess Charlotte.* She was off the coast of Greenland. And one of these freaks almost rolled 'er over. Killed a bunch of the mates. Some of them they never even found."

The rest were suddenly silent. Then a young apprentice, not much older than the boy, spoke up.

"My old man was off Cape Horn, back . . . oh, 30 years ago, I guess, in that clipper . . . the . . ." He stopped, frustration evident in his tightened features.

"The *Trident,*" the old sailor finished for him, softly, almost whispering. Everyone looked at him. He waved their attention away, taking a long pull at his bottle.

"Yeah, that's it," continued the young sailor. "The *Trident.* One of those things just took the whole damn bow off it. Just like that." He snapped his fingers.

"What happens," the Swede said to the boy as an instructor might say to a pupil, "is that you get perched on top of the thing, like we did tonight. But if you're in one of them big clippers . . . Hell, it can only take it for a second or two. Then it . . ." he shrugged. "It just snaps."

The crew fell into a sort of reverie, perhaps recreating in their minds the image of the thing which had dominated their collective vision for those awful, paralyzing moments. The boy, halfremembering something he had heard the old sailor say, now asked him quietly: "You were in another one, weren't you?"

The old sailor took another pull at his bottle, and started speaking, as if he and the boy were the only two in the cabin.

"Yeah. That's the second one I've seen. They said . . ." His eyes took on a distant look, and the boy realized he was seeing the other one again. "They said it was the biggest rogue — the biggest *wave* — they ever measured. *Scientifically,* that is." He almost sneered the word. "It was a Navy frigate, the *Erie,* back in '33. I was jest a squirt then, like you. But there was this naturalist aboard who said it was a hundred feet from trough to crest." He paused. "An' I b'lieve it. Every goddamn foot of it."

The boy at first hesitated, then decided to speak anyway.

"But . . . but a hundred feet! This one was bigger'n that!"

The old sailor smiled. "Yep. It was," he admitted. "But there was somethin' . . . special . . . about that other one."

"Special?" the boy whispered.

"There's things in the sea that the scientists, with all their fancy instruments, will never explain. But that don't mean they ain't real."

The Limey laughed nervously. "What are you saying, old man? That these waves are . . . *supernatural?* That's — 'ow d'you blokes say it? — that's *bull.*"

"Bull, yourself!" the Swede interrupted. "Let him talk."

And the old sailor *did* talk then, his habitually taciturn tongue loosened by the whiskey. He spoke of things that he had seen in his half-century and more at sea, and of other things that he had only heard of, sometimes in whispers. He spoke of myth, and of heroic sailors from a time when myth still lay within memory. Of times, indeed, when myth was still in the making.

" 'There were giants in the earth in those days'," the old sailor quoted cryptically, slurring the words slightly. "An' in the seas, too. They say three-quarters of the world is water. An' some mighty unusual things can be hidin' in it. You c'n laugh at the stories of the old seafarin' men and their mermaids, an' serpents, an' . . . all the other monsters of the deep. But they didn't make them up. There was always somethin' there, in those seafarin' tales. Chris Columbus himself spoke of mermaids, but he saw *somethin'.*"

The old sailor put the bottle to his lips again, tilting it higher than before.

"Sirens . . . giant whirlpools . . . ghost ships. . . . There's things that, if you're around long enough, some of them you'll see. And you won't talk about them, 'cept maybe to other seafarin' men. Most of them you'll jest hear about. But there's still *somethin' there.* You'll realize that, finally. There's things in the depths that aren't like anythin' on land. They say there's worms on the bottom of the ocean, hundreds of feet long. They got things that live down there so deep that when they're hooked an' brought up, they explode. But down below, before they exploded, they *glowed,* in all that blackness. But they explode by the time they get to the surface, so you c'n only make out bits 'n' pieces of them. But y'get the feelin', lookin' at them pieces, that if you put them back together . . . Well, you wouldn't *want* to put them back together. You jest wouldn't want to *see* somethin' like that."

The old sailor paused to drink again, and the boy shuddered.

"You heard of the Tower of Babel," he finally continued. "And you heard how it was destroyed. It was blasphemous, that tower. *Insolent.* Now think about the *Kronos.* They crowed that it was unsinkable, an' they called it the *Kronos.*" He snorted. "Hell, the name alone was enough t'sink it . . . to *guarantee* it'd go down."

One of the others started to protest, but the old sailor waved him down. "Yeah, I know it wasn't a rogue that did it, but the point is, *it made somebody angry.*"

The boy didn't understand, but he assumed, hoped, that he would someday.

The old sailor continued, seemingly on a completely different subject, "Sure they always happen in rough seas. Sure. That's because *they make the rough seas.*"

"What the Hell are you saying?" the Swede demanded, oddly frightened. But, again, the boy did not understand.

The old sailor put the bottle down and sighed. When he finally spoke again, it was with perfect sobriety.

And genuine awe.

"All right. In the middle of that wave, that enormous wave, I saw a light. A big light."

"I didn't see it," the boy protested. "I was right there. . . ."

The old sailor smiled at him gently. "No. The one in '33, on the *Erie.* I saw a light. Not very bright. It seemed . . . it seemed to be . . . within the wave itself, about halfway up. But it didn't shine any light outward; it jest seemed to glow there, green, like the mornin' sea. At first I thought it was a ship — a gaudy lighted yacht of some sort, caught inside the fury of the wave."

The old sailor himself shuddered, and fear prickled silently among the staring men.

"But then I noticed, about twenty feet farther along the slope of the wave, *another* light, jest like the first . . . jest as high. An' then I realized it: these things weren't ships. They weren't pitchin' or rollin'. They weren't movin' up, or down into the trough. They weren't movin' at all. They were *stationary . . . within* the wave. No, they weren't ships. *They were eyes.*"

After a moment of what the boy felt as almost a *solid* silence, everybody in the cabin seemed suddenly to speak at once.

"You were seeing things, old man."

"Didn't you once report a mermaid off Marseilles?"

"A little too much grog that night, eh?"

The taunts and joshing continued until, quite suddenly again, the crew evidently decided — as a man — to break it up and hit their bunks. The banter was good-natured, but there was a renewed nervousness evident in their voices.

After they had left, the boy heard it, low and distant.

It was a roar, such as the sea might make. But . . . it was not the sea. Perhaps it was merely the boy's too-fertile imagination, brought on by the "tot." But he heard a definite roar, a distant roar, in the now calm and tranquil sea. A roar perhaps of complaint, of frustration, of — perhaps — hunger?

The boy, now alone in the cabin with the old sailor, looked to his companion for insight, for solace, for comfort. The old sailor simply smiled back at him, lowering the bottle.

"Hot damn," he said quietly. "Made it again." And he closed his ancient eyes.

Ω

WHERE THE SUN STAYS FOR THE WINTER

by Nina Kiriki Hoffman

My foster mother gave me a riddle on my twelfth birthday that sent me climbing to the top of the apple tree in the inn's back yard even before the sun was up. "Where does the sun stay for the winter, Mila? Where is it locked up and kept? Look for your present there."

I sat on the apple tree's broadest branch and looked down. The tree's bark felt gnarled and cool against my bare feet and hands. The dew was thick in the grass below, leaving my footprints plain from the kitchen to the base of the tree, green prints in silver. I smelled woodsmoke and baking bread and morning. The sky was purple, shading to lavender along the eastern hills — courting colors, my foster

father called them, when the stars were still out and the sky went velvet; the sky was courting the sun. The moon's prongs pointed up over the edge of the hills. A drift of black smoke rose from the kiln beside Travis the potter's house. Ma got up before the sun on baking days; Travis stayed up all night when he did a firing, to feed wood to the kiln whenever the fire needed it.

The world was morning-still. I heard one of the horses in the stable kick its stall. I glanced toward the inn. Light glowed in the kitchen window. There was Ma, peeling apples at the counter, and slicing them up for my birthday pie.

That had given me a clue. Pa had told me that

apples took sun inside, and that's how they got so nice and fat and sweet. But here I was, on the highest branch of the apple tree, and I didn't see a single present up here.

I stared toward the east and watched the moon lift free of the earth. The wind talked to me about how green and fresh the grass was, and how good the bread Ma was baking would taste. Maybe this was my present, to be up here in the air when the sun rose, so I could see how beautiful it was. But that seemed like cheating. In the four years since I had come to live with Ma and Pa, on birthdays and Christmas they had given me something I could hold.

The sun followed the moon up the sky, washing away the purple and lavender, bleaching it into blue. As its first rays touched me, I saw a last-year's wrinkled, winter-bitten apple hanging on a nearby branch, golden in the sun. Maybe this was my gift. I lifted a hand and the apple dropped into it at my touch.

I lay back on the branch, holding the little apple. My stomach growled. I'd been so excited by my riddle I had left the kitchen carrying only a slice of bread for breakfast, and I ate that before I climbed up here.

Locked sunlight. I rubbed the apple against my shirt, then bit into it. It tasted sweet. Then there was another taste, one I had never tasted before in my years of eating apples in pie and sauce and cider or just off the tree. It was a taste like the smell of a spring night. I felt sad and knew I wanted something but I didn't know what it was, which was how I felt most spring nights. Only this sadness was stronger and deeper.

I ate the rest of the apple. When I finished it, I felt so sad I cried. I turned over and lay on my stomach on the branch, hugging it and sobbing. The sun touched my shirt with warmth. I pressed my cheek against rough bark and noticed how the tears moved over my face once they left my eyes. Was this my gift, sadness? I thought that was something I would get for one of my later birthdays. I lay and listened to the sadness inside me. It had a voice like water flowing over stones.

After a while I sat up and rubbed the tears off my face with my sleeve. I took the apple core out of my pocket and picked the tear-shaped seeds out of it. If sadness was my birthday present, and if I decided later it was a good present, I wanted to be able to give it to other people. I tied the seeds up in my handkerchief and put them in my pocket.

"Mila!" Ma called from the kitchen door. "Time to serve breakfast!"

In the common room, I found only one of our guests up. He smiled as I put a plate of eggs and bacon and hot buttered bread in front of him. He held up his white common-room mug for refilling. I got the coffee pot from the serving table and poured more coffee for him, then went back to the kitchen.

"Did you find your present?" Ma asked me as she braided bread.

"Yes," I said.

"Did you like it?"

"I don't know yet." I looked at her kind, rosy face, her eyes green-gold like ripe apples, her gray hair tied back so it didn't fall in the bread dough. Her apron had flour dusted on it, and small crusts of dough. Was sadness a good gift? If it was, why didn't I know it yet?

"Mila? Louisa?" Travis the potter's voice called from the common room. Ma put her thumb-print on the end of the bread braid to fix it on the pan, and then we both went out to see him.

Ma beamed at Travis, whose arms and leather apron were smudged with black ash. "Have you said a proper good morning to Travis yet?" Ma asked me.

"Good morning, Travis," I said.

"I thought you'd be by earlier, Mila," he said. "Louisa said she'd send you. But since you didn't come, I brought this over for you." He held out a mug like the ones he'd made for Ma and Pa before I came to the inn.

Wordless, I reached for it. It was brown around the bottom, rising through lighter shades with shiny flecks of glass in them to a circle of gold around the rim, a few drops of gold splashing down around the sides. The handle was sturdy and fitted comfortably into my hand. When I looked inside, I discovered a tiny gold owl in the bottom.

"I thought it was time you had your own mug," Ma said.

"Oh, thank you," I said, going to hug her. She smelled of flour. "It's beautiful," I said, to Ma and Travis. I had been here four years, drinking out of the white common-room mugs like any other guest. Now I felt like I belonged.

"I thought you said you found your present," Ma told me as I studied my mug again.

"I thought — oh! The kiln is where the sun spends the winter?"

"If Travis cuts enough wood."

"I got the riddle wrong," I said. "Thank you for my present," I said again, and offered to get everybody coffee or cider or milk so I could drink from my new mug.

Sitting at the table with Travis and Ma, my hands around something made just for me, I thought about sadness. Until I felt so sad, I had never felt this happy. Ω

VALENTINES

by Nina Kiriki Hoffman

Susan sat twisting the silver-gray ribbon in her hands and staring at what her unwrapping had revealed. Malcolm, across from her, sat on the couch with his arms crossed over his chest and half a smile on his face, but only half; the other part of his expression displayed his uncertainty.

The gift was a clockwork heart, with a soft doubled tick that mimicked heartbeat. She bit her lip and leaned closer to examine the heart. Its smooth surface consisted of silver, brass, gold, and copper puzzle pieces, interlocked with such precision that the cracks between them were nearly invisible. Here and there tiny inset rubies shone. She reached out a hesitant hand, touched the heart's cold surface, jerked back, then closed her hand around the heart and lifted it from its black velvet cushion inside the wooden box. She turned the heart over in her hands. "It's — really pretty," she said.

Malcolm's smile flickered and died.

"Clever," she said. "Amazing and beautiful."

"Touch the jewel on the top," he said.

She did, and the heart opened, to display satin-surfaced gears and cogs enmeshed in the ticking away of seconds. She watched the movements, striving to understand. There was a message here. She knew she was deaf to it.

"It's wonderful," she said. "So intricate. The craftsmanship is incredible."

Malcolm glanced away, toward the window. Outside a gray Christmas reigned. "Thanks," he said, and looked back at her and smiled — more than half a smile, but not quite a whole one.

"Open yours," she said, afraid, now. She had given him the one thing she thought he'd want, and now she wasn't sure anymore.

He took out his Swiss Army knife, opened the scissors, sliced away the red ribbon, sliced through the tape that kept the pink wrapping paper tight around the wooden box. He opened the box and stared down at her present, with no expression on his face. She watched. Tears brought tightness to her throat. She realized that her present was dripping. A little red trickled out over the neatly removed pink wrapping paper, leaving a tiny trail.

He reached into the box and took out her heart. In his hand it looked soft and terrible, threatening to break or bruise. It stained his fingers. He cradled it in both hands. "Thanks," he said, a little hoarse.

How often she had asked him to show her his heart. She looked at the artifact in her hands. No matter how beautiful it was, it was still an imitation. And now she had shown him hers, and he didn't know how to handle that, either. "Oh, Malcolm," she said, "I'm sorry. I guess I was pushing too hard. Maybe we should take it slower."

"You don't understand," he said, gently laying her heart back in its box. "Anyway, thanks for trusting me this much."

"I wish . . . I wish you could trust me."

He stared at her a moment, then looked down at the rug. After a deep silence, he untucked his shirt and lifted it enough to show the scar on his chest. "I did," he said.

She held his heart up to her cheek, trying to warm it, despairing of ever learning its secret language.

Ω

THE SHARK

The Great White God
Comes from the deep,
Choosing his own sacrifices.

There is nothing to say to him,
No plea for mercy.
He is The Other.

Beware the sea,
The sailboat's dip and flirt with the wind,
The sparkling beach in summer.

Cling to the land.
There are Gods older than man.

— Margo Skinner

CECILEY IN THE SUPERMARKET

by Nina Kiriki Hoffman

Since the remodeling, the supermarket's produce department had taken on a pool-hall aura, dark ceilings with directional lighting over blocks of jewel-like produce, which were positioned just too close to each other to fit the new double-wide shopping carts between. Mounds of red tomatoes, Sunkist colored oranges, earthy potatoes, and green-black avocados were heaped under the lights like billiard balls sorted according to color. Mist machines over the salad vegetables gave the impression of cigarette smoke, though the air smelled wetter and less flavored.

Ceciley, a large woman in a green shift, peeked beneath the husks of untrimmed corn-on-the-cob, looking for the freshest kernels, ones which would bleed corn milk when punctured with a fingernail. She smelled them, too, so as not to pick an ear too old. Youth was no hindrance — the younger the better. Tiny kernels like baby teeth, pale kernels with only a hint of color to presage the bold yellow of old corn. Their tenderness would please her husband.

No, that wasn't quite right. Their tenderness would please who her husband ought to be. Ralf was never who he ought to be. Who knew what would please him? Perhaps the heads of babies cooked over an open fire. Maybe a salad of chrysanthemums. She shrugged and thumped watermelons. She never knew what to pick up at the market.

As she was turning over steaks to see which one had the least fat, a young man behind the counter in the meat department reached out and pointed to a chuck roast. She looked up at him, annoyed. He had the bloodied white paper apron of a meat cutter, and the small square paper hat. His eyes were intensely blue. He smiled as though he had never practiced anything else. She smiled back because she appreciated energy well spent. He came closer. "I could give you a nice piece of meat," he said.

She straightened. "You wouldn't say things like that if you knew my husband," she said.

"What? Oh, no, I didn't mean it that way. I could trim one of these and re-price it."

"What would you expect in return?"

"Another smile," he said.

"You're a connoisseur?"

"There's a word I never expected to hear in the meat department."

"Surely restaurant cooks shop here? Or do they?"

"No. Usually they have their own supplier. What do you say? A slice for a smile?"

"Somehow that sounds threatening," she said.

"Why not try it? Brighten my day."

"I don't want to be in charge of anybody's day but my own," she said. She picked up the likeliest steak and gave the young man a farewell smile anyway.

She was looking at the colors of queen-size pantyhose, pulling the samples on over her hand to see what flesh tone she ended up with, when the young man approached again. He had ditched his apron and his hat. With his blond curls unveiled, he looked cherubic.

"One more smile?" he said.

"What does a person have to do to get rid of you? Rub your nose in it?"

"I wish," he said, glancing toward her hem.

She frowned. "If you don't leave me alone, I'll call the manager."

He tapped his name tag. MANAGER, it said beneath his name — Mark Galliacci.

She sighed. "All right. What *is* your problem? You like large women?"

"Is that a problem?"

"Hmm."

"I was watching you from up there." He pointed up at some windows she had never noticed before, high in the back wall of the store.

"Watching me smell corn? You *are* perverse."

"Just appreciating you. I like the way you move. Has anyone ever told you that before?"

"Are you trying to score points for originality? You'll never beat Ralf."

"Who's Ralf? Your husband? I don't believe it for a minute. No wedding ring."

"There are covenants and covenants," she murmured. She stared at the young man. "When was the last time you had a date?"

He looked confused. "Yesterday," he said.

"A large woman?"

"Not large enough. Not as beautiful as you." He leaned closer.

"Well," she said, "you can follow me home and take your chances. If that's what you really want."

He lifted her hand and kissed the back. Then he kissed the palm. Then he licked the palm. "Please," she said, snatching her hand away. "Not here."

He followed her up to the check stand and bagged all her groceries himself, smiling all the while. The checker, a pretty redhead, glanced sideways at him, then at Ceciley. She shook her head slightly.

"Does he do this often?" Ceciley asked her.

"Whenever he gets encouragement," said the checker.

"Then it isn't just me. Hmm." She paid in cash. Suppose the boy never came back? She didn't want to leave her name and address in a drawer here where he worked.

He carried the two sacks of groceries out to her maroon Karmann Ghia and put them in the boot. "You know, this really isn't safe for you," she said. "You never can tell what my husband will do."

"Maybe he'll join us," said Mark.

"There may not be any 'us'," she said. "Just because you have a charming smile doesn't mean I want to see more of you."

"But you'll let me come home with you?"

"You certainly are persistent."

"It usually works."

She opened the passenger door of her car. "Climb in," she said.

"Will you give me a ride back to the store afterwards?"

"Probably not."

"I better take my own car and follow you."

"What'll I do with your car after I murder you and slice you up for shishkebobs?"

Even his eyes paled.

"My husband is such a picky eater, I'm always trying new recipes. He's so thin. But strong. Strong as a horse. Maybe two horses. He needs meat to keep his strength up."

He wavered, then smiled. "You're beautiful when you're fabricating."

"You should see me when I'm lying."

"I want to. I'll go get my car. It's a green Gremlin. Don't leave until I pull up behind you."

She tossed her purse into the car and climbed in behind the steering wheel. Perhaps she should start the car and drive off before he appeared. On the other hand, Ralf might like this boy. He liked strays. What he did with them was another matter. She turned the key in the ignition and pedalled the gas, but before she put the car in gear, there the boy was, in a green flat-booted car behind her.

She sighed and started home.

She never knew what to pick up at the market.

Ω

Statement of Ownership. Management, & Circulation required by 39 U.S.C. 3685.

Title of publication: *Weird Tales*®. Publication number 0985703. Date of filing: 1 October 1992. Frequency of issue: Quarterly. Number of issues published annually: 4. Annual subscription rate (in the U.S.A. and its possessions): $16.00.

Complete mailing address of Known Office of Publication, & of the Headquarters of General Business Offices of the Publisher: both at PO Box 13418, Philadelphia PA 19101-3418 (4426 Larchwood Ave., Philadelphia PA 19104-3916). Full name of Publisher: George H. Scithers. Full name of Editor: Darrell Schweitzer. Full name of Managing Editor: Carol Adams. Complete mailing address of Publisher, Editor, & Managing Editor: PO Box 13418, Philadelphia PA 19101-3418.

Owner: Terminus Publishing Co., Inc. Names and addresses of *all* stockholders: George H. Scithers, 4426 Larchwood Ave., Philadelphia PA 19104-3916. Mary Betancourt, 410 Chester Ave., Moorestown NJ 08057. Leslie Smith, 1209 Miller Ave., Ann Arbor MI 48103. David J. Williams III, 5079 Blacksmith Dr., Columbia MD 21044. Darrell Schweitzer, 113 Deepdale, Strafford PA 19087. Yale F. Edeiken, 137 North 5th St., Allentown PA 18101. There are *no* Bondholders, Mortagagees, or Other Security Holders. This is *not* a Non-Profit Organization authorized to mail at special rates.

Extent and Nature of Circulation: (**Average** number of copies during preceeding 12 months, Actual number of copies of single issue published **nearest** to filing date)

A. Total number of copies: Average 9064, nearest 8534. B. Paid or requested circulation (1) Sales through dealers and carriers, street vendors, & counter sales: Average 4041, nearest 3789. (2) Mail Subscription: Average 3224, nearest 3261. C. Total paid and/or requested circulation: Average 7245, nearest 7050. D. Free Distribution by mail, carrier, or other means: Average 34, nearest 35. E: Total distribution: Average 7279, nearest 7085. F. Copies not distributed (1) Office use, left over, unaccounted, or spoiled after printing: Average 1058, nearest 624. (2) Return from news agents: Average 727, nearest 825. G. Total (Sum of E., F. (1) & F. (2): Average 9064, nearest 8534.

I certify that the statements made by me are correct & complete:

George H. Scithers, Publisher.

SKINNED

by Jimm Gordon

Zeb straightened up with a groan and fisted his aching hip, sure that February in Antarctica couldn't be any more frigid than in Montana. The metal pins that held his leg together seemed to suck the cold into his marrow despite the simmering woodstove in the corner. Outside, the wind slashed at the drift-flanked quonset hut. The radio announcer cheerily quoted the chill-factor as eighty below, but promised that there would be blue skies and warmer weather tomorrow.

"Bullshit," Zeb mumbled as he bent over to put another tiny stitch in the .22–250 hole that ruined an otherwise gorgeous coyote pelt. Bought as damaged, by the time he finished it would bring top dollar.

A thrum deeper than the wind's moan prompted him to put the pelt away, force himself up his diamond willow cane and hobble over to the small window set in the tin door. Through the frost-glazed glass he watched a beat-up blue pickup with a mangled front bumper and yellow passenger's door come bucking through the drifts. Injun wagon was the only word to describe it.

He recognized the driver a moment later; grunted when he saw it was Big Pow, and his fingers stroked the hilt of his belt-knife. His profit margin was too low to turn away any customer, but . . .

The halfbreed forced his way out of the pickup and rummaged in the bed of the truck for a moment, then turned, shouting and slashing at the wind with a pronghorn antler tipped with sprig of sage. Zeb tried to see the markings carved into the horn, but couldn't identify which of the many Blackfoot spirits Big Pow was trying to ward off. Probably Wind-sister, he decided.

Big Pow tucked the charm inside his coat and yanked a bundle from the back of the truck, no longer concerned with whatever threat he'd perceived in the wind. Zeb chuckled mirthlessly, remembering the winter he'd spent trapping in the Tobacco Root Mountains with the Little Dogs band of the *Siksika* — the Blackfeet. Wincing as he made his way to the grading table, he wished that old White Calf were around to prescribe something for his hip that would *work*.

The winter of '56–'57 had been a good one for trapping. Cold to prime the furs, but with little snow to hinder the trappers. Elk and mule deer were in plenty, so the camp fed well and didn't have to dig into the meager store-bought emergency supplies until a February blizzard came to bury the mountains in heavy snow. The wind blew savagely for days and the people huddled around tiny wood-preserving fires chewing pemmican and jerky: waiting for the storm to break.

Zeb hadn't minded the confinement because he had fallen in love: Snow Crocus, the big-eyed, honey-mouthed daughter of Zeb's trapping partner, Robert Smokey Door; four-year-old sweetheart who had captured his heart the first time she'd made herself a seat in his lap at supper and fed him the best of the pot with chubby fingers. She pulled at his beard, giggling when he pretended to bite her fingers. She called him Many Beads because of the wide, brightly-beaded wampum belt he sported, and made him promise it as a wedding present when she got big enough to marry him. When he looked at her smiling face a feeling that he'd only experienced when surveying God's creation from the top of Grinnell Glacier came over him — awe and humbleness to be in the presence of such perfection.

One evening she crawled into Zeb's lap, as she was accustomed to, her sparkling eyes bright with fever instead of laughter. Before midnight the family had crowded around the bed where she lay whimpering and exhausting her tiny body with thick coughs.

White Calf had come knocking at the cabin door before the eastern sky had begun to lighten, saying that he had smelled sickness on the smoke.

Zeb hesitantly offered the medicine man the aspirins he'd just dug out of his first-aid kit, explaining that they were good for bringing down a fever, but that he wasn't sure of the dosage for so small a child.

White Calf had gravely accepted the small brown bottle. "I am familiar with aspirin, Many Beads. It is made from the inner bark of willows, which we've used for fevers since the beginning of time."

Zeb fretted as the old man examined his little darling, his concern lessening a bit when he saw Snow Crocus quiet at White Calf's gentle touch on her little-girl's brow.

From under his coat the shaman took a much-decorated parfleche, and unfolded it, not objecting when Zeb leaned forward to examine the collection of twisted roots, leaves, twigs and less identifiable things it revealed.

"We will use your aspirins to help with the fever," the shaman explained, shaking two white tablets into his wrinkled palm. "Also warrior's root to slow her heart which flutters like a frightened sparrow, and spruce buds and yarrow for the cough."

He pulverized the ingredients with the hilt of his knife and sifted them into the pot of steaming water he'd asked Robert's wife to prepare, giving instructions for how long it should steep and how often to give the child draughts of the elixir. Zeb was reassured by how the medicine man diagnosed and prescribed much like any white doctor.

Then White Calf turned to Zeb with a glint of humor in his eyes. "This is where Blackfoot and white medicine differs." With that he took the big knife used to crush the medicine and gashed his thumb, letting the blood drip onto the fire and beginning a long round of atonal chanting.

Zeb listened for a moment, then slit his own thumb and picked up the simple chant feeling that somehow the blood and song were profoundly right for the situation, and at their worst they couldn't hurt the girl.

The chant ended when the blood clotted. Through the smoke White Calf had looked at Zeb for a long while, and — seeing a glimmer of understanding there — had explained:

"The medicine is for the disease, the blood to appease the unhappy spirit."

White Calf waved at the smoke and continued, "I know you do not believe. White men ignore the spirits. They have lost their ability to feel them. This has made them powerful in some ways — weak in others.

"The Blackfeet can feel the spirits moving among us. We know they are there the way you know the wind is blowing. When they are happy, we are happy; when they are angry, they must be appeased; sometimes they can be persuaded to be helpful. Remember this, Many Beads; it is better to try to appease a spirit than fight it."

White Calf had risen and left without waiting to see if Zeb had understood anything that he had said.

Big Pow banged the door shut behind him and stood a moment, blinking and inhaling hugely. The air in the dimly lit fur-room was woodstove-warm and rank, with a queasy, predator's-den reek. Clusters of rich fur — sunset-colored fox, pale ghosts of coyotes, dark chocolate mink, mottled bobcats and lynx — hung along the walls like fetishes guarding a shaman's cave.

"Middlin' cold," Zeb commented.

Big Pow grunted and walked over to flop an old canvas sea bag onto the table. He scanned the room, visibly gauging how much money was represented along those walls. Again Zeb's hand caressed his knife.

"You are a rich man, Many Beads," Big Pow sneered, slurring the nickname into a near-insult.

Zeb kept his words cordial. "Not hardly, Pow. My customers are rich. I'm just a poor old trader that pays too much and gets too little." He put his hands on the counter firmly, "Show me what you've got to trade."

Big Pow looked down from his six-feet-four-inches, frowning at the edge in the crippled trader's voice, but opened the bag.

Zeb caught his breath as a thick roll of silvery plues was pulled from the shabby canvas bag. Even folded and unbrushed they were some of the finest beaver pelts he had ever seen. Only the icy ponds and streams of Glacier Park could produce beaver so pale and rare.

Zeb squinted up at the halfbreed, but said nothing. Taking a few beaver from a national park was far down on the list of laws Big Pow regularly shattered.

Ruffling long guard-hairs with sensitive fingers and gauging color and quality with expert eyes, Zeb graded them solemnly, then measured the plues with a grease-stained yardstick, adding lengths and widths for sizing.

"#1 X-pale," he scribbled on the flesh sides along with the sizes: four average, thirty blankets, two super-blankets — all perfect. Big Pow, or his squaw, knew how to handle fur.

"This all you brought for me?" he asked, pretending to figure their worth in a pocket notebook. A dickering gambit, he already knew close to how much they'd bring back east and what his opening bid was going to be.

Big Pow's lips opened, and a gold incisor glinted. "Lock the door."

Zeb looked up and matched the hulking trapper stare for stare. "I don't deal in anything illegal."

"I know. Lock the door."

Zeb held the other's eyes for a few seconds more, then limped to the door and locked it. When he turned around Big Pow was laying another pelt onto the table.

"What the Hell are you trying to pull?" Zeb growled as he stomped toward the table and reached for the hide. "A green cougar. My ass!"

He snatched the pelt up, intending to throw it on the floor like trash, then froze. As his fingers touched the delicate guard hairs he felt his heart lurch, and knew in his bones that it was *real*. The fur was the finest he'd ever seen; soft as a kit beaver's down, but long and luxuriant; able to hold in body-heat better than goose down. But the colors were impossible: satiny silver-green. It lay there shining as genuine as emeralds in platinum.

Zeb considered that it might be the dyed skin of a snow leopard for a moment, like the one he'd marveled at in the big fur show at Harrod's; but even the pelt of that ultimate fur-bearer would look like a mangy jack rabbit's compared to this.

Zeb squinted up at Big Pow, but the half-breed stood fingering the bear-and-eagle claw mandala that hung from a thong around his neck, his face a tanned leather mask.

This is for real, Zeb thought. This is my chance. It'll only come once. "I'll give you eighty dollars."

Big Pow snorted. "This ain't no beaver blanket. Forget it. What'll you bid on my plues?"

Zeb forced himself to put the wondrous softness down and turn away from it. His hands ached to snatch it back up.

He shook his head mournfully — the traditional start of the dicker. "Twelve hundred, Pow. Beaver's down this year."

Big Pow snorted again and narrowed one eyelid.

"Well, maybe eighteen — if you throw in this one." Zeb's hand crept back to stroke the silken smoothness. "That's a fifty dollar average. You won't do any better at Beckman's." He spat a gob of tobacco juice on the much-stained cement to clear the name of his main competitor from his mouth.

Big Pow leaned forward and spat himself, just missing the fur trader's boot.

"Twenty-five hundred."

Zeb choked. His fingers worked the ultra-fine hairs between them.

"Only way I could do that was if you throw in the castors. And I'll still be taking a bath on the deal."

Big Pow's yellowed fangs showed. "Twenty-five. As is."

Zeb's common sense screamed for him to walk away. "Keep the beaver. I'll give you three hundred for this oddity by itself."

"Twenty-five. All or nothing, Marler."

Of their own will, Zeb's hands gathered up the pelt and placed it on the shining beaver; as a priest might settle a communion cup on an altar cloth. Cursing himself, he opened the battered tin cash-box and counted out twenty-five hundred dollars in bank-fresh hundreds and fifties.

Big Pow licked his thumb and insultingly counted the bills again while Zeb glared. They spoke not another word as Big Pow strutted to the door and Zeb stumped over to lock it behind him.

Slowly he returned to the table, sure that now that his money was gone some glaring flaw would meet his eye to show him for a fool, but the pelt lay like a pool of liquid treasure on the table, its surface shining like that of a deep lake on a windless day; hinting at unguessed depths.

"I hope to Hell you are real," Zeb murmured.

Without warning a spasm of crushing pain grabbed his hip, nearly forcing him to his knees. He clung to the cane with clenched teeth until it passed. There was a storm coming, all right, despite what the radio johnnies said.

When the spasm had faded to the normal throbbing ache he squeaked open the lid of the cash-box and sighed. The deal with Big Pow had about wiped out his operating money. The trading season was over for him one way or another.

His mind drifted back to his cabin in the Big Belts. If the oddity was genuine it might bring enough for him to retire on and buy back the land he'd sold to pay off the hospital. He let the dream shine for a moment before reality reminded him that the mountains were no place for a cripple. That life was closed to him.

Packing his furs for transport took two hours. When he had them ready he returned to special pelt and let his fingers and eyes feast on its glory till the window in the door showed only star-pricked black. Not daring to leave it behind, he wrapped it in heavy brown paper and slid it inside his shirt. When he walked out into the wind it tingled against his skin, making the hairs on his body prickle up.

Home was Room 314 in the Empire Hotel. Once the pride of Great Falls, now its rooms went for twenty-seven dollars a week: no cooking in the rooms; transients welcome. The place smelled of moldering velvet and better days.

Zeb kicked the empty short-dog that lay in front of his door down the hallway and unlocked the ancient dead-bolt, shuddering at the phlegmy coughing that sounded through the wall across the hall.

Once safe from prying eyes, he pulled the package from under his shirt and unwrapped the pelt with shaking fingers.

He hissed and stepped back. It glowed. Really glowed, like Halloween paint. An aura of pale blue lay on it, like thin morning fog. Tiny sparks winked here and there on the tips of mussed hairs.

"What in Hell are you?" he whispered.

A jolt of cold pain bit his hip as if in reply.

"Hello Zeb, whatcha eatin' tonight?" Burt called to him as he entered the dimly lit Stables Bar and Grill.

" 'Lo, Burt. Give me a bacon cheese and a bottle of beer, please."

He eased onto one of the red-vinyl stools and laid his cane on the counter; dug a cigarette out of his pocket and stared into the smoke as if it might hold an answer to his questions.

A man flopped down on the stool beside him and banged an empty beer bottle down, shaking Zeb from his thoughts.

"Ho. Many Beads. My friend. Will you have a drink with me?"

"Evening, Joe." Zeb grinned. "You already drink up the money I gave you for those coyotes this morning?"

Joe Comes-at-Night laughed and said in his soft Blackfoot lilt, "No, my friend. I would be dead if I drank up all the money you paid me. I gave it to my woman. I kept fifty dollars."

Zeb hoped that was true. He'd waved to Joe's wife and the brood of brown-faced kids waiting in the pick-up while their father traded his furs.

"Bring one for Joe," he said when Burt placed the long-necked brown bottle in front of him, judging from experience that the invitation to have a drink meant that Joe was tapped out.

"You are a good man, Many Beads," Joe said.

Zeb wound up buying Joe dinner as well. He bought for the rest of the evening. Joe was good company, and Zeb didn't feel like going back to his room right away. He blamed the feeling on his stiff leg.

"You know what happiness is, my friend?" Zeb said through the warm glow of his fifth whiskey-with-beer-chaser. "Happiness is a cabin high up Hound Creek in the Big Belts. Trout stand in line to grab your hook and the beaver are pale as the winter moon. Bull pines roar and aspens whisper."

He took a melancholy swig.

"I had it once and lost it. I'll be going back now. Once I'm settled in those hills I won't come out again for love nor money."

"A man who settles down in a lodge needs a squaw to cook his elk and skin his beaver," Joe slurred. "Maybe you should ask this one to go with you," he leered as the barmaid came to clear their empties and set a fresh round down. She rolled her eyes and sauntered away. Zeb and Joe admired her gait as she crossed the room.

Zeb raised his shot glass. "Here's to the jiggly-pocketed women of the world — God love 'em." They knocked back their drinks and laughed, pounding the table at their wit.

Joe belched and smacked his lips at the flavor. "So, my friend. You have had some luck? How will you buy this perfect land?"

"I bought a pelt today that will make me rich enough

to retire," Zeb bragged.

Joe looked astonished. "One pelt? Of what, a white medicine buffalo?"

Zeb lowered his voice and motioned Joe's ear close to his lips. "I don't know what it is. Looks kinda like a cougar, but the fur is long and silvery green. Some animal that's never been discovered before. I'm betting that the Smithsonian or National Geographic will pay a fortune for it."

Zeb sat back ready to accept Joe's congratulations, but the Indian was sadly wagging his head.

"You have been tricked, my friend. The buyer of skins got skinned himself."

"What the Hell is that supposed to mean?"

Joe hesitated, then answered, "The animal you describe is a spirit animal, not a real one."

"My ass. I've got the pelt back in my room."

Joe shook his head slowly. "*Staau Ai-kokutuyi-mistakists-katsu. Staau Sikstakiu-ixts-Koku'tyi-kitssta'aiks,*" he informed Zeb mournfully.

"What?" Zeb asked. "*Staau* is spirit. You said, "spirit of the mountains with teeth," or something. What do you mean?"

Joe squiggled his bottle on the table, making wet rings.

"C'mon, Joe, it's me, Many Beads."

Joe looked up and stared at Zeb, the visible traces of his drunkenness gone. When he spoke, his voice was so low that Zeb could barely hear it. "It is something that grandfathers tell about. He-Makes-The-Ice-Mountains-Sleep. Biter-Of-Souls.

"At the beginning of time, *Napi,* the Good Man, put a spirit in the Backbone-of-the-World to keep the ice mountains from coming down and covering the land of the Blackfeet. A fierce spirit-cougar with blue eyes and green fur." He shrugged and made a lop-sided grin. "It is just a story."

Zeb felt a chill finger run down his spine. "You come back with me and look at it," he insisted. "It's no fake. And it damn sure ain't no ghost."

Joe shrugged and they got up.

"Who did you buy this pelt from?" Joe asked once they'd stepped outside and the frosty air had cleared away more of the booze-fog.

"Big Pow."

Joe stabbed at the air with his fingers and spat. "He is bad medicine. His mother was a Raven woman — evil. He kills eagles and bears. Sells their parts and leaves the bodies to rot."

"I heard animals aren't all he's been known to kill."

Joe shrugged. "Mostly white men. That is not as big a crime." They laughed and shared Zeb's last cigarette as they walked across the icy street to the Empire. The fur trader didn't try to shake off the hand that gripped his arm at the slick spots, but he cursed and fumed inside.

Zeb took the package from under his mattress once they were in his room, unwrapped it slowly, then stepped back.

Joe's eyes grew to the size of eggs. He moaned, backing away until his spine slammed against the wall. "Zeb Marler, you must put this on top of a

medicine pole and leave it," he husked.

"My ass. I damnear bankrupted myself to buy it. I respect your religion, Joe, but I'm not going to break myself."

"*Sikstakiu-ixts-Koku'tyi-kitssta'aiks* is very fierce. You must do it for your own safety," Joe pleaded. "It is not dead. Can't you see the spirit light that shines from it?"

Zeb snorted. "If it's a demon, how the Hell did Big Pow get a hold of it?"

"Perhaps he found it sleeping and stole its skin."

"A man needs to have an awful light touch to be able to steal a critter's hide without waking it up," Zeb observed.

"*Sikstakiu-ixts-Koku'tyi-kitssta'aiks* sleeps once every hundred years. When he sleeps, he sleeps deeply."

Zeb tried to put his hand on Joe's shoulder, but the Indian flinched away. "Come on, Joe. I believe that your people have seen this kind of animal before and it's awful rare, but it's just an animal, like a beaver or bobcat."

Joe inched along the wall until his hand rested on the doorknob. "Many Beads, I tell you true. *Ai-koku-tuyi-mistakists-katsu* will be coming for his skin. He has the medicine of the ice mountains; do not doubt it."

Zeb shook his head. Joe wasted no more time trying to convince him, nearly tripping in his haste to get out the door.

Zeb shook his head as the rapid footfalls faded down the hallway. Demons. Ghosts. Still, it was a good story. Having a legend to go with the pelt would make it all the more valuable.

Yawning, he bolted the door. It had been too long a day and he'd drunk too much. Weariness descended on him like a load of flour sacks. He smoothed the pelt, reveling in its feel and beauty. He felt a wild urge to cover his naked skin with it; bathe in its power; steep in its mystery. Instead he laid the paper over it and fell into his bed. He watched the hint of blue glow that came through the folds of paper until sleep came.

Eyes. Eyes in the north and west; burning with blue fire and knifing through the darkness. It moves with a blizzard on its back; surrounding it, concealing it, pelting it.

Down from the mountains of ice. Down through the tree-line; through the foothills of gnarled-fingered aspens and onto the plains. The wolf hides his face into his tail and whimpers. The grizzly rouses with a snuff from his winter's sleep and softly moans.

Across the coulees and buttes it sweeps. A murderous rumbling undertone rips the limbs from river-bank cottonwoods. Where the eyes touch, ice-knots shatter.

It rests for a brief moment on the bluffs above the wide valley, glaring at the spill of lights that hold back the night. It lashes its storm-tail and shrieks — rage and hunger — then pounces down from the cliffs and onto the city.

Zeb jerked awake as the wind crashed against the hotel. "Sonsabitches!" he cursed. Those assholes at the

Weather Bureau were never right.

He winced at the raging pain in his hip and back as he got up and peered out the window. The snow was coming down so hard that the street light on the corner was a faint glow.

He stuck a finger in his breast pocket to find a cigarette, then stopped and leaned toward the glass.

Far out there was a blue light. He wondered, what the Hell could be bright enough cut through this blizzard?

The light moved closer, resolving into two ovals. They rushed at his window. Zeb stumbled back against the far wall and threw up his arm to cover his face.

The storm exploded into the room like a demon. Zeb felt flying splinters of glass thud into the wall around him. Sparks of pain dotted his body.

A snarl cut through the shriek of the wind. Zeb opened his eyes and wailed. A . . . cat . . . glared at him from across the room: massive as a tiger, skin gleaming through the storm-light like frozen pearl. Snow coiled outward from its body like thick white snakes. Wind howled from its maw. The eyes ate at his soul with teeth of ice. From a lower fang, whipping in the wind, hung a familiar wheel-shaped medallion on a blood-stiffened cord.

Zeb edged toward the door. His hip banged into something. The dresser. He slid his hand along the top, through the little drifts of snow on it. His fingers touched the crackle of paper, slid beneath it to entangle themselves among silken strands. Cold fire burned his fingertips.

He pulled the fur from under its covering and held it toward the creature. "What's yours is yours, *Staau.*"

The cat snarled — *not enough!* A rock-like paw flashed out to smash the cane, and Zeb fell heavily onto the floor.

Numbed by the cold and terror, Zeb struggled into a sitting position and pulled his boot-knife; opened his shirt and slit a line from breast to navel. Cold bit into the wound like a flame. He rubbed the pelt's whiskers in the steaming blood. He croaked out the chant he'd learned from White Calf long ago.

The cat stood stiffly unmoving in its blizzard, watching with those eyes. It moved forward to place a paw on Zeb's belly. He groaned at the tearing pain, but kept chanting, determined to face death with open eyes.

Sikstakiu-ixts-Koku'tyi-kitssta'aiks growled softly and turned its soul-eating eyes away. Zeb gasped in relief as the pressure was removed from his stomach. With a howl, the creature snatched up the pelt in its teeth and hurled itself out the window.

Zeb slumped down, the wind no longer there to hold him up. The skin at the edges of his wound was blackened as if by fire from the beast's paw. His bones felt as if they'd been shattered and reglued. Across the floor his cane lay, splintered and useless.

He pulled himself up the side of the dresser to his feet, letting out a small scream of agony. The thought came to him that it might be better just to lie there in the snow and die. At least it wouldn't hurt as much.

But the part of him that had forced him to crawl from the face of Chief Mountain when the fall had smashed his leg pushed him to make his way to the door, to warmth and life.

When he got the door open and felt the rush of warm air, he turned to look into the room again. It definitely looked as if some ice demon from Hell had smashed around in there.

He noticed his footprints in the snow. Something was odd about them. Where was the scuff and twisted print from dragging his crippled leg? The tracks were straight and sure. Unbelieving, he pressed on his hip. It hurt, but no more than the rest of him. He looked down to see that the foot no longer turned in.

He laughed and walked a few sure steps in amazement. The chant he had learned from White Calf had been one of healing; the ceremony, one of supplication and appeasement.

"*Ya-ta-hay, Staau,*" Zeb murmured. "Thank you for your gift."

He strode down the hallway, feeling suddenly suffocated by the hallway, the hotel and the city. . . . Feeling too large to be hemmed in by their narrow trails and coulees. He needed to walk across mountains, tasting clean air and eating before a hunter's fire. And, by God, he would.

Ω

WHATEVER IT IS

What is it that whispers in the night?
It is not the wind — it is not the wind.
What is it that darkens the window pane,
Vaguer than shadows, veiling the light?

What is it that keens a sad refrain,
Mournful as souls that have suffered and sinned?
What is it that cries in the pelting rain?
It is not the wind — it is not the wind.

It is not the wind with sepulchral chill,
That sighs through the branches, barren and dead.
It is not the wind that sweeps over the sill
To stand, a dark giant, beside my bed,

Where quivering, I lie, my blood cold
    and thinned.
Whatever it is, it is not the wind.

— **Stanley McNail**

BUCK, GLORY RAE, & THE THREE LITTLE PIGS

by John Gregory Betancourt

The day they move in, I give them till dinnertime before paying my traditional welcome-to-the-house social call. I should be jaded, inured, the way people flow through these doors; but each new arrival strikes me as keenly as a church bell pealing on a still summer morning.

Glory Rae answers my knock. She has her hair up in a red handkerchief and over her shoulder I can see the wreckage of the living room, buried waist-deep in boxes.

"Can I help you?" she asks.

I hold out a foil-covered dish. "I just wanted to welcome you here, Mrs. Osterman."

She accepts my present, looking puzzled. "Do I know you?"

"I live next door," I say. "I hope you don't mind, but I called the realtor and asked your name when I saw the **Sold** sign. I'm really glad you got this place — it needs children. A pity about the Johnsons having to leave so suddenly."

"I heard Mrs. Johnson had a nervous breakdown?"

"Something like that, yes. She claimed this house was haunted and went all to pieces over it."

Glory Rae laughs. "I don't believe in ghosts."

"I can't really say, myself. I must know plenty of people who've seen strange things . . ."

"My uncle used to drink, and he'd see the little people."

I smile. "I wouldn't know about that. But poor Ruth, it really shook her, thinking this place was haunted. It's always sad when it happens to someone so young." I nod for emphasis. "But I didn't come to mourn the loss of one set of neighbors, I came to celebrate the coming of a new one. A very pretty one, if I may be so bold."

She smiles back, raises a corner of the foil, and takes an appreciative sniff. "Tuna casserole?" she asks.

"I hope you like it."

"It's very kind of you," she says, backing up a step. "Won't you come in?"

"I know how busy you must be . . ." That's the way you play the game, give them a chance to escape.

"No, really, I could use a break."

"If you're sure it's not an imposition?"

"Of course not, Mr. —?"

"Call me Buck." I smile. And reel her in.

Glory Rae's husband is dead, it turns out; she doesn't offer details and I don't pry. I can find out anytime I want, anyway: her kind is always so easy to read. She works as a receptionist in a factory to keep her children fed and clothed, and dreams of going to Beauty School. I have a sort of knack with people, and she opens up at once, thoughts and words spilling over each other so fast I have trouble keeping up. And as we talk, she oozes that special type of charm women have when they're looking for a husband. Not that an old geezer like me — age 666, thank you, and mostly retired these days — would be fair game. But I can tell she's hunting.

My first glimpse of Glory Rae's children comes when they tumble down the stairs in a laughing, giggling heap. They seem all light and sunshine; like their mother, they have startlingly blond hair, but cropped short and with tails in back. She's dressed them alike in bib overalls, and from the moment I see them all I can think of is the Three Little Pigs.

I have no sympathy or patience, but feign it well enough. Children have always disturbed me. They see with a clearness their parents never know.

Back, back through the years I can still see them: bunched like rats around my coal-cellar door in their knickers and high-button shoes and little red caps, a midnight gathering, each dared by another to come, all giggling and telling horror stories of the old man inside. "He worships Satan," they whispered then. "He eats human flesh, and he poisons all the dogs and cats he catches in his yard."

True, true, *but how did they know?*

Glory Rae introduces her brood one by one. I nod politely to each, Joey (age 3), Ricky (age 6) and Patrick-not-Pat (age 8).

"You can call me Buck," I say, and smile.

Joey hides behind his mother and peeps out, wide eyed. Patrick and Joey mumble a hello. They are all clearly uneasy at my presence. Perhaps they sense something about me which their all-too-sane-and-rational mother cannot.

Run, little pigs, or I'll huff and I'll puff and I'll blo-o-w your lives down. I grin at each and ruffle their hair. They dance back out of reach.

The casserole leads to my staying for dinner, exactly as I'd planned, and as we sit around the kitchen table (again lost in a sea of boxes), I feel the age-old call to the hunt. Glory Rae has a strength, a vitality, that makes my mouth water and my hands shake. I long to taste it, to tear it from her. With no husband around, it will be easy, not the slow seduction I needed for Ruth

Johnson.

Slowly I let my facade of age slip away: the gray recedes, the hairline inches forward, the teeth grow straighter, ever so slightly whiter. Am I 65 — or 50? 50 — or 40? I can see the doubt begin to creep into her eyes; she reappraises me. *Perhaps he might make a good husband after all.*

Yes, yes, this is what you want. I can feel it. But you must ask me, I cannot take what you do not give.

She licks her lips, hesitates. "Buck —"

That night, I make love to Glory Rae. I am thirty going on thirty-five, handsome, confident, everything Bill was to her. The game is over. She can refuse me nothing now.

There is a certain inevitability about everything I do, in more than the physical act of entering her body, of caressing her, of devouring her soul. I have centuries of practice and experience to draw upon. She is mine, as surely as hundreds of others have been mine.

She screams in pain/pleasure, and I smother her lips with kisses, my mind piercing hers. I see all the layers peeling back, and at the core lies a lost and lonely woman. Grew up in a small town. Met Bill at a church dance. Married him, followed his career (architect, how trite) around the country. Allowed herself to be wooed into the domesticity of housewivery. Then — Bill dead in an automobile accident, so sudden, and how sweet the tang of loss.

I drink it all in, and when there is nothing left, push deeper, into primal feelings. *Lust. Greed. Ambition. Love.*

Ah, love. Her children swim here, larger than life, alongside a glowing Christlike icon that can only be dear departed Bill Osterman. How perfect the skin, how piercing the eyes, how loyal and sympathetic the expression. Idealized, pasteurized, blended with God and Daddy and dreams. And perhaps hidden somewhere just a tad of reality.

I suck that in, too, make it part of me. It buries (for a time) my own true self, buries the darkness within that threatens to overwhelm all that I once was. For a second I am alive —

Then Glory Rae moans and abruptly lies still, eyes fixed on the ceiling. *Empty.* No more dreams, no more ideals, no more pleasures or pains or joys or fears. Just a bland sort of grayness inside.

I touch her cheek softly, wistfully, wishing I were human, wishing I were Bill. Sated, I withdraw.

I dress, walk catlike down the stairs, let myself out.

Next morning, as I lie abed, I can easily imagine the scene next door:

Glory Rae is asleep, her skin ivory, her breath coming soft and rhythmic, hair haloed around her head. How peaceful she seems, how deathlike her sleep.

Suddenly one of her children comes in. Suppose it's Joey. He climbs up beside her, all light and motion, and shakes her awake. She turns blank eyes on him.

"Mommy," he pleads, "it's breakfast time."

"Breakfast . . ." she murmurs, and begins to rise with mechanical grace, pulling on housecoat, houseshoes. The fires within her have dulled; her mind has chilled. She looks around, but I am gone. Was I real? Uncertainty flickers through her. But it no longer matters, so quickly it fades. As everything will fade now, in her drab, soulless life.

It's all so familiar. The lack of dreams, perhaps she will notice that as she lies abed at night. And perhaps she will notice her sudden loss of appetite, of ambition. But surely it's nothing Valium cannot fix if she goes to a doctor.

Little Joey tugs her arm, gets her moving toward the kitchen.

It happens this way every time. I sigh.

How beautiful Joey is, the image of Bill Osterman made young and small.

Then for the barest moment I feel a pang of guilt. No, I am not beyond these emotions; I feel them more keenly than any human, since I feed on them, need them to survive. Perhaps that is the worst part of my eternal curse: with every soul I take, I become a little more human.

Bill is part of me now, the dream Bill, the idealized Bill. I revel in the life I — *he* — created: how sweet little Joey is. Now, hunger slaked, I can appreciate the finer things. Little Joey, partly my son. How I . . . *love* you.

It makes my skin crawl, but I know the truth. My needs outweigh my morals. Next time I hunger, I *will* come for Joey, a wolf wrapped in the skin of a father returned from the grave.

And I will suck him dry. Ω

ANTONIUS BEQUEATHED

by Tanith Lee

Silvesta was late for the funeral. She wore a black costume, long black hair, and pale violet gloves.

The old chateau lay in a forest and was not quite simple to reach. A private plane had deposited Silvesta at the forest's edge. From here she had had to continue on foot along a winding and in spots rather overgrown track. The forest was nearly black, dense with pine and larch and hung with ivy. Sometimes the faces of wolves might peer out at Silvesta, or a hare bound away. Birds sang in the trees and frogs croaked at hidden pools. Otherwise Silvesta saw no life for two hours, until she reached the gates of the chateau, an impressive building of stone, with round, crenellated towers and galleries of windows.

An elderly servant admitted Silvesta and led her up into a wide hall on the second floor. Here the other mourners were assembled. The priest had already addressed them, and they had begun to follow him out of the room. Silvesta joined the end of the procession. She knew nobody there. Everyone wore black and a stern expression, but none were in tears. The corpse, which was that of an aunt of Silvesta's she had never met, was borne on a bier draped in purple, by four tall young men in black top-hats, and wearing masks, of an owl, a fox, a locust and a crocodile.

The party went up many flights of stone stairs, with griffons carved on the bannisters, and eventually emerged on to the broad flat roof of a tower. Here the chateau dead had been buried for years.

All around were long granite vases, some six feet high or more, from the top of which spilled varieties of prolific flowers. In the centre of each flower bush might generally be discerned a brown human skull, each in a different stage of decay.

The priest took up his station by a flowerless vase five and a half feet in height. As he spoke the words of the service, two gardeners shovelled some rich black soil into the empty vase. Then the four top-hatted, masked young men drew Silvesta's dead aunt from her bier, and lifting her high in her lace frock, let her down slowly into the jar until only her head showed above the rim. The gardeners quickly filled in the vase with soil, and packed it tightly around the dead woman's neck until even the pearls in which she had been buried had disappeared.

The priest concluded his words and folded his hands. A hunchback appeared and went to the vase. From a bag he took some white seeds, like grains of rice, and climbing up a small step-ladder, put them carefully into the mouth of the dead aunt. The chief mourner, a gaunt woman with beautiful false teeth, tipped the hunchback a little bouquet of notes.

Everyone went to the dead aunt, and sprinkled about her head some fertilizer from a crystal scoop. Most had to ascend the step-ladder to do so, and the more decrepit ones had to be assisted up and down, making feeble anxious sounds.

When this ceremony was over, the mourners moved below again into the house. A light rain had begun to fall on the forest. Silvesta paused to look at the vase of a recent death, whose head had not yet completely rotted. From its greenish dough a myrtle had started to grow strongly. These were perhaps the remains of her uncle, who, the previous year while out shooting, had been killed by pigeons.

In the hall of the chateau the funeral guests were given cakes and wine, and then the will was read by the chief mourner.

Silvesta paid little attention to the will. She had no expectations of it. Instead she gazed at the stained glass pictures in the tops of the windows, which showed scenes of violence and murder from the Bible.

"And to my niece, Silvesta," said the chief mourner suddenly, with a snap of her beautiful teeth, "for her special care and protection, I leave Antonius."

All the other mourners raised their heads and stared at Silvesta.

Silvesta said: "What's that?"

"It is being brought," said the chief mourner.

Just then the door opened and in came two of the servants, propelling a large silver cage on wheels. As the cage rumbled nearer, it was possible to see inside an armchair, in which sat a very ancient, slender, white and almost transparent old man.

The servants opened the door of the cage and the ancient old man got up from his chair and came out. He stood beside Silvesta.

"This," said the chief mourner, "is Antonius. He is now yours."

"But what am I to do with him?" exclaimed Silvesta. None of them answered, and so she turned to the old man himself. "What am I to do with you? Surely you belong here?"

"I am yours," said the ancient man in a voice like a thin shaving of steel.

"This is ridiculous," said Silvesta. "I don't accept you."

"It was your aunt's dying wish," said the chief mourner.

Silvesta smoothed her gloves, and left the room. She descended the chateau and let herself out of the door. As she walked towards the gates, in the fine rain, she was aware of a narrow white shadow at her heels. The ancient man was following her.

Silvesta re-entered the forest. The canopy of the trees was so thick no rain fell through, and very little light. The ancient man glimmered behind her. Silvesta turned.

"It's a long walk. You'd better go back."

"I am yours," said the ancient man, "Silver Star."

Silvesta quickened her pace. Surely he could not keep up with her for two hours?

But the ancient man, Antonius, did so.

Now and then, the wolves looked out of the pines, but Silvesta barely saw them, she was so disturbed. She hurried until finally she was running, but Antonius trotted after her; his ankles might have rested on springs.

At last she came to the edge of the forest and saw her plane waiting on the meadow.

"You must go back now," said Silvesta firmly.

"I am yours. I shall go with you."

"There's no room," said Silvesta.

She walked to the plane and got in, and the ancient man climbed in after her. She tried to push him out but he was both resilient and adamant and somehow he had arrived in the seat behind her.

Presently the plane took off with Silvesta and Antonius aboard, and flew back to the city.

Silvesta lived in a marble block overlooking the river. She was a designer of unusual clockwork animals, whose creations were very popular. Even the Mayor was often seen with a furry orange flamingo with two heads which Silvesta had designed for him.

The apartment had a studio, a bedroom, a garden room, a bathroom and a kitchen. It was full of plants, masks, weapons, statues, small trees, architectural finds, books, jigsaws, games, dolls, and furniture. Now there was also Antonius.

Antonius sat down in Silvesta's peacock chair and switched on the television. He dialled the sound up very loud. Once the television had been put on like this, it was never off, except for a few brief moments when Silvesta turned it off. Then Antonius would turn it on again.

Antonius did not sleep, so the television was also on all night.

Because he had no teeth, Antonius did not eat anything solid. He would therefore go to the kitchen and put everything he could find into the blender, whole oranges, cashew nuts, cold chicken, zucchini. He made these gruels several times a day, and often during the night.

Occasionally he would go about and inspect Silvesta's rooms. He would take down swords and spears and leave them lying in a tree, or the bath; or books, which he hid in cupboards. He put a doll into the washing-machine and started it.

When Silvesta left the apartment, Antonius would follow her. Sometimes she would rush across busy intersections, but somehow he always kept up. She could not lose him in the most crowded store.

He spent two hours every morning in the bathroom and two hours every evening.

He wore Silvesta's clothes, without asking her. They fitted but did not suit him, and he spilt orange and cashew gruel on them.

"I want you to go!" shouted Silvesta.

"I am yours," said Antonius.

One morning, after her normal sleepless night, Silvesta went out, and as always Antonius followed her.

She led him to the centre of a savage park where half-wild tigers were allowed to roam, and most visitors stayed in their cars.

"Do you like this tree, Antonius? I hope you do."

And so saying, Silvesta handcuffed Antonius to a low bough.

Then she went for the day to the sea.

That evening, when she returned, two florid kind people were waiting at her apartment door with Antonius.

"We found him for you in the park," they said, beaming. "How worried you must have been."

"He was handcuffed to a tree," added the florid man. "The things these old fellows do!" And he winked at Antonius, who was wearing Silvesta's golden skirt and four-inch heels.

"One of those naughty tigers was licking his feet," put in the florid woman. "I gave it a Choco-Bite."

After a month, Silvesta brought some of her acquaintances to the apartment and showed them Antonius.

"What a wonderful old man," they said.

They told Silvesta how exquisite Antonius was, added things to his gruel, turned the television up even louder for him, and soon went away.

Silvesta did not sleep and could not work. In her studio she could hear the television even over the blasting music she played, and the sounds of the blender breaking again on a meat bone. In the city shops Antonius came after her like a ghost. In the elevator mirrors she saw his white image, behind her left shoulder.

Exhaustedly she conducted him to an antique tea party, and two lovely cobwebby old women took a fancy to Antonius. But, as they presently informed her, "He says he belongs to you."

Silvesta packed a bag by stealth. She left her possessions and her apartment, evaded Antonius, and flew to another city. On the third day a police escort howled into the street beneath her hotel, and next Antonius was brought up to her room.

"Here you are," they said. "How worried you must have been."

In the second month, Silvesta remembered something. She went to a firm of specialists who twelve days later delivered an amazing cage. It had a remarkable bathroom cubicle that required no maintenance, and in the open area was a comfortable armchair. It was quite difficult to get Antonius into the cage, but the burly men managed it, glaring at Silvesta afterwards and mutely accepting her large tip. Through the bars Silvesta slipped tiny earphones into Antonius' ears, and then turned on the television picture for him.

A blessed silence filled the apartment.

Silvesta worked in her studio all day on a blue feathered buffalo that sang Strauss. In the evening she made Antonius a gruel of roses, onions and Mozzarella cheese — one of his favorites.

Antonius did not eat the gruel. He sat staring at the silent television that only he could hear, and large silver tears slipped down his white pure ancient face.

"Why?" said Silvesta. "What more do you want? Do you want to drive me mad?"

That night in the silence she could not sleep. At dawn she let Antonius from his cage. He went at once to the apartment bathroom where he remained two hours. Then he came out, splattered the kitchen with avocado and halibut, turned up the television to gargantuan pitch, and concealed a Samurai sword in the arbutus.

Antonius followed Silvesta to a dark glass building in the lower area of the city.

Seated on one side of a desk, with Antonius standing at her left shoulder, she detailed what had occurred.

When she had finished, she signed a paper, and a vast volume of notes changed hands.

Then two gigantic men came in. They wore snow white and looked impossibly wholesome. They lifted Antonius between them, and carried him away. He did not protest.

Silvesta said, "But he'll be well treated? Loud television, and his gruels . . ."

"Of course."

When Silvesta emerged from the building of dark glass, she went up in a helicopter to a high place. She sat there for hours surrounded by cedars and syringa.

When she got back to her apartment, she was tense and wary, but no one was waiting. No one came.

Some days passed, and some nights. The silence was profound. It grew and blossomed. Silvesta had a firm of professional cleaners in to see to the kitchen. When they had gone every trace of Antonius was obliterated. A last crossbow surfaced from the humidifier. All was calm.

Silvesta had dreams of a white figure riding after her on the back of the blue buffalo. She drank heavily for a month, until she no longer saw Antonius behind her shoulder in the mirrors of elevators.

After that she made the Mayor a yellow lemur with three tails, the Earth turned, and Silvesta rebecame herself. She donated Antonius' cage to a famous aviary.

Some new apartments had gone up in the middle of the river. In the topmost one of these, the party was to be held. Silvesta, in a long white gown, joined some of the guests, who were gazing down from the balcony at a brown jade slice of river lapping the base of the building eighty feet below.

One of the guests had a striped parrot on his shoulder which was a design of Silvesta's. The parrot went through its tricks, and the guests questioned Silvesta about her work and her success. She was a celebrity, and they treated her with astonishment and great respect, so a transparent wall seemed to form all about her, isolating her from everyone.

It was the mode to drink a mauve wine, that tasted like cold iron, and Silvesta did not drain her goblet.

On the table was a pot out of which a pretty miniature tree was growing. The tree bore fruit the shape of tiny lemons and the colour of pomegranate hearts. In a dish lay a heap of the fruit already plucked. The hosts invited the guests to sample it.

"This is my aunt," said the hostess, pointing at the small fruiting thing. "It's the latest method. They shrink the cadaver and pop it in a pot. Then they plant one of these little trees. A lovely memorial. And the dearly departed can always be with you."

She petted the tree, and went on to confide she made a jam from the fruit, and leading them to an enormous fish tank peopled with fat black finny ovals, she demonstrated the feeding of the jam to the fish. The fish plainly relished it.

"They're carnivorous," said the hostess. "I suppose the jam . . ."

Some of the guests did not seem pleased that they had chewed and swallowed fruits nourished on an aunt's corpse.

But Silvesta sank into a reverie, remembering all those years ago, when she had attended the burial of her own aunt in the vase. As she was doing this, the other bright guests leaving her alone inside her walls of transparency, Silvesta passed before a tall skeletal mirror. She stopped in surprise. In the mirror was a very old woman in a long white dress and long white hair, and wrinkled ashen skin. It was Silvesta. Seventy years had gone by since the funeral at the chateau. How quickly and playfully they had gone, changing her one iota at a time, and now suddenly here she was. Silvesta studied herself with interest. At her back a few of the guests spoke of her complacently, knowing her as well as an heirloom. She was extremely deaf now and could not hear what they said.

Silvesta turned from the mirror and moved towards the door of the apartment. The host and hostess regarded her exit benignly, for an old and eccentric celebrity was permitted to behave as she wished.

Out on the street, Silvesta summoned a helicopter. She noticed how streamlined and shiny it was, an unfamiliar model. The helicopter rose into the peach-bloom sky, and bore her away to the building of dark glass which, over seventy years, had added further angular terraces to its heights.

She was driven by a strange compunction, perhaps of guilt or sorrow, she did not know.

When she had reached the inner chambers of the building and explained her case, she had to wait more than an hour while computers sorted through the institution's records. Finally a man with a beaded scalp entered the room and opened a file before her which Silvesta could no longer read. He read aloud to her solicitously.

"No," said Silvesta, "you've made a mistake. I've only come for the remains. He was an old man then. It's been seventy years."

"Yes, yes," said the beaded man, soothingly. "But you see, we have it here. A room with a bath and television. Gruels ten times a day. Money has been extracted automatically from your account."

Silvesta had made so much money she had not missed these payments, evidently.

"If it's true," said Silvesta.

"But it is."

"Then I should like to see him at once."

"Someone shall take you to his apartment."

Silvesta said that she would prefer that the unbelievably elderly person be brought to meet her here.

The beaded man set off to see to this, and another half hour went by. Silvesta sat still on a couch, watching a moving news mosaic on the wall about countries she had never heard of. Then an ancient man, pale as ice, was guided into the room.

Silvesta stood up. She was utterly astounded. He had not changed as she had done. He was just the same.

She went towards him hesitantly.

"Antonius?" she asked, in her reedy voice.

"I am yours," said Antonius, "Silver Star."

Silvesta took him in her arms.

Since she no longer slept, Silvesta and Antonius would sit up all night, watching television with the sound very loud. Sometimes they played games, and now and then one of them would take something from its place in the nine roomed apartment, and hide it somewhere for the other to find. Although Silvesta had kept all her teeth through the wonders of modern dentistry, they were very fragile, and she was happy to eat the exciting gruels she or Antonius prepared in the unbreakable blender. For two or three hours in the morning and the evening, they companionably bathed together in the bathroom. They had no secrets from each other. They talked and talked, about everything. He never called her Silvesta, but always Silver Star.

Quite often they went out, and wandered the city hand in hand. In the park they fed the tigers; these beasts were now quite tame, although they occasionally attacked cars. As Silvesta and Antonius rose together in the elevators of stores, Silvesta would point to Antonius in the mirror. "There you are."

Antonius smiled.

One day they visited a display of mechanical washers, wearing each other's clothes, and put a bag of oranges into the works. Juice and pulp sprayed the audience. Silvesta and Antonius hurried away before they were caught.

In secret, Silvesta left Antonius in her will to the daughter of the Mayor. Then she hid the will in a lacquer box, and went to watch Antonius watching television. Ω

WEIRD TALES TALKS WITH NINA KIRIKI HOFFMAN

by Darrell Schweitzer

Weird Tales: You are a somewhat newer writer than most of our featured authors, so, could you start off by telling the readers something about yourself and how you got started?

Hoffman: I've been writing since I was ten or eleven. I started writing a ghost story because I couldn't find enough books to read that I really liked. I was writing for my own pleasure. This ghost story went on for something like ten years until it got to be five hundred pages long. I'd go back and reread the parts I liked the most. Now I see that it's not a book at all. I started writing like that, and then every night before I'd fall asleep I'd make up serial stories. The next night I'd make up the next chapter. Sometimes I'd stay up all night because it was so interesting.

Then, when I was twenty-five, I took a story to a convention workshop. I'd taken some courses on writing in college — but they never tell you anything about how to prepare for publication. They didn't tell us how to mail things out or market or anything like that. People would just sit around and critique each other, but not in any informed fashion. So I went to this convention workshop and that was the first time I'd actually heard anything that I could use to try to get the story into shape. I didn't sell that particular story at that time. But Eileen Gunn, who was on that panel, thought it was a great story. She kept bugging me about it. Finally I showed it to Jessica Salmonson. She bought it. That was my first sale.

This was around 1981. I started taking stories to conventions on a regular basis. In 1982, a bunch of us in Moscow, Idaho — these were members of the science-fiction club — were sitting around saying, "We want to be writers. We don't know how, but we're going to start a workshop." So we did. The members included Dean Wesley Smith, a guy named Steve Fahnestalk who now lives in Edmonton, Lori Ann White, Victoria Mitchell — she has a *Star Trek* novel out now — and some other people. We got together every Tuesday night, and pretty soon those who were determined to actually sell something scared off everybody else, and it was just the core four members, Lori, Steve, Dean, and me. We all took stories to the Norwescon short-story workshop. That was a really rude awakening, because all the pros got together and started talking about the people who submitted stories and said, "These are really wretched stories. What do we tell these people? Do we want to tell them how to fix these stories or how to write in general?" Lori and I were in the workshop where they put the worst stories.

I stumbled across one of these professionals, Dick

Kearnes, when he was in the hall talking to someone; and when he found out that I was in that workshop, he said, "What do you want me to tell you?" and he gave me a choice: "Fix the story, or learn how to write." I said, "Well, I guess I want you to tell me how to fix the story." It was like he had a bet with someone else, and they'd said I'd rather learn how to fix one story than learn how to write.

But in any case, he and George Guthridge and J.T. Stewart came in and they'd decided they were going to tell us how to write. So they told us the Scott Meredith seven-point plot outline, which I had never heard before: things like, you have a beginning, a middle, and an end, and specific things happen in each part. I had never heard that before, but a little light went on. Also, they workshopped my story, and I felt terribly wounded and then I was riding home — it's a seven or eight hour drive from Seattle back to Moscow — and I started getting madder and madder and madder! I decided I was going to fix that story and I was going to sell it and I was going to prove something to those guys.

So I went home and I thought about the seven-point plot outline and I remembered all the things they'd told me in critique and I fixed the story and I sent it off to *Asimov's* and they bought it. It's the only time I've ever sold anything to *Asimov's*.

That was my second sale. Then Dean and I decided we wanted to go to the Clarion Writers' Workshop and find out more, so we both went that summer. We learned a lot. That, basically, is how I got started.

WT: You are one of the clearest examples of someone who emerged through writing workshops. There are professional writers who hold that workshops are a bad idea and you'll come out as part of a group-mind. You've heard all this, but obviously it's not true. Possibly you're uniquely situated to tell us why.

Hoffman: I've heard that when people go to Clarion they all come out homogenized and they all write the same things. I haven't experienced this. I read things by various Clarion graduates and none of them seem alike to me. I think people take their individuality into it and they get whatever they can out of it. When I was there, I heard completely different things than what Dean heard, even though we heard the same speeches. We were each picking up what we were ready to hear and ignoring the rest, which didn't apply to us at that point. People pull out of these experiences what they're ready to work with. I took a lot of notes, too. If I go back and look at my notes, I find things I can understand now that I wasn't ready to incorporate at that time.

As far as what makes me different, I don't know. I

think that what I want to read in a story is different from what I find in books. So that's the kind of story I try to write.

WT: I suppose it's hard to qualify what makes a typical Nina Hoffman story. Well, they're usually short, and they usually involve somebody in a psychologically odd situation — such as the one *Weird Tales®* ran about the woman visited by the ghost of her future self which tells her to kill herself —

Hoffman: Not quite like that —

WT: It *sort of* starts that way — which only proves my point. How would you describe a typical Nina Hoffman story?

Hoffman: I'm interested in people who are under pressure. I am interested in writing about people I like, that I'm intrigued by. I've gone through a long process. When I started writing, before I knew how to put a story together, I'd just think of some character. I'd think, *this person is really neat. I really want to find out what he does. Let's put her in a haunted house. Let's have him walk down the street because I really want to find out what he'll do. She's so much neater than I am.*

That was a lot of it. I'd make up these people who were smarter. They were braver; they were stronger; they could do all these really neat, magical things. Then I'd try to figure out how they would respond in all these situations that I would be scared of.

That's really evolved a lot. I still have this whole stream of writing that I just write for my own pleasure, and it will never see the light of day. But when I'm trying to create something that will work for other people, I start with a person with a problem. This goes back to that Scott Meredith seven-point plot outline. But I want them to be people I'd like to spend some time with, so I can write about them and really figure out what happens to them next. At the same time I may have an idea I want to think about. I wrote this really weird story about abortion called "Life Sentences," which is in *The Year's Best Horror* this year. It was a matter of *What do I really feel about this whole topic?* I use stories to explore issues. I want to find out what they might mean to me.

A lot of the time the material is coming from some place I don't understand. It's from another source that I think of as beyond me. I ask the question. I put it out and get the answer back.

It's a weird process. It does start out with character-with-problem, then a situation, but then, if I can't figure out what's going to happen next, I take a nap, and usually when I wake up, I think, *Yeah, the next step is* — Or, I lie in bed thinking, *Well, let me consider these characters some more. Who are they? Where do they come from? How would I really feel if I were in that situation?*

I like to explore people. I don't know if they're very realistic people, but they're intriguing to me.

WT: Are these characters aspects of yourself? I should think that, considering how many stories you've written, you would either have to deliberately make *this* character different from *that* one, or else the cast would go into reruns very quickly.

Hoffman: [Laughs.] What do you think?

WT: I think there must be an element of deliberate artifice in this. Is the presence or absence of such artifice

the difference between what you write for yourself and what you write for the public?

Hoffman: I can tell you one thing. I came from a family which had seven kids. There was also a housekeeper and her daughter. So I came from a big household. Now this is one thing that I tend to do over and over again — you haven't seen this because it's the stuff I haven't submitted yet — but I'd write about this big house full of people, not consciously based on my family. I have several of these "households." In one of my novels, which I've got to rewrite before I can sell it, there is a whole community of really weird, magical people, and there's a town with all these interrelationships. I like to have a whole bunch of people who have to relate to each other on a family level. Then the characters get out and have little stories about themselves.

That's where "Exact Change" came from, for instance. Those are two characters from some big, central thing that I wrote for myself.

The story "Little Once" that was in *Weird Tales®* — that's the origin story for a character I know as a grownup, that creepy, monster guy. He's in other stories. So all these things connect. In the "Ceciley in the Supermarket" story, Ceciley is the one who married the guy who was a baby in "Little Once."

So, if anyone ever does a concordance, or if I do, all these things connect on another level. All these groups of people I have been making up since I was twelve years old are actually creeping out into the world in the form of these stories.

As far as how they're different from each other, I think I observed a lot of people interacting on a lot of really weird, dysfunctional levels while I was growing up. I think that comes through in the fiction too.

WT: There are three theories of the origin of authors. One is that they are born that way; another, that they are made — they acquire authorship through training — and a third is that they're *bent.*

Hoffman: I think bent has a lot to do with it. I wonder about this because I see my siblings being very creative also. I think we had a hard time growing up, but the pressure and the environment led us to take these channels to expressing ourselves.

WT: If you're sufficiently famous one day, will the public ever see that submerged mass of stories — the rest of the iceberg, rather than the tip you've been showing us?

Hoffman: It's gotten lately so that I write a bunch of novellas and I show them to people I know, and they really like them. The response I've gotten has been really positive, so I'm getting less and less afraid to show the stuff that's close to my heart.

I think that when I write stuff now, the result does come out closer to something that's marketable, just because that's the way I've been working for the past nine years.

But I don't think I'll ever show people the teenage stuff where I didn't have any idea what a story is. Wait till I'm dead.

WT: Surely the ones closest to your heart are the ones which will carry the most conviction and therefore have the most emotional power.

Hoffman: Yes, I think that's true. I think things are working out now so I can give the heart stories out to the world, if the world is interested.

WT: One major element in these stories is obviously the autobiographical. But what is the function of the fantastic element?

Hoffman: The fantastic element keeps me from getting bored. It provides a spin that I suspect couldn't exist in real life, so I can keep playing with things. It's also a matter of asking for answers from my own mind. The stories teach me. I don't know what's going to happen ahead of time, though I may have a vague, cloudy idea of how the whole shape of the story will be. I write them to find out what happens next. The fantastic gives me whole other areas of play. It's a way to examine things. It gives me a tool.

WT: Which isn't there in literal realism.

Hoffman: When I contemplate writing something mimetic, based on what I perceive life to be, I just get bored from the start. I think about writing in other genres, and I never do, at least I haven't so far.

WT: To get back to the idea of artifice, there is something in fiction which is deliberately made up. This is how we distinguish between fiction and folklore. Folklore lacks the element of *deliberate* invention, and so a folk tale only seems fantastic to people who don't come from the same cultural background. In a fantasy, as opposed to a folk tale, there's an agreement between the author and the reader that this is a made-up story. So, a story, any story, requires a self-conscious and deliberately artificial element to it. Possibly this is what was lacking in the ones you were writing as a teenager. So, for you, now, what is the degree of deliberately making it up, as opposed to the degree of genuine feeling?

Hoffman: One of the things I have learned to do is to supply tension. I used to hate to do anything mean to my characters. I didn't want to afflict them in any fashion. I wanted them to be safe, because I liked them a lot. What I've learned is that tension is what pulls the reader through, that people who are in trouble are very intriguing. The reader is looking to see if the characters will survive various weird experiences. Somehow that gives us information we need. That's why a story gets read all the way through. You're reading to find out if these people will survive, if these people will solve their problem or gain their goal. That's something I had to learn in order to sell stuff.

WT: It sounds like something they shunned in the college courses, the p-word, *plot.*

Hoffman: [Laughs.] I don't think I had any college courses that were quite that weird. I went to Santa Barbara City College and they were a little more practical than that. But they didn't really know how to communicate about it.

WT: Perhaps this was because, unlike the writing workshops, the college writing courses were not actually taught by writers.

Hoffman: They weren't taught by writers, and selling stuff for money was not something that most people thought was a good idea at that time. We didn't even talk about sending things in the mail. We'd just turn things in and read them and talk about them.

WT: Do you still participate in workshops? A usual result is they leave you with a desire to teach.

Hoffman: I go to a weekly workshop every other week. There's a workshop in Eugene, Oregon, that's been running since 1987, and I drop in there. I don't usually turn stories in because I discovered later in my workshopping career that when I would turn stories in, I would hear them critiqued and then I'd take the stories home and put them in a drawer. So that wasn't working for me. I started realizing that the stories I didn't workshop were the ones I'd rewrite and send out. And they'd sell, or a lot of them did anyway.

So workshops stopped being valuable to me. But I do participate in workshops at conventions because I feel that I know the pitfalls, that I can tell people some basic things which will help them. I do like to teach.

WT: Do you think workshops will benefit all new writers, or are there people who, while they may have talent, just don't belong there?

Hoffman: The second. I think workshops work for some people and not for others. It really depends on your temperament.

WT: How much reading in fantasy fiction did you do before you started writing? Did you have a solid background in the field?

Hoffman: I read a lot of science fiction. I started going to the library a lot when I was a child. I got wonderful stuff there, Andre Norton, Alan Nourse, Edgar Rice Burroughs. I read some Robert Heinlein, not that early-on, but a lot of great stuff for kids. So I read all the stuff in the children's section of the library, and then I started reading grown-up books. I read all the science fiction I could find, and I read fantasy. I was reading five books a week.

But the more I started to write, the less SF I was reading. I don't know why that is, but when I would go to read something to relax I would read something a little less challenging than science fiction. I'd want to find something that didn't demand anything.

I still read a lot in the Young Adult field, because I think there is a lot of exciting writing going on there. That doesn't deter me the same way that the challenge of science fiction does now.

WT: What are your tastes in horror fiction?

Hoffman: I don't read horror very much. I talked to Kim Antieau about this. She doesn't read horror either. She writes a lot of it. We seem to have horrific things to say.

WT: Therefore you're not writing in the genre just because it's commercially hot. There are people who just sit down and say, "Well, horror is selling now, so I'll write horror." Usually the result is a formulaic imitation of Stephen King. You know, there's this small town which is menaced by a Thing, but only the kids know about it, and the parents don't believe them, so after several bloody deaths the kids have to confront the Thing on their own . . .

Hoffman: Actually, Dean Smith and I tried to figure out how to write Minute Mysteries for *Women's World.* It was like fifteen hundred words, five hundred bucks; it sounded great, so we'd sit around and try to figure out how to write them. We'd write them and send them off, and sometimes they'd come back with a little "Sorry" on the bottom of the form, but we just couldn't get the formula down. That's the closest I've come to trying to write to a particular formula. Usually I just have to write what's bugging me at the time.

But I also think that the fiction I've written that's appeared isn't generally a clear reflection of what I've written because I've also written a lot of stuff that didn't sell or that I never sent out. I have a lot more fantasy in my files than I do horror. The horror is the stuff that sells right away. The more spooked I am by it, the more icky I think it is, the sooner it sells.

WT: I should think that you have two contradictory impulses at this point: one to read up on horror fiction to see what everybody else is doing, and another *not* to read up on horror fiction, so you'll avoid influences and remain unique.

Hoffman: Somewhere in the middle. There are some books I'd really like to read in the horror field. I read some Stephen King. I have read some V.C. Andrews, but they had this weird, icky fascination that I don't like to see in myself. I'm creepily fascinated by the books, but I hate the fact that I like them and I'm just not going to read them anymore.

I would like to read the Dell Abyss line. I have some of those books at home and I'd like to see what Jeanne Cavelos is doing. That looks intriguing. I've read some Steve Rasnic Tem short stories that I find just incredible. The stuff that we're publishing at Pulphouse I usually typeset or proofread, and there's a lot of horror stories there that I find fascinating.

WT: How about your novels? You've mentioned writing novels. Have any been sold or published?

Hoffman: I haven't published any books except two collections of short stories so far. I have some novels with my agent. I have one big fat book and seven or eight novellas. One of the novellas is under consideration with an editor at this point. I don't know if I've sold it or not. The rest of them need work, but I'll be getting them out pretty soon.

WT: Are you thinking more in terms of what you have to do to further your career at this point?

Hoffman: As much as I try to think about that, it doesn't seem very natural to me. It feels like nice things are happening. I don't feel like I have to go out and agitate for them. They just seem to happen.

WT: Can you think of any incident in your life which influenced your fiction and made you turn out this way?

Hoffman: I grew up in Southern California, which is a very weird place to grow up. There are fads which sweep across the state like wildfire, and they change everybody around and then they are gone. You think that each one is going to be permanent, it's going to be the final answer, and then something else comes along. So you can never trust what's going on because you know subconsciously that the next thing that comes along will sweep it away.

This is the way my mother lived. She would always be looking for answers and hoping that she would find something that would fix the family.

In the late '60s there was this thing called Co-counseling. That's when lay-people get together and one person is the listener and another is the person being counseled, and they switch roles halfway through the

session. This took over half my family. Suddenly they were doing this thing. There were all these guidelines. They'd go off to workshops and learn how to be co-counselors, and whenever they were upset about anything they'd run into the back bedroom, and one of them would cry and scream and rage for a while because they were discharging the negative emotion before it clouded their thinking.

So I had two brothers and two parents and a couple of others who went off and underwent this process, and it seemed as if each went away as one person and came back as someone else. I was completely creeped out by this. It was part of wondering, *What is reality?*

WT: This indeed is why reality is not all that certain in your fiction.

Hoffman: [Laughs] That's something you've noticed . . .? This *Invasion of the Body Snatchers* type of thing — I think that's a really basic fear, that people will come back as something else. You won't recognize them and they won't take care of you. Actually, Co-counseling had a very positive influence on my family because they got rid of a lot of behaviors that were destructive and menacing, but they were somebody else and I wasn't used to them.

WT: I suppose that's why we're all afraid of brainwash cults.

Hoffman: I didn't have that knowledge at the time. The Moonies weren't around yet. But it was spooky.

WT: The curious thing about horror fiction is, of course, that the more spooky and disturbing it is, the more we *like* it.

Hoffman: I've wondered about that. I don't understand why people ride on roller coasters. I hate them. I don't understand why people scare themselves. I think there's an adrenaline rush, some sort of high they get, but I don't like it.

WT: But you do it.

Hoffman: I have theories about this. I read in the psychology field because I always want to figure out why people do what they do. There's this whole thing about identifying with the oppressors. As a child I was terrified of horror movies. I'd have nightmares. But I'd sneak down and see them whenever I could, and I'd get my brothers in trouble because they let me watch horror movies. Then I'd go screaming to my mom and say, "My brother let me watch this movie." Then I'd have horrible nightmares and my brothers would get in trouble. Still, I was fascinated by it. Then, when I grew up it was as if I were invoking my powers of darkness and scaring other people, as if I'm becoming this abuser or oppressor. That's so buzz-word, but sometimes I think that's what I'm doing. [Laughs]

WT: It's been suggested that horror fiction is a *safe* scare. You're going to a place you couldn't explore in real life, but in fiction, you can.

Hoffman: I like that theory too. I heard Steve Barnes talk about that, where he pointed out that the audience goes to the horror movie and they scream, *"Don't go in there! Don't separate! Turn on the lights!"* But the characters are always too stupid . . . so we all know we'd do better.

WT: I would suggest that we're not actually scared by movies like that because they're so stupid. The ones that actually scare us are the ones which are genuinely intelligent, like *The Haunting* or some of the better Val Lewton films.

Hoffman: The original *Night of the Living Dead* is like that. The people are all real. They all have their own agendas, but they band together and try to work things out. I found that one terrifying and extremely well-crafted.

WT: Have you ever come up with a story which is either too frightening to write or too frightening to publish?

Hoffman: I tried to write a horror novel. It turned out to be so creepy that . . . it became a novella. It's under consideration right now. I'll be very curious to see how people respond to it if it does come out. It's all the horrible things I could think of. Maybe there are deeper depths of terror, but I haven't gotten there yet.

WT: It may be like Co-counseling, only you're doing it with yourself.

Hoffman: I do believe that's true. These things are helping me solve my own problems. My mother used to be very upset. She said, "Don't show your therapy to the world." But if the response I get from people is that it works for them, then it's all right.

WT: Does other people's "therapy" in their fiction work for you? If you come away from the story with some greater understanding, then it must have worked for you.

Hoffman: There is a Susan Palwick story I've read that was really great. It's about a mother trying to take care of her kid on one of those days when everything is going wrong, and the puppy's barking and everything like that. You wonder why do mothers put up with this stuff.

Ultimately in the story you don't know, but I just thought it was so amazing to see her put that on the page. It's so true.

Then there's a Steve Rasnic Tem story that's going to come out in an issue of *Pulphouse*. It's about this man writing these stories he doesn't dare show his children. They're all based on fairy tales, but they're all creepy. It raises the basic question of *How do we take care of our children?* That intrigues me a lot.

And there is some David Bunch stuff. He did some completely creepy stories for literary magazines in the '60s, and we're doing reprints of those. They're completely *awful*, but they're very good, and they make me think.

WT: They also make you feel. It seems to me that making you feel comes first. Thinking comes later. But if you aren't emotionally moved by the story, no amount of message or thought-content will keep the reader interested. Any story you remember is a matter of how you felt when you read it.

Hoffman: I think that's true. If the story makes you feel, you turn it into a memory which is part of your internal works. The stories that made me feel I remember more often. They come up in various situations. They come back. They haunt me.

WT: Do you ever write as exorcism, so that something which haunts you will stop haunting you, now that it's on the page?

Hoffman: Yes, I do. I write because something won't leave me alone, because it just keeps manifesting itself whether I want it to or not. There are all these things I've written when I didn't know why, and finally I'd figure out that there was this stuff going on and I was trying to deal with it. This is the best way I know to deal with it. Things terrify me and they shock me. I keep working on ways I can believe people operate, the most charitable way I can believe.

I read Alice Miller's books. She wrote one on why Hitler turned out the way he did, *For Your Own Good*. For me it helped explain why people go on doing these things.

WT: What are you writing now or do you plan to be writing in the near future?

Hoffman: I've finished a collaboration on a young-adult novel with Tad Williams. It's going to come out from Atheneum, we hope, sometime this year. I intend to rewrite my novellas and novels and get them into a shape where they're ready for an editor to look at. We'll see where that goes. I want to write more books. I want to write more short stories. It's not a very clear picture, but I do know that I've set my schedule so I have a couple days a week to write. I've been trying that for about a month and it's really working.

WT: Let's tell the readers where they can find your stories.

Hoffman: I've had a lot of work in *Pulphouse*. I've had stories in *Weird Tales*®, of course. I've had stories in *Amazing Stories* in the small, digest form. I've also been in Charles L. Grant's anthologies and several others.

I suppose if I have any secret agenda in writing it's that once in a while I think I have a clue about how people work, and I want to let others know. I wrote this story called "Waiting for the Hunger," which appeared in Charles L. Grant's *Doom City*. It was about a vampire with an eating disorder. She's a binge-eater and she can't stop. She needs to find help because she hates doing what she's doing. That was a product of an experience I had, where I went to a hospital for people with eating disorders. I went through the program there, and it was really great information. I just wanted to be able to give that to people.

WT: To some extent, a didactic agenda.

Hoffman: I hate terms like that because I don't like reading polemics. I don't want to get in anybody's face, but I hope the underlying message is hope, empowerment, that people can take charge of their own lives.

WT: Thanks, Nina. Ω

THE SWITCH-BACK

R. Chetwynd-Hayes

The Ray Heywood Story has been told so many times in some form or another, it is now one of those supernatural legends that bear comparison with the Marie Celeste or the Flying Dutchman. Of course, the factual foundation on which the legend stands is very frail indeed, and I am certain there is no more than one person alive today (now that my beloved wife has passed over) who is in a position to relate the true story.

That one person is me.

So I place not so flexible fingers to typewriter keys, while offering up a prayer that my brain is still capable of marshalling facts, rebuilding the memory of a world that we young blades found after surviving the most terrible war in history, and temporarily raising the dead from their graves to bear testimony to what I am about to relate.

But I must wander a little further back into the mists of time. Ray Heywood was my platoon sergeant. May I stress that the relationship which exists between platoon sergeant and platoon commander, despite the mighty gulf that separates non from commissioned officers, is a close one. Once the battalion goes into action, even more so, for something under an ounce of lead could remove a second lieutenant from the scene and elevate the sergeant to his place.

Heywood was one of those fortunate beings who are blessed not only with a magnificent body, handsome face, and able brain, but also with that mysterious extra we call charm, which usually meant that at least ninety-five percent of his fellow beings were prepared to lean over backwards to please him.

He had a mass of golden curls and large blue eyes that always seemed alight with a good-natured, slightly mischievous twinkle. When anyone displeased him, that light slowly died and was replaced by a baleful glare. Then strong men trembled. But I never knew him to raise his voice or place any man on a charge.

Me he managed with respectful firmness. In fact looking back I now realise that most of his soft voice "suggestions" were only saved from being interpreted as "orders" by a few well-placed sirs. Frankly I was extremely grateful for any suggestions or orders he cared to issue, for they all paid off, and I am pretty certain that without him, I would have dropped any number of clangers, that could have resulted in the loss of men's lives.

Then VE day came, to be followed three months later by VJ day, and all of us came to realise that we had come through alive and intact, and there was no reason to suppose we would not remain that way until the old man with the scythe came to pay us a personal visit. Frankly I couldn't believe my luck and continued to regard each new day as an unmerited bonus for a very long time. Ray Heywood entertained no such qualms.

Even when the mortar bombs were whistling down on us in front of Caen, I heard him declare that the one with his number on it would never be made. "I will never be killed by bullet or shell," he told me with all seriousness. "I will outlive this war."

"How can you be certain?" I asked.

He shrugged. "One just knows these things. At least I do."

In March 1946 the battalion, after a rip-roaring party, was disbanded; and its component parts went their various ways, in the majority of cases never to meet again.

But former platoon sergeant Heywood gave former lieutenant Mansfield a job.

I had always assumed that his family were well-heeled, for he often spoke about an uncle who appeared to own vast estates in the north of England, but I was quite unprepared to discover what a big shot he was himself. He made no bones about offering his one-time superior officer a job; in fact his letter emphasised — tactfully — our changed relationship.

Dear Philip,

I hope you don't mind my using your first name, but Mr Mansfield sounds too formal and is apt to remind us both of times every sensible person wants to forget. I bumped into Frenshaw the other day, who not only gave me your address, but the news that you are at rather a loose end these days.

I wonder — would you care to join my lot up here? Did I ever tell you that my family more or less own Heywood Motors? Anyway your one time square basher has been clobbered with the job of managing director. Why? Heavens above knows, unless it be that I own more voting shares than the rest of the mob.

Anyway, how would you like to be my PR man? Not a bad old number, selling the company image to the press, throwing the odd cocktail party — should be up your street, and we won't fall out about salary.

If agreeable ring the above number any time after six. We can then arrange for you to spend some time at the family pile and get to know everyone.

Hope to hear from you soon. Ray.

As being "at rather a loose end" meant being jobless and near broke, it did not take me long to swallow whatever driblet of pride I still retained and ring Ray Heywood at the number indicated on his heavily embossed notepaper. I was greatly impressed by hearing what had to be the butler announce "Heywood Residence," then after I had given my name and stated my need to speak to Mr Raymond Heywood, was rather flattened by: "I will ascertain if Mr Heywood is at home."

The ensuing silence was interposed by clicks and harsh breathing sounds, terminated by that respectful but arrogant voice, saying, "You are through now, sir."

Ray Heywood's voice throbbed with charm, if I may be permitted such an expression, while it also radiated the same gentle authority, that in all probability marked the change in Charles II after he had re-mounted the throne of his ancestors.

"How marvelous of you to call, my dear old sir. I have been hoping so much that you would. And of course . . . But I'm not allowing you to get a word in edgeways. Be on CO's orders. Please say your piece. Are you taking up my offer? Coming down this week-end?"

I said: "I would most certainly like to discuss the matter with you."

"Absolutely splendid. You must allow me to lay on transport. Expect a vehicle around fourteen hundred hours on Friday. Your place is just off Bayswater Road, isn't it? Great. I really am looking forward to seeing you again. Bye now."

And he hung up. My contribution to the conversation had been eleven words.

An ancient but stately Rolls collected me on time the following Friday, and I sat dead centre on the back seat, where lulled by the gentle purr of the engine, I soon fell asleep. I was awakened by a gentle nudge and a gust of cool air. The chauffeur had the off-side door open and was leaning in.

"The County Hotel, sir. Mr Heywood has arranged for dinner to be served for you here, sir."

I just managed to stifle a: "Good God!" and replace it with, "Right. I see. And what about you?"

He gave me the suspicion of a smile. "I am provided for, sir."

"Dinner" proved to be whatever I chose from an extensive menu, and I decided that if my late platoon sergeant could afford to send a ruddy great car two hundred miles to fetch me, a thumping great bill for dinner would not do him any great harm. So I went the whole hog. Gin and tonic, starters, grilled fillet steak served with asparagus, button mushrooms, and baked potatoes; all washed down by a bottle of Roederer '28. Rum-baba and liqueurs followed. And not a food ration coupon in sight. Those who could afford to eat out did not worry about such things.

By the time I again entered the car the world in general had assumed a rosy hue, and I was not all that steady on my feet. Needless to say I had sunk into a deep sleep before we had progressed another mile.

When I next surfaced the hands of my watch pointed to a quarter to nine, and the car stood before an imposing flight of steps that marked the front entrance to a strange house.

Heywood Manor was not an old house; in fact it was very new and hideous to behold. Imagine a Hollywood producer's idea of a Tudor Castle built of red brick, with a few Plantagenet bastions thrown in for good measure. Then add the flight of black marble steps that terminated in a colonnaded porch.

If the exterior was eye-catching, the interior can only be described as mind-boggling. A hall lined with white pine panelling; an immense cast-iron brazier, seemingly packed solid with artificial, electric logs; suits of oxidized-brass armour; while man-made fibre mats littered the highly-polished floor, waiting to up-end the unwary visitor.

Ray received me in what was supposed to be an early Elizabethan study, shook me firmly by the hand, then pulled a flute-backed chair towards a huge dog-ironed fireplace where real logs spluttered cheerfully.

"Scotch was always your poison, dear old sir, as I remember. Help yourself from the small table on your left. Don't be put off by this awful house. My Grandfa-

ther's idea and we his descendants have been shouldering the blame ever since. By the way — I do hope the County gave you an at least passable dinner."

"Fine," I replied, then raised a hand when he displayed distinct signs of continuing a one-sided conversation. "May I please ask you one or two questions?"

The slow, well-remembered charming smile lit his face. "Which is a nice way of telling me I talk too much. Fire away — anything at all."

"Please tell me — why on earth did you enlist as a ranker in a not very distinguished infantry regiment and content yourself with the rank of sergeant? Frankly in your shoes I'd have dodged the services altogether and remained at home to run the family business. Yours was surely a reserved occupation?"

He half filled a whisky glass and added a splash of soda, which reminded me that I had never seen him drink anything stronger than shandy-gaff when he was in the battalion; then he chuckled.

"Frankly, running a bloody great show like Heywood Motors didn't appeal to me. Still doesn't. I suspect there's a touch of Lawrence of Arabia in me; I get a kick out of being ordered around. The war enabled me, at least for a time, to indulge this kinky trait, until some bloody company commander decided I was equipped to shoulder responsibility. I let them edge me up to sergeant, but I refused to go any further. Apart from anything else accepting a commission in wartime is a dodgy business. It's a well-known fact that the sniper always goes for the chap with a pip on his shoulder."

"You pulled me out of one or two messes," I pointed out.

He smiled again. "Well, to be honest, there was a kind of helplessness about you that sort of twanged me heart strings. In fact, the thought of you stranded to fend for yourself in Civvy Street rather haunted me. That's why I took the trouble to find out where you were and what you were doing."

"Not very flattering," I objected.

"But, dear old sir, you have a gift beyond price. You bring out the best in everyone. It becomes a pleasure to help you. But you must be worn out. Let me show you to your room. There you can freshen up, then — if it so pleases you — join the family in the large drawing-room. Not in the least frightening, I do assure you. Just a wee bit pathetic."

He jumped up — there seemed to be more nervous energy than I remembered — placed a hand on my shoulder, and gently propelled me out of the room and across the atrocious hall and up a flight of stairs. My room was actually equipped with a four-poster bed that could be shut in when thick tapestry curtains were closed; and several electric lamps had been made to look like guttering candles in green enamel candlesticks. At least the bathroom, which was situated to the left of the fraudulent Tudor fireplace, did not pretend to be other than it was, a fact that Ray was not slow to stress.

"Grandfather never took a bath; didn't believe in them, so all bathrooms are fairly recent extras. But, take your time. If you want anything — ring for it. The kitchens are manned practically round the clock and can cater for most tastes. The three main meals — breakfast 8:30, lunch 13:30, and dinner 18:30 — are served in the dining-room. If for any reason you're late for any of 'em, not to worry. OK? No rationing worries here."

I nodded, then managed to conjure up a "Yes."

"Fine. See you in the large drawing-room — second door on the left, as you leave the staircase — when you're good and ready."

I took him at his word and soaked in the bath for at least half an hour, while pondering on the peacetime edition of Roy Heywood. The charm was still there, if more flamboyant than formerly, but the man seemed to be harder, more artificial, showing signs of strain. I could understand that running a vast business would most likely result in a personality change.

But the question slid across my brain as I chased an errant bar of soap under pink-tinted water: had I ever known Ray Heywood? Charm is nothing more than a pleasant veil that could well be hiding a far from pleasant character; and I had so admired the sergeant, I was fully prepared to accept him on face value. Come to think of it — we were all acting a role during the war. Mainly that of a coward pretending to be brave.

I dressed and went downstairs.

The large drawing-room lived up to its name, creating the impression that a small electric car would not have been out of place to convey the visitor from one wall to another. However the fifteen people present had arranged their chairs in a neat half-circle, thus permitting Ray Heywood an unimpeded view of each face from his position a little to the front, where he reclined in an item of furniture that bore a passing resemblance to a throne.

He did not get up, but waved to me when I entered the room.

"There you are, dear old sir! Look here, one of you — Anne, you're the youngest, drag a chair into line." An extremely pretty girl with a mass of blonde hair did as she was bid, but before I could be seated, Ray again raised his voice. "This is Philip Mansfield, who used to be my platoon commander. Now he's going to do a really first-class job as my PR man. It's damned silly my introducing you to this lot. You'll never remember their names. Anne of course you won't forget; and Uncle George, who has a glass growing out of his right hand, sort of sticks in the memory, but the rest will make themselves known when needful. Have you settled in?"

I nodded more than necessary. "Indeed yes. Very nice."

"Great. If you want a drink just raise the right hand. A being will glide out of the shadows and minister to your needs."

And by turning my head I saw that there was a man attired in a white tunic and black trousers, standing by a cocktail bar, who presumably was keeping a watching brief for any raised hands. The consideration for creature comfort was so elaborate in this house as to be ridiculous.

A small man with snow-white hair and bright blue eyes, which were magnified by rimless glasses, cleared his throat before speaking.

"We have a perfectly adequate PR department, R.H. Frankly I'm rather at a loss to see where Mr Mansfield is going to fit in."

"Philip, my dear Charles, will be my personal representative," Ray said quietly. "He will be answerable only to me."

Charles — at least three of them now could be identified — created a bleak smile. "Are we to understand Mr Mansfield's task will be to publicise your image? Glorify Raymond Heywood?"

Ray laughed gently, and I could swear his eyes glittered with malicious amusement. "Good heavens no! As you should know I dread publicity as does the snowflake the rising sun. But it so happens that I have a few ideas of my own that I would like to toss around, and prefer not to put them through the normal channel."

Charles tilted his head and addressed the ceiling. "As does the snowflake the rising sun. I must remember that one."

"Herewith I give you the copyright," Ray said gravely. "You may sell it for what it will fetch." He turned his head and directed a sardonic smile at a thin young man with a large nose. "Rodney, I understand that you have been criticising my practice of testing Saturn on the Switch-Back."

Rodney — were they all Heywoods? — assumed an angry expression.

"It's a damned silly thing for the chairman and managing director to do. Particularly the way you do it. Weatherby says you took Saturn up to one hundred and eighty-three yesterday. You know the Switch-Back needs resurfacing. I've nothing against you killing yourself, but the Saturn is an expensive piece of machinery, and I'd hate to see it go up in flames."

Ray Heywood nodded with apparent approval. "I do respect good honest hate. Fear not for the expensive piece of machinery. It is well-insured. So is your chairman and managing director. Apart from which the engine talks to me. I will know if it's been monkeyed with."

Rodney growled something that sounded like "Bloody mad," and Anne Heywood laid a hand on my arm.

"I expect you're wondering what this is all about."

I nodded, aware that several other voices had started what promised to be a first-class row, and Ray was sitting silent, his face lit by the well-remembered charming smile.

Anne spoke softly in my left ear. "Let's leave them to it and take a seat at the cocktail bar and have a well-deserved drink."

"An excellent idea."

We left the gesticulating, arguing half-circle and, clambering up onto tall stools, ordered gin and tonics, which the man in the white tunic served, before taking up a position some six feet away, to continue his watch for raised hands.

Anne began to explain the situation. "That lot can be loosely described as family. Uncles, cousins, and what-have-you. I'm Ray's second cousin; my father, who was his first, got himself and my mother killed in an air raid. I hope that's clear. The point is, all of us own shares in Heywood Motors, some more than others, but Ray has controlling interest. Is that right? His grandfather left him over fifty-one percent of all voting shares, which means whatever he says goes. Now Rodney, Uncle Charles, and quite a few of the others hate him like poison."

I said, "I can hardly believe that. A less hatable man you will never meet."

She nodded. "I know what you mean. That famous charm. But when money and power are involved, charm does not always work. Also, I think that Cousin Ray gets a kick out of making some people hate him. He torments Rodney until the poor boy is glassy-eyed with shame and rage. And he does it — I know this sounds mad — so charmingly, Uncle Charles said it took him twenty minutes to realise he was being insulted."

"Why are they sitting in a half-circle?" I asked.

"Ah! I wondered when you'd ask. This is a kind of unofficial board meeting. There's one about once a week. Ray lets them blow off steam, then tells them what he intends to do. Real board meetings are very much cut-and-dried affairs."

"What about this business of driving a car at breakneck speed on the — what was it? — Switch-Back?"

She widened her eyes and gripped my arm. "You know — that place is real scary. It's just beyond Marston Wood. A real racing circuit. Grandfather Heywood built it. Both sides curve up into a fairly steep slope; and, way at the top, trees have grown and seem to be reaching down to grab the cars as they go past."

"Is it much used?" I asked.

"You've heard Ray uses it to burn up the concrete with his favourite car — the Saturn. Otherwise a local racing club often ask permission to practise on it."

It was at this point the meeting (if it could be so called) broke up, and Ray made his way towards us. He raised Anne's hand to his lips and did not release it afterwards. She blushed slightly and looked up at him from under long eyelashes.

"I should imaging that my charming cousin has been putting you in the picture. Couldn't have a better instructor. She has a woman's love of gossip, married to an observant eye." He released Anne's hand and nodded to the barman. "Double on the rocks, Marvin. Come on you two, don't let me drink alone."

Anne shook her head. "Will you excuse me, Ray? I feel worn out and would love an early night."

He did not look at her. "As you please. Sleep well, and may sexy dreams attend you."

I think she would have stayed had he made a point of it, but as he remained motionless, she backed away, gave me an almost inaudible good night, then turned and ran towards the door. Ray spoke again.

"Would you love an early night as well?"

I gave him a tactless reply. "As a humble employee, I can't afford to."

His head jerked round, and I stared into glacial-blue eyes. "Don't you dare say that again. You're here because I need a friend at my back. A pack of hungry wolves are planning — are always planning damn them — to pull me down, and — blast my soul — I just can't help baiting them."

"Who ran Heywood Motors during the war?" I asked, in an effort to divert him onto a less dramatic track.

"Oh, the family headed by a couple of experts appointed by the War Office. We were making aeroplane engines, you understand. Now we're back on peacetime production and, what is more, making a bid to lead our field, our potential is limitless. I'm in the hot seat. Everyone thinks they need me, but few want me."

"I'm sure that's not true," I said. "There's bound to be friction in a family like yours, particularly when big business is involved. Greed and envy play Hell with finer feelings. But I cannot believe everyone actively dislikes you."

He began to laugh softly. "Good old sir! You only knew the sergeant who was enjoying a more than slightly dangerous holiday. Now I'm engaged in an only minutely less lethal war. And on occasion I'm forced to imitate the tiger. But you look worn out. Go to bed. Tomorrow, as Scarlett O'Hara so aptly remarked, is another day. See you at breakfast."

He drained the glass which had been placed before him, slammed it down on the bar, then turned and walked quickly from the room.

The entire family were seated round the breakfast table next morning, that is to say after they had served themselves from the long sideboard, where I found three kinds of oven-warm bread, coffee, tea and chocolate, devilled kidneys, bacon, eggs, and thin slices of liver. Two attentive footmen stood by to help the indecisive make a selection. I thought long live the black market.

Ray sat at the top of the table, looking handsome, self-confident, and in an exceptionally good mood. The same could not be said for the majority of those who slumped in straight-backed, well-padded chairs and toyed with the excellent food. Uncle Charles (surprising how that soubriquet seemed to suit him) gave me something akin to a glare when our glances met, Rodney looked as if he had had a rough night, while a fat man with a bald head sat with closed eyes, beating out a rapid tattoo with a spoon on the table. Fortunately Anne was seated on my left and quickly identified this impromptu musician.

"That's my second cousin, once removed — I think that's right — Morris Heywood-Makepiece. He's director in charge of design and knows he's a genius. I should imagine he's having creative pains right now. If you really want to cause some excitement, tap him on the shoulder and ask him to pass the salt."

"I wouldn't dare. Who is that oldish-young man with thinning hair, on Mr. Heywood-Makepiece's left?"

She made a gurgling sound. "What an apt description. He is oldish-young, isn't he? That's Morris's son. He believes God speaks through his father's mouth."

"Philip." Ray Heywood's voice made me look up. "I've a treat in store for you after breakfast. Meet me in the hall at nine-thirty. OK?"

"Right," I said.

"I know what the treat is," Anne whispered, "and in your place I'd find an excuse to dodge it. He's going to drive you round the Switch-Back at something like a hundred and fifty miles an hour."

I may have exclaimed: "Good God!"

"Mind you," Anne added, "he's a great driver. I only went with him once, and watching him is really weird. He does seem to become part of the car, and there's a kind of mad grin on his face. I was terrified, but somehow knew there was no way that car would crash with him at the wheel."

"I would appear to be in for an experience," I murmured.

Anne nodded. "I'd say yes to that. Take my tip, and don't look at the speedometer or Ray. Either watch the road in front or close your eyes. Then maybe you'll hear the engine talking. I did. Sometimes it purred like a contented cat; at others it seemed to be angry, but only in the way a woman is angry with a lover who takes her for granted."

I frowned and gave her an enquiring glance. "You're not having me on?"

Her blonde hair danced like wind-tormented corn when she shook her head. "No. I suppose it must have been the result of an over-excited imagination, but it seemed real enough at the time. Well, I guess you'd better go and get ready. Put on a thick pullover. There always seems to be a Hell of a wind blowing over the Switch-Back."

I took her advice and joined Ray in the hall some half an hour later wearing a polo-jersey and a thick sports jacket. He nodded his approval.

"Take care of the outer man and the inner will take care of himself. Let's get started. It's quite a walk through the woods and . . . But of course you don't know what's in store. Or do you?"

"A ride in your super motor car," I suggested.

"Of course you were sitting next to Anne, who appears to have taken a shine to you. Woman, thy name is frailty. Yes, I'm going to take you for a spin in Saturn, if, that is to say, you can trust yourself to the care of a maniac."

"You have driven me in a jeep enough times," I pointed out.

"Ah! A jeep! A pussy cat. Riding a lion is a different matter. At least there's no land mines on the Switch-Back."

We were walking through a sweet-smelling pine forest, with needles crunching beneath our feet, while from some distance off came the sound of a strange cry that must have been made by some bird, or maybe an animal, but in my disturbed state, I could have sworn it was my name being called by someone in deep distress. Ray did not appear to have heard it, for presently he said:

"I doubt if Saturn will ever be put on the market. I keep adding, improving, until she's more of a racing car than a family saloon. No respectable *paterfamilias* could possibly be turned loose with such a monster. Do you know she'll edge a hundred and ninety if pressed.

She doesn't like it and gives me Hell, but she'll do it — maybe more."

I looked at him with growing unease, but having decided to take whatever came my way, there seemed little point in expressing alarm. We crested an incline and began to walk down towards a fairly wide ditch that was spanned by a stout wooden bridge.

"Once we've crossed the dyke," Ray explained, "and surmounted that slope, we'll see the Switch-Back — or some part of it. I suppose only an eccentric millionaire like my grandfather could have afforded or wished to build such an oddity. It's not really a race track, not being wide enough, although a local club does practise on it. No, the old boy, like me, was infected by the speed bug and loved nothing better than to tear round doing his ton — that being the best he could manage in his day."

We crossed the bridge that had a bronze plaque fixed to the left-hand rail, which had the inscription etched in black enamel: IN MEMORY OF ANTHONY RAYMOND HEYWOOD. 1859-1937 . . . and Ray stopped and polished the surface with the sleeve of his jacket.

"Himself," he said with a wry grin. "I suppose he was a ruthless old bastard, but he was very decent to me. Called me young Navarre. Made sure I had control of the entire caboodle once I came of age, which was a year after his death in 1938. Come on — feast your eyes on the Switch-Back."

We climbed up the furthermost slope, then descended a few yards and stopped. Yes, I know that many thousands of sensation-seekers have made that journey since and looked down on that narrow stream of concrete that runs like a strip of grey ribbon along the floor of a natural valley, curving gently round into a perfect oval, but I doubt if anyone has seen it in quite the way I did on that autumn morning.

The wind chased a cloud across the sun — and a shadow that bore some resemblance to an old man with long hair went scurrying along the Switch-Back. I thought: death looking for a victim, and hoped to Hell it wouldn't be me. But that had to be pure imagination, as was the impression that the tarmac had — when viewed from a certain angle — a sinister glow. But Ray continued to guide me down the slope until we came to a flight of steps that curved down into the hillside and terminated in a vast underground and brilliantly-lit room. A man attired in green overalls came out of a glass-sided cubicle and actually knuckled his forehead.

"Morning, Mr Heywood — Sir."

Ray waved a hand between us. "Tim Binns, who thinks he's the best mechanic in Britain — Philip Mansfield."

I was given a grimy hand to shake and a gap-toothed grin, but not a knuckled forehead. Then he turned to Ray and asked: "You'll be taking Saturn out this morning, Mr Heywood?"

"Yes, Tim. How is she?"

"Purring as sweet as you please. I'll not deny she's a bit frisky. Maybe try to bolt for open spaces, the second you put your foot down, but you'll know how to handle that."

Ray murmured something that sounded like, "Bless

her," then ordered in a normal tone of voice, "Right, take her nightie off," which resulted in us being led to what looked like a long, canvas-covered hump. Tim bent down and inserted his forefinger in a large ring and ran it up and over the hump, causing a zip-fastener to part, gradually revealing that unholy monstrosity — the Saturn.

The original designer (Mr Heywood-Makepiece? perhaps) may have had a super-de-luxe family saloon in mind, but it had long since passed into the realms of the fantastic. Low-slung, streamlined, certainly fitted with a wide passenger seat at the back, a transparent plastic roof, which created the impression that the entire structure might be distantly related to a jet plane. The paintwork was a bright-red that reflected and elongated my own image; rotund, jet-black tyres, the radiator edged with chrome: Saturn (who seemed to have had a sex change) suggested latent power, a downright wicked disposition, and utter contempt for anyone who rode in her — with one possible exception.

"Get in," Ray ordered. "This is our fun period. A long work day follows."

If there had been a choice I would have forgone the fun and started straight in on the work, but seemingly I slid onto the front passenger seat without will or effort on my part, blacked out for a few seconds, to be awakened by a terrible roar that might have come from the throats of at least six hungry tigers.

Ray Heywood sat some three feet to my right, his hands resting on a leather-bound steering wheel, while he revved the engine and shouted into a small microphone that reared up from the instrument panel.

"Tim, she's talking loud and clear. Not too happy about that new oil, but will take it. Stand clear — I'm going out."

The gear lever slid into place, and I became aware that we were moving slowly forward; a patch of daylight grew gradually larger; blue, green, and red lights gleamed from the instrument panel — and Ray was still talking.

"You've done a fine job, Tim. She's rearing to go and hinting at all sorts of good things. Don't think she's cottoned there's a passenger aboard. May play up when she does. Right, about to greet the glad morn."

The car gathered speed. The patch of daylight became a rectangle, then we were out on the Switch-Back; emerged from a tunnel that had been driven obliquely into the hillside. Ray allowed the engine to tick over and pointed to the scene that reared up all around us.

"Isn't that something?"

The Switch-Back curved up to a curtain of trees and bushes on the left and tall grass on the right, looking not unlike an immense gully that would have been half-filled with water, were it not for the grid-covered storm drains, set at regular intervals dead centre of the track and adding — in my opinion — to the hazards of driving at very high speeds. I said so.

"If one of those grids works loose, you would really take off."

Ray shrugged. "So would I if a log or a tree blew down from the top. Tim drives along the track each morning looking for trouble. Anyway I always do a slow lap before opening up. So not to worry. Here we go. . . ."

We glided forward, and the engine roared briefly until he shifted into second and top gear; then a low, sated purr that reminded one of a large and dangerous cat that is for the time being regarding its keepers with condescending favour. The "slow lap" was done at around 45 miles per hour, and I noticed that in places leaves had collected over some storm drains, but Ray did not bother to report the fact over the two-way radio. Then we were back at the starting point, and his voice rose to a higher pitch.

"OK, Tim — we're going for the stars."

After a pause Tim's laconic voice replied, "Right, sir — make sure you don't reach 'em."

My God! Suddenly I was pushed back into my seat, the engine replaced its contented purr by a fast-rising shrill scream; a roaring wind pounded on roof and windscreen; an invisible giant whose one wish was to fling us up . . . up . . . up and over the rim and into the forest, so that those who control the universe could truly say: "They do not exist."

For that was the great truth that came to me as the needle crept round the illuminated dial: Man and all his works have no place in the annals of nature. Life is life is life is life and was never intended to be planned, trimmed, have roads driven across it, flown over, delved under, or even thought about. Creative dreamers often subconsciously realise this and bring to flower the seeds of self-destruction, whereas men like Ray shout their defiance to the stars.

I tore my gaze from the track that raced towards us, gave the speedometer one quick glance, and noted that the needle was edging past 130 — then looked upon the face of Ray Heywood. It was transformed by a maniac's grin. Clenched teeth bared, eyes gleaming and all but bulging from their sockets, the face dead white, save for the forehead where inflated veins stood out like blue-black streaks of blood on a field of snow. Then he spoke from behind clenched teeth.

"She . . . has . . . promised . . . me . . . one . . . one day . . . one . . . nine . . . three . . ."

Terror clamped an icy hand over my heart. Ray Heywood was in love with speed and the car which created it, and now that the speed was approaching one hundred and fifty miles per hour, he had become a living extension of the engine. He spoke again in that eerie harsh whisper, while the car quivered and the engine's scream rose to a higher pitch.

"No . . . more . . . than . . . one . . . nine . . . three . . . not . . . safe . . ."

So, even while under the influence of this terrible obsession, his inborn commonsense still retained a vestige of control. It told him that to drive this car beyond one hundred and ninety-three would be more than just dangerous. So far as I was concerned we had been courting danger from the very moment the needle passed the 60 mile per hour mark.

Suddenly the engine cut out. All sound ceased, except for the wind which continued to buffet roof and windscreen; neither did the speed perceptibly decrease until we had glided round a curve. I shot a glance at

Ray. The maniac grin had gone and was now replaced by an expression of intense annoyance.

"Damn and bloody Hell! A length of wire overheated and burnt out. I could feel it go. Well, we should be able to coast back into the pits, then Tim can take over." He looked at me and grinned. "Sorry, old man. Bad luck for your first spin round the Switch-Back. Never mind, we'll try again in a day or so."

"If you can spare the time," I said, silently resolving that nothing on earth would get me into that hellish machine again.

"I'll always find time for Saturn," he replied. "But I do appreciate she's not everyone's cup of tea. Nevertheless, my dear fellow, you've had an experience that is granted to few." He swung the car round into the entrance. "Remember, fear is a major emotion that has been much under-rated. Like pain it warns the body of danger, but unlike pain it can be controlled and directed into one particular channel." He applied both foot and hand brake, then opened the side door. "But here comes Tim looking sorry for himself." He placed a reassuring hand on the mechanic's shoulder. "Not to worry, Tim. Wire burnt out. Gremlins at work. Or maybe Saturn did it herself. Perhaps dear old sir didn't suit her ladyship. You know what she's like."

Tim helped his employer clamber from the car. I was left to manage the best I could.

"Don't you fret, Mr. Heywood. I'll work on her all day and night if need be. I don't understand it. I replaced all wiring last week."

Ray touched his nose with a pointed forefinger. "You must listen to me, Tim. Her ladyship was put out. Now she's sulking, so you'd better put off replacing the wiring for at least twenty-four hours. Now I must push off. I want to show Mr Mansfield the watch-tower, before going back to the house. Take it easy, Tim. Don't let the factory bods put on you."

The man grinned while watching his employer through narrowed eyes. "No fear of that, Mr Heywood."

We walked back along the tunnel, then strolled up the track until we came to a flight of concrete steps that led to a tall wooden tower, which reared above the tallest trees. By the time we had stepped out onto a sunken path that ran through the pine forest, I was panting like a worn-out steam engine. Ray pointed to a staircase that spiralled up through the frame and finally gave access to the tower itself, that must have been at least a hundred and fifty feet above.

"I'll not ask you to climb up there, but take my word for it — from the tower you have a view of the entire Switch-Back."

"Worth the climb, I'm sure," I asserted without total conviction.

"And of course the surrounding countryside," he added. "One day, when the weather is fine, you must try it."

I followed him out of the wood and back to the house, not at all happy with this new facet of his character. Once again I found myself comparing the sergeant with the tycoon (which I assumed he was) and not being able to match the two. Although now I came to think of it, a tycoon hiding himself in the ranks could be interpreted as an unreasonable act, Lawrence of Arabia notwithstanding.

But during the rest of the day he displayed a shrewdness and complete mastery of his business that I could not equate with the near madman who talked to a motor car. He guided me round the vast factory and explained the intricacies of the assembly line in a language that even I could understand, and I noticed that the factory floor staff greeted his arrival with enthusiasm, and all seemed most anxious to catch his eye. The famous charm still worked with the other ranks.

I sat in on a board meeting, comprised mainly of the family group I had met the night before. But now there was a great difference. Ray Heywood became the dictator, the tyrant, whose voice took on a staccato bark and permitted no opposition to his will. The platoon sergeant in a bad mood, with a bleak look in his eye that made strong men tremble.

Then we were on our way back to dinner, and I became aware that the genial host-employer drove the Aston-Martin at a moderate speed, observed all the rules of the road, and displayed no signs of communing with the engine. Instead he talked of a subject very dear to an employee's heart.

"We haven't had time to discuss your salary and perks. I was thinking of £5,000 a year, you live in the house, have full use of a company car, which means free petrol, oil, and maintenance. How does that suit you?"

"Very generous," I replied with deep sincerity. "I can only hope I will justify your generosity."

He spoke without removing his eyes from the road. "In one way or another you will. Every penny. I do assure you."

"Nothing will please me better," I replied. "But when do I start? Today I have been little more than a paid guest."

The ghost of a chuckle — his eyes mocked me from the rear mirror. "Nevertheless you have started. Your mere presence in this car is a form of employment. Sitting beside me in the dining-room and eating a dinner has to be classified as a prodigious labour. Following me round the factory this morning, then sitting in on a board meeting, merited a fat bonus."

"You would not care to explain all that?"

"In a short while there'll be no need. In the meanwhile concentrate on Uncle Charles and Rodney. The others growl, occasionally snap, but are comparatively harmless. Or perhaps not. One day you may have to decide who are the guilty."

"If you feel this way about your own family," I demanded, "why bait them?"

"Because angry men, like drunkards, reveal more than they intend."

He did not speak again until we were ascending the steps to the hall. Then he murmured:

"They may kill Caesar, but never still his ghost."

The Heywoods dined in style and quantity. All the men wore dinner jackets and the women some kind of evening gown; but even Anne was not certain who everyone was. I counted forty-five people seated round the long table, all of whom seemed to be whispering or listening to earth-shaking secrets, except for Ray, who addressed mundane remarks to me in a low voice and frowned at anyone who looked in our direction. Presently a belated light of understanding struck me. I leaned forward until our heads were only a few inches apart and spoke in a low voice.

"You want them to think I'm more important than I am. Your personal assistant, for example. Sharer of secrets."

"Or successor," he added. "The dark horse who has arrived from nowhere and sits on Caesar's right hand."

"And so takes whatever is in store for Caesar," I murmured.

"What! Cut off the arm and leave the head still functioning! No, you are merely speeding up the action. Fear not, dear old sir, you are not of the stuff from which ghosts are made."

Irritation made me raise my voice. "I refuse to believe that anyone wishes to harm you physically. You're more likely to kill yourself in that car."

It was uncanny. All conversation died along the table, all faces were turned in our direction, eyes seemed to glitter with anticipation, but only Uncle Charles spoke.

"Quite right. If you have any influence with the wretched fellow, make him blow that dreadful contraption up. It will never be a commercial proposition and will sooner or later reach for the sky."

"That car will never kill me," Ray said slowly and loudly, as though intending to etch his words on every brain present. "Unless she's interfered with. Do you understand? If I die in Saturn, it will be because someone has got past Tim and buggered about with the most foolproof car in the world."

Uncle Charles lowered his head in actual or pretended embarrassment, and I thought — if they want to get rid of him, there will be no need for murder — and Ray creased his face into a smile and went on in a quieter tone of voice:

"Not that I am expecting anyone to be so foolhardy, particularly anyone at this table." The smile broadened. "And I do not expect to be taken seriously after downing half a bottle of old claret."

Anne, who was seated on my left, whispered, "The retainers don't give a damn. But don't let it worry you, nothing is for real in this house. Outside — maybe."

I turned my head and looked down into her blue eyes. "Explain that. Who are the retainers? Why is nothing for real in this house?"

She shook her head. "I don't know. Wine wisdom. I take it in with every glass. Wait a minute while I grab a few strands of reality from a mountain of phantasy. You and I must be real, because we respond to each other. Ray must be real, because without him this entire structure would fall to pieces. But the others . . . ? I wouldn't be too sure. I mean — take another glass of wine, close your eyes, and wait for the roaring darkness to quieten down, then blink three times — and there's only shadows sitting at this table. Plus the retainers."

"Again I ask . . . ?"

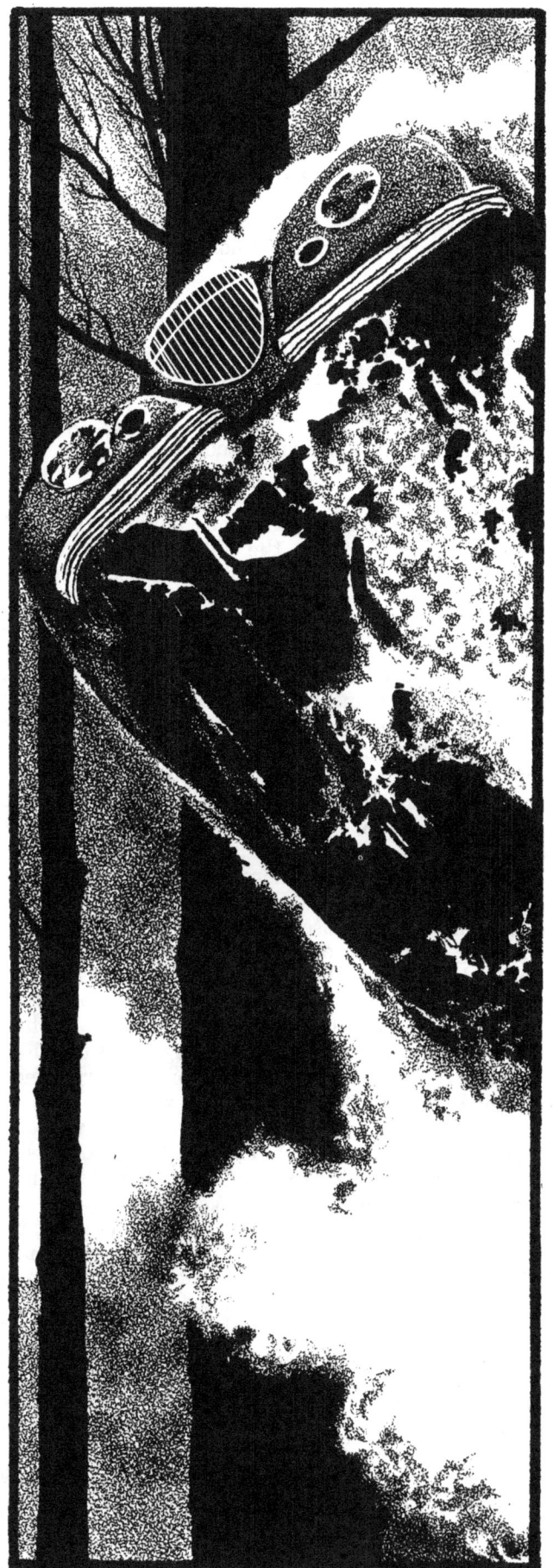

"Thin men who dine off the crumbs dropped from a rich man's table. Jobbers, service men, beggars in dinner jackets. They expect a thousand-pound tip and considerably more for special services rendered. But such creatures could not swear to their own reality, let alone those who employ them."

"You are straying beyond the frontiers of credibility," I protested.

"Good wine is no judge of reality. Neither am I."

Ray leaned over and laid a none too steady arm on my arm.

"Is my beautiful second cousin soused? Pickled? Looking at the world through a glass of red wine?"

Anne giggled and whispered in my ear. "If tonight were tomorrow night — then he wouldn't be here."

"Not exist?" I asked.

She shook her head very slowly. "Oh, yes. Ray will always exist — in one form or another."

If a tipsy Anne meant what I think she meant — then she was wrong. Ray gave me a guided tour round two subsidiary factories the following day, ate his dinner that night, and so far as I knew slept peacefully in his own bed.

But his confidence that the Saturn would never kill him proved to be entirely misplaced. Having, the next morning, reached a speed that Tim maintained was somewhere over one hundred and ninety miles per hour, the Saturn suddenly swerved, turned over several times, then exploded into roaring flames. The remains of my one-time platoon sergeant, which for some reason I was asked to identify, were most horrible to look at and impossible to equate with a formerly handsome and healthy body.

The entire family, retainers, servants, and hangers-on, all expressed and displayed signs of deep grief; and one might have supposed that the deceased had never been regarded with other than respect and affection during his lifetime. The inquest, presided over by an urbane coroner, who Anne informed me was a distant connection of the family, passed smoothly, while witness after witness testified or suggested that Ray had died trying to ensure that Heywood Motors turned out the best and safest cars in the world.

I was prepared to pack my bags and depart immediately after the cremation, but the reading of Ray's will, or rather a codicil that had been signed the day before his death, brought about a change of mind.

Having insured against death duties, he left fifty-two percent of voting shares, divided between Anne, Tim, and myself. Anne also inherited the house and half a million. Tim was requested to remain at his present post and maintain both the Switch-Back and the Saturn. I thought that he had been relieved of the latter duty, which surely made nonsense of the first. But when I spoke to him on the subject, he shook his head.

"Mr. Ray wanted me to remain here for a purpose, and remain here I will. That business of me owning those voting shares doesn't mean a thing. I'll make you my proxy, and you can use it to vote any way you please."

"But what on earth will you do with yourself all day?" I asked. "There's no Saturn for you to maintain now."

"There's other cars the factory like to try out here, and I usually give 'em the once-over, after the mechanics have done their worst. Then there's Model K which the racing club is hoping to perform wonders with, one day. My time will be well-occupied."

Mine certainly was. I had not the slightest idea how to run a great company, and although with Tim's proxy and Anne's backing I could have dominated the board if I so wished, there was little point when I did not know what to dominate it for. Uncle Charles offered to buy my shares for a respectable sum, and why I hesitated is still a matter for serious conjecture, because my one and only ambition was to salt away enough money so I need never face that foul evil called work again. Maybe I entertained some hope that the offer would be increased if I hesitated, or an even better one would come from another quarter.

Then one evening I received a telephone call from Tim.

He spoke in a low, rather tremulous voice. "Could you come down to the Switch-Back early tomorrow morning, sir?"

I said, "What do you call early?"

"Just after six. When it gets lightish."

"If it's important I do so — OK. Care to tell me what it's all about?"

I could hear his breathing, and it sounded quick and shallow, like that of a man who is under some intense excitement. Then he said, "Not now, if you don't mind. Just be here early tomorrow, and I'll explain then."

He had used an internal phone, so there was no dialling tone when he hung up, just complete silence. But I slammed the receiver down, for suddenly there was a feeling that if I held it to my ear for one second longer, another voice would have spoken.

I did not sleep well that night.

A cold wind blew through the pine wood and over the Switch-Back when I arrived a few minutes after six next morning, and slowly descended the curving steps to that vast, brightly-lit underground space. Tim was waiting in his little glass-sided office.

"Cup of coffee ready, sir. Get it down, because we're going up to the watch-tower and it'll be mighty cold up there."

I half-emptied the mug he gave me. "Not me. I've no head for heights."

He shook his head slowly. "I don't think you understand. Mr Heywood is back on the Switch-Back. Driving the old Saturn — doing all of a hundred and ninety."

I stared at him goggle-eyed for some little while, before saying: "Don't talk such utter rot, man."

He went on as though I had not spoken. "Started two days ago. I saw Mr Ray in the Saturn, crouched over the wheel — that funny look on his face, and — Lord Almighty — it was all so real. And Mr Mansfield, you've got to come up into the tower where you can see the entire track, and see for yourself."

I was frightened — terrified — and therefore angry. I shouted, "Being down in this place for years on end has cracked you, man. The Saturn finished up as a heap of twisted metal and Mr Ray — two handfuls of ash."

When he next spoke it was with a voice that a parent might use to a backward child. "That I well know, sir. And I also know I've seen Mr Heywood twice, driving the Saturn along the Switch-Back. Just one lap. Then he disappears — car and all. And you — and maybe Miss Anne — must see him too. Or I'll really go crazy, for this is not the kind of thing a man can keep to himself."

I clasped shaking hands to my forehead. "I don't want anything to do with this ridiculous business. I came here because Ray asked me to, and I knew that whatever the job was he'd do all the thinking, because he always had. Then I found myself being used as a front man in a particularly vicious family war. Now . . ."

"Mr Ray wants to tell you something very important, sir," Tim said gently. "I think he's tried to reach you in other ways, but only him driving Saturn full out will work. So you come along with me, sir, for he'll soon be driving that one fast lap."

I shook my head violently. "No, I can't. If what you say is true, then that's one more reason. I haven't the strength to look upon a ghost."

Anne came into the office and kissed Tim gently on one cheek, then smiled at me. "Yes you have, Philip. You'll be surprised. When Tim told me — only you and me — I was terrified and felt just like you. Then I knew that if I didn't come and see for myself, I'd be passing up a unique experience. And that's life, isn't it? Experience. Taken often and in small doses."

"But someone you have known . . ."

"Ray was of the stuff from which ghosts are made. He knew it, so did I, and you must have sensed it. And a friend in life is surely not less a friend in death. So come along and try to enjoy your unique experience."

She took me by the hand while Tim slipped the strap of a pair of binoculars over his head. "You have a way with words, Miss Anne. Always had. There's no doubt that you're the man of the family, now Mr Ray's gone."

"But not departed," she said, tightening her grip on my hand. "Let's hurry. We've got that awful ladder thing to climb yet."

I remembered and started to protest. "But I've no head for heights and . . ."

"Neither have I," Anne confessed cheerfully, "but you'll be surprised how curiosity overcomes fear."

Again she was wrong. My fear was too great to be overcome by anything, while my curiosity was absolutely nil. I cannot believe there ever has been a more frightened man on this planet than the one who started to climb that awful spiral staircase, which in due course — after much prodding and encouragement from Anne — arrived up and out on to an open-sided observation cabin. Fortunately it had a waist-high wooden wall on all sides and a gabled, shingled roof, which gave it at least the illusion of security, even if the entire structure did sway in the wind.

Tim placed what I am certain was meant to be a reassuring hand on my hand and shouted: "See the entire Switch-Back . . . a large oval carved out of the lower slopes. But we've only got a downward view, but when Saturn takes the curves, she — Ray — will mount the slope . . . then you have a brief view through the side window."

I nodded, being very conscious that I was beset by three fears. That the wind might blow me over the low wall; the climb down again; the spectral appearance of Ray and his car. I believe there was the thought that if the latter proved too much for me, I could always close my eyes.

I may have adopted this excellent idea, for suddenly I was looking down on what seemed to be a toy car with a transparent roof that raced along the track, presumably without sound, although that may have been smothered by the wind, knowing that Tim was attempting to thrust a pair of binoculars into my hands. Time was wasted while I fumbled to get the damned things adjusted to my eyes, then finding the car (which I was not all that keen to do); the rear wheels of which kept sliding into my line of vision, then out again; eventually I had the entire thing captured in a moving frame, albeit only for a short while.

Taking the curve, so that he was halfway up the slope, and I could see him so plainly he might have been only a few feet away, crouched over the steering wheel, then he turned . . . He did indeed . . . turned his face in my direction . . . and there was the maniac's grin, but it could well have been a dead man's grimace. And oh my God! I knew he was looking at me.

Then I jerked the binoculars from my eyes, and I believe there was the muffled sound of a crash, but Tim insisted on shouting in my ear: "Did you see him? Did you see him?"

I was incapable of making a coherent reply, and presently Anne and Tim somehow got me down to ground level.

A sense of duty is a dreadful burden.

More cruel, distasteful, and stupid actions are committed in the name of duty than any sensible man would deem possible. I was reared on a mental diet of Lord Nelson, Florence Nightingale, Captain Oates, and that stupid little wretch who stood on a burning deck, and hence have a very strong sense of duty. After my hair-raising experience in the watch-tower, it gave me no peace.

It reasoned that Ray had given me a job when I most needed one, had left me what amounted to a lot of money, and had trusted me. Now it would seem — if Tim was to be believed — he wanted to contact me and would continue to drive that ghost car over one lap on the Switch-Back until I did something about it.

Anne expressed an opinion that reinforced that put forward by my sense of duty. "If I had to guess, I'd say Ray is trying to tell you, or someone, that the accident was no accident. Also, who did the dirty on him. Maybe not, but you or someone should try to find out. If he really wants to contact you, I mean."

I sighed deeply. "So do I. I was rather hoping you

would talk me out of it."

"I would like to, but I don't think I really should."

I thought deeply for a few minutes before coming to a decision. "There's no way anyone is going to get me up in that tower again, apart from which it is far too high for a good look at the driver. Not that I am all that keen to have a close view of him, but if some kind of contact is to be made, he's got to be — well — near."

Anne nodded. "True. But how will you go about it? Stand on the track?"

I shuddered. "God forbid. No, I was thinking that perhaps Tim could find me a viewpoint just above and facing down the track. Then I'll have . . ." I could not continue for I suddenly realised exactly what I would have — a full view of that ghastly face, every detail revealed as it drew nearer, complete with its dead man's grimace.

Anne sensed my horror and squeezed my hand. "Seeing is not all that bad. Touching is so much worse. We'll go down this afternoon and see Tim."

Tim nodded when I explained what was needed. "Easy enough to give you a little bay on the straight run to the first curve. Even so you'll only have the Saturn in view for about ten seconds. Best sighting will be when he passes you. For two seconds you'll only be about six feet apart. Miss Anne, if you're going along, how about taking a movie camera with you."

"Absolutely not," I interrupted. "I want no ghoulish record of this awful business. If that is Ray out there, I want him to let me know who and how, then sheer off. Then I will spend the rest of my life trying to forget."

"You're right, of course," Tim agreed. "And I don't suppose anything would have shown up on the film. I understand that ghosts don't as a rule. Anyway I will get some blokes busy building the bay. I don't suppose it'll be ready in time for tomorrow morning. May have to wait until the day after."

"Make it as quick as you can," I replied. "I'd like to get this business over in the shortest possible time."

"It's not entirely in my hands," Tim replied. "I can't guarantee Mr Ray will run every morning. He missed yesterday for example, but was there this morning. I'll ring you when everything's ready."

Somehow the story got out. Looking back I realise it was nigh impossible to keep such a phenomenon a secret. The woods were open to the public, and any number of people could have been looking down on the Switch-Back when Ray did his post-death lap. Including someone from the big house.

Uncle Charles approached me that evening and asked a direct question.

"What's all this about Ray haunting the Switch-Back?"

I swallowed — how the Hell do you know? — just in time, shrugged, and said: "So — it's started already! Bound to happen. What is he supposed to do? Walk down the centre of the track, looking for his car?"

Charles looked at me through narrowed eyes. "No. Drive the Saturn one lap, then disappear. Early in the morning."

"Well, I've been down on the Switch-Back for the

past two mornings and damned if I saw him. Oh, come on, surely you don't believe in ghosts."

He said, "No, of course not. But I can't help wondering why you were out there at sunrise. Not a pretty view at this time of year."

"Maybe I was looking for a ghost that never appeared. Strange, no matter how much one may jeer at such a story, there's always a faint hope that it might be true."

He nodded. "That's a fact. Then you'd say it's not worth my while getting up for an early trudge through those woods?"

"Most certainly not."

He laid a hand on my shoulder. "Then I'll stay in bed and leave ghost-hunting to more enterprising types like you."

There was a supercilious grin on his face when he turned away and walked quickly down the corridor. I wasted no time in telephoning Tim.

"Have you started to build that bay yet?"

"No. Getting the men . . ."

I spoke quickly. "Don't. There isn't time. The story about Ray haunting the Switch-Back is already making the rounds. Charles Heywood was thinking of going out there. In two days the place will be cluttered up with sightseers."

His voice was unnecessarily loud when he spoke.

"What do you suggest, sir? Call the entire thing off?"

I sighed deeply. "I'd love to, but I can't. It's as though Ray is beside me, trying to make contact. Is there another car you can lay hands on that will better one hundred and ninety miles an hour?"

"Yes. The Model K. It's a racing car that belongs to the Brightfield Racing Club. I've got it here under wraps. Why?"

I hesitated, because what I proposed to do could result in either loss of life or sanity, but the spine-chilling idea was deeply embedded in my brain and refused to be dislodged. I cleared my throat.

"There's only one quick solution. Go out on the Switch-Back, and match him speed for speed — so we're driving side by side."

The ensuing silence was eventually broken by Tim's rasping voice. "Good God, man! Have you ever driven at near two hundred miles an hour? A moment's inattention — such as being distracted by something coming up on your off-side — and you'll follow Mr Heywood's lead — go up and over. One ghost car is enough."

I shouted: "Do you suppose I want to go out there? My bowels heave at the very thought. But I've got to. Do you understand? Bloody well got to."

A few seconds later he spoke in a calmer voice. "You'd better come out here so we can talk this over. And bring Miss Anne with you. At least she'll be dead against this."

"And so am I. But I'm still going to do it."

To this day I remember very little of my third journey to the Switch-Back, due I suppose to my brain refusing to consider the suicidal action I was proposing to take. I really only came back to full awareness when

Anne guided me into Tim's office.

He spoke to Anne. "Have you talked him out of it?"

"How could I? He hasn't said a word to me since we left the house."

He turned to me. "Look, sir, I'm old enough to be your father, so I'll speak plainly. You have much to be thankful for. You came through the worst war in history unscathed, are blessed with the three treasures that should guarantee happiness — health, wealth, and youth. Now you're planning to put the lot into the melting pot. If Mr Ray were here he'd say the same."

"But is he saying the same now? It seems to me that he is leaving me no option but to go out there and match his speed. As I see it, that must be the only way he can tell me — in one way or another — who was responsible for that crash."

Tim thought for a long time before replying. "If someone tinkered with that car without me knowing, then only God knows how they did it. I checked everything from tyres up before Mr Ray went out. The track itself was dry. Surely the truth is he asked too much from Saturn. She was never intended to do more than a hundred and twenty. It was his added improvements that made the extra speed possible."

"Then why is Ray haunting the track? Before he died he kept hinting that someone was after him; and, for my money, that someone succeeded. If I've got to take a bit of a risk to find out who the bastard is, then I'd be all kinds of yellow rat if I didn't take it."

"God protect a grateful man," Tim murmured.

"Philip," Anne said quietly, "don't imagine that you owe Ray anything. He was using you, as he used everyone. You were brought here to frighten the family. With your arrival came rumours of a take-over bid, a merger. Only Ray himself really knew what he intended to do."

Tim creased his forehead into a frown. "I liked and admired him more than any other person I have ever known. But frankly, looking back, I think he was a bit mad."

"Shall we take a look at this car?" I suggested. "The one you call Model K."

Tim sighed and led the way out of the office and across the expanse of concrete to a wide bay where a racing car stood. It had four immense tyres, a slender but long radiator, a wide cockpit, and a chassis that tapered off into the likeness of a fish's tail. Tim walked round this mechanical marvel, then looked at me with a wolfish grin. He spoke with the voice of an aggressive stranger:

"This baby has at least twelve tigers packed in under her cowling, that most reluctantly obey a driver who knows what he's doing and has years of experience to back him up. If a greenhorn attempts to do more than sixty — they slaughter him. Now, how much experience have you got in driving a contraption like this?"

I considered the question for a few minutes.

"About two years. Two prewar years, of course; and I never clocked anything like two hundred. Around one-twenty, but that was on a crowded track, and I was always scared stupid. I should add my father was Sir James Mansfield, and he was the best teacher ever."

Tim looked at me with renewed interest. "Ah! That makes a difference. The son of Britain's one-time speed king should have an even chance. I would suggest you and I go out for a trial run. No dramatic speed, not with me aboard, but just to get you used to the car and her funny little ways, to say nothing of the track itself."

"I suppose there's no chance . . . ?" I began.

"He only makes one lap on the day he appears. So far as I can judge he comes into being — going full out — anything from five minutes to seven and five minutes past. I suppose there must be a reason for the fluctuation in time, but I can't imagine what it can be."

"What do I do?" Anne asked.

"There's a small army walkie-talkie by the entrance, and I've rigged up another in the car. Both are tuned in for mutual broadcast and reception, but I'd like to try them out when the car is in motion. You can man the one at this end."

I put a driving helmet on, then climbed in behind the steering wheel and started the engine. It had been a long time since I had driven a racing car; and, despite my brave words, the prospect of pushing this roaring monster up to a hundred and ninety-odd miles an hour made my blood run cold. I did not even think of what would be alongside should this bizarre experiment be successful.

Tim settled into the seat beside me, wearing a helmet equipped with earphones; then the Model K roared up the slope towards that patch of daylight, and I felt like a man astride a horse that would throw him whenever it so wished. Once out on the track I felt a little more confident, for there was a seemingly unending stream of grey concrete ahead, with gently curving slopes on either side, and here were no walls to extravagate the build-up of speed. Tim shouted a warning:

"There's no need to risk your life twice or mine once. Just keep her down to a civilized speed, and get the feel of the car and track."

I did three laps at an average sixty-five and was beginning to enjoy myself when Tim nudged my elbow.

"That's enough," he shouted. "Take her in. I've got to work on this radio. Nothing is getting through."

I completed the next lap before gliding into the entrance, remembering that hair-raising ride in the Saturn with Ray; the day he said, "I'll always find time for the Saturn," and "OK, Tim, we're going for the stars," yet denying that he would ever do that.

I braked to a halt well within the vast underground room and switched off the engine, then slid from behind the steering wheel and joined Tim who had made a much faster exit. We both waited for Anne who was staggering under the weight of a portable walkie-talkie.

"Fine old mess-up," she complained. "I've been out there twisting knobs and yelling my head off and not one intelligent word did I get out of the thing."

"I did ask you to leave the knobs alone," Tim protested gently. "No wonder I couldn't get reception."

"But your voice was so faint, and I thought that a slight adjustment would put it right, but all I got was that sound of frying eggs."

I interrupted what threatened to become a pointless argument.

"Anne, put the set down on the car bonnet. I've some experience of these things and can usually get them to work."

This was pure showing off, for although I had been sent on a RT course, I had forgotten almost everything I had been taught. However, I turned one knob from left to right, was rewarded by a roar of static, dimly aware that Tim was adjusting the car model in a like manner. Suddenly we all heard a voice that seemed to be trying to make itself audible over the static, or perhaps it would be more accurate to say through it. Extremely faint, even though at times I got the impression it was shouting, we gradually deciphered what seemed to be a series of numbers.

"I make it out to be zero . . . seven . . . zero . . . five," Tim said.

"Nine," Anne corrected. "I'd swear the last number is nine."

"Must be a private code," I suggested.

Tim shook his head. "But it's on our wave length and co-ordinate numbers. Listen to him. Seems to be doing his nut. Adjust your set one degree to the left."

Scarcely had I obeyed this instruction than both sets sent out a veritable bedlam of sound; static roared like a vast crowd of enraged football supporters — and through it came the distinct tone of Ray's voice.

"Philip . . . tomorrow . . . zero . . . seven . . . zero . . . five."

My name and the four numbers were repeated three times, before that well-remembered voice and the static faded away, to be replaced by complete silence. Tim depressed the on-off switch several times.

"I'd say," he said quietly, "all the valves have blown."

"What did it mean?" Anne whispered.

"Ray will put in an appearance at five minutes past seven tomorrow morning," I replied with praiseworthy calmness. "But why he couldn't have given us a more straightforward message is beyond me. Name some names, for example."

"I'm not up on ghosts," Tim confessed, "but my sister, who is a regular sitter in the Hoxley Circle, told me that communication is very difficult and a spirit is very lucky if he or she gets a few words over. And they make sense."

"But I have still to risk my neck tomorrow morning," I protested. "But at least we now know exactly when he will come into being."

"Take a bit of working out," Tim said thoughtfully. "You've got to remember he — I don't know how to put this — starts at a hundred and ninety-odd miles an hour. You must be doing that, or faster, to draw level. So . . ."

"Can you do your sums later?" Anne asked. "Philip, if you must do this, at least take Tim with you."

"The answer to that one, is no," Tim stated firmly. "As I said before, I respected and liked Mr Heywood when he was alive, but I've no intention of getting a close-up view of him now he's dead, particularly in a car driven by someone who must be unbalanced to even consider such a project anyway. Sorry to speak so plainly, sir, but that's the truth."

"Then you drive the car," Anne insisted.

I raised a protesting hand. "Hold it. This is strictly a two-man show. Tim and me. Anne, I don't even want you anywhere near the track. Where will you be, Tim?"

"Up in the watch-tower. From there I can give you the tip over the radio, the moment he comes into sight."

"You can't stop me watching," Anne stated. "I'll be up in the watch-tower with Tim, and God help him if he tries to stop me. I'll maintain an icy calm, even if you're spread all over the track."

I kissed her gently. "Don't worry. Nothing will happen. Ray always looked after me, particularly when I was technically in the driving seat. Now that I will be in fact, should fully arouse his protective instinct."

"Yes, if what comes into being out there is Ray Heywood as we knew him."

I shrugged. "None of us are as we were at the last meeting."

I did not go down to dinner that night, not being in a mood to dine among those who were fast coming to the conclusion I was nothing more than a sheep well worth shearing. Even now I can only surmise what Ray's plans for me had been, if indeed my role was to be other than that of morale booster, but the fact remains that once he was dead, his former associates soon lost whatever apprehension my initial appearance had caused.

Surprisingly I slept well that night, although next morning I felt tired, drained of energy, and a great disinclination to face the ordeal which awaited me. As I walked through the woods, this grew into something not far short of a waking nightmare; my imagination presenting a trailer of the main event, in which I drove the car at a suicidal speed, while a thing that had little in common with the Roy Heywood I had known leered at me through the side window.

Tim remarked on my appearance the moment I set foot in his office. "You look dreadful. Why not call the entire thing off? That will make Miss Anne happy."

"No way," I said brusquely. "Where is she?"

"Up in the watch-tower, sitting on a walkie-talkie. I insisted. Down here she would have created a scene, which is the last thing you want. Now, there's not all that time to spare, so sit you down and I'll explain the layout as I see it."

I sank into a chair and accepted a cup of steaming coffee which he pushed across the table.

"Mr Ray giving us the exact time he's due to appear will be a great help. If — that is to say — that is what he intended that list of numbers to mean. We know he comes into being immediately outside the entrance to that tunnel at around one hundred and ninety miles per hour. The Switch-Back is just under three miles long, so the entire lap will take something under a minute. Ample time to get killed in, but not a great deal to successfully drive a car full out, while trying to hold a conversation with a man who has been dead for over a week. Do you get my point?"

"Clearly," I said.

"So, you must draw level with him in the quickest possible time, which means — and hear this — allowing one minute to build up speed, another two point seventy-five to reach the entrance — and by the grace of God and me risking my neck in testing these bloody and possibly quite wrong calculations — you'll be driving side by side from the very beginning."

"You've been testing the car out there on the Switch-Back?" I asked. "Despite all you said?"

He nodded. "There can only be a spoonful of sanity between us. But please understand this. No more after this morning. This must be the one and only trip. Find out what Mr. Ray wants — or give up."

"You have my promise. But tell me this — how will I communicate?"

He removed the empty coffee cup. "If I get you out there on time, doing the right speed, then my job's done. Spooky intercourse is yours. Right — let's get you ready."

I know very little about what makes men act as they do, why the habitual coward suddenly masters his fear, but I do know that as Tim helped me to put on padded jacket and trousers, rubber boots, and finally the gleaming helmet, I no longer cared what happened to me out there on the Switch-Back. But I was most anxious to meet whatever fate was reserved for me, and — so to speak — get it over.

Once I was behind the steering wheel, Tim plugged in two leads to a built-in radio and explained how it worked.

"The microphone is fitted to the lower part of your helmet, so all you have to do is speak. The earphones are all but covering your ears — so just listen. By six-fifty I'll be up in the watch-tower with Miss Anne. When — whenever anything appears, I'll notify you and give location. Right?"

I adjusted the goggles and gave him an idiotic grin.

"Right."

I knew he never really expected to see me alive again, and if it had been possible for me to give the matter any coherent thought, I would not have expected him to see me alive again. Yet, I could not wait to get out on the Switch-Back. The car roared along the tunnel, and I really believe that if I had closed my eyes, some instinct would have steered it towards that patch of grey light. A glance at the illuminated clock told me the time was six-fifty-three, which meant I had twelve minutes to do a practice lap, then gradually build up speed so as to be doing around one ninety at the right place and the right time.

The Model K glided out of the tunnel and on to the track; became a vigorous animal hungry for speed; snarled impatiently when I changed gear, then leapt forward when my left foot touched the accelerator. Tim's voice admonished me.

"No need to go mad. Keep her down to under forty until I give the word. I may say it's bloody cold up here and Anne sends you her love."

That distorted, but still familiar voice was oddly comforting, creating the illusion that I was no longer alone and whatever horror came to me would be shared by two companions. I completed one circuit of the track,

had passed the entrance, before Tim spoke again.

"Take her up into the eighties. Gradually — there's plenty of time."

I again glanced at the clock. The hands now pointed to two minutes past seven. Three minutes to the moment of truth — if we had translated Ray's figures correctly. The car seemed to rejoice when the speedometer needle began to creep round the dial, for the engine raised its voice to a triumphant scream, the tyres hummed a gay, if a tuneless song, that changed into a shriek of rapture when we (the car and I) mounted the slope to swing round a curve.

"Up to a hundred and beyond," Tim's voice filled my head. "Ease her up . . . faster . . . faster . . . you're doing fine. Two minutes to zero. When you reach one-two-zero — hold it."

My body merged into the quivering car, my hands became an extension of the steering wheel; and under, in front, and over me was a terrible, but exhilarating power that might kill, but would never destroy.

Tim's voice again. "It's now or never. If now — then go full out. Ram your foot down . . . that's it . . . Be prepared to cut slightly . . ."

I dared not remove my gaze from the track in front, for the car had become a shrieking monster that seemed to be only just resisting an urge to overturn; and what was the point of Tim shouting: "Not so high — keep on the lower slope," when the power was in charge — not I?

"You're on the home track . . . entrance coming up . . . look out for HIM . . . too fast . . . five seconds too fast . . ."

The tunnel entrance flashed by, and I had started the essential lap when Tim's voice all but blew my ear drums in.

"He's right behind you . . . left hand down, cut speed . . . *He's Right Behind You.*"

The earphones went dead, and I became aware of movement just beyond the off-side window; a gradual merging into view of a bright-red bonnet: and — Oh God! I did not want to turn my head to the right, for only He and possibly Tim knew what speed I was making, and no man would wish to see what was crouched over the steering wheel. But I could not resist fearful temptation; a momentary change of viewpoint; and I saw him . . . I did . . . I did. . . .

Face, dead white, looking at me, wearing the maniac's grin, teeth bared, eyes bulging, deep lines carved round the mouth and nose. A facsimile of a mask created by death? The ghost of a corpse? Ray Heywood himself occupying a do-it-yourself body? One theory is as good as another, but that brief glimpse was enough to make the hair stand up on the back of my neck — what followed will haunt me for the rest of my days.

Static crackled in the earphones and through it came Ray's voice; speaking slowly, conveying a hint of mockery.

"What you lack in brains, Philip, you make up in guts."

I had read somewhere that no one has yet held a conversation with a ghost. I had assumed that was because the ghost for some reason always remained silent; it had not occurred to me that the live one — the seer — might be incapable of speech. I think my vocal cords were frozen by fear, the rest of me being engaged in keeping the car on a straight line and negotiating curves. That voice went on.

"Did you imagine that someone had tinkered with Saturn and sent me up and over? I told you that was impossible. She would have told me. No, I fooled them all. I sent myself up and over."

I must have drawn slightly ahead, for suddenly I saw his face looking at me from the rear mirror. I might have screamed had any kind of vocal action been possible. The voice became a harsh whisper.

"Lonely in life — lonely in death. Badly need friend in life — even more badly needed in death. Besides — you mustn't hurt the family. Mad in life — sane in death."

We were rushing towards the final curve, and the face in the mirror was even more hideous to behold: now a blank white mask lit by ice-cold eyes.

"Philip — it is so easy. When you mount the curve — keep going up — leap towards the stars. I will help you. Help . . ."

The bright red bonnet drew level again, and I knew he was looking at me from behind his steering wheel; head turned towards the left, that terrible cold glare bridging the distance between us. I mounted the slope as we began to race round the curve, dimly aware that the tunnel entrance lay a mere half a mile ahead, so the spectral lap must soon come to an end.

But the red mudguards were coming nearer, and I automatically swerved to the left, went a little higher up the slope, and when I jerked my head right, tried to send him a look of silent appeal, those eyes were dead — dead as those of a fish on a fishmonger's slab.

The tyres screamed and the car shuddered and I must have been seconds away from that death he wished for me, when Tim's voice exploded in the earphones: "Right hand down — steer into him."

Possibly it was the sound of that familiar voice that saved me, although what it said should have been a deciding factor, but I am certain had that brief instruction been uttered by anyone else, I would have been incapable of following it.

The red car with its transparent roof was crowding mine, and I almost imagined I could hear teeth-jarring grinding of metal when, with a mighty effort of will, I turned the steering wheel to the right; sent the car hurtling down to the track below, there to spin round several times as I frantically applied the brakes. The fact I did not turn over must be classified as a minor miracle, but so far as I was concerned, the moment it shuddered to a stop, black oblivion took me into its kindly embrace and I temporarily lost interest in ghost cars and whatever drove them.

I took Anne's hand in mine, and Tim stared intently at the Model K that stood a few feet beyond the glass walls of his office.

"Ray must have been suffering from some kind of persecution complex," I said. "He most probably did

believe that certain members of the family were plotting his death, but would do it in such a way they would never be implicated. By beating them to it, after making a public statement to the effect that if he died on the Switch-Back it would be because someone had interfered with the Saturn — it was intended to bring dire suspicion down on those who were guilty by intent."

"But no one assumed that his death was other than an accident," Anne pointed out.

"One person did. Me. The not very bright platoon commander who could always be controlled. Advised. Instructed. My role was that of prosecutor. Stoker of the fires of suspicion. And it would have worked, too, had he not started to haunt the Switch-Back."

Tim turned his head and looked at me with a certain grudging respect. "Why did he do that?"

I smiled grimly. "It would appear that death cures all ills. Mad in life — sane in death. He said so. Freeze the ego that has just formed an irrevocable purpose. Get me out on the Switch-Back, and kill me before I could harm a single member of the family. Such is the fruit of sanity. But I can understand why he wanted a friend. He will be very lonely for a very, very long time."

"You mean we haven't seen the last of him?" Tim asked.

I smiled again and ignored Anne's shudder.

"I should imagine that many people will see the ghost of Ray Heywood in all sorts of places."

Time has proved me right. My suggestion that the Switch-Back be destroyed was disregarded, so stories — true or otherwise — of Ray driving the Saturn at unbelievable speeds, usually at sunset or sunrise, abound. But he is not confined to the Switch-Back. Report has him terrifying local residents as he races silently along country lanes, or causing a nasty accident on the M1 motorway.

He has also been seen on foot. At least three independent witnesses have told hair-raising accounts of meeting him in the pine forest, presumably on his way to the Switch-Back; all testified to the dreadful grin that appeared to be etched on his face.

I was amused to see that the television people have taken an active interest in the affair and actually planted a camera in the watch-tower — now built of reinforced concrete — where a commentator waffled away for half an hour, relating the more lurid tales, promising to break off when — and if — Ray appeared in his mechanical apparition. Regretfully my one-time platoon sergeant and friend did not oblige.

However, I can but hope that this account will reach a sufficiently large audience to kill those scurrilous tales that have grown up round the name of Ray Heywood over the years. The worst being, in my opinion, the one allegedly based on confidential information (whatever that might mean), that he committed suicide because of unspecified crimes that were about to be brought home to him. It was a bad government that first decided a dead man could not be libelled or slandered.

I will close on one more interesting point. I went to

see Tim just before his death last year, and it was he who brought up the matter of Ray Heywood and the stories which had caused us so much distress. Presently, to keep the conversation alive, more than anything else, I said:

"To this day I haven't understood how I came to drive a great racing car at near two hundred miles per hour. Particularly when one remembers what was coming up on my near side."

Tim chuckled. "You never reached anything like two hundred. In fact I'd be surprised if you clocked much over a hundred. And when I told you over the air that Ray was just behind you, he seemed to deliberately slow down so as to draw you both back to something

under eighty."

"Then he tried to kill me."

Tim shook his head. "I don't think so — not now. The purpose of the exercise was to panic you and me. He wanted you to kill him — again. When you swerved into the Saturn it turned over and burst into flames — before disappearing. One could say you killed a ghost."

"Then what the Hell is it that goes roaring down the Switch-Back and other places? Are all these stories the result of over-heated imagination?"

Tim grinned impishly. "Not necessarily. What everyone now sees is the ghost of a ghost."

Ω

PRISONERS OF THE ROYAL WEATHER

The royal sun illuminates
the spires and cupolas
of our illustrious city.
It reflects brilliantly
from the whitewashed walls
and coruscates blindingly
on the king's gold armor,
yet never does it shine
upon beggars or thieves.

The royal wind perfumes
the night with the velvet
of cognac and frangipani.
It tousles the tawny locks
of sacrificial virgins
and dares to rumple
the king's jeweled mane,
yet never does it reek
with the stench of corpses.

The royal rain waters
our gardens and limns
the streets with crystal.
It mists like gossamer
in the palace grounds

and washes the stains
from the public square,
yet never does it fall
if the king is on parade.

The royal snow is pure
and refreshingly cool
as our lord staggers
with drunken eyes ablaze
from the smoky inferno
of some ornate dining hall.
It blankets the city
with sovereign silence,
yet never does it chill.

The royal clime envelops
and mandates all of our days.
And four times each year,
often more than that,
the king issues an edict
when the seasons change,
yet never does he forecast
the nature of his tempests
or whom such storms will claim.

—Bruce Boston